WINNER TAKE ALL

WINNER
TAKE
ALL

A NOVEL

T. DAVIS
BUNN

DOUBLEDAY
New York · London · Toronto · Sydney · Auckland

WATERBROOK PRESS
Colorado Springs

WATERBROOK
PRESS

PUBLISHED BY DOUBLEDAY

A division of Random House, Inc.

1745 Broadway, New York, New York 10019

DOUBLEDAY and the portrayal of an anchor with a dolphin are
trademarks of DOUBLEDAY, a division of Random House, Inc.

WATERBROOK and its deer design logo are registered trademarks of
WATERBROOK Press, a division of Random House, Inc.

THIS BOOK IS COPUBLISHED WITH WATERBROOK PRESS
2375 Telstar Drive, Suite 160,
Colorado Springs, CO 80920, a division of Random House, Inc.

Cataloging-in-Publication Data is on file with the Library of Congress

ISBN 0-385-50370-9 (DOUBLEDAY)
ISBN 1-57856-530-8 (WATERBROOK)

February 2003

First Edition

1 3 5 7 9 10 8 6 4 2

For Thom and Becky Bradford
With Love

WINNER TAKE ALL

CHAPTER

1

TOURISTS MEANDERED DOWN the brick walk, laughing in the way of people who had spent too much money not to have a good time. Dale Steadman licked his lips and searched the close Carolina night. Across the street beckoned the last remaining bar from Wilmington's bad old days, a Barbary Coast dive whose music thumped in time to his own lurching heart. Gas lamps flickered and mocked him with shadows that threatened to reveal Erin coming from both directions at the same time. When she finally appeared, dancing across the bricks and waving excitedly, Dale could not even raise his arm in response. He watched heads turn up and down the street, some because of her poise and beauty, others because they recognized the newly arrived celebrity. Dale accepted her kiss of greeting, followed her into the restaurant, and knew a strong man's terror at watching the world slip utterly out of control.

The Wilmington harbor area had known its share of hard times. Two decades earlier, the streets fronting the Cape Fear River had been home to some of the raunchiest dives this side of Trinidad. Back then, even sailors off the rusting bulk carriers had walked in pairs. Eight Front Street was a product of recent renovation, with French cuisine served in a pre-Revolutionary War warehouse. The waiters liked to thrill the tourists with tales of former nude bar dancers and the three Hudson Bay outlaws who had carved each other up with bone-handled scimitars. But tonight the candles and the gas wall lamps glowed like ghosts of the here and now, and Dale found scant room for bygone days. Across from him, Erin showed a vulnerable enchantment that was all her own, a waif in Hermès silks. As the waiter took their orders, Dale wondered anew why this world-renowned opera diva had ever come to marry him. Or how he had ever let her go.

They talked of her recent roles at La Scala and Vienna's famed opera house. Candles brushed her features with featherstrokes of youth, as though she were forever seventeen. Erin had been born in Germany and raised in Belgium. That night her accent was an erotic purr. They talked of his recent appointment as chairman of the New Horizons board. They cast those special looks across the table. They pretended she had never abandoned him, leaving for a role in Paris and never coming back. At least, she pretended it had not happened, and he pretended to let it go.

Erin was an odd mixture of softness and edges. Her nose was far too strong, a single line drawn from forehead to tip. At a certain angle she hearkened back to a distant age of hunter-gatherers, which was perhaps the source of her ruthless intent. Whatever she needed to dispatch, she did so without a solitary hint of remorse. She ate what she killed. And she murdered with grace and song.

Erin carried a childlike zest about her. She ate with a gusto that was her trademark in everything and brought the burning to his gut once more. She responded with the rounding of her dark eyes, still open to his signals and reading them before they were ever fully formed. After ten and a half months of hellish pain, an hour back in her company was enough to chain him once more.

She drank sparingly, but encouraged Dale to go the distance. She had always professed to love his drinking and his cigars and his hunting, calling them manly traits in an emasculated world. He was a winner and a giant among pygmies, she had often said, compliments he had always loved to hear from her lips, for the words had usually triggered nights of astonishing passion. Erin had been the first ever to release him from the prison of restraint. The one and only.

The first difficult moment came as they were finishing the main course. She tossed out the question with a casual glance at other tables, little more than an aside. "Who is keeping you company these days?"

He was saved by what in earlier times had been a constant barb, but now was a windfall. An older couple approached with pen and smiles outstretched. They had seen her recent PBS opera special and read about her in the *New York Times*. They were thrilled to meet her.

Just so delighted. Erin resumed the role of star and signed their pages, then dismissed them as pleasantly and swiftly as only a diva could.

She turned back to him. "Am I meant to be jealous already?"

"I don't want to spend our time talking about this, Erin."

"No. Of course not. My prim and proper husband dislikes any hint—"

"Erin. Please."

She lifted her wine and drained it. She had scarcely tasted it before then. She did not ever drink very much. The dreams came after that, and the terrors. He knew the dreams, but he could only guess at the reasons. Which made her adolescent beauty even more remarkable. Not even having a child had diminished her lissome radiance. It was only in moments like this, when her features tightened in anger or distress, that she aged from a perpetual seventeen to her actual thirty.

Erin's dark eyes did not so much focus upon him as take aim. "My glass is empty."

"Sorry." He refilled hers, then his own. "Congratulations on your recent success, by the way."

"A smooth change of subject. Very smooth."

"Not to mention the front page of the Sunday *Times* Arts and Leisure section. Quite a coup."

Three years ago, Erin had come to New York hoping for a chance to make it at the Met, the crown of America's operatic world. They had met her first week in New York and his second, two outcasts to the Apple's high society. The magnetism was mutual and instantaneous. Or so he liked to think.

Entry into the New York Metropolitan Opera had never come for Erin. She had hammered upon the backstage entrance with all her might. She had paid her dues by singing every American venue that would have her, from San Francisco to Miami to Chicago. She had gained accolades from virtually every place. But still the Met did not grant the invitation she so desperately craved.

Dale had followed whenever and wherever he could. Theirs had been an international romance, a fairy tale that fit well into the European magazines. Pictorial spreads appeared in France and Switzerland and Belgium, where opera stars were granted the same status as the Hollywood imports. Beauty and the Beast, was how the German magazine *Bild* put it, a backwoods hick from a town redolent of slave labor and brown lung. Dale disliked admitting it even to himself, but he had occasionally asked himself the same question. Why had this woman, who could have had almost any man in the entire world, ever married the likes of him?

Now she was back in Europe. His love had not been enough to keep her content. This was only the second time she had returned to America since their divorce. The other occasion had been to record a PBS special as the precious innocent in *Carmen*. The telecast had received to-die-for publicity when the *New York Times* had blasted the Met's new lead conductor for refusing Erin a debut. As a result of the *Times'* coverage, PBS had gained the largest audience for a televised opera in history.

Dale had not even known she was in the country until he read of the upcoming broadcast. He had gotten so spectacularly drunk the third act remained a scotch-scented blur.

After a two-bottle dinner they had a couple of brandies, or at least he did. Erin sipped twice from her glass, then poured the remainder into his own and said, "Tell me about the break-in at the house."

"You can't still be reading the Wilmington rag."

"My press agent has instructions to pass over anything she can find about you. Local man foils armed robbers by knocking them both cold, wasn't that how they put it? Front page above the fold." Erin toyed with the lay of her pearls and the spaghetti strap of her dress. She sounded almost shy. "Perhaps I shouldn't keep such close tabs on you, but I couldn't help myself."

"I was terrified. But only after it was over. Before there wasn't time for thought."

Her smile flickered in the candlelight, ephemeral as myth. "Did you really knock them both out?"

Dale related the bare bones because she seemed so interested, even though the episode still gave him severe night sweats. Apparently he had caught the pair just after they had broken into the house, for nothing had been touched. Erin leaned across the table and pressed him for more. Her intensity caused the afternoon to become vivid once more. He had come home early to discover the nanny bound and gagged on the kitchen floor. Dale had then spotted the two men upon the landing by the baby's room, which was why he went utterly berserk. He had grabbed a nearby lamp, catapulted up the stairs, and taken them both down. Only afterward had he seen their guns. But it would not have mattered anyway. The bigger of the two men had been gripping Celeste's doorknob with his gloved hand. The memory still drenched his vision with blood and fear.

Erin reached across and snagged his hand and scratched the surface with one fingernail. Back and forth, the proprietary gesture of a woman in comfortable possession of her man. "Let's go back for a nightcap."

He wanted to say it probably wasn't a good idea. But the light in her eyes kindled a volcano of hurt and craving in his gut. Dale could not deny her. It was his greatest failing. That and the knowledge she could control him only because he still wanted so badly to believe.

Erin drove, as was their habit when he had been drinking. She rested one hand upon his seatback, where she could play with a wayward curl of his hair. Their careful silence saved him from confessing how time had become a blunt weapon that crashed against the walls of his life, shattering and homicidal.

When they turned off the state road and entered the tree-draped darkness, she came as close as she ever had to probing his wounds. "I'm so sorry for the way I spoke to the press."

"Lied," he corrected, but without heat.

"Lied," she agreed, settling his hand into her lap where he could feel the pulsing warmth. "Lied and lied and lied again. But what was I supposed to do? I had hoped that if I didn't return, didn't contest the divorce, they wouldn't discover anything until it was all old news."

When they rounded the final corner, Dale regretted not having turned off the timer switch and the outside spotlights. The house stood upon its own moon-draped island, a mockery of cream-colored stone and dismembered fantasies.

As they started across the plank bridge connecting his island to the main road, Erin rolled down her window and let the brackish perfume sweep over her. "Things weren't working out between us, you knew that as well as I did. Why give them any reason to gossip? Abandonment was a perfect reason for the divorce. If I'd come back, it would only have opened us to the risk of reporters sniffing out a story."

The bridge had been part of his gift, a way of making the home he had built for her as perfect as he could make it. The Cape Fear delta had once been a world connected by such wooden scaffolds, where barefoot boys could fish and crab and dream of better days ahead. The house was to be a waterborne palace where he would share the best of his world, and shield them from the worst of hers. Now, as the thick boards drummed softly beneath his tires, he could only manage a single word in response. "Abandoned."

Wisely, Erin let the topic drop into the silver-black waters.

After he had paid the sitter, Erin walked up with him to see the baby. Or rather, she watched as he checked on Celeste. It was one of the most remarkable things about her, and the hardest trait he had been forced to forgive. Even now, as she stood beside him and stared down at their daughter, he could feel the utter lack of connection between them.

As they left the room, he asked once more, "What happened to you as a child?"

She gave him the same blank gaze she had always responded with when he tried to pry, and pulled on his hand. "Come let me pour you a drink."

They settled on the glassed-in veranda, the lights so low they could study the play of moonlight on water and the glow of Wrightsville Beach across the bay. He watched her pour him an oversized single malt, slip off her shoes, and pad across the carpet to where he sat. Her eyes were so dark that it was only when he was close enough to taste her lips that he could make out the colors, and the moods, and the faint flickers of anything other than calm craving. Her long hair was a shade or two off black, depending upon the light, and framed her face with ardent precision. Her lips were astonishingly pale, her skin almost translucent. Her few freckles were so blanched they disappeared with the faintest frosting of powder. Or emerged when Erin wished to look her youngest. Her most alluring. Like now.

She folded herself down so that she rested on the carpet by his feet. She wrapped her arms around his calves, leaned her chin upon his thigh, and asked in as mournful a tone as he had ever heard, "Where did it all go so wrong?"

She could have been reading the brand upon his heart. He took a hard slug from his goblet, the liquid fire a mimicry of the heat raised by her words.

Erin leaned over him, her eyes hooded with the satisfaction of his response. Her lips were as warm and welcoming as he remembered. As he could never forget. The taste was of honey and the scotch's smoky sorrow.

Dale was back inside the dream for the first time in almost a year. He stood in the stadium for the seventh and final game of his professional football career. The rest of his teammates were huddled and huffing from the previous play. Dale took a moment to look around the stadium, almost as though he knew what was about to come. The capacity crowd shouted with one continuous voice. The pennants shimmered, the band's brass instruments flickered under the lights, the grass was impossibly green, the evening incredibly pure.

That much had actually happened.

In the dream, the quarterback shouted words Dale did not hear. Dale started to ask what he was supposed to do, but the team was already moving into formation. He shouted for them to wait, but the ball was snapped. The quarterback turned and slapped the ball into Dale's gut. Dale wanted to run. He knew that was his job. But his feet were caught. The grass had turned into vines, and the vines writhed and hissed and bared venomous fangs.

Then he was struck. Just like it had actually happened. One from the left and low, the other from the right and high. His bones crunched, low and high, and once again Dale heard them go from inside his skull.

The defensive linesman who had broken his collarbone rose first. He looked down at Dale, pinned to the ground by a fractured hip, and grinned. He said something lost to the blaring whistles and the shouts of his own teammates. Then the linesman reached down and given Dale's helmet a little farewell pat. Just as had actually happened.

The dream sequence's pattern was so well grooved Dale could be trapped inside and still watch it as he would a training film. At least now there was no pain, even as time slowed and the refs clustered and the doctor did his slow-motion dance across the turf toward him. The crowd's roar changed now, from frenetic and thrilling to hungry. He was trapped on the ground, the latest morsel for them to devour. He had actually lain there for about five minutes, while the team doctor shot him full of painkillers and fitted a steel brace to his neck and back, in case he had fractured his spine. In the dream he usually lay there for aeons, watching the crowd disperse with his team, and the seasons change, and the snow fall and cover him utterly. But tonight the doctor grabbed his arm and shook him hard, screaming for him to *wake up, wake up, wake up.*

Dale opened his eyes to discover that Erin was shaking him awake. But his head was pounding and the world was impossibly shattered.

Erin tore back the covers and began dragging him out of bed. "Get up and *help me!*"

Erin hauled him to his feet by sheer force of her indomitable will. Dale's dismembered brain snatched frantically at images, all of them disconnected and painful. From the hallway, the smoke alarm gave off the high-pitched peeping of a terrified mechanical bird. In the distance he might have heard a baby screaming, which should have had him flying down the hall. But his legs didn't seem to want to connect with his thoughts.

Erin let him go, and he bounced off the bed's corner post before slamming into the hardwood floor.

His two old injuries both started flaming again. For an instant, as the pain thudded louder than the shrill peeping, he wondered if somehow the dream had managed to finally breach the barrier and enter his nighttime world.

Erin slapped his face and *screamed* at him. "*Move!*"

This was something she had never done. Not even in their worst moments, right after her arrival in Wilmington, two months pregnant and panic-stricken at becoming just another has-been, a woman who once was famous. Back when he finally realized his love could never compete with her voice and her career.

Then he smelled the smoke.

Dale lurched to his feet. He almost fell, but caught himself with a two-armed embrace of the bedpost. Erin was only half dressed and her hair hung tangled about her face. The baby was there in the room with them. Celeste lay upon a towel on the floor, squalling and kicking in panic. His daughter watched him with eyes that pleaded for him to pull himself together.

"*Hurry!*"

Then he *saw* the smoke.

Somehow he managed to get into his pants. He struggled with a shirt Erin handed him, then flung it aside. He slipped into the first shoes he found, from two different sets and on the wrong feet. But it didn't matter, because the smoke was *pouring* under the bedroom door.

Erin had the baby in her arms, wrapped in a wet towel with another draped around her head. Erin handed him a third, but he couldn't make it work and still see where he was going. So he tossed it down. Then he had to pick it up again after he opened the door and met a solid, billowing wall.

The smoke was acrid and it *burned*. He peered down the hall but saw no flames. He started forward, pulling Erin along behind him. The smoke's heat was something unexpected. His mind remained disconnected, like sparks flying up and disappearing into the final night.

He moved on reflex alone. Dale entered the guest bedroom over the slanting sunporch roof and rushed to the window. When he could not get it open he broke it with a chair, tearing out the entire frame and terrifying his baby girl even further.

He stepped onto the roof, almost lost his balance, then turned back for the child. Erin refused to hand her over, but instead let him help her step out. Together they scrambled around to the north side, where the smoke was less intense. They slipped over the lip of the roof and climbed down the trellis.

They stumbled across the back lawn and down to where his yacht was moored on the canal dock. It seemed to take forever to quiet the baby, but it had to be done before he could even hear what Erin was saying. "You have to call the fire department."

Even now that his heart no longer threatened to shatter his ribs from the inside, he still could not make his brain connect properly to his tongue. "Automatic."

Though the word came out slurred and distorted to his own ears, it was enough to catapult Erin to her feet. "What?"

"They installed a new security system after the break-in."

She turned panic-stricken eyes toward where flames began pushing through the kitchen window. "I can't be seen here! Not by anyone, not now! The press will eat me alive!"

Erin cupped his chin with both her hands, weaving her head so that it stayed centered upon his wandering gaze. Or perhaps it was merely his internal focus that moved. "You can't take care of the baby in all this, not without a home. You understand that, don't you? I'll go and take the baby until things are settled down. Can you understand what I'm saying?"

Dale was trying his best, but the drink still had his brain in a vise that squeezed all thoughts into a boiling mash.

Erin took a moment to pull her clothes right. Then she picked up Celeste. Their daughter immediately started to fret. Dale's one last coherent thought, before he slipped back into the welcoming blankness, was the fury that crossed his former wife's face as the baby began to squall.

CHAPTER

2

THE FIRST TIME *she sees the darkness revealed, the child is seven years old. It will be another seven before she has a name for what she sees. If she has to name it now, it would be terror.*

She has to dress up for dinner, and beneath her sky-blue dress she has on a starched petticoat and white socks and polished black shoes. She wears a matching velvet-silk ribbon in her hair. Her mother comes in at precisely six-fifteen to make sure she is dressed. Her mother has a cigarette in one hand and a drink in the other. She leaves lipstick stains on the rim of her cigarette as she smokes. The ice tinkles in her glass as she stands over her daughter and surveys her above the rim of her drink.

"Head up straight. Okay," her mother says. "Now give me your best curtsy."

That usually means there will be important people for dinner. Tonight her mother has a flat void in her gaze. Her mother has very pale eyes. But sometimes they grow dark and shadow-filled. Like now. Instantly the child knows it is going to be a very bad night.

The sick fear begins to flood her legs, and she flubs the curtsy. But her mother's attention is already downstairs. She rolls herself off the doorframe and leaves without another word.

The child knows something is wrong inside her family. People tend to think that a seven-year-old child is not worth noticing. So they show her things they assume she cannot understand. The child has a space behind the parlor sofa where she has built a little corner all her own. A wormwood table with legs narrow as fairy pillars backs up against the pale velour sofa. They know she is there, or at least they should. She crouches there almost every evening before dinner.

There isn't much the child can do for fun, dressed as she is. So she takes two of her favorite dolls and she slips beneath the Irish linen tablecloth. The table bears two crystal decanters, one for her father's scotch and the other for her mother's gin, along with a beaded silver ice bucket and a lead-crystal bowl filled with roses. Her little hideaway is filled with the scent of fresh flowers and light filtered through the damask. It should be a perfect fairy palace. She is supposed to only come in this parlor with her parents before dinner, or when her mother orders her to help serve tea to guests. But on rainy afternoons she sneaks in so she can create a world of soft light and perfumed bliss. But tonight the prince and princess do not transport her to a more beautiful and happy land. No matter how she moves them about or whispers words for them to say, her hands hold two plastic figures with lies for smiles.

"You went out to the tracks again, didn't you."

"Of course not."

The child's fingers slip, and the plastic man with the sparkling crown and perfect teeth falls to the carpet. She picks him up and tries to concentrate harder. But the words from beyond the damask will not leave her alone.

"I had a conference that took all afternoon."

"Where?"

Her father rattles the ice in his glass and walks over. She can see her reflection in the polished toe of his hand-stitched broughams. "At the office. Where else?"

"I called the office. They said you left before lunch."

"I went out for lunch with the boys, then we met in the conference room on the eleventh floor." Her father poured and poured and poured. "You want me to sketch you a diagram of my afternoon?"

As soon as her father moves away, the child can hear the tread of her mother's high heels thunking softly across the Chinese carpet. As she refills her glass, smoke from her cigarette drifts down and under the damask. "I can't believe this is the best excuse you could work up. Or maybe you just don't care enough to try anymore."

"This is some welcome. Here I am, working on the biggest deal of my entire career, and you're hounding me over where the conference took place."

"Harry, I spoke with Deveraugh."

"You called the chairman's office? You got some nerve."

"No, Harry. He called here. Wondering if you'd taken sick." A long drag on her cigarette. "Want to rethink your little tale?"

When her father speaks again, his voice holds a hard edge from the whiskey still in his throat. "So I took a little time off. So what."

"How much did you lose this time? A thousand? Five thousand?" Her mother grinds out her cigarette so hard the crystal ashtray beats musically upon the sideboard's top. "Ten?"

"It's my money."

"No, Harry. It's our debt. Here I am, juggling bills like crazy, hoping we can make it through another month. And what do you do but go out and blow us deeper into the hole."

"Like you don't know how to spend." He sets down his glass, or tries to, but misses the table's edge. The glass thumps on the carpet and rolls toward the child, spilling ice and the last caramel drops. "One afternoon at Saks and you can outspend the Pentagon."

A slender hand with fingernails dyed a deep blood red reaches for his glass. "You're such a loser, Harry. Such a—"

The child flinches even before the blow, as though she knows it is going to come, only not precisely when.

The strike holds a musical quality. Bells chime and jingle, for her father has struck with the phone. Then more bells, for her mother careens against the sofa-table and drags off the damask and the crystal in her fall.

She catches herself on her hands and knees, turns, and gives her child a single look. This look frightens the child more than anything else that night. For her mother is smiling, sharing with her daughter a furious satisfaction.

Her mother rises and announces in a vicious hiss, "You will never touch me again."

She leaves the room without another word.

Her father walks over, plucks his decanter off the floor, then stands in the puddle of spilled scotch as he fills his glass. Only when he ambles back to the room's opposite side does the child crawl across the carpet and out the door.

The next morning, her mother comes into her bedroom. The flat void is still in her eyes and her voice. Powder is caked over her features, and her hair is coiffed so that it falls across one side of her face and down her shoulder. But when she leans over, the child can see that the ear is very swollen. The skin around her eye and cheekbone is also puffy. Her mother grips the child by both arms. "If anyone ever asks you, we have a perfect family. Your parents are the best mother and father anybody could ever have."

"But—"

She shakes the child violently. "Say it!"

"A perfect family."

"And who has the best parents in the world?"

"I do."

"Don't you ever forget it." Her mother rises and leaves the room.

Later that day, the child throws the prince and princess doll into the trash. The maid, an illegal immigrant from Ecuador with three small children, hastily retrieves them. That night she and her husband spend hours talking about the strange habits of rich people, and how they teach the lesson of waste even to their young.

T HE PHONE RANG and Marcus Glenwood glanced out his window as he slid upright in bed. The stars were still a faint wash against the western border. He had been awaiting this call for over a month. Ever since Marcus had made the horrible error of asking Kirsten to marry him.

That particular night had been a gift of fabled perfection. Not even Kirsten's customary reserve had been able to resist the enchantment. After an intimate dinner they had walked Raleigh streets perfumed by a coming summer storm. When he had reached for her hand, she had responded by wrapping an arm around his waist, drawing close, and laying her head upon his shoulder. Not even that had been enough, however, and a second arm had reached across to form a ring of union around his middle. Then she had sighed his name, sung it almost, so comfortable with him and the night she had turned his name into a melody of promise. So he had asked her. Boom. Surprising himself almost as much as her.

Kirsten had said nothing for a time, but even before the arms had retreated he could sense her withdrawal. The past four weeks had not improved matters. The further they moved to time's relentless tread, the quieter she became, the more repressed. Which was why he had been dreading this call.

So before Marcus answered, he took a moment to settle his feet upon the floor. He felt the coolness of time-honed wood and fixed himself firmly in the here and now. He stared out the back window at trees not yet detached from the night and hoped for wisdom. Then he picked up the phone.

"Marcus, good, I was afraid it would be your answering machine and I didn't have idea one what I was going to say. Are you awake?"

It was a woman's voice, and familiar. But his relief that the caller wasn't Kirsten left him unable to identify anything further. "Totally."

"You know who this is?"

He did then. "Judge Sears."

"At four-thirty in the morning it's Rachel, all right? We need to talk."

Rachel Sears was a fragile-looking brunette with piercing emeralds for eyes. She was also a district court judge and a friend. In the past two elections, a number of women had shoved aside the dinosaurs who had come to assume the bench was theirs by right. These new judges were introducing a novel brand of compassion and judicial sharpness.

Marcus took a hard breath. "I'm here."

"Yesterday a young woman caught me outside the court. She was crying and lost, and had two babies doing the frantic routine at her legs. You got the picture?"

"Yes." It was a common enough scenario. Single mother, poor reading skills, drawn to court by some legal document that terrified her. The bored Highway Patrol officer who pulled detail at the information booth downstairs, a duty they all loathed, likely as not had sent her to the wrong floor. In the central foyer by the elevators she would confront a series of yard-long computer printouts listing the day's cases by courtroom, randomly assigned and not in alphabetical order. Between four or five hundred names in all.

"She's being evicted. I glanced over the document. Pretty standard stuff, failure to pay for ninety days, three warnings. Now she's been locked out. Her belongings have been confiscated to pay back rent. But something about this one bothered me all night. Then an hour ago it hit me. Just by chance, I mean, this is in the million-to-one category, I had another eviction cross my desk three weeks ago. I've got the case file in front of me now. Similar deal, young single mom, preschool kids. The same southeast Raleigh address, thirty-four units in the complex. With me so far?"

"Are you at the office?"

"Came in to check the facts, see if my mind was playing tricks from lack of sleep. It wasn't." There came the sound of rustling papers. "The first woman refused a court-appointed attorney, she wanted to make sure she had a chance to tell her story in court. She accused the landlord of soliciting sexual favors in exchange for rent."

"Nothing new there." Tenants facing eviction were a clan that shared information and tactics. Nothing frightened most landlords like the prospect of public shame.

"Their details match to a surprising degree. Both mothers are black and in their late teens. Both claim they were offered nice apartments for half the going rate. Both say once they were settled in, the landlord propositioned them."

Marcus recalled the first time he had tried a case in Judge Rachel Sears' courtroom. The woman had become a mother only six months prior to being elected to the bench and was still fighting the postbirth weight battle. The robes had left her looking both dumpy and frail. Then she had seated herself upon the dais, and the skin of her face had pulled back so taut that her lips had almost disappeared, as though she was consciously shedding every vestige of laxity. From mother and friend to wielder of power.

"I continued the case over to this morning. I also obtained the names and addresses of three other women who this defendant claims had the same thing happen to them."

A robin took roost just outside his open window, and mocked the dawn's treachery with song. "You want me to obtain affidavits and confront the landlord in open court."

"The young lady gave her previous address as your side of Rocky Mount. I arranged for a shelter to take her and the children last night. But she needs someplace semipermanent." Judge Sears read out the names and addresses. "Marcus, do I have to tell you anything more?"

"This phone call never happened," Marcus confirmed.

He disconnected, took another breath, and dialed Deacon Wilbur's number from memory. As he listened to it ring, his mind wandered back to his waking thought, and the fear that Kirsten's call would be to say she was leaving him for good.

He and Deacon collected the young woman and her babies, spoke with two of the other women, then headed downtown. By the time they arrived on the Wake County courthouse's third floor, the babies were squirming and cranky.

Her records claimed Yolanda was nineteen. The elder of Yolanda's two children, a boy, was almost two and looked huge in her arms. The daughter was about six months old and far lighter in skin tone than her brother. Yolanda crossed the foyer with the blank-faced sullenness of one who was well used to living without hope.

Marcus staked out the stairway while Deacon stood sentry before the elevators. Deacon Wilbur was a retired black pastor who revealed his seventy-plus years in the gaunt caverns at his temples. Deacon had never studied much besides the Bible; his formal schooling had ended at nine when his sharecropper daddy had ordered the boy to join him in the fields.

There had been a period in Marcus' life, separated from the present by a mere knife's blade of time, when sorrow had been both crippling and constant. As he drove back from a weekend on Figure Eight Island, his car had been struck by a truck and his two children killed. His wife had used their subsequent divorce to brand him with further public shame. When Marcus had finally begun emerging from his own dark pit, Deacon Wilbur had been there to shed light upon what Marcus had almost decided was a hopeless and intolerable climb.

The older child started mewling again. Deacon turned to Yolanda and spoke softly. She snapped from her internal funk long enough to hand him the boy. Deacon held the child with a grandfather's experience, bouncing him slightly on his hip, and paying the fretful sounds no mind whatsoever.

Hamper Caisse emerged from the stairwell so deep in conversation with his client that he almost collided with Marcus before he saw him. "Marcus, why don't you go find some other place to park your sorry carcass."

"I have some affidavits you may want to see."

"Don't go waving your papers in my face. You want to see me about something, you come to my office."

"These affidavits relate to a case you're trying this morning." The man seeking to hide behind Hamper was a caramel doughboy and minus a neck. "Would you happen to be Mr. Duane Dean?"

"Don't say a word to this man."

Yolanda spotted them and emitted a terrified wail. The babies caught wind of their momma's distress, and began caterwauling.

"Mr. Dean, I am about to present evidence before Judge Sears that you have made a practice of extorting sexual favors in lieu of rent, then falsely impounding your tenants' property."

"Back off, Marcus, while you still got use of your legs."

"I would imagine that Judge Sears will be issuing a warrant for your arrest." Marcus offered Duane Dean the affidavits. "Your situation would be vastly improved by seeing to this matter immediately and permitting this woman to return to her apartment."

Hamper slapped the papers from Marcus' grasp. "You're way out of line here, counselor!"

Deacon set down the child and swooped in to confront the landlord. "How can you do this to one of your own kind? You been going around preying on our children, taking them like you would a nice piece of meat." The pastor was a scrawny bundle of rage and time-blackened iron. "Don't you be shaking your head at me, I know what I'm seeing. I know!"

"Who is this nutcase?" Hamper moved to block Deacon's inexorable approach. "Get him away from my client or I'll have him arrested!"

Deacon shunted Hamper Caisse aside as though the attorney held less substance than a shadow. He pressed Duane Dean tightly against the scarred cinder block wall. "How old are you, sir? Forty-five? Fifty-five? You know how old this child is? What is your *problem*? You think you're gonna come into my town, take advantage of my flock? I got some news for you, sir. I'll tear your house down with my two bare hands!"

"Threats!" Hamper was playing to the theater now, waving his arms enough to make his tie dance like a silk snake. "Y'all hear that? He's threatening my client with bodily harm!"

"I'll expose you to the newspapers! I'll talk to my friends in the police and the sheriff's office. This might be Carolina, sir, but it's a new day. Yessir, a new millennium. We got us some friends now, and we'll turn every one of them against the likes of you. You hear what I'm saying? We'll hunt you down where you live!"

Duane Dean emitted a rodent's squeak, clawed his way around Deacon, and fled down the staircase.

"Duane, hold up now, we're due in court!"

Deacon turned on the lawyer. "I've got something to say to you, sir."

Hamper Caisse had the haggard features of a dedicated chain-smoker and the pale eyes of a luminous ghost. His voice held the rough hoarseness of one who lived for theatrics. Everything about him—vision, direction, dress, motion—was disjointed and awkward. He did not seem to connect with anything fully, not even himself, until he entered a courtroom. Before the bar, Hamper Caisse came into his own. He roared, he laughed, he juggled the jury's emotions. Then he departed, untouched by all but the thrill of trying another case. He was said to have a wife and children, but he took no social engagements and was always seen alone. His paperwork was abysmal, his memory shoddy, his morals absent. He took everything that came his way, from traffic violations to rape. He would defend anyone. He reassured even the most pathological sadist by the utter absence of questions in his gaze.

Hamper tried for indignation, but it flickered and died in the face of Deacon's rage. "You just keep your distance!"

"You might *think* you have the right to do whatever you want with my people." Deacon's voice would not have carried far, save for the fact that the third-floor lobby now held its breath. "The book learning and the power you think you got makes anything you feel like doing just fine, don't it. Tell me I'm not talking the truth."

Marcus gathered up his affidavits and moved a half step away. Anyone who could silence a courtroom dramatist needed no help from him.

"You might *think* you can control the cards, on account of who you are and who you know." Deacon moved closer. Hamper had the choice of backing up or rubbing chests.

He backed.

Deacon kept on coming. "You might *think* you're a powerful man, given the color of this no 'count skin you're wearing like a cheap suit. But my God knows just *exactly* who you are. Oh yeah. He knows *exactly* what you've done." Another step. "My God is a *great* God." And another. "He's an *awesome* God."

He pushed Hamper around the corner and into the center of the lobby. "He's bigger than anything you know, or anything you have, or anything you've ever done. So I'm gonna pray to my God for your no-good, rotten soul." Deacon leveled the only weapons he had at his disposal, his gaze and his voice and his trembling finger. "Your nasty, stinking, depraved, and *wicked* soul."

When the elevator doors pinged open, Hamper flung himself into the crush. The cries of those at the back were cut off by Deacon rising to a full-on pulpit roar. "But let me tell you this. If I *ever* catch you anywhere near my people again, I'll have this entire *world* in the streets!"

A deep black voice from somewhere behind them belled out, "Say it, brother!"

"I'll have them marching on your home! I'll have them crying for your head!"

A woman's voice took up the background cadence. "I *say* amen!"

"You think you know some folks? I'll call the politicians who're just *begging* for our votes. I'll tell them just exactly what it is you and your filthy friend's been up to. You think you can do this to my people? You're wrong! It is *not* going to happen." Deacon had to lean over to fit his epitaph between the closing doors. "I'll expose you for the scum you are!"

When the doors cranked shut, the silence lasted a profound moment. Then the entire lobby began cheering. It was the first time Marcus had ever heard applause in the Wake County courthouse.

Deacon turned around, his features seared by his own flames. He spoke to the cowering young woman. "Come on, daughter. Let's go watch Marcus clear up this mess. Then we gotta find your children someplace healthy to live."

They left the courthouse and went by the apartments, where Yolanda's unit was now open and the landlord nowhere to be found. After they had gathered her belongings, Deacon asked her to introduce them to every other young woman living there. Marcus came in twice to take affidavits from women enduring the exact same treatment, then retreated back to his car. The stench of abject hopelessness was too strong for his paltry spirit to withstand for long. Deacon was made of stronger stuff, however, and did not reemerge until every one of the women had received his message. Whether they wanted it or not.

Yolanda remained morosely silent the entire journey back to Rocky Mount, save for two sharp outbursts when her children grew so boisterous she could not ignore them. Deacon used Marcus' phone to call ahead, then turned around to say, "I'm taking you by your aunt's home. She's agreed to take you and your children in for a time."

"She don't like me none."

"She's family, she's Christian, and she knows what's right. She's disappointed in you, the same as I am. You know that, don't you?"

Yolanda might have nodded, or she might simply have jerked in time to her son's bounces on the seat beside her.

"Child, you've known me since you were a baby. I changed your diapers. I married both your momma's sisters. Look at me, daughter. I even helped you learn to *walk*. Why on earth didn't you come to me before now?"

Yolanda found something beyond the car window of morose fascination, and said nothing. Marcus studied her in the rearview mirror, and wondered if having so much sorrow inside such a young form stripped away the ability to weep.

"It breaks my heart to see people I love go out there and make bad choices," Deacon went on. "I know you've been abused. I know you've been taken advantage of here. Turn around and look at me, girl, I'm talking to you."

She tilted her chin upward, but the defiance was such a paltry show she did not even convince herself.

"This ain't just about that man back there. You knew exactly what you were getting yourself into. Don't you shake your head. The fact that you've got these two children sitting here says you know all there is to know about using your body." He turned around long enough to say, "Pull up in front of that red brick house there."

Before Marcus cut the motor, a heavyset black woman he recognized from church pushed through her front door. They gave each other a solemn nod, but neither felt this was a time for neighborly waves.

"I am angry with you, child. I'm upset. Same as your aunt here. We know you've been doing wrong. All this trouble we've been having today is on account of bad decisions you've made yourself."

The boy spotted the older woman standing on her front lawn and let out a squeal of delight. Yolanda leaned over to open his door, almost masking her shattered tremble.

"Everybody makes bad decisions, daughter. That's why Jesus walked upon this earth, to help us with these bad times, especially the times that are all our fault. But from this point forward, you gotta play it straight. You need to start thinking about what kind of legacy you're gonna be leaving for those children. You not careful, you'll be watching them do the same things with somebody else. You hear what I'm saying?"

She whispered, "Yes, Deacon."

"Marcus and me, now, we've put ourselves on the line for you. So this is how it's gonna be. If you don't want to live by our rules, we'll love you just the same, and we'll pray for you with our last dying breath. But we're also gonna get those babies taken away from you, and we won't be having you around us no more. You'll just be left to suffer the consequences. Those are your choices, daughter. Now go say hello to your aunt."

It wasn't until the young mother was enfolded into her aunt's arms that she began to weep. The great heaving sobs only made her look more fragile than before. The older woman gave Deacon a long look over her niece's head, but did not say a word.

As the young woman fought to regain control, Marcus helped Deacon unload her belongings from the trunk. Overhead the clouds were massing for a serious summer downpour. The air was thick with humidity and dread.

When Marcus returned from the house, Yolanda was waiting for him by the car. She spoke so softly her lips scarcely moved. "That white man back there, the one Deacon lit into."

"You mean your former landlord's attorney, Hamper Caisse?"

"He was one of them always coming round. Messing with a lot of the girls. Scaring them bad with what he'd do if they talked 'bout what was going down."

"If you'd be willing to testify to that under oath, I could try to have him disbarred."

She hefted a bundle larger than she was and headed for the house. "I don't want to be *thinking* 'bout that stuff no more."

CHAPTER

3

THE AIR SMELLED OF superheated asphalt and coming rain. Marcus was pursued the entire way home by the rumble of gunfire over the horizon. He pulled into his drive just as the first drops started falling, big pelting bullets that pursued him across the lawn. The Victorian home had borne a striking resemblance to its owner when Marcus Glenwood had returned to Rocky Mount soon after the accident. The place that now served as both his office and home had stood derelict and empty with treelimbs lancing the walls. Windows had cupped shards of old glass like segments of teeth in an unearthed skull. Marcus had done much of the rebuilding himself. Eighteen months of hard labor had proved a sweaty therapy against the ghosts that had chased him from Raleigh and the high-wire act of big-time law.

Kirsten stood waiting for him on the wraparound veranda. Today his research aide and would-be fiancée was sheathed in gray silk, elegant in design and European in cut. Eyes the color of crushed lilacs watched his approach, giving nothing away. In the day's dim light her white-blond hair shimmered with a glow of internal fires, the enigmatic beacon of a future he had mistakenly thought was theirs to claim. Of all the uncertainties in his life, the worst by far was not knowing if Kirsten would show up again. Or even call to say she was gone.

He took the front steps in two bounds, slapped the rain off his briefcase, set it aside, and stepped behind her. Marcus wrapped both arms around this living mystery and lowered his head so that it rested upon her shoulder. Kirsten was a quiet woman by nature, a trait some counted as weakness in a society that prized noise and empty opinions. He could spend an evening in her company, count the number of words they spoke on both hands, and feel replete. If only he could find the proper words to make her stay.

"You need to put on a clean shirt. You smell of the courthouse."

"How does the courthouse smell?"

"Fear and ashes and burnt sulfur." Her voice was scarcely louder than the water streaming off the veranda roof. "Hurry now. He should be here any minute."

"Do I want to know who?"

"No, but I need to tell you." She stepped out of his embrace. "The chairman of New Horizons."

A pair of crows mocked him from the nearest tulip poplar. "The new guy, what's his name?"

Netty, his secretary, called through the screen door, "Dale Steadman. The man called just after you left this morning. Personally."

"You should have phoned and told me."

"We know what kind of morning you've had. You didn't need to be adding another worry like this one."

Thunder rumbled from the far south. Closer to hand a car pierced the slate veil and angled into the drive. Kirsten turned him toward the door. "Go, now. You're wearing sweat stains I can see through your jacket."

Two years ago he had waged courtroom combat against New Horizons, the world's largest producer of sports apparel. The press had called it a victory, and for a match-flare of an instant Marcus had stood illuminated upon the stage of public attention. But the young woman who had uncovered how a New Horizons factory used slave labor had come home in a casket. Her parents still had moments when their features would slacken and the loss of their only daughter would drill a hole through the center of their gazes. The case still wound its way through the appellate system, an endless maze created by frantic teams of New Horizons attorneys. Lawyers could spend lifetimes keeping their clients from ever shelling out a single dime, and be proud of their manufactured futility.

As he reknotted his tie, Marcus recalled the little he knew of his visitor. Dale Steadman was a newcomer to the scene, appointed chairman after New Horizons became the whipping boy of both the press and the human rights campaigners. Marcus' case had breached the company's armor. Their factories became the center of protests right around the globe. As a result their stock had nosedived. Dale Steadman was the former owner of a high-end sports apparel company that had been acquired by New Horizons just prior to the case. He had been foisted upon the company by panic-stricken stockholders as the new chairman. His initial steps toward cleaning up the corporate act had been viciously opposed within the company.

Marcus knew the house so intimately he could sense the change downstairs, as though the newcomers tramped across his own bones and not the conference room floor. He dreaded what was about to unfold. The air of his conference room would be as highly charged as a thunderstorm's ground zero, when invisible particles lifted hair like tentacles seeking the oblivion of a direct hit. The chairman of New Horizons would sit flanked by his senior legal team. They would deliver whatever news they carried with the precision of laser-guided bombs, study his reaction, then depart to measure and prepare the next skirmish. Maximum damage with minimum exposure. Appellate court cases were the modern-day equivalent of the Hundred Years' War.

But when he entered the conference room, he was confronted by the astonishing sight of a single man.

Dale Steadman sat so that he could stare out the open window, where the diminishing rain chimed and rustled. Kirsten sat beside him, angled so that she could observe both the guest and the day. Marcus' tread sounded loud as drumbeats as he approached his new adversary. "Mr. Steadman?"

"That's right." Dale Steadman rose and shook Marcus' hand, revealing a fighter's bulk beneath his tailored navy suit. "Thanks for seeing me."

"As we have repeatedly informed your attorneys, I have turned over the New Horizons case to the firm of Drews and Howe. What you see here is my entire practice. We're not equipped to manage an appellate battle."

His guest turned back to the open window, as though the reason for his visit was to be found in birdsong and rain-lashed wind. "I don't recognize these trees you're putting in here."

"Crepe myrtle." Marcus slid into his seat. "They replace a giant elm your lackeys destroyed when they tried to burn down my house."

Kirsten leaned forward and said, "Repeat for Mr. Glenwood what you just told me."

Marcus studied Kirsten's face. Her sympathetic tone was jarring. New Horizons had kidnapped and murdered her best friend. If asked, Marcus would have said their new CEO would never draw anything from her save loathing.

"My ex-wife has stolen my baby girl. We've been divorced seven months."

Netty entered and began pouring coffee. When Marcus remained silent, Kirsten asked, "Your ex-wife has abducted your child?"

"Three weeks ago."

"You have custody?"

"That's right."

"And your ex-wife?"

"She never showed any interest in Celeste until the publicity started."

Marcus continued to watch his fiancée, wondering how she could be so captivated by a tale that to him made no sense whatsoever. Kirsten asked, "What publicity?"

"My ex-wife is Erin Brandt."

"I've heard that name."

"She's an internationally famous opera star. A soprano. Sings all over the world." Dale Steadman uttered the words with the steady toll of a funeral bell. "Erin tried to keep our divorce a secret. But the European press found out somehow. There was a spate of articles."

"How long ago was that?"

"Five months."

"What does Ms. Brandt have to say about these allegations?"

"I haven't had contact with Erin since she stole Celeste. I kept hoping all this would work itself out. It's insane, I know. I've known it all along."

Kirsten glanced at Marcus, offering him the chance to take over. When he remained silent, she continued, "You haven't contacted the authorities up to now?"

"Three days after the fire, I heard from her lawyer. A spiteful Raleigh man by the name of Hamper Caisse. The lawyer said that if I made any move at all, they would convene a court hearing to reveal how drunk I was the night of the fire." The man spoke with the disjointed precision of addressing internal ghosts. "They'll call witnesses from the fire department and the police. They will have people from my community reveal how my drinking has been a matter of concern. They will question how such a man could possibly be left with responsibility for a baby. He said if I'm willing to work things out amicably, then I need to show some patience."

"But you think this offer is a lie?"

"Totally."

"You are saying your former wife has abducted your child and now seeks to mask the fact through false representation?"

"That's it exactly."

"Why?"

"Excuse me?"

"You said she didn't care for the child or contest your receiving full custody."

"That's right."

"So what has changed?"

"I have no idea."

"Before the events of that evening, when did you last speak directly with your former wife?"

"Almost a year ago. She left to sing in Paris and never returned. Finally I filed for divorce on the grounds of abandonment." Dale Steadman scooted a manila file across the table and addressed Marcus directly for the very first time. "I hear you're the patron saint of lost causes, Mr. Glenwood. I need just such a fighter in my corner."

CHAPTER

4

T HE CHILD'S MOTHER *and her mother's mother have never gotten along. Somehow just being around the older woman is enough to fracture her mother's immovable façade. When they are together, the old woman usually goes out of her way to say nothing. But a single smile toward the child, a word of quiet praise, and her mother begins a screeching tirade about meddling where she is not welcome. The child has only seen her grandmother twice in the previous four years.*

But the child hears from her. Every birthday and Christmas, a card arrives with three tickets for some Broadway show. What happens to the tickets, the child has no idea. The child's dreams of escape often center around the absent old woman.

Over the eight months leading to her thirteenth birthday, the child observes a change in her school friends. One by one they enter a different realm, a place that beckons with an allure as powerful as fury. They smirk together in the halls around school, giving little hand signs and one-word beacons that mean nothing to the child, except to show she is an outsider here as well. Until she is invited to join.

Four months before her thirteenth birthday, they invite the child to a sleepover. Her mother lets her go because the family is one of the most powerful in the city. Even her father, who pays almost no attention whatsoever to her activities, is impressed to hear where the child is spending the night. He starts in on his desire to have the man as a client. Her mother shuts him up with a single scathing remark.

After her mother drops her off, it takes the child almost half an hour to realize there are no adults home.

The child finds another couple of girls her age who look as lost and frightened as she feels. Together they move into a small corner of the living room, over by the blaring sound system. A movie is on the wall-sized television, but the picture is just meant for background lighting. There are almost three dozen girls tightly segregated into two groups—the majority are friends of the older sister, who is sixteen. The younger girls are barely tolerated. Especially after the boys arrive.

As the child watches, drugs and drinks spread around the room. Hash, pot, coke, speed, a new designer pill called ecstasy, wine, a couple of the older boys even bring champagne. This is a rich and generous crowd. Several times the boys come over to where the children crouch and urge them to have a toke, a sip, a dance. The older girls find this bitterly hilarious.

The child listens between the songs as other parents are scorned and dismissed. She sees the way others speak of their homes. She finds malignant comfort in not being so alone.

By the third party, it all seems pretty much normal.

Gradually her friends become restricted to girls from these gatherings. The child watches as one by one these friends allow themselves to be pulled into the game. That is what they call it, especially when around people who aren't included. The girls who depart from the no-fire corner begin urging the child to come on and join the game. The child can't say exactly why she resists. But it seems to her that they are becoming replicas of those they despise. Gay and lively on the outside, bitter and drugged within.

Even so, the child knows it is only a matter of time.

The night after her sixth game, she watches her parents with the detached interest of an eternal refugee. Their house is filled with a crowd of other false faces. The child helps the maid serve drinks and watches as her parents offer these strangers reptilian grins and chatter they do not even hear themselves. When the guests leave, her parents strip off the happy masks and reveal a steadfast hostility. They slide over to two opposing sofas, the last drinks charged like late-night ammunition. Her mother's final cigarette adds to the smoldering cauldron. They snipe carefully, little wounding bullets that have been collected and charged over the night's course.

Two nights later the child becomes trapped in a taxi with them. They are returning home from a party where the hosts had a clown act for the children, when a torrential downpour halts all traffic. For tor-

turous aeons she remains locked between them on a seat that smells of a hundred thousand miles of angry chatter and thwarted dreams and rain splashing against the window. The child tries her best not to hear a thing. Just the same, she inspects herself afterward in the bathroom mirror, and is astonished to find she does not bleed from the wounds to her heart. As she lies in her bed that night, the child decides there is no reason not to go ahead and enter the game.

Then four days later, her grandmother dies.

At the reading of the will, which the lawyer insists the child attend, she learns that a trust fund has been set up in her name. An education fund, the lawyer calls it, to be released upon the child's seventeenth birthday. One hundred and ten thousand dollars, every cent the grandmother has remaining after a long and lingering illness the child has not even known about. Her parents observe her with mute astonishment as the lawyer describes the precise terms of the child's ticket to freedom. She is to have total control of the money. Until the release date, she has the sole right to determine how the funds are to be preserved. Although the child does not understand much of what is said, the lawyer's words hold the delicate perfume of a foreign love song. She understands the most important thing, however. Silently she chants the phrase the entire way home while her parents fight viciously, for they have received nothing.

Total control.

The funds are moved into a passbook savings account. That night she calculates the amount of interest she will have accrued by her seventeenth birthday. She writes the sum down on a slip of paper. One hundred and thirty-seven thousand, four hundred and twenty dollars. She hides the paper in the back of her desk drawer, where she can take it out and look at it whenever she wants.

Two weeks later, she enters the school's student counselor's office and announces, "I want to graduate a year early."

The woman is heavyset in the manner of one who has long resigned herself to a life of uncomfortable chairs and bad air and school food. "Aren't you a little young to be planning such things?"

"No."

"Do your parents know about this?"

"No. They can't ever know."

The woman is neither dumb nor new to her job. "Is there a problem at home we need to talk about?"

"No. We have a perfect home."

"I see." This is not the first time the counselor has heard that one either. She rises from her desk. "Wait here a moment, please."

The counselor comes back with the child's records. "Are you serious about this?"

"Very."

"Well, the first thing you're going to have to do is improve your grades. Which means applying yourself a good deal harder than you have so far. Can you do that?"

"Yes."

The child's terseness does not seem to bother the counselor at all. "We can increase your load a little, put some meat in here and there. What about summer school, are you up for that?"

"All right."

"Let's say we give it a couple of months, then if you stay serious about this, we'll have another chat." When the child rises from her seat, the counselor adds, "Sometimes the hardest lesson to learn is when to ask for help."

"There's no problem," she replies and leaves the office.

And there isn't. Not anymore.

She severs all connections with her friends and the game. In fact, she stops almost everything that is not directly tied to school and her work. That term, she receives one C and manages to raise the rest of her grades to B's and A's. The crowd of former friends rename her Casper. The next term, she receives her last B ever. By that spring her former friends no longer even greet her in the hall.

Two weeks before her seventeenth birthday, she graduates with honors. Two universities offer her full rides. She accepts the offer from Georgetown because they agree to defer her entry a year.

The day she turns seventeen, she gives herself a ticket to Europe as her birthday present. Her parents do not even know she has left until they receive her one and only letter, sent the week after her arrival in London.

Two months later she has made her way across France and down the length of Italy. Her passport and a wad of traveler's checks are stuffed deep inside her backpack. She likes introducing herself as Casper, and by the time she arrives in Rome it is the only name she uses. She makes no plans further along than the next seventy-two hours. She wears Gortex ankle boots and high wool socks and hiking gear and a Gypsy kerchief sewn with silver spangles to hide her hair.

She meets some Dutch backpackers at the hostel in Naples who invite her to take the train over to Bari. From there they will catch the two-day ferry to Athens. On the train ride they talk about mystic beaches untouched by tourist hordes—the southern coves of Crete, Cleopatra Island off Turkey, Lamu Island near the Kenyan coast, Niias in Indonesia. The child listens and laughs and shares a wineskin of fiery red. As the day trundles on, she aches with the realization she has finally found a reason to use the word happy and mean it.

If only she could hold on to that feeling a little while longer.

The second night of their boat crossing, three of the backpackers drug her wine and rape her repeatedly on the upper deck between the two smokestacks.

All she remembers afterward is their drunken laughter and the way smoke keeps rising to stain the star-flung sky.

T HE NEXT MORNING, Kirsten worked in Marcus' front garden forming a periwinkle border around the central elm. She dug between the roots and tried to hold to a circular formation. A high summer wind blasted through a cloudless sky. Heat squeezed sweat from her forehead like a weightlifter working a sponge. Why she remained here at all was a question that only aggravated the fissure in her brain. Two warring factions battled in fierce mental salvos. Impossible choices. Impossible decisions.

Six months ago she had started working as Marcus' research staffer. Almost immediately the neighbors had taken her presence as a sign of something deeper in the making. They welcomed her with flowers and shrubs from their own gardens. It was the clearest possible message both of her own acceptance and of the affection they felt for Marcus.

It was also a quiet signal of their watchfulness, for never did she receive the next gift until the previous one was planted. Half this neighborhood attended Deacon's church. While they were far too polite to say a thing, Kirsten knew the eyes were scouting carefully. Her comings and goings were the subject of the same stream of gossip as their own children. This she knew from Netty, who had heard the mildly approving chatter at the supermarket checkout counter.

The only exception to the community's cordiality was Deacon's wife, Fay Wilbur. She was inside right now, doing her thrice-weekly cleaning. The woman had said nothing, but Kirsten sensed the storm brewing. Fay eyed her with the same distaste she would a worm among her vegetables. There was going to be a reckoning. It was only a matter of time.

Her internal foment and the day's searing wind masked the man's approach entirely. Then a shadow fell over her and a man's voice said, "You just gotta be the Yankee dolly they warned me about."

Kirsten scrambled to her feet. "Can I help you?"

"Soon as they heard I was stopping by, they said I was gonna fall in love with this dolly and I might as well get used to the idea right fast." He was a redheaded behemoth with a blade for a face. All his features slanted sharply toward the arrow of a nose, the angles so tight even his forehead appeared retooled. The swept-over curl of greasy red hair almost met with his eyebrows, which only accented the barbed glint to his eyes.

When his gaze drifted down her sweat-stained front, Kirsten shifted her grip on the trowel. "I asked you what you wanted."

His grin ridged out in taut compression until his eyes almost disappeared. "Just came by to deliver this check. You ain't so rich you'd pass up some extra greenbacks. Not with Glenwood camped over here on the trashy side of the river."

"I don't recognize you as one of Mr. Glenwood's clients."

"That's all right, dolly. We know Marcus." A blast of wind pried back the sleeve of his rumpled jacket like the lid of a filthy gray jar. Tattoos crawled down his wrist and over the back of his hand. "Somebody oughta told you by now, it ain't healthy to do your planting in the high heat."

She took a step away, backing toward the porch. "Unless you are registered as a client I can't help you."

He tracked her, moving closer in the process. "I'm the one doing the helping, or I would, if you'd stop this two-step across the lawn."

"Are you or are you not a client?"

"I'm what you might call an interested third party. Never had the occasion to meet old Marcus personally. Couldn't hardly pass up the opportunity to call on the man himself when I heard he was knocking on New Horizons' door again."

She kept her face to him and tried to angle her backward motion toward the house. "Please come back another time and talk with Mr. Glenwood directly."

"You don't look all that busy to me." He paced lightly along with her. "Hot and bothered, maybe. But I've always liked my ladies to glisten."

Kirsten aimed the dirt-flecked trowel straight at the man's heart and screamed, "Netty!"

Quick as a striking cottonmouth, the man snatched the trowel from her grasp. He tossed it in the air and caught it at shoulder height, such that it was now aimed for a downward killing blow. His grin was a distillation of menace.

"What on earth's going on out here?" The front door slammed back. "Sephus Jones, are you messing with that lady?"

The grin relaxed a trifle. The man leaned down and jammed the trowel so hard it disappeared into the earth up to his fist. He then reached into his jacket and plucked out an envelope. He whipped forward and jammed it into the front pocket of Kirsten's shorts. In and out so fast she did not have time to scream. "Deliver that check to Marcus for me, will you?"

"*Sephus!* You leave that woman alone!"

Kirsten scampered for the front steps and Netty's comforting fury. Her entire frame was trembling so hard her footsteps were as unsteady as an infant's. She could still feel his hand in her pocket.

"I'm calling the police, you don't get offa my lawn!"

The man cast Kirsten another tight spark from those half-seen eyes, and said, "You have yourself a nice old day, now, you hear? Oh, and tell Marcus for me I'm glad to hear he's decided to dance another tune with us. *Real* glad."

The two women watched him saunter to his idling truck and drive off with a tattooed wave. When Kirsten's breathing stopped shuddering, she said, "He said New Horizons sent him."

Netty squinted into the sun-drenched distance. "I'm not the least surprised."

"You know him?"

"Know of him. Sephus Jones."

"He threatened me."

"Yeah, that sounds about right." Netty's face bore the pinched quality of someone looking for a place to spit. "Folks around here refer to him as Skunk. Whenever he's disappeared off for a spell, there's no question but Sephus has been sent up. Again." She pointed to where the envelope's corner poked from her shorts. "What's that he planted in your pocket?"

"A check." She used two fingers to pull the envelope free. "My guess is it's a retainer from New Horizons for Dale Steadman's legal fees."

"You want me to burn it?"

Kirsten entered the front hall and set the envelope upon the side table. She then headed upstairs for the guestroom shower. Sephus Jones' imprint was on her skin like a rising bruise. "I think Marcus should see it."

"Why spoil the man's Friday? I could dig a hole and bury it out there by your plants, he knows where it is if he's interested."

CHAPTER

5

T HE WAKE COUNTY COURTHOUSE was just another Raleigh downtown high-rise, banded across its center by three stories of windowless concrete. These middle floors housed prisoners awaiting trial
and those sentenced to anything less than ninety days. A second jail
had recently been erected across the street and was connected by a
fourth-floor walkover. The courthouse foyer was a tidal wash of everything wrong with the legal system. The currents moved in predictable
fashion, rushing in at half-past eight, out at noon, in at two, out at
five. When Marcus arrived, the lines at the metal detectors were ninety
strong. Marcus waited while a rat-haired mother with a squalling baby
explained to a bored deputy why her common-law man really didn't
mean to kick the kid. Staffing the courthouse information desk was
one of the most hated duties a deputy could pull. The accused and
their families loved to use the deputies as a captive audience, practicing
their spiel before moving upstairs to the judges' chambers. The deputy
waited for the mother to draw breath, then directed her to the crèche,
as no children were permitted in family court unless called there by the
judge.

Marcus asked, "Any idea where I could find Anita Harshaw
today?"

The deputy gave him a Teflon scan, swiftly classing Marcus as one
of the legal opposition. "She usually hangs out on the third floor."

"Thanks." He slid around the crush waiting for the elevators and
took the stairs. On the third floor he entered a linoleum and fluores-
cent realm. Two windowless lobbies were filled with grim tension and

confusion. Lawyers stood in clusters, smirking effigies in slick suits, telling jokes and shaping last-minute deals.

Anita Harshaw was an alpaca-draped blonde who lived and breathed divorce work. She outweighed Marcus by a hundred pounds and accented her size with bulky knits. The attorney spotted his approach and greeted him with "If it isn't the roller-coaster kid. What is it today, Marcus, you on the rise or the fall?"

"I want to talk with you about a case you handled."

"Is it privileged?"

"Probably not."

"Then I'm happy to dish out the dirt." She stepped out of earshot from the other lawyers. "Who's the target?"

"The former Erin Steadman."

"Couldn't possibly be privileged. Seeing as how I never even met the lady."

"And now she's taken other counsel."

"For what?"

"Custody dispute."

Up close the woman had a rich floral scent, an unexpected hint of femininity. "You're kidding me."

"Tell me what you know."

"That'll take about five seconds. The lady calls from somewhere foreign. Germany, wasn't it?"

"Düsseldorf."

"See, you know more than I do. She gave me three sentences. Handle the case. No visitation rights, no argument, no alimony, no publicity. Fast and quiet."

"She didn't show up for the hearing?"

"I just said I've never met the woman. So who's handling her now?"

"Hamper Caisse."

She caught her smile before it was fully formed. "Heard about your set-to the other day. Did they really give that old pastor a cheer?"

"Standing ovation."

"Sorry I missed that one."

"Any idea why she'd make a case out of custody now?"

"Not a clue. The lady wanted this thing to die a quiet death and disappear."

"Publicity," Marcus repeated from his talk with Dale.

"I told her that was the last thing on anybody's agenda, and I could still represent her interests and seek partial custody."

"She said no?"

"Wouldn't even let me finish the sentence."

Marcus hefted his briefcase a trifle. "The file makes no mention of who was counsel for Dale."

"On account of how Steadman represented himself. Man showed up looking like the sacrificial lamb. One thing I do remember. When the judge granted him custody, Steadman broke down right there in chambers. Only reason I didn't feel worse about not going for his jugular."

"Thanks, Anita." Marcus started to turn away, then asked, "Any idea why the divorce hearing was set in Raleigh?"

"Same thing all over again. Too much risk of publicity down Wilmington way."

"Can you give me your impression of Dale Steadman?"

"Other than clearly loving that child, I didn't have one. We were in and out of Judge Sears' chambers in less than five minutes." The dark eyes glinted with experienced humor. "You looking to build a case or find a way out?"

"As soon as I discover the answer to that one," Marcus replied, "I'll let you know."

The courthouse's rear doors opened onto the Fayetteville Street Mall, a pebble-dash haven for lawyers and bureaucrats and bums. The previous day's rain bubbled off the surface, turning the air into a sauna laden with molten asphalt and car exhaust. Marcus selected an empty bench beneath a shade elm and pretended to watch the slow-motion theater. If only he knew what to do.

A voice behind him said, "I guess I got it wrong."

"Excuse me?"

"The Steadman case. You're not handling it after all." The young man had a complexion of cinnamon-laced latté. He wore a summer assortment of high fashion—sharply creased gabardine trousers, striped shirt of Egyptian cotton, flash tie. He approached, but did not offer his hand. "Omar Dell, court reporter for the *News and Observer*."

"You are definitely jumping the gun here."

"I called your office. The lady I spoke with did not deny that you were working for New Horizons."

"Who was that?"

"I did not get her name."

"You call that a confirmation?"

"Oh, I already had the confirmation." Pianists' hands held a gold pen and leather-bound pad. "I was just looking for comment."

"Sir, you are encroaching on my territory." Despite all logical reasons to the contrary, Marcus found himself drawn to the man. "You look more like a hotshot trial attorney than a reporter."

"I've been working this beat for almost three years, looking for my ticket to glory." Dell's even features showed a dead-set determination. "Last time you created a publicity hurricane, I got shoved aside. This time I'm not so junior."

"You see television cameras hanging around here?"

"They'll come. My aunt goes to Deacon's church. I've been hearing the stories about you for two years. Putting you and New Horizons back together is like sticking the detonator into a hydrogen bomb and turning the key."

"But like you said," Marcus pointed out, "I'm not certain there's a case. For me, at least. And if there is, I won't be working for New Horizons."

Dark eyes did a partial melt, his disappointment was that keen. "Couldn't help but hope, even when I saw you sitting out here."

"Where else should I be?"

"You mean to tell me the man's doing an end run around Marcus Glenwood?" Omar Dell gripped Marcus' arm and dragged him from his bench, out into the hammering heat, across the concrete anvil, and into the wash of false coolness. "Hurry now, there's not a moment to lose."

As soon as Marcus entered the courtroom, he knew Hamper was dressed for combat. The attorney had a series of tailored silk suits, shades of gray or palest pastels, and kept for days of serious war. Hamper had the flamboyant gestures of a frustrated actor, and used his dress as he would a good prop. These suits shimmered with each motion and had mesmerized many a jury. Lawyers who had mistaken Hamper for a fool sneered when they spotted him so clothed, called him Mirror Man, and pretended not to fear meeting him in court.

When Marcus and Omar Dell slipped into the courtroom, Hamper was saying, "Outside the scope of the divorce hearing, the couple made a private arrangement to jointly share custody."

Judge Sears watched as Marcus strode down the left-hand aisle, pushed through the barrier, and set his briefcase down upon the empty attorney's table. "Mr. Glenwood, do you have business before this court?"

"I have been asked to represent Dale Steadman, your honor."

She frowned at Hamper. "Did you not just inform me you had attempted to contact opposing counsel?"

"Yes, your honor." Hamper did his best to swallow bitter dismay. "That is, the records showed Mr. Steadman had no representation."

She gave Marcus a moment to settle, then returned her attention to the file on her desk. "As I recall, there was no mention whatsoever of any such agreement in the divorce decree."

"There was no need, your honor." Hamper waved a sheaf of papers. "As this document shows, Ms. Erin Brandt and Mr. Dale Steadman had already agreed on joint custody. Everything was fine, as far as my client was concerned. Then her former husband went back on his side of the bargain."

Judge Sears waved him forward and accepted the document. She leafed through the pages, then said for the record, "I have before me a notarized document signed by both parties and dated seven months ago. Mr. Glenwood, I assume you have a copy of this agreement?"

"This is the first I've heard of any such thing, your honor."

Hamper passed over a second copy and suggested, "Maybe you need to establish a better line of communication with your client."

"That will do, Mr. Caisse."

"Your honor, this agreement states clearly that the couple agree to joint custody. The dates when Ms. Brandt are to have the child were left out because they agreed to work around my client's singing sched-ule. Which is precisely why they did not bring this to the court's atten-tion during the divorce. Ms. Brandt is an opera diva and sings all over the world. This open-date arrangement was only natural."

Marcus pretended to review the document. All he could clearly focus upon was his client's signature on the final page, the notary's seal, and the question ringing through his mind as to who Dale Steadman really was.

Judge Sears set the document aside and demanded, "You are now filing a motion to enforce this agreement?"

"That was Ms. Brandt's original intention, your honor. But when she returned home last month to try and determine why the agreement was not being followed, she found her husband drunk and dangerously out of control."

"Objection," Marcus said. "Hearsay."

"Your honor, I have witnesses here to show that this scandal is in fact the latest incident in what is a very worrisome trend."

Marcus pointed out, "It is not customary to have live testimony at these hearings."

"What they have to say is so important we wanted the court to hear for itself why this child should not be allowed to spend another single hour in the company of this dangerous man."

"Mr. Glenwood, would you care to respond?"

"Your honor, I thought this was going to be a simple matter of requesting an emergency motion for *ex partae* custody." *Ex partae* was an appeal for the court to take physical custody of the child. This temporary injunction could be requested by any interested party—parent, relatives, foster care, social workers, even the court itself. It granted the court time to determine whether the child was endangered in any way. In this case, the court would require the child to be returned from Germany and delivered into the court's care, from which a custody ruling would be made.

"Sounds reasonable," Judge Sears said. "Mr. Caisse?"

"We object in the strongest possible terms, your honor. Because of the seriousness of the situation that would face the child if returned to the father, we ask that you hear what my two witnesses have to say."

She glanced at Marcus, waiting for an objection. But Marcus remained uncertain what path to take. Given enough room, he was certain Hamper Caisse would grant him the perfect out.

"Proceed, Mr. Caisse."

"I call Bert Warner to the stand."

The assistant chief of Wilmington's fire department was a veteran of hundreds of courtroom battles. Yet his bland Southern drone could not remove the potent quality of that night. By the time he finished describing what he had found at the Steadman dwelling, the crammed courtroom held to a rare hushed state. "We searched the house and found no sign of anyone. Then we discovered Mr. Steadman passed out on his back lawn. We weren't certain exactly what he was saying, but we gathered the child had been taken somewhere by the mother.

The man was so drunk or drugged we had to wake him up four different times. Each time he just repeated himself, saying something about the child, then passed out again."

Hamper Caisse found one word to be especially delicious. "Drugged."

"We found no sign of illegal substances in the house. And the man smelled of alcohol. But he was so far gone . . ." The chief shrugged. "The fourth time we woke him up, he spent a while surveying the house, then asked us to help him back to his boat. He passed out again there."

"You made this journey up from Wilmington on your own accord and at your own expense, did you not?"

"Yes."

"Could you tell the court why?"

"I have three daughters of my own. The youngest has just turned two."

Hamper resumed his seat. "Your witness."

Marcus' natural curiosity overcame the desire to distance himself. "Sir, did you happen to find any evidence of the fire being deliberately set?"

"Nothing that first night. When we returned the next day, Mr. Steadman had already called in workers. Mr. Steadman said he would cover the cost of reconstruction himself, rather than wait for us and the insurance people to sign off on our investigation." His tone expressed clearly what he thought of the whole process. "Said he wanted to have the place ready when his daughter returned. Which is why I decided to come and testify."

"No further questions."

"You may step down, Mr. Warner."

"Your honor, I call Russell Dermont to the stand."

Dermont was an oddly assembled man. He matched Marcus' six-four frame, but draped it with an additional hundred and fifty pounds of pure lard. His chin was lost in the pouch that obliterated the knot of his tie. His silver hair formed a waxed wave over a very large dome. His palm-sized ears were so flat they looked webbed to his skull. Delicate lips appeared stolen from a smaller woman.

"You are chairman of Dermont Industries, is that not correct?"

"Yes."

"You also served three terms as president of the Wilmington Chamber of Commerce."

"That's right."

"We are indeed most grateful that you would take the time to join us today, sir." Hamper rose and began pacing. Each foot was lifted with exaggerated care, his knobby knees bunching beneath the shimmering suit. "How long have you known Dale Steadman?"

"Ever since he was the star fullback at the University of North Carolina at Wilmington. Met him a few times, usually when he was invited to some city function or another. He's come and gone several times over the years. The first I knew about him showing up in town again was when he bought that island off Towles Road. Paid a ton of money from what I heard."

Even the witness paused in anticipation of Marcus' objection to the evident hearsay. But the impetus was not there.

"You say he paid over the odds," Hamper Caisse prodded.

"That boy just spent and spent and spent. Place has got a six-car garage, boathouse, poolhouse, and his very own old-timey plank bridge. Word is, the bridge alone cost him half a million dollars. Spent almost four million more on the house. Had two architects and three contractors working on it at one point or another. I know on account of how one was my cousin. Had to have the best of everything. Got this one room just for a piano. Thing cost four hundred thousand dollars, I know that's a fact on account of how it was in the papers. Boy was plain crazy. Spent his money like a drug king."

This time, even Judge Sears turned and waited for Marcus to speak up. When he remained silent, Hamper drew his little two-step closer to the witness stand. "What does the local business community think of Dale Steadman?"

"They don't think any more of him than they have to."

"Now that is a strange thing to my ears. I mean, here you've got Wilmington's only former pro football player. A homegrown hero like that, I'd expect you to say he's been ushered into the top echelon."

Dermont had the restless quality of a man dealing with a deep-seated irritant, one he could not entirely suppress. He kneaded the chair arms, shifted his weight to emphasize the end of each sentence, crossed and uncrossed his legs, straightened his tie, pulled at the skin that ticked by his right eye. "When he came back to town, there were folks who invited him and his new wife just about everywhere. He was offered a chance to join the alumni committee, the local clubs, you name it. He turned them all down flat. Those of us who remember the first time he came back, we just held our peace."

"Why is that?"

"Because Dale Steadman is a shyster and a flimflam artist. You can't believe a word the man says."

This time Marcus felt forced to say, "Objection."

"Withdrawn." Hamper Caisse did not bother hiding his satisfaction. "What can you say about his home life?"

"Lady found out he was a crook and a cheat. She left him. Word is, he beat her something awful."

"Objection."

Hamper did not wait for the judge to sustain. "There has also been mention made of his drinking."

"All the time."

"Were there drugs?"

"Lot of it going around." Dermont used both hands to adjust his belt, girding himself for the main assault. "Not long after he started his little textile company, Steadman got himself into a serious financial tangle. He'd maxed out at the bank. Went hat in hand around the local community, begging for a handout. Nobody wanted to help him, of course. Why get involved in a company that's going under? Just be throwing good money after bad. So we were all watching and waiting for the ax to fall, when suddenly the guy is flush again. There was some rumor of an old buddy from England bailing him out, but Dale never bothered to explain it to a soul. Which makes you wonder if it wasn't another source, if you see what I mean. Man had to have gotten his money from someplace."

Hamper's return to his table was a triumphal march. "Your witness."

Marcus lingered over the cage he was drawing upon his legal pad. To not respond was to declare himself uninvolved. Which was tempting. But that would leave Dale Steadman unsupported and defenseless. Which was something Marcus would not do to a panhandler. Much less a father, no matter how poor a father he might be.

Judge Sears broke into his reverie with the warning "Mr. Glenwood, I see no reason at this point not to proceed with a custody ruling."

Marcus rose to his feet, certain now he was hooked, hauled in, gutted, and descaled. "Your honor, as I stated in the beginning, I merely intended to apply for an *ex partae* order."

"Do you have any questions for this witness?"

"How am I supposed to, your honor, when this character assassination has hit me utterly out of the blue?"

She turned to the witness. "You may step down, sir."

Hamper waited until the Wilmington official had stepped through the barrier and seated himself in the front row to declare, "Your honor, Marcus Glenwood is not the star of this show, much as he would like us all to believe otherwise. This is about protecting a child."

"The child your client abducted," Marcus pointed out.

"She had no choice," Hamper shot back. "None."

"The same child," Marcus continued, "Ms. Brandt previously abandoned."

"She did not abandon the child, your honor. That is a misconception fostered by her ex-husband. The custody agreement proves this. The person who deviated from the plan was the husband."

"My client denies this, your honor."

"Let me get this straight. This is the same client who denies ever abusing her?"

"Absolutely."

"Or the baby?"

"Your honor, I object to these baseless accusations."

"Oh. Wait now." Hamper paused long enough to cast Marcus a malicious glint. "This objection is being made by a man who couldn't even protect his own children in their hour of direst need?"

The judge revealed a serrated edge to her Southern cadence. "You will apologize to counsel, or you will be censured by this court."

"Of course I apologize, your honor."

"Not to me."

"Marcus, excuse me. I simply got carried away by the concerns of this moment."

"Mr. Glenwood, do you have a motion that you wish to place before this court?"

Marcus recognized the offer of an out. "Only that this matter be carried forward until next week so that I might have time to prepare."

"So ruled. I am away Monday. I expect you both to be here first thing Tuesday with answers to questions I haven't dreamed up yet." Judge Sears applied her gavel. "Next case."

Marcus' intention to waylay Hamper Caisse outside the court-room was stymied twice over. The attorney was instantly snagged by a frantic client. Then Marcus found himself confronting a very excited Omar Dell. Which was not altogether a bad thing, he decided. There were certain risks to assaulting another member of the bar in the dis-trict courthouse lobby.

The court reporter said, "That man just tried a smash and grab."

"I still can't see why you're so interested in a custody dispute."

"I told you before, Mr. Glenwood. You're nothing but fireworks and fame in the making." The man's eyes held a joy too fresh for this courtroom. "Give me something. There's bound to be some lead you can pass on that won't breach your client's confidentiality."

Marcus nodded a grim commitment to the case. "In time."

CHAPTER

6

IN ATHENS, THE YOUNG WOMAN *starts to make a formal complaint to
the police. But she walks away when the looks they give her and the
questions they keep repeating filter through the lingering fog of drug
and pain. She leaves Athens the day her passport and traveler's checks
are replaced, both of which the Dutch backpackers have stolen.*

*She spends almost two months running from herself. Then she
wakes up in a Barcelona hotel with a vicious sangria hangover, and she
can't even say what country she is in, or how long she has been there,
or why she continues to leak tears even in her sleep.*

*When she arrives in Switzerland, late September rains have trans-
formed the highland roads into rivulets of fading autumn colors. She
finds a waitressing job in Zermatt's top hotel. That lasts until the
maître d' makes it plain there is only one way she will be allowed to
stay.*

*She moves to a bar at the base of the Valais glacier, the local hang-
out for ski instructors and Matterhorn guides. She meets the Swiss version of a cowboy, a rancher from the Ticino province, with smooth
Italian ways and eyes like electric night. She lets him get her drunk and
do whatever he wants. But he does it only once, and he leaves immediately after. There are a couple of others who try, and she no longer sees
any reason to put up a fuss. But something they find in her leaves them
unable to stay the night, or return, or even speak to her the same way
afterward. What it is exactly, she can't say. From her side, the moment
they begin their moves, the Dutch backpackers' drug seeps out of some
secret recess deep at the center of her being, and turns her utterly*

numb. *The only sensation she can recall afterward is watching the smoke rise and stain the eternal night.*

By the start of the high season, she has been adopted as an unofficial mascot by the local ski troop. They all compete to teach her, all save the ones who have been with her for a night or an hour. They name her Schwisterli, *little sister in Swiss German, and they find her absolutely fearless. They take her down the most difficult black slopes long before she is ready. She learns by falling and rising and falling again. They share with her the thrills of following the international slalom circuit, of racing supercharged bikes on snowbound Alpine roads, and of drinking thimblefuls of espresso spiked with* Pomme, *the fiery Valais apple brandy. And they protect her from any outsider who might otherwise try their wiles on the lovely white-blond apparition with no past and few words and a gaze like shattered sapphires.*

Toward the end of the season she sends a letter off to Georgetown University, requesting that they postpone her place and scholarship for a further year. She makes a halfhearted attempt to describe her European experiences in a positive light, then halts when the effort to look back makes her sick to her stomach. Georgetown responds so swiftly it almost seems as though they have been expecting her letter, saying the place is still hers, but not the money.

The next step is the easiest of all.

When the month of spring mud announces the end of the winter season, she packs her bags and accepts a ride to London. Some of the instructors are headed for the international nightclubbing circuit. Once the high snows melt and the skies clear, they will return as mountaineering guides. Until then, they are tall, muscled, young, and rippling with good Swiss cheer.

Their first night in a new club off Piccadilly, they introduce her to the international elite. The talk follows a tragically familiar path along beaches with clubs—Majorca, Sardinia, Rhodes, Lanzarote. This time, she enters the scene with eyes wide open.

The next night she returns on her own. And the night after. She accepts an ecstasy tab from someone, then follows him up to the dance floor. A while later he realizes she is neither dancing with him nor hearing his shouted comments. She does not even notice his departure. In fact, she is not dancing to the music at all. She is too busy writhing to the thoughts that glide about her brain like eager snakes.

Maybe she is inherently bad. This fact would certainly make sense of what otherwise is just a set of random events that direct her life. Maybe there is a dark and tainted portion of herself that rules supreme. All she can say for certain is, looking inside means confronting a colossal bleakness. Depression and a vague self-fury hover just beyond her vision, always eager to clutch and smother. She opens her eyes, surveys the flashing lights and the thunderous din, and reflects that maybe this is where she has always belonged.

By the time she returns to the group, she has decided it is time to stop fighting the inevitable, and give herself over to the game.

She spends four months doing whatever comes her way. Her looks and availability draw the attention of the flash crowd. The fact that nothing seems to impress her only makes them want to shower her with more. An older man gives her champagne and coke and diamonds and a ride to Capri in his private jet. He lasts eleven days. The diamonds are sold and the funds placed in her account. Why she saves the money at all, she has no idea. Georgetown becomes just another myth somewhere beyond the game.

Another player draws her into a modeling agency. Her blond beauty and utterly detached air perfectly suit the current mode. She spends the next three months allowing herself to be flown and painted and dressed and positioned and photographed. The girls and boys in this arm of the game are the same, only more elegantly so. They speak the empty chatter. They make swift little liaisons they pretend are important, at least for the moment. She becomes part of a crowd that hails one another in airports and clubs and studios with excited greetings and a desperate need to find the familiar wherever they go.

In early December she returns to Zermatt. Things are the same, yet different. Calls from modeling agencies keep coming in, taken at the café because she does not bother to connect her apartment's phone. The Alpine guides pretend that she is still one of them, yet they are all preparing for a departure she refuses to accept.

Finally she leaves for a modeling gig in Geneva, just one day. But that leads to a studio in Zurich, then the runways in Milan and Paris and Brussels. And before she knows it, April is dawning, and a million miles away the highland snows are gone.

Over the next five months Kirsten Stansted travels twice around the globe.

One night in early September, the agency puts nine of them into a suite. Kirsten can't care enough to recall either the clothing line or the magazine, even the city. They go to some club. A handsome young man and a beautiful young woman resume a romance they have started somewhere else. Only in the limo taking them home, the woman discovers that the young man has been with another. And the young man discovers the woman is taking this far worse than expected.

The next morning Kirsten is awakened by a chorus of screams and the sight of the young woman sprawled dead in her bathroom.

After the police finally depart and the agency's lawyer makes them sign forms nobody bothers to read and the hotel expels them and they are off to another day's gig, one of the other women consoles the handsome young man by saying, "Don't blame yourself. She forgot the first rule of this game, is all."

The next morning, Kirsten leaves for Washington.

FTER HER CONFRONTATION with Sephus Jones, Kirsten brought in
her gym bag with the change of office clothes and showered in the
upstairs guestroom. Marcus had said nothing when she had deposited
her makeup in the big home's unused bath. But his silent pleasure had
been so vast she had grappled for days with a renewed urge to flee.
How could she tell Marcus that he was someone else's perfect catch?
Especially when she remained so viciously at war with her own desires.

She returned downstairs to be confronted by the crumpled envelope resting on the front hall table. She could still feel the man's lightning jab into her pocket, the roughness of his fingers on her thigh. She
debated calling Marcus at the Raleigh courthouse to tell him . . .
What? That New Horizons remained an enemy? That she had finally
decided it was best to return to Washington? She sighed her way into
her desk at the rear of Netty's office.

Research on Dale Steadman took no time at all. The man had left a
trail of headlines. The local Wilmington paper called Dale Steadman
the epitome of a self-made man, the product of two university lecturers
who were both mortified to discover they had sired a behemoth who
loved to do battle. He had been an all-state fullback, then played one
season of pro ball before injury permanently sidelined him. He had
gone on to earn a real degree at Duke, in accounting of all things. He
had then returned to Wilmington and established a textile company
specializing in high-end sports fashion.

Fay Wilbur chose that moment to come thumping through the
office's rear door. Deacon's wife was a rail-thin woman who never
stopped moving. Kirsten could feel the woman's glare on her back, an
acidic torch that just begged for battle. Fay banged the dust mop
around the room, striking every available surface and glaring constantly at Kirsten.

Netty was heads-down at her own computer, her desk at the
office's far end. When Fay finally harrumphed her disgust and departed, Netty said, "That woman is dead set on giving me hives this
morning."

"It's not you."

"You know what's going on here?"

Kirsten did not reply.

"Well, the woman's in a state, is all I can say."

Kirsten returned to the research. Three years later, New Horizons had bought Dale out. He started spending more time in New York. He sat on boards and did some consulting for U.S. textile companies seeking to avoid moving their operations overseas. He met Erin Brandt. They pursued an international romance, they married. The Steadmans built a home in Wilmington and subsequently divorced. One child, a daughter.

The phone rang. Netty answered with "Marcus Glenwood's office. Just a moment please." She cupped the phone and called, "Fay, it's for you."

The thunking halted. "Who's that calling?"

"Your daughter. Line three."

The mop was dropped with a clatter. The two women exchanged a glance as Fay picked up the conference room phone and snapped, "What is it now?" She was silent a long moment, then, "I can't tell you any more than I did the last time. I get to it soon as the man walks in the door."

Fay slammed down the phone, picked up her mop, and started up the front stairs trailing smoky epitaphs.

Netty rose from her desk with her mug in hand. "Never thought I'd need to run a gauntlet just to freshen my coffee."

As she was leaving the office the phone rang. Netty snagged the phone on Kirsten's desk. "Marcus Glenwood's office. I'm sorry, Mr. Glenwood is in court this morning." She listened a moment. "Who may I say is calling?"

Netty gave Kirsten a curious glance. "What is this in regard to, please?"

Netty listened a moment further, then pressed the mute button and said, "Senator Jacobs' office wants to talk with you about the Steadman case."

"Me?"

"He even knew your name. Should I say you're not available?"

"This is growing worse by the minute."

"What is?"

Kirsten reached for her receiver. "Kirsten Stansted."

"Brent Daniels, Ms. Stansted. I run the senator's local operations. We understand your office is about to become involved in an international custody dispute."

"That is for Mr. Glenwood to say."

"Then our sources have it wrong?"

"How did you get my name?"

"Ms. Stansted, I don't know if you're aware, but there are over six hundred cases where American courts have assigned custody to one parent, only to have the child abducted by the other and shielded from being returned by the German court system."

"Sir, I asked you a question."

"This is a direct violation of the Hague Convention on Children. It has become a matter of concern to the Senate Foreign Relations Committee. We have been looking for a landmark case to force the German government's hand." There was the rustle of pages. "The senator is hoping to be in Raleigh this weekend. Could you ask Mr. Glenwood to stop by the senator's local office and let us discuss the matter?"

"I will pass on your message."

"Something your office might not be aware of, Ms. Stansted. Erin Brandt will be leaving for London sometime late Sunday evening. She's been contracted to perform at Covent Garden, which is the way the Royal Opera House is usually referred to. It's her only scheduled visit outside Germany this summer. Just a little something to establish our bona fides, give your boss a reason to stop by. Shall we say Sunday afternoon around five?"

As she hung up the phone, Fay banged her way down the stairs, quarreling with the railing and the front hall mirror before heading back into the kitchen. Netty said, "Deacon should get a place at heaven's front table for putting up with that woman."

Kirsten rose, picked up her cup, and headed for the rear doors. Netty watched her with astonishment. "You can't possibly be needing caffeine that bad."

Kirsten found Fay peering angrily into the refrigerator and muttering to herself. "Can I help you with something?"

Fay reached in and snagged a plate with cautious disapproval. "What is this mess here?"

"Fresh tofu. Bean curd."

Fay Wilbur was a smoldering wick of a woman. She shook the plate, making the white curd glisten and wobble. "You're feeding my boy white Jell-O?" She gave it a careful sniff, and her features wrinkled even further. "Land sakes, this stuff is long dead."

"Put it back, please."

"And what do we have here." Fay set the plate on the counter, but kept her gaze inside the refrigerator. "Would you just look at this mess."

Kirsten moved close enough to be able to see what she was pointing at. "That's fresh basil. And Brie."

"How much did you pay for this wine?" She pulled out a bottle, raised her eyebrows at the label. "I know my boy didn't go and buy this 'less somebody was telling him to. He's got more sense than that."

"Excuse me? *Your* boy?"

"Ain't nothing in this whole kitchen to keep body and soul together." She set the bottle back, and asked the cool interior, "Tell me something, child. Can you cook?"

"I don't see—"

"This is not a difficult question. I want to know, can you cook. Don't tell me you think you can keep my boy happy with moldy cheese and wine. What are you bringing to the table, other than some fine looks and sweet blond hair?" She swiveled around, using the refrigerator's open door as a place to settle. "All I'm asking is, what is my boy gonna find himself living with, once them looks of yours start to fade."

"This is none of your concern."

"I saw you out there working the front garden this morning, acting like you belong. Didn't hardly have a thing on, them shorts hiked up where nobody ought to be looking, nothing on your arms but sweat. No behind on you at all. You probably starving yourself to look like Twiggy."

Kirsten crossed her arms. "Twiggy's long gone."

"You will be too, you keep on like you're going. My boy needs himself a wife and a mother for his children. Not some fancy young missie from up north that don't have a clue how to make a man feel like a man."

"Marcus hasn't said a thing to me about looking for a mother."

Fay made a noise down low in her throat. "You thinking just because I'm old, worn out, and black, that means I'm dumb too? This is my boy we're talking about here. I love him just as much as if I'd birthed him myself. If you got something to offer, honey, I ain't seen it yet."

With Fay's fists on her hips and her elbows cocked, she looked like a blackbird ready for battle. "I'm a ways removed from my boy's starry-eyed mood. He thinks you're gonna make him a good wife on account of how you're this pretty young thing. But life's taught me to look beyond the glamour and the glitter. I've listened to six babies scream through my nights. I've had forty-two years to get used to worrying over unpaid bills and kids that don't come home when they should. I *know* what struggling does to a mind and a marriage." One wing elongated enough to rake the air between them. "You don't know nothing about nothing. And that's the truth."

Fay moved a step closer, stalking her prey. "Why don't you tell me something, while you're at it. Just exactly who is this doing the loving here?"

Kirsten backed away, or tried to, but was halted by the pantry door.

"You're hiding something. Ain't you now. Tell me the truth. What is it you don't want nobody to know?"

This was what she had been looking for, why she had entered the kitchen, a reason to say a permanent farewell. But nothing emerged around the choking force that clenched her throat. She could not understand it. Here was her departure ticket on a platter. The woman had declared open war. Fay was asking the question Marcus had not dared to utter, the one to which she would never give an answer. Never. All she had to do was what she wanted. Leave.

"From the outside you don't look like nothing but successful. You're white, you're rich, you're beautiful. But I seen past all that, child. I seen what's the truth. Inside you ain't nothing but a mess. Come on now. Let's you and me just get to the bottom of this. Tell me what's got you so tore up inside."

The first either of the women knew of Marcus' presence was the slamming of the refrigerator door. *Wham.*

Fury emanated from Marcus like a silent bellow. Kirsten had never imagined him capable of violence until this moment. What the old woman saw in his features backed her up a full yard and more.

Marcus said, "You're going to leave now."

Fay did her best to hold on to her own ire. "This girl here ain't nothing but smoke."

"Wrong. This *lady* is more than I ever deserved."

Kirsten felt as defeated as she ever had in her entire life. The opportunity had been given, the excuse granted, the door opened. She shook her head. Impossible situations. Impossible moves.

"If you ever speak to her again like that . . ." The grip he took on his thoughts clenched his face like a fist. Marcus took a hard pair of breaths, then started from the kitchen.

"Marcus." Fay's features crumpled as she reached toward his departing back. "I got me a bad worry."

He stopped, but did not turn back. "What."

"My youngest grandson, he's been caught taking a gun to school." The old woman's voice settled down one shattered octave. She angled her words toward Kirsten, offering the only apology she was capable of just then. "What is a seven-year-old child doing with a gun?"

"He's being held downtown?"

"I 'spect."

"What's his name?"

"Jason." Fay was no stranger to pain. But she had little experience with weeping. The tears she shed seemed to melt her eyes. "Don't go telling Deacon. It'd break his heart. He thinks the world of that boy."

"All right, Fay." He was already stalking away. "I'll have a word with the sheriff."

Kirsten had no choice but to follow him down the hall. "Marcus. I have to talk with you."

"Can it wait?"

"No." She pointed to where the check lay in the crumpled envelope and described what had happened.

"New Horizons sent a goon over here to threaten you?"

"Netty knew his name."

His secretary appeared in the doorway behind him. "Sephus Jones. You heard of him?"

"No."

"Pull up enough rocks around here, you'll come across him sooner or later."

Marcus turned to her. "I'm sorry, Kirsten. For Fay, for this latest New Horizons mess." He cast a dark glare back toward the kitchen. "I can't understand what got into her."

"I can."

Marcus pushed through the front door and started down the stairs. Netty called after him, "Should I call New Horizons and say you're stopping by?"

He stuffed the check in his pocket. "Don't tell them a thing."

CHAPTER

7

MARCUS DID NOT FOCUS UPON his surroundings until he started up the bend past Deacon Wilbur's church. As he turned into the New Horizons campus he inspected the brick centerpiece with its brass nameplate. On his first visit two years earlier, Marcus had been chased off by two men armed with baseball bats and lawyer-eating pickups. The chipped corner where he had bounced his SUV when fleeing for his life had been carefully repaired, but the spot was still visible. Marcus slowed and took a few deep breaths. A frontal assault would get him nowhere but crippled.

He was uncertain how he felt about finding Amos Culpepper leaning against his patrol car in the New Horizons headquarters parking lot. Sheriff Amos Culpepper had appeared soon after Marcus had arrived in Rocky Mount, back when Marcus had been so desperate for trustworthy allies he could not have named the need, only the hunger.

The rangy sheriff had one metal-tipped boot propped on the bumper. Darren Wilbur, Deacon's nephew and the sheriff's newest deputy, was bent over the open trunk. Amos surveyed Marcus from behind mirror shades, his face an unreadable cop's mask. When Marcus opened his door, he demanded, "We going to have trouble here today?"

"No."

"You sure about that?"

"I'm just going to return a check."

"Should've used the mail." Amos stepped over in front of Marcus, blocking his way. He was two inches shy of Marcus' height, but his stern demeanor and buff cowboy hat raised him up to a giant's stature. "Last time you marched in there they cleaned your clock."

When Marcus had taken on New Horizons, Amos Culpepper had saved both Marcus' life and his home. They remained friends in the manner of two men who took their professions seriously, and knew there would always be the risk of them standing on opposite sides of the courtroom. "Did Kirsten call you?"

"Matter of fact, she did. Good thing we happened to be in the area."

His deputy emerged from the trunk. Darren Wilbur was a huge man who covered a severe stutter with silence and muscles. The pump-action shotgun looked dwarfish in his hands. It was a riot model, with a snout of a barrel and a ten-shot clip built into the butt. Darren nodded a tight greeting as he fed in shells. "Afternoon, M-Marcus."

"This is not happening."

"Wrong again, sport." Amos stepped closer, inserting himself firmly into Marcus' space. "Are you absolutely certain you have a valid reason to be here?"

"I've been asked to represent their chairman." He studied his reflection in Amos' sunglasses, and saw a man distorted by a world of half-truths. "I was told it was strictly a personal matter. Then this morning they send a man around to my house. He accosted Kirsten in my own front yard, Amos. I'm fed up with being led around by the nose. I need to find out what's happening."

The sheriff radiated a professional disapproval. "Here's how it's going to play. We're walking in there together. We're going to find your man, we're going to have a word, and then we're turning around and walking out. Together the whole way. And you're going to promise me this is the last time you ever set foot in this place."

"I can't do that."

A trio of business executives passed them, the men in gray and the dark-suited woman carrying an artist's oversized portfolio. They made round eyes at the sight of Darren, tall and dark as a latent volcano and armed with his buff-black weapon.

"It'd be right tempting to call you ten kinds of fool." Amos extended his hand toward Darren. "The communicators working all right?"

In response, Darren handed his boss a walkie-talkie, then slipped another one into his pocket and threaded the earpiece up through his jacket. "Channel t-three."

Amos opened his jacket, slipped the walkie-talkie onto his belt, and twisted the knob. "Testing, one, two."

Darren gave him a thumbs-up.

Marcus protested, "This really isn't necessary."

"Don't you even start." Amos pointed them toward the head-quarters. "I'm telling you the same thing I say to all my new recruits. Your first job is not to get shot."

"They wouldn't try anything here."

"Course not. Ready to roll?"

The newer headquarters building had been redesigned after the court had convicted New Horizons of colluding with Chinese slave-labor factories and abducting Kirsten's best friend. Marcus crossed a public area done in soothing pastels and Southern tweed and approached a young woman seated at an oversized partner's desk. The inlaid leather centerpiece had been carved out to hide her phone system. The walls behind her displayed blowups of three overseas factories, as pristine and well groomed as holiday spas. The receptionist looked terrified.

Before he could speak, the rear glass doors slid open. A trio of blue-jacketed security emerged. "Can I help you, Mr. Glenwood?"

"I'm here to have a word with your chairman."

"Mr. Steadman is not in this afternoon." They stood an arm's length apart, hands caught before them, legs slightly spread. "I need to ask you both to turn around and make your way—"

Amos Culpepper dangled his badge an inch from the man's nose. "Why don't y'all just slow down. We're concerned about all the infractions we noticed on our way in here. We might have to write up every single car in this lot, invite them down to the local lock-up to explain all the broken headlamps and erratic driving we're going to find when they start leaving this afternoon."

To his credit, the muscle did not flinch. "You're rousting the entire workforce?"

"Not unless you roust first." Amos had the country lawman's ability to shout at a whisper. "I'm inviting you to reconsider, is all. We want to pay your chairman a visit. You say he's not in. We'll settle on, who will we settle on, Marcus?"

Marcus drew out the check, and read the name printed beneath the signature. "Lynwood Hale."

"Now, you see how reasonable we are? Why don't you just call ahead and say we're on our way upstairs."

When the guard hesitated, Amos moved so fast Marcus did not even see his hand in motion. One moment he was standing there with his badge dangling in the muscle's face. The next, and he had the badge in one hand and the young man's walkie-talkie in his other.

Amos froze the other two guards with a look, then motioned with the receiver. "Make the call."

The guard retrieved his radio and turned away. One of the other men demanded, "Are you carrying?"

Amos made the raising of his gaze into a polar crossing. "Sir."

The man's neck was so muscled it formed a continuous angle from his ears to the tips of his shoulders. But he was unable to meet Amos' eye for long. "Sir."

"I'm an officer of the law, son. I'm always armed." He prodded the first man's shoulder with a knobby finger. "We're ready to roll here."

The guard had turned sullen by things moving from his control. "This way."

"That's more like it. See how reasonable everybody can be when they try?" When one of the trio tried to step behind them, Amos halted him with "You just move on ahead there. I'll bring up the rear."

"But I'm—"

"Don't get me any more riled than I already am, son. Move out."

Heads popped out of cubicles up and down the interior hall. All five men crammed into one elevator. Amos kept his back to the doors and held the muscle against the rear wall with his gaze. The Muzak drifting down from overhead was less suited to the tension than gunfire.

The executive floor was as muted in tone as the reception area. Beige curtains hung the length of the exterior steel and glass wall, dimming both the light and the view. As Marcus gave his name to the senior secretary, Amos Culpepper stepped over and swept aside the drapes. Marcus found himself steadied by the glimpse of the timeworn church and a cemetery resting comfortably in broad meadows of summer green.

"Mr. Glenwood?" The paunchy man used a pomade on his hair Marcus could smell from across the room. "I'm Lynwood Hale, director of finance."

"Which is the chairman's office?"

Hale pointed to the double doors behind the secretary. "Through there. But he's not—"

"Show me."

Lynwood Hale waved a manicured hand toward the secretary. "Escort the man, Sandra."

Marcus followed her back and through the doors. The lavish interior held all the warmth of an empty hotel suite. Marcus did a slow sweep, but could find nothing that indicated who occupied this chamber. Marcus stood over the polished rosewood desk, empty of even a calendar. "Does he never come in here?"

When she did not respond, Marcus crossed his arms and waited. Showing he was ready to make this an all-day affair.

"He comes."

"How often?"

"Most days."

Marcus swept a hand over the desk's bare surface. "What makes him so secretive he won't even keep his calendar in his office?"

The finance director had waited as long as he was willing. "That's all right, Sandra. I'll take over now."

Marcus reached into his pocket and drew out the check. "This check was brought by my house today."

"This is a large company, Mr. Glenwood. Despite your best efforts to the contrary, we are also very successful. My department issues a large number of checks every day."

"Let's talk about this one. Somebody had it delivered by way of some old-style muscle."

"You'll need to see our attorney about whatever . . ." He squinted more closely at the check being dangled in front of his face. "Where did you get this?"

"Did you order this made up? Or did Dale Steadman?"

"I'm not authorized to discuss such matters with an outsider."

"But you're authorized to send me money."

"Don't try and tell me you're so high and mighty you're adverse to being paid for your work." The man made a grab for the check.

Marcus jerked back just in time. "First you want me to have it, then you want to take it away? Sounds to me like we're looking at a case of in-house forgery."

"Give me that!"

"First you tell me what's going on around here."

The man had a felon's eyes, dark no matter what the color. "You're nothing but a corpse looking for the open grave. You want to keep the money? Be my guest."

"I'm considering pressing charges against Sephus Jones for trespassing and felonious assault." Marcus shredded the check and tossed the fragments into the man's face. "If there's any way to tie him to you personally, sir, I am going to nail your hide to the wall."

As Marcus started toward the door, Lynwood Hale hissed, "The company is delighted with Dale Steadman's problems. You hear what I'm saying? Dee-lighted. You go right ahead and run with this thing just as long as you like. We'll look forward to seeing you keep this man busy for ages."

"You're telling me this case is your way of avoiding Dale Steadman's proposed reforms? That's why you had your hired gun accost my assistant?"

But Lynwood Hale was not finished. "You just tell your client, sooner or later he's gonna stumble. He's gonna find himself exposed and feeble. We'll be there and ready. You go tell Dale Steadman what I said."

———

Once they had rejoined Darren, Amos observed, "I smell a few singed feathers, but I don't see any sign of scorched flesh."

Marcus said to them both, "Fay Wilbur told me her grandson's been detained for carrying a gun to school."

Amos asked his deputy, "This your cousin?"

Darren looked stricken by the news. " 'Fraid s-so."

"He as big as you?"

Darren shook his head. "Deacon's b-build, my b-bad attitude."

Amos said to Marcus, "Here I thought all you country lawyers did was shoot the dog and walk the breeze. Or maybe it's the other way around."

"Fay is worried sick."

"I expect she is." Amos said to Darren, "Sounds to me like we ought to pick up this young'un, take him for a ride out to Wendell."

Wendell was home to the largest state pen, notorious for its boot-camp attitude. Local police departments often took young repeat offenders for a walk down Melody Lane, as the central hall was known. The felons always sang the young boys a very warm welcome.

Marcus said, "There's a local hardcase by the name of Sephus Jones."

"You're mixing with some bad stock there, Marcus."

"He's the guy who harassed Kirsten. I'd appreciate it if you could find out where he might be found."

"I'll see what I can turn up." Amos climbed into the passenger seat, rolled down his window, and gave Marcus a little of the heat he had revealed inside. "Show a little intelligence from now on. You got anything you feel has to be done around here, you call for backup."

CHAPTER

8

As usual, Reiner Klatz compressed his fifty-three-year-old body into clothes designed for sleeker greyhounds doing the Königsallee strut. He called goodbye to his wife, left his apartment on the fashionable Oberkasseler Weg, and drove across the Rhein Knee Bridge. Parking around the opera house was impossible as always. Reiner left his new S-class in the Carsch-Haus underground lot and hoofed it to the Kö, as the place was known to locals.

The Königsallee and its surrounding lanes made up the primo shopping region of all northern Germany. The main drag was about a kilometer long and was split by a moat, useless medieval bridges, a fountain Wagner would have swooned over, and shops selling cashmere socks. Reiner Klatz made it a point to be seen daily somewhere along its length. He flitted about, far too busy to sit down and actually *say* something. The greyhounds all knew him, of course. The blue-hair set liked to kiss the air by his cheeks. But his chance to really shine, the one occasion when all the Kö's spotlights swiveled and followed him down the lane, were opening galas at the Düsseldorf opera.

To say the least, the Düsseldorf opera was not Paris. Nor Vienna nor Berlin nor La Scala. But beneath this first rank huddled a second tier, provincial houses and some which pretended to be far more than that. Of all these houses, Reiner considered Düsseldorf tops. Hands down, without qualification. Premier of the second league. And that, as Reiner would tell anyone who cared to listen, was not a bad place to be.

Düsseldorf was unable to retain rank upon rank of opera stars. But those it did engage were counted among the best. Where La Scala might have twenty divas under long-standing contracts, Düsseldorf had three. Yet these three had all starred at La Scala at one time or another. And Glyndbourne. And Berlin, Nice, Paris, Rome, and the Royal Opera House. One had even sung at the Met.

Reiner spotted the duchess in time to wipe the bitter cast from his face. Thinking about the New York Metropolitan Opera House, even for an instant, was enough to ruin a perfectly good day. The duchess seethed through the Königsallee summer crowd like the *SS Bismarck* through dinghies in some teeming third-world harbor. This week's pair of personal attendants and her private secretary skittered along behind.

The duchess planted herself in front of Reiner and blared, "I want you to explain to me how it is I cannot have the director's box!"

"A lovely day, is it not, your highness."

"Stop with this nonsense. Do I look like a fool to you?"

"Never have I thought—"

"Then do not cloud the air with blather!" The duchess was the real thing—real title, real money, real power. She was built like an aging Wagnerian alto, with a bovine figure that would have caused a rampant steer to blanch. "I spoke with the director again this morning and he informs me that the box is still untaken!"

"Please excuse me, highness. I have sought twice to alter matters with Frau Brandt. But with the chancellor coming . . ."

The duchess balked. Although the chancellor's power was far younger than her own, it was of a realm she could not safely attack. Which was of course why Reiner had mentioned him. But in truth the chancellor had been refused the box as well. Which had almost given Reiner a stroke. But Erin had insisted. And when Erin insisted, particularly the day before a gala opening, there was nothing Reiner could do. When she had returned from the United States and agreed to start back at Düsseldorf, Erin had written into her new contract that the director's box was hers by right for every gala event in which she starred.

For now, however, the box remained strangely empty. Which was baffling. Erin had personally written the chancellor and explained in her precise convent-taught script that this was an event of national importance. The Düsseldorf opera was going on an international tour, in which Erin was singing just twice—tonight at their sole performance in Germany, followed by the Royal Opera House in Covent Garden three nights hence. It was the first time the Düsseldorf opera had been invited en masse to Covent Garden, and there she would be singing before the Prince of Wales. To Reiner's delight, the chancellor had accepted. Yet not even he would be seated in the director's box.

Reiner extricated himself from the duchess and scuttled along the Kö. As he passed a news kiosk his eye was caught by the local rag, which naturally had Erin's photograph on the front page. Reiner had almost come to blows with the managing editor over the coverage they had given Erin in her moment of direst need. At least, that was how Reiner had put it, standing over the woman's desk and screaming so loud he had drawn people from two floors below. Erin Brandt could sing anywhere she wanted. The paper had publicly lamented the fact when Erin had departed for America two years earlier.

Anywhere, that is, save the Met.

Standing over the managing editor's desk, Reiner had shrieked and wailed and torn his Seelbach cashmere jacket over how Erin had been treated upon her return. The same paper that had wept poignant tears over her departure had spread tales of a bitter divorce and an abandoned baby. Was it true, the managing editor had dared ask. True? Who cares what was the truth? Erin Brandt was a star! Stars were *expected* to misbehave!

To an opera diva, the Met was the ultimate prize. Yet Erin had never been granted the starring role she truly deserved. Not even when she moved to America with this as her goal. Not even when she paid her dues singing to rave reviews in Chicago and San Francisco and even before the President at Washington's Kennedy Center. Not to mention a variety of more mediocre stages—Atlanta and Miami and Phoenix and Dallas. Dallas! But nothing had done any good. Seven long months she had bowed and scraped and licked their societal boots. To no avail.

No wonder she got herself pregnant and let that horrid man drag her down to Wilmington, North Carolina. Reiner shuddered as he took the backstage stairs two at a time, recalling his one visit to Swampville, as Erin now called it. When Erin announced she was returning to Europe and singing and him, Reiner could have wept from sheer joy. He should have. Really.

When he entered the star's dressing room, Erin was the calm at the center of a force nine gale. That was one of her greatest gifts, facing the horrendous pressures of a major live performance and remaining the ice queen. Reiner inserted himself into the crowd, and waited.

The dresser was busy with yet another final fitting. During the previous day's dress rehearsal, the stays had snagged and bitten until Erin had bled quite profusely. Yet Erin had seemed not to notice the blood oozing from beneath her left arm, until Reiner had pointed it out and almost fainted in the process. Afterward she had claimed she was too involved with the music to notice anything so minor. Now the conductor and the makeup man and the wig mistress all gaped in horror at the stain. Even after a frantic dry cleaning the bloody shadow remained. By this evening it would become another component of the lady's legend.

He waited while the conductor discussed two minor changes to her opening aria. When Reiner's chance came, he gave it to her hard and fast. At such times there was no alternative. And Erin had insisted upon knowing immediately.

"Marcus Glenwood," he announced.

Erin tilted her chin in his direction. After all these years, he still could be awed by the intensity of her concentration. "Yes?"

"He could not be worse news."

Erin brushed the seamstress' fingers aside and announced to the room, "Give us a moment alone, please."

When the door swung shut, Reiner went on, "By all accounts, Marcus Glenwood is a stealth bomber. Quiet and Southern and polite. So mild-mannered it would be easy to dismiss him out of hand. But the man single-handedly took on the world's largest sports apparel company *and* the Chinese government." He tried to keep the alarm from his voice, for the last thing he needed was to stoke Erin's fires. "And he *won*."

Erin surprised him once again, however. Most things about this entire episode managed to shred her calm as nothing else, transforming her into a feral vixen with the powers to turn any assailant to stone. But today she simply gave him a cool smile.

"Give me the phone, *Liebchen*."

"Who are you calling?"

"The man who promised to occupy the director's box and I fear is not coming after all. Go stand guard outside my door, that's a dear."

Reiner did as he was told. He bestowed a smile on all who passed, as though all was right with this abnormal cosmos called opera. He knew Erin as the most consummate actress he had ever met, stage or screen. Even so, her calm left him wondering if perhaps, this time, things might actually work out.

CHAPTER

9

MARCUS TOOK THE INNER BELTWAY around Raleigh, then headed east on what had formerly been a simple country lane. The new four-lane was presently farmed by tracts of new houses that sprouted with the speed of high-velocity weeds. Six miles farther out, carefully shielded by acres of elm and holly and scrub pine, stood the city's last remaining quarry. Marcus made his way past a string of idling dump trucks and halted where a crew of roughnecks had toned down their speech because of the deputy sheriff standing nearby.

Darren Wilbur offered Marcus a hand like a flat-blade shovel. "H-how you doing, sir?"

"Pressed for time. I'm due in Wilmington to meet a new client. Appreciate your doing this."

"M-mind stepping t-this way?"

The offices said all there was to know about the quarry business. The exterior walls were slatted shingles of tree bark, stripped off trees used as supports for the original shafts. That was back in the thirties, before the dozers came equipped with diamond-tipped blades which carved up the surface rock like hot wax. Just crossing the yard and climbing the back stairs turned Marcus' black loafers a wintry shade of pale.

Outside the closed door, Darren handed Marcus a bulky file. Marcus read the name on the jacket. "Sephus Jones."

"Amos t-tracked him down through h-his parole officer."

Marcus opened the folder, scanned the first page. "This man's been charged with grievous bodily harm, armed robbery, abduction of a minor, assault with intent, and extortion?"

"A-assault and abduction're the only ones that s-stuck."

He slapped the file shut. "You sure we don't need some backup here?"

Darren showed a very rare smile. "I believe we're c-covered."

"There anything I could use as a lever?"

"M-man was picked up again l-last week."

The quarry's blast whistle sounded as Marcus reached for the door. Then the air concussed about him and the dusty road shivered as if a school of predatory creatures foraged beneath the surface. When the subsequent silence was broken by a bird's tentative all-clear, Marcus pushed open the door and walked inside.

The man seated at the table leaned back so that sunlight through the door struck his body but not his face. The backs of his hands bore prison tattoos. More artistic bands of blue and purple dye wrapped aboriginal designs about his wrists and drew daggers up both forearms. Dancing upon his right arm was a snake-haired Medusa. A sunburst with a warrior's face protruded from his shirt's open front. "Ain't right, you bothering me here where the whole world's gonna know."

The deputy merely shut the door and leaned against it. Almost instantly Marcus had to fight off the urge to gag. The smell emanating from the man coated Marcus' tongue and the back of his throat like putrid enamel. A year's worth of body odor was mingled with a drenching scent so overwhelming Marcus required a moment to identify it as English Leather. The man must have bathed in the stuff.

Marcus gave the room a careful sweep. A wall calendar advertising either thong bikinis or tires counted days off the previous April. The walls were rough-hewn and pegged with overdue bills and yellowed call sheets.

Sephus Jones planted his boots on the corner of the empty desk. "And just who exactly do we have here?"

Marcus pulled a straight-backed chair up close. "You should know. You were in such a powerful hurry to meet me yesterday."

"Marcus. My man." Sephus Jones had eyes so pale they fed upon the shadows, glimmering with a beast's fervor. His hair was dyed a cheap reddish orange that almost matched his dime-sized freckles. "Nice little dolly you got yourself there."

Marcus set the file on the desk between them and flipped to the last page. "Says here you're a two-time loser, Sephus."

"You decide you're done with the dolly, how's about I have a taste?"

"From what I understand, you've been recently brought in on something new." Marcus lifted his gaze. "Don't tell me that hasn't got you sweating."

"Chump change. I was holding a bag for a buddy."

Marcus looked over to where Darren stood by the wall. Just crossing his arms was enough to stretch the uniform's shoulder seams. "Hundred c-caps of ecstasy. Arrested in f-front of a j-junior high."

The dust-matted window emitted a light like a fading lantern's glow. A bare bulb glowed from a wire dangling off the ceiling. Neither was enough to press the shadows back very far. "Why don't I shoot a couple of guesses your way," Marcus suggested. "The earlier arrest has resulted in court orders to stay well away from schools, parks, the works. Which means you're now facing a double-barrel charge."

Sephus Jones unsnapped the leather holder hanging from his belt and plucked out a bone-handled knife. He pried open the largest blade and began paring his fingernails, reflecting what light he could muster into Marcus' face. "There mighta been some mention made a while back. I don't rightly recall."

"Jailers in these parts don't take kindly to convicts who've messed with children. They know better than to lay a hand on a prisoner. But they're going to take great care in selecting your dance partners. One night awaiting arraignment should be enough to remind you of that fact." Marcus leaned his hands on the desk. "How am I doing so far?"

"If you came looking for new business, I'm just sorry as I can be." His grin was empty of all save the stretching of skin. "I already got me all the lawyers I can use."

"This is what you call a carrot and stick meeting. You help me, I talk shop with the DA. You don't, the deputy here is going to arrest you on charges of assaulting my girlfriend."

"Just another helping of chump change, bub." He flicked whatever he had on the knife's tip in Marcus' direction. "I didn't touch the dolly."

"All I want," Marcus replied, "is a name."

"What, you grown dissatisfied with the one your own daddy offered you?" He returned to his knife and his fingernails. "Now that's a pure shame."

"New Horizons didn't send you over to my place. And the check you brought was a forgery." He took strength from the slight check in the knife's motions. "Just tell me who set you off against me."

"That's the trouble with you lawyers. You see conspiracy behind the simplest deal. I did a favor for a friend. That's all there is to it."

"Who is the friend?"

"Always did have a terrible head for names." He closed the knife, stowed it away, slammed his boots to the floor. "We done here?"

"You're really so concerned about protecting somebody that you'd risk further indictments?"

"Ain't concerned about it at all."

Marcus rose to his feet, eager now for a breath of untainted air. "I'll give you a day to think about this."

"Five seconds'll do, bub." He rose to his feet, offered a final grin. "But you feel welcome to come visiting anytime you like."

Marcus left the office and stomped down the stairs. Back in the parking lot, he propped one foot on his front tire and used his hand-kerchief to smear around the dust. "All he's given me is a load of questions I don't need."

"Y-you want me t-to arrest him?"

"No. He's right. We won't be able to make an assault charge stick." Marcus started on his other shoe. "The man's too confident to be sitting in there on his own."

Darren waited until Marcus slid behind the wheel to say, "T-that's what they pay you for, to p-put together the p-puzzles."

CHAPTER

10

DALE STEADMAN'S LIBRARY BAR was built into a corner opposite the rear French windows. Sunlight played a reflector's game off the dual mirrors and the crystal glasses and the bottles. Dale studied his own fissured reflection. None of the guilt or anguish showed, only a stone-flat gaze and features that had gained fifteen years' worth of creases in the past eleven months.

He dropped ice cubes into his highball glass and poured in two inches of bourbon. He knew he should wait until after he had met with the attorney. But the worry and the strain and the huge empty house were bearing down hard. And the silence. Before, there had always been music. He had told the architect that every room had to be wired to a central system. Every single room, even the seven bathrooms, even the kitchen pantry. The house had thirty-four rooms and over three hundred Bose speakers. The amplifier was the size of a double oven and hulked beneath the cellar stairs. He had dreamed of the moment when Erin would step across the threshold and hear her favorite aria soaring from every room. A welcome fit for a queen, one guaranteed to woo her and bind her firmly to her new home.

He had been wrong before, but seldom so completely.

Dale poured another two inches, then added more ice. He carried the glass and bottle and ice bucket over to the sofa. Despite the plastic sheet blanketing the entire northern wall and the air conditioner on full blast, the room still stank of oily ashes and sawdust. The contractors were gone for the day. He missed their chatter and hammering and the tinny radio and the saws. He knew he should move out, find a place where he was not plagued by the ghosts of past errors. But he could not think beyond the one next step.

He glanced down and was surprised to find his glass empty. He poured another couple of inches, decided he didn't need to bother with ice. The bourbon had a different heat when taken straight, a liquid smoke to match the flames he saw every time he shut his eyes. Dale glanced at his watch. The minute hand was cemented to the same place it had been since his arrival home, or so it seemed. This one final glass, he decided, then he wouldn't have any more until after the meeting.

He stared out the rear windows past the slate patio to where the sun was turning the Intracoastal the color of a blast furnace. Despite the constant rush of cold air, Dale was sweating heavily. He looked down at his glass, and watched how the tremors in his hand cut fierce little ripples across the bourbon's surface. The glory days, was how he had always thought of his move back to Wilmington. The start of how things should have been from the beginning.

The sound of tires drumming over his private bridge drew him to his feet. Dale picked up the bottle and glass and carried both into the front hall. He fought to bring his chest and his emotions back under control as the car pulled around his drive. When he was certain he could hold the bottle steady, he poured another glass. Then he set it on the side table untouched. He just wanted something to anchor the moment, and the one after.

The drive from Rocky Mount to the coast had been a journey through aeons. High-tech modernity was soon replaced by an atmosphere of crinoline and molasses. East of I-95, they traversed a region where older men still tipped their hats to passing ladies, where sidewalks were used as an extension of front parlors, and tobacco remained undisputed king. Kirsten kept her face turned toward the summer greens as she first recounted her telephone conversation with the senator's aide, then summarized her findings about Dale Steadman. The efficient researcher briefing the top guy. A perfect picture, minus the heart.

"UNC-Wilmington had a football team up until ten years ago," Kirsten related to Marcus. "They axed it in favor of soccer and other equality sports. Dale Steadman was a walk-on the team's fourth year."

"Where was he raised?"

"Burgaw. A reporter at the Wilmington newspaper described the town as, blink and you've missed all the fun." Her hair caught the sunlight and teased him with the afterglow. "According to the same reporter, Dale took the UNC-W team from the swamps to the treetops. He won the conference title his junior and senior years, more or less single-handedly."

"Now I remember where I'd heard his name before."

"The paper dubbed him the Wilmington Wonder. The Bengals took him in the second round. But during the final game of the regular season, he was hit bad and broke both his collarbone and his hip. He was stretchered off, never to return."

Kirsten recounted Dale's rehabilitation and MBA and return to Wilmington without referring to her notes. "The company barely held its head above water for three years. Then Dale hit pay dirt when, of all things, a leading maker of wedding gowns offered him a long-term agreement. They liked his precision sewing, they wanted an American supplier. Dale's turnover doubled in eleven months. Four years later, New Horizons bought him out." She pointed ahead. "That's your turn. The Steadman residence should be four miles down on the left."

Marcus halted at the traffic light, studying her and the vast distance between them. Her skin glowed with the fabled luminosity of a perfect blonde. The open file in her lap did not quite cover the stockinged legs emerging from the sky-blue linen skirt. Her lips were as pale as her lashes and just begged to be kissed. Kirsten turned to him then, and recognized the hunger. She did not draw away. Instead, the gemstone gaze melted with resignation and fear.

The question was out before he could halt it. "Who hurt you?"

Her lips parted, reaching not for words but air.

"Did it ever occur to you that maybe the only answer is in trusting me? Just for a moment, long enough to separate me from whatever it is you're carrying around inside?"

Kirsten began trembling. He could see the tight shivers attack her frame. He reached over, but halted his hand in midair when she flinched from the coming touch.

A horn honked behind them.

Marcus took the turn and drove a tunnel of country greens down to where the road forked. A half-mile farther on, he started across a long plank bridge that led to Dale Steadman's private island preserve. Before them rose a faux French manor of cream-colored brick, with gray shutters and a peaked slate roof and eleven dormer windows on two floors. Marcus cut off the motor and sat there.

He hated the fear she showed him. Hated how vulnerable she looked, unable to move yet awaiting his next words as she would a vicious blow. Which was why he swallowed down what he wanted to tell her, and instead merely said, "I think you should take the meeting with Senator Jacobs."

He could see she was tempted to refuse, and knew with dagger-like certainty she was close to departing. "All right."

"I might need more time down here to map out a strategy with Dale."

"I said I would." She ended the discussion by rising from the car.

The front portico was domed in the manner of a European palace and ringed by ornate columns. The manor's south side was gutted and blackened, such that a dozen windows watched their arrival like charred and wounded eyes. As they started across the drive, Dale Steadman opened the front door. Marcus realized instantly the man was drunk. Dale observed their approach with a bleary gaze, muttered a half-formed greeting, pushed off the doorway, and shuffled inside.

Although the rooms through which they walked were relatively unscathed, the stench of cold ashes was everywhere. Tools were piled by sawhorses and lumber. Plastic tarpaulins split the central hallway and covered the south-facing doorways. Dale led them into a rear parlor that ran the length of the house. Three walls were fashioned as a rich man's study, with panels of oiled walnut and burl. A spiral brass staircase rose to a long balcony fronted with bookcases. The fourth wall was a ribbon of French windows, through which Marcus could see slate decking and the precision of professional gardening. Beyond the lawn, the Intracoastal Waterway sparkled with a carnival's myth of easy living and only good times.

As Kirsten followed Dale over and settled him into a sofa, Marcus' phone rang. He stepped back into the hallway. "Glenwood."

It was his secretary. "I couldn't find you a hotel at any price. It's summer, it's the weekend, it's the coast."

"Now that I'm here, I can't wait to get back," Marcus replied. "Any luck on that other matter?"

The previous afternoon Marcus had given Netty a list of Wilmington attorneys he had met over the years, and asked her to call around and see if anyone would meet with him. "One lawyer by the name of Garland Perry. Now Judge Perry."

"I don't remember him."

"He couldn't place you either. But he knows Mr. Steadman, and it didn't add a good flavor to his Saturday to hear why I was calling."

"But he'll see me?"

"Only if you can be there in a half hour's time. He's on his way out of town."

"Call him back and tell him I'm coming."

He slipped his phone into his pocket, reentered the back room, and asked Dale point-blank, "How drunk are you?"

Strangely, the New Horizons chairman gave his response to Kirsten and not to him. "Still looking for that place where it won't matter anymore."

Kirsten focused upon Marcus, finishing the triangle and keeping him from saying what he was thinking, that Dale was wasting everybody's time.

Dale only slurred his words a small amount. "You'll have to excuse me. I'm new to this game."

"Which game is that?"

"The one where I have mercenaries going to war in my place. I've always fought my own battles."

"Your ex-wife is working hard to keep custody of the child."

Dale used the hand holding the glass to punch himself upright, leaving a dark bourbon stain on the sofa's arm. He weaved his way over to where he stood before the central glass doors. He was burly, loud, and almost comic in his glorious wreckage. "That makes no sense whatsoever."

"Why do you say that?"

The bourbon stained his mouth with golden tears. "Erin never cared about the baby. Not till the publicity started."

"That doesn't jibe with the fact that she has hired a courtroom brawler."

"Hamper Caisse."

"That's right. Yesterday he brought in witnesses who attested to your unfitness as a father."

Dale's next gesture collided with the window. "That makes even less sense."

"That they would condemn you as they did?"

"No. That Erin would go to all this trouble."

"You're not worried about your good name being demolished in open court?"

"Only got room for one worry right now. And that's not it."

Kirsten spoke up for the first time. "Marcus is a fighter. But you've got to help him."

"Show me how."

Marcus extracted the custody agreement from his pocket. "Your ex-wife's attorney has presented a notarized agreement to the court, claiming you and she settled the issue of your child privately." He waited while Steadman gave the pages an owl-eyed scan. "Is that your signature on the last page?"

"Absolutely." He tossed the pages to the floor. "And I've never seen this before."

"You're claiming Erin Brandt's lawyer lied in open court?"

"Somebody sure did."

"Sir, I dislike carrying on important business under these circumstances."

Dale Steadman carried his laugh into his glass. "That makes two of us."

"I have to see a local attorney about a matter. Then we'll be leaving for Rocky Mount, since I couldn't find us a hotel room. I'll come back tomorrow and we'll try again. I'd appreciate it if you would try and be sober for the occasion."

"Stay here." Dale tapped his tumbler on the window. A long wooden finger stretched into the Intracoastal Waterway, molded into fable by the setting sun. A magnificent yacht was moored at the end. "The guest room's not redone yet, but that thing out there sleeps eight. I bought it for Erin, she begged me for one, then never stepped on board except for cocktails at sunset. Be nice to see somebody in love out there for once."

Marcus glanced at Kirsten, but found an unreadable stare. "Thank you, sir, we are most grateful for your invitation."

As Marcus rose from his chair, a sudden thought occurred to him. He did a careful search of the room, then said, "Kirsten, could I have a word?"

When she joined him in the front hallway, he was still intent upon his search. "What is it?"

"Stay there just a moment, please." Marcus walked to where the house was dissected by the plastic tarpaulin, swept it aside, and stepped through. Sawdust and old ashes drifted in the air. The house's articles had been stuffed in packing crates and draped with more plastic sheeting. He unpacked several boxes in different rooms, until he was certain his search was both futile and discomfiting.

Kirsten called from the hallway, "Marcus?"

"Just a minute."

"What are you doing?"

"Looking for something. Don't come back, it's filthy."

When he stepped through the plastic drape, Kirsten asked, "What did you find?"

"Step outside with me."

He waited until they were removed from the man's influence to say, "There is no sign of the child."

"What?"

"Not a picture, no mementos, dolls, toys, nothing."

"The baby is sixteen months old, Marcus."

"Listen to what I'm saying. There's *nothing*. We arrive to find the man drunk. His only response to the custody document is a slurred denial. What kind of father does that imply?"

"What do you want me to do?"

"I'm going to meet this local judge. See if you can find some reason for me not to drop this case."

Wilmington's old town held an aura of carefully preserved history, capturing through struggle and money a past that never was. Gone were the seedy bars and topless joints and the beer wagons' rutted tracks. Wilmington had entered a second heyday, fueled by two Hollywood studios who had fled the union-dominated west coast and a sudden upsurge in high-tech business. The ancient coastal oaks had been trimmed back, the rotting wharf district restored, the pre-Revolutionary houses as carefully done up as a bevy of aging brides.

Marcus turned by the church where the British military had stabled their horses after taking the manor next door for General Cromwell's residence. He pulled into the drive of a house only slightly smaller than a full-blown plantation.

As Marcus left his car, the Wilmington judge appeared on his front veranda. "Thank you for agreeing to meet me, sir."

Garland Perry was thirty years senior to Marcus, and proclaimed his staunch membership of the old school by appearing on a Saturday afternoon in starched white shirt and suspenders. He removed the pipe from his mouth. "I don't normally like to do business on a weekend. But your secretary indicated this could not wait for next week."

"I have to be back in court on Tuesday. You might have heard I've been asked to represent Dale Steadman."

"Rumors to that effect have been circulating 'round here." The judge rapped his pipe against the nearest pillar. A dark smudge suggested this was a long-held custom. "Personally, I find the idea that you'd take the side of a former opponent very repellent."

"This case has nothing to do with New Horizons."

"So you say."

Marcus remained standing upon the front walk, looking up the three stairs to the older gentleman. "Are you opposed to my handling this case, or my representing Dale Steadman?"

"Mr. Steadman has the right of every citizen to legal aid, I suppose." He blew hard on his pipe, then stowed it in his pocket. "But there are any number of lawyers out there."

"He came to me."

"Then I question his motives, as I do your own."

"What do you have against Dale Steadman, sir?"

"Nothing more than any number of local people. He's brash, he's a drunkard, and he's a stain on our good city." He met Marcus' gaze for the first time. "My advice, sir, is you'd be well served to send him packing."

Marcus took Highway 132 back out toward Pine Grove. He drove past the Wilmington Golf Club, then took the Greenville Loop Road out to Towles Road. It was a round-the-elbow sort of drive, but he needed time to think. The absence of clear answers made for much disorder and no resolution. Near Dale's plank bridge, Marcus halted and got out. Back behind him the day's final glow bid him a pleasant farewell. The surrounding marshland was dotted with stick figures of salt-blasted deadwood. Their inky branches pointed him toward every step of the celestial compass, which only reflected the state of his cluttered mind. A pair of redwing hawks screeched from either side of the bridge, as though they'd selected Marcus as their feast and now sought to scare him from cover. Up ahead, the night only accented the house's damage. The northern half gleamed a yellow welcome. The south side was nothing but shadows and mystery.

The front door opened as he pulled through the stone entrance and into the circular drive. Even from this distance Marcus could see Kirsten's distress. He climbed the stairs and asked, "What's wrong?"

In reply she took his hand and led him inside.

"Where is Dale?"

"Asleep." Kirsten drew him through the front corridor.

"Tell me what's wrong, Kirsten."

"I asked him your question for you." She drew him up the stairs and halted by the middle landing's only door. "Look in there."

A ring of keys dangled from the lock. Marcus twisted the handle.

The room was crammed floor to ceiling with Celeste.

Boxes spilled photographs and teddies and kittens and dolls. Crates were stacked so high the bottom ones were crushed almost flat. An antique rocker was lost beneath a pile of smiling stuffed animals. The little desk held a trio of plastic mixing bowls filled to overflowing with pewter teething rings, pacifiers, and plastic infant's toys. The roller crib was a single mass of fluffy angels. Silver frames had been roped together like plates and piled upon the diaper table so that one leg had given way, and the table was now supported by a high-backed chair.

"He wouldn't come in here," Kirsten said from behind him. "Wouldn't even look. He just gave me the keys and stumbled off to bed."

Marcus cut off the light and shut the door. "Why does this make you so sad?"

She continued to stare at the closed door. "Is it possible to love too much?"

"No. I don't think—"

"What about the pain? What about all the worries and all the things you can't keep shut up inside anymore?"

The questions were too important to be discussed in the middle of an ash-soaked stranger's home. Marcus draped his arm around her shoulders and steered her back down the stairs.

"What if loving this much only gives the world a way to crush you again?"

"Again?" He opened the central French doors and led her out into the night. The gravel path was bordered by ankle-high lamps, such that their way was clear yet the starlight remained undiminished. "Who hurt you the first time?"

There was no mistaking the panic in her voice. "Answer my question, Marcus."

He guided her out onto the dock. He tried to pitch his voice so that it mirrored the water's calm lapping. "We need to learn to trust one another, to have confidence that such a hurt won't ever come. And if it does, then it will be from some outside source, and we will face it together."

At the boat's side she finally balked. "That's not good enough."

"Kirsten, we're arguing over a future that hopefully won't ever come. It's been an exhausting day. In the morning these things will—"

"What if I can't learn to trust you?"

Muted light glimmered off her overwide eyes. "What are you saying?"

"What if I shouldn't be here?"

"Kirsten, I believe with all my heart that you are heaven's gift."

His words only pushed her farther back down the pier. "Then you're not seeing who I truly am."

"So show me."

The path's light seemed too much for her, as she canted away from the illumination and angled off into the grass. "What if I can't?"

"I will work to earn your trust." When she only fled more swiftly, he called, "Years, if need be."

Marcus heard her slam the car door. Gravel scattered like shotgun pellets as she rounded the drive and headed away. He stepped into the boat, burdened by the weariness of just another defeat at the hands of someone he loved.

CHAPTER

11

T HE NIGHT REFUSED TO DEPART of its own accord. Around four Marcus dressed and went out to chase it away. He stretched long and slow, the sea breeze faint as a sleeping woman's breath, the air so warm he left his sweatshirt on the poolside table as he started his run.

The plank bridge thunked a series of musical wooden notes beneath his tread. He followed the road along the water's edge but saw nothing save huge stone gates and more floodlit manors. Streetlights cast the willows and sea oaks in malarial tints. Beyond them, where the road turned inland and the houses became less imposing, broad rises of magnolia and elm formed inkstains upon a starlit sky. For a time Marcus was able to outrun even his thoughts. There was a singular purity to a predawn run. Every promise still held the potential of fulfillment. Even now.

Back at the yacht, he took the narrow stairs down into an opulent central cabin. He called both Kirsten's apartment and her cell phone, but received no answer. Then a thought occurred to him. Marcus dialed the number for Deacon's home, reflecting that perhaps a shred of joy could be found for someone who needed it almost as much as he did.

Afterward he showered and made coffee in the yacht's over-equipped galley. On the upper deck he was greeted by a soft world quilted together by mist and gray light. From this angle the morning fog appeared as the water's uppermost layer. Marsh islands hung suspended in both time and space. Overhead a jet painted a long finger-trail aimed straight toward dawn's rising tide. Across a narrow channel rose Masonboro Island, its high-backed hills the result of dredging the Intracoastal free of silt. The dunes glowed sable and expectant, while overhead gulls sang a sea-born chantey.

Marcus sat there long after his coffee had grown stone cold, until the sun split the horizon into an eruption above and heat below. Whenever possible, he had refused divorce and custody cases. There in the dawn's light he recalled one particular instance when the work could not be avoided. A longtime client had discovered his wife with not one outside lover, but six. The man had been utterly devastated. Time after time he had asked Marcus how it was possible to live with someone for seventeen years and not know them at all.

Gradually the July sun began searing his skin. But there was a clarity to this position, a pressure to see everything with morning's purity. Kirsten was the most irritatingly secretive woman he had ever met. She held a huge portion of herself clenched impossibly tight. He would like it otherwise. He desperately wanted her to share all with him, even though he was certain her secret would prove to be appalling.

Here in this gift of quiet Sabbath space, he asked himself the carefully avoided question. What if she refused? Marcus set his cup aside. It was not like he needed a lot of time to think this through. The morning's importance had lain with confronting the issue. The answer was immediate.

Whatever she chose to give him would be enough. Half of Kirsten's heart was a thousand times more than he had ever expected, or deserved.

He walked across the gangplank and took the gravel path toward the house. Finally he had an answer for that long-ago client. You lived with someone and never knew them fully because the alternative was unthinkable.

When he crossed the rear patio, Marcus found two men in Dale's kitchen alcove. Dale Steadman had recovered from the previous day's binge with well-practiced speed. An older man stood like a wraith beside him, holding himself with the fragility of one guarding eggshells.

Marcus stepped through the doorway and announced, "We need to talk."

"I hope it is to tell this gentleman that you cannot in any way be associated with this case." The stranger had a patrician's nose and the highbrow British accent to match. "A more atrocious set of circumstances I could not possibly imagine than to have this be dragged into open court."

Dale offered Marcus a half-full pot. "Like a cup?"

"Black."

"Marcus Glenwood, Kedrick Lloyd. Kedrick happens to be the eighth earl of Tisbury, and my oldest friend. He introduced me to Erin." He handed Marcus a mug. "Then told me I was a fool to marry her."

"Which you most certainly were."

"No argument there." He bent down and retrieved a bottle of cognac from beneath the sink. "Anybody else feel like a spike?"

Marcus said, "Don't."

"You telling me what to do in my own house?"

"If you want me to take the case, I am."

"Gentlemen, really," Kedrick Lloyd protested. "Neither of you can possibly be serious."

Marcus walked around the central station and took the bottle from Steadman. He dropped it into the gleaming waste can. "These are my terms. You are going to be in court every single day this case requires. We have to do everything possible to counteract the impression Erin's attorney is painting."

"You're going for it?"

"I'm not finished. You lay off the sauce and you join a local AA." Marcus made every word a challenge, half hoping the man would refuse. "You must prove to Judge Sears that the claims against you are false and malicious. And by taking the time to appear you demonstrate a greater commitment to your child than Erin Brandt."

"This is preposterous!" The hand that rose to wipe Kedrick's mouth was pale as a linen shroud. "It has obviously escaped your local boy here that international custody cases are notoriously difficult."

Marcus asked, "Are you an attorney?"

"Kedrick is a patron of the arts," Dale replied. "He is vice chairman of the board of the New York Metropolitan Opera. Which makes him an expert on everything. If you don't believe me, just ask him."

"I know the ways of the world, unlike your hired gun!" He had still not glanced Marcus' way. "Dale, listen to what I'm saying. Even if you win here, you will lose. Believe me. I have friends who have been tied up in such cases for years. It will rob you of your life."

"No chance," Dale replied. "That's already been taken from me."

"Hopeless," Kedrick muttered, starting from the kitchen. "Senseless, preposterous, hopeless. You realize, of course, he will milk you for every cent you have, then vanish."

"Just a minute, please," Marcus said. "I need witnesses who will testify on Mr. Steadman's behalf. Could I ask you to appear Tuesday in—"

Kedrick did not even turn around. "I will not grace this obvious act of prostitution with a single further instant of my time. Good day to you both."

When they were alone, Dale said, "Kedrick is dying. Leukemia. He's down here to sell a couple of hotels and start some last-ditch treatment over at Duke." His voice held the hesitancy of one fearful of hope. "You're serious about taking me on?"

"I meant what I said. You're going to have blood tests on a regular basis. The first time you show anything stronger than aspirin in your system, you get yourself another lawyer."

"Yes. All right. Agreed."

"Let's go back to a point I tried to make yesterday. On Friday your wife's lawyer came up with a fire chief and the former head of the Wilmington Chamber of Commerce."

"Let me guess. The fire chief said I was blind drunk and the businessman suggested I be burned at the stake."

"Pretty much. Then yesterday I met with a local judge by the name of Garland Perry who basically agreed with them."

"No surprise there. There's all sorts of levels to a society like this one." He took a hit from his mug, then shook his head over the absence of what he sought. "Once you've been cast to a role by the old guard, they grow testy if you head in a different direction."

"You're telling me none of what these people said about you is true?"

"I never had a chance of acceptance in this town. I was too ambitious, too tough, too full of newfangled ideas about workers' comp and such. Then I brought home this foreign lady I met in New York. Man, I was history."

"Come Tuesday morning, I'll refute their testimony with evidence to the contrary. Either that, or any chance we have goes right out the window."

Dale's hands were too big and too busy to be contained upon the counter. They sent him traipsing around the kitchen, scattering little touches here and there. "I'll try to come up with some folks who'll speak on my behalf."

"Your British friend is right, by the way. This case has virtually no chance of succeeding."

"Then why are you helping me?"

To that Marcus had no definable answer. "You mind if I borrow your boat for a while? I've got some friends who should be arriving after lunch."

Early that afternoon, Fay Wilbur's car rattled across the plank bridge and pulled up in front of Dale's waterside palace. Deacon rose from the car, gave the house a single astonished glance, then hustled around to unload the wheelchair from the trunk. A face like a shriveled gourd protruded from the driver's window and shrilled up at him, "Marcus Glenwood! You ought to hang your head in shame!"

"Hello, Fay."

"Don't you sass me! My man's supposed to be preaching at the revival tonight! He's got hisself people wanting to hear about the Lord, and you're taking him off sinnin'!"

"We couldn't do it without him, Fay. He's the only one who knows where the fish are."

"Don't you go blowing any smoke my way! This here's nothing but a wrongness in the making!" An arm straight and angular as a dried tree root took aim at the man settling into the wheelchair. "And shame on you, Charlie Hayes, shame! With the Angel of Death hovering 'round, you oughta be busy getting your house in order!"

"Seeing you always makes my day complete, Fay," Charlie Hayes assured her.

"I ain't taking none of your smoke neither! Anybody close as you are to meeting your maker oughta be a little busier with the things of heaven, sir!" She waited until Deacon pushed the wheelchair farther down the drive, then lowered her tone somewhat. "Marcus honey, come over here a second."

When he approached the car window, a knobby hand caught him in a rough-palmed vise. "I can't tell you how sorry I am for that other day. I had no call speaking to your lady friend like I did."

"Maybe you did, maybe you didn't."

"Well now." Dark eyes penetrated deep enough to see he did not care to discuss that further. "I heard what you and that sheriff fellow did for my grandson."

"Amos is a good man."

"I just want to thank you both." The hand gripped tighter. "You're family, you hear what I'm saying? Near as any of my other kin."

She rammed the car into gear and sprayed seashells into the sun-polished air. Deacon walked over, revealing an ability to appear dignified even in tattered khakis and a sweat-stained cap. "Fay felt a singular need to deliver her message personally."

The stick figure in the wheelchair complained, "It's not polite to keep a dying man waiting."

Marcus hefted a load of gear and pointed with his chin. "The boat's around back."

"Worse than ill mannered, it's downright risky. I might croak and load you down with guilt you can't do a thing about."

Deacon settled the cooler into Charlie's lap, then gripped the chair handles. "Come on now. Be nice."

"Can't." Charlie Hayes was a retired federal appellate judge and Marcus' oldest friend. He was also two weeks away from his second round of chemo. "They're about to load me up with more of that venom in a bag. All you got to do is look in the doctor's eyes to know this chemo business is nothing but a painful waste of time."

Deacon complained to Marcus, "He's been like this for weeks now. Every other word out of that mouth is about dying."

Charlie demanded, "Is your intention to let me and the fish both perish of old age?"

Deacon gripped the handles of Charlie's chair and pushed it over the uneven surface. As they rounded the house, Dale Steadman appeared on his back patio. Marcus offered, "You're welcome to join us."

The man returned to his home without another word.

Marcus shrugged to his friends and said simply, "Client."

Charlie cast a jaundiced eye about the home's smoke-scarred southern half. "Looks like we got us a good tale in the making."

The thirty-seven-foot cruiser drew murmurs of astonishment from both men. Marcus helped Charlie over the transom and into the white-leather starboard seat. The twin diesels rumbled soft as well-spent money as he cast off fore and aft. Marcus reversed down the slip and into the waterway, then turned north, standing tall and shirtless on the open bridge, for all the world just another rich playboy doing his summer thing. He accepted a cap from Deacon, lathered sunscreen on his shoulders, and pretended that his heart was not lurching to the absence of a lilac gaze.

The boat remained silent for quite a time, as the three men set some space between them and all they had left behind. Deacon's face was a dark working of stone and deep-running emotions. Charlie watched the waters with the slow-blinking care of one who took everything in aged caution.

When they departed the crowded Sunday thoroughfare and began threading their way through marsh islands south of Wrightsville, Charlie asked, "Is this new case of yours as interesting as it looks?"

"Maybe." Marcus outlined what he knew of Dale Steadman's situation.

When he finished, Deacon hummed a deep note and said, "New Horizons. Hard to feel much sorrow for anybody messed up in that place."

The boat was far too large for a day's outing on the inland waters, but Marcus wanted the air-conditioned cabin in case Charlie needed a place to lie down and rest. This trip was much more about doing Charlie Hayes a service than about catching fish. Other fishermen in standard bass boats glared angrily, taking him for an outsider with more cash than sense.

Deacon helped Charlie settle into one of the padded rear seats. He set a can of live bait at his feet and a pole in the holder to his right. He pulled a Coke from the cooler and swept the ice off the can. From his place behind the wheel, Marcus could hear Charlie fussing at the pastor, telling him to stop pampering him so and go thread his own hook. Deacon took no notice of the man's words, just kept on bustling about until Charlie had greased his face and cast his line and assured Deacon for the fifth time that he did not want a sandwich.

The Pamlico Sound was a wind-fractured mirror. The marsh islands weaved frantic little dances, singing wind-whispers as waves lapped in cymbal clarity about their edges. Marcus kept the motor down as close to idle as it would go, and weaved through the lily pads and the sawgrass. Deacon pointed out a kingfisher diving from fifty feet, a silver-gray bullet that made hardly a splash upon impact. Marcus crossed a patch of deep water and anchored in close to a larger island where a crop of dead trees rose bleached white as old bones. The scrub pine and wild dogwoods around the southern border offered them an overhang of shade. In the sudden silence a hoopoe chanted a waterborne greeting.

The boat had only two rear chairs, so Marcus made himself comfortable upon a life preserver on the side railing. He threaded a nightcrawler onto his hook and slung the line overboard. Charlie harrumphed a cough that tore at his gut. Marcus and Deacon exchanged a glance over the old man's head, then went back to watching their lines. In the distance, crows cawed crossly at the day's tragic imperfections.

The shaded waters about their boat were darkest green and utterly still. Which made the eruption even more startling. One moment the loudest sound was the buzzing insects, and the next a fish that looked a full ten feet long shot straight out of the water, rising so high Marcus feared the line was going to catch on the branches. He was so startled he fell off the railing and sprawled on the deck. He heard Charlie's line zing from the reel and two old men shout with fishermen's glee.

Charlie had his pole pointed straight out, just letting the fish whiz out every last inch of line. Marcus scrambled across the deck and came up hard against Charlie's seat back. He reached over and tilted the pole skyward.

"What the . . . Get your hand off my pole!"

"You're going to lose the fish!"

Charlie used one hand to swat frantically at Marcus' arm. "I been fishing since before you drew your first breath. Let go of my pole!"

"Jam your thumb on the reel there, you're down to your last ten feet of line!"

"You touch my pole again and you're gonna be driving this rig without some fingers!" Charlie heaved on the pole, finally setting the hook. "Go on, stand back over there outta range!"

Deacon had one long-fingered hand across his mouth, from behind which bubbled a low humming laugh. His eyes were squeezed almost shut with pure pleasure. "Lay into him now, Charlie. You got him."

"Doggoned right I do, if this little child here with milk dribbling off his chin'll keep his distance." Charlie reeled and pulled and reeled some more. "Was that fish as big as I thought?"

"Looked like a silver whale to me." Deacon wiped his eyes. "My, my, I thought we were gonna have bloodshed there for a minute."

"Lucky you didn't leave the tackle box where I could grab the bait knife." Charlie was puffing and red-faced but his hands moved with the fluidity of a lifetime's experience. " 'Bout to have laid me out in the box, when that thing leapt up."

Deacon was up on his feet now, watching as the line angled up higher and higher. His voice rose to pulpit level as he sang out, "Look there, now! He's coming up again! Hold him hard, Charlie!"

The large-mouth bass was impossibly huge. It did not leap so much as explode, tossing water across the forty feet separating him from the boat as he furiously sought to throw the hook.

There was a moment's gasping silence, then Deacon breathed, "Lawdy mercy, Charlie, you done hooked yourself the granddaddy of them all."

"I didn't see that," Marcus agreed. "Did I?"

"Charlie, don't tug on him quite so hard, else he'll break your line. Marcus, you unleash us and start that engine." Deacon never turned from watching the line and the water. "This old man knows his water, sure enough. He's down there hunting himself a root where he can tie you up good."

Marcus hauled up the anchor, moved to the wheel, hit the starter, then turned to follow Deacon's hand signals. The man kept two fingers resting on Charlie's line as he held his other hand overhead and directed Marcus. Slow and steady, hard right, hold there, reverse again—his only words directed to Charlie in the chair. "Pull in steady like, wind up that slack, ease off now, let him have his head here, that's it, okay, he's breathing easy now. Wind in steady, keep the line taut. He's hunting still."

Charlie was huffing so hard Marcus could hear the bitter phlegm catch and break over the motor's rumble. But he was winding steady, in tune with Deacon's words, anticipating the directions even before they were spoken. Which was why Deacon stopped talking at all, doing nothing now but directing Marcus at the wheel, leaning over the rear transom, squinting at the line and the water.

The fish broke a third time, but it was a feeble effort, for he was tiring. So was Charlie. The old man's khaki shorts and T-shirt were drenched two shades darker. His breathing was one step away from a constant coughing fit. His arms trembled so from the effort of handling the pole and the fish that his upper body shivered in harmony. But there was no question now. This was his fight. His fish.

Marcus heard a change to Charlie's labored breathing, and knew with a friend's wisdom that he was about to give in. Soon he would have to go back and take the pole, which would break the old man's heart. He could not decide which would be harder on Charlie, to lose the fish or have somebody else land it. Deacon glanced his way, the same question there on his face.

Then the pastor turned back and cried, "Hold on, Charlie! He's coming in now! Marcus, you cut that motor and get back here with the net! Yeah, here he comes, wind hard, Charlie! Wind hard, man! You got him!"

Marcus gripped the net handle and leaned over the stern next to Deacon. The preacher was hand-feeding the line now, helping Charlie haul in the almost dead weight. The fish came up through the dark waters almost motionless, a flicker of gills and rear fin his only signs of life. "You just watch out, he might break. This is one wily old fish."

But the fish waited in weary resignation as Marcus dipped the net. He slipped under the bass, settled him in, and drew him out of the water.

The bass was so large he filled the net and spilled out both ends. Marcus needed both hands to heft his load over the transom and lay him down on the deck.

Deacon's hand slipped back over his mouth as he hummed his deep-throated laugh. Charlie sat in his chair, heaving hard, trembling so that when he tried to set his pole on the deck he dropped it with a clatter. He took three tries to shove his glasses back up his nose. When he reached for a Coke, Marcus needed to unpry the hands and flip the top himself. Charlie took a snorting gulp, choked slightly, drank again. Then he leaned over and stared at the fish. He asked hoarsely, "How big do you reckon?"

"Got to be near on fifteen pounds," Deacon said, shaking his head in wonder. "That there is an emperor fish if ever I saw one."

Charlie took another swallow, stared at the fish a moment longer, then said, "Slip him back, son."

"I don't have a camera," Marcus pointed out. "Nobody is going to believe we caught this thing."

"Don't matter a bit, does it, Deacon?"

The preacher was already bent over the fish, prying loose the hook. "Ain't no need to say a word about this to a soul. This here's our tale. Ours and ours alone."

As they threaded their way back through sun-dappled waters, Marcus found the day darkened by Kirsten's absence and his own lack of answers. Charlie must have caught the smoldering drift, for as they approached the Steadman manor he pushed himself out of the rear seat. With Deacon's help he shifted over to the one directly beside Marcus. "All right, son. Now tell me what's troubling you so."

Enclosed within sunlight and sea breeze and the concern of good friends, Marcus found the ability to say, "I'm afraid Kirsten is going to leave me."

Charlie and Deacon exchanged a single look. Charlie said, "She's always struck me as a fine young lady."

"She's a good woman who doesn't always do good things. She's pushed by storms I can only guess at. Which makes knowing what to do here very tough."

"Maybe you can't do a thing, son," Charlie said. "Except survive her passage."

"Listen to you with your doom and gloom. That ain't what the boy needs to hear." Deacon reached into the cooler and plucked out one of the cans bobbing in the melted ice. "The question is, are you man enough to love her *hard* enough? Can you accept your need for wisdom that ain't yours and never will be? And then can you use it when it's given?" Deacon said to Charlie, "Now you just tell me I ain't right."

Charlie took the can from Deacon's hand and raised his face to the sun, his Adam's apple bobbing as he drank.

Deacon asked Marcus, "You know why she seems intent on going?"

"The closer we get, the more frightened she becomes. From some few things she's said, I gather she's chased by something in her past. Something bad."

"So you haven't done anything to bring this on?"

"I asked her to marry me. Does that count?"

"You're not hearing what the man is saying." Charlie leaned forward and poked Marcus in the ribs with the hand holding the can. "Do us all a favor here, son. Try and set the lawyer in your head to one side."

Deacon chuckled low in his throat and took a step back, so as to study the two of them.

"Just for a moment," Charlie went on, "I want you to put aside the portion that says, I'm going to think this through and come up with the right course of action, on account of how I'm in control here. Listen to the love in your heart. Don't even ask for logic. Just listen. See if there's a different answer waiting for you."

The answer sprang up fast and unwelcome. Marcus shook his head, not to Charlie's words, but to his own internal response. "That's no help at all."

Charlie settled back in his seat, his features clamped tight in the vise of exhaustion and ill health. "Sometimes love is a gift that's got to be dug from the pit of old woes. When we first fasten on it, what a burden that gift can appear to be."

Marcus said nothing more as he slowed and turned into Dale Steadman's dock. Beyond the emerald lawn, Dale watched through the kitchen's rear window as Deacon stepped onto the dock and tied them up fore and aft. All Marcus' present fears seemed crouched beyond the smoke-stained corners, feeding off the mysteries and doubts.

Marcus cut the engines and handed the first load of equipment to Deacon. He piled the remaining poles and the cooler on the pier, brought a plastic bucket and rag up from the galley, and began sluicing the deck. Charlie remained seated in the white leather chair, his back to the house, sipping occasionally from the soda. As Marcus worked, he found himself recalling a time when he had spent three hours watching the reflections of an afternoon rain form colorless trails down his kitchen wall. There had been a certain comfort in the ephemeral scroll and knowing there was no message to be discerned, no further tragedy to savage him. He let the old man be.

Marcus drained the bucket over the rear transom. He stepped onto the dock just as Deacon disappeared around the house with the final load of poles. Marcus headed down to where Charlie's wheelchair waited at the foot of the dock. He knew his current melancholy was partly due to the day now ending and the prospect of summers where Charlie Hayes played no querulous part. But there was more that troubled him, much as he might desperately wish otherwise.

The response to Charlie's water-borne question had come to him with the instantaneous force of a bullet to his gut. But it was also precisely what he most wanted to avoid. The answer had been simply, give her up while he still had the power. Let her go. Then if she returned, it would be freely and fully. His entire body clenched tight over the agony of such willful loss.

He was midway along the dock when the entire world seemed to catch its breath. Then the boat erupted.

The surrounding marsh grass shone as though the water itself had turned to fire. Then a giant's hand reached out and slapped him headlong off the pier, and buried him beneath the flaming waters.

CHAPTER

12

KIRSTEN EXTENDED her morning routine until three in the afternoon. She cleaned her little brick townhouse from top to bottom. Her music system pumped so strongly she could feel the bass rattle the sink through the scouring sponge. The house did not need cleaning and she scarcely heard the music at all. But it reduced the threat of hearing the phone ring, of having to speak with Fay, of someone from church asking where she was. All the things she was desperate to avoid.

At four she ate a bowl of fresh-sliced fruit and unsweetened yogurt. She took her time dressing. A deft hand with the makeup, just a touch of color, her hair was never a problem, a serious dress and modest jewelry. She put part of the Sunday *Washington Post* into her briefcase in case the senator's aide made her wait. She checked her reflection one further time, and saw a lovely and poised young woman whose gaze was the only part of her exterior she could not control.

At a quarter to five she locked her front door and stepped into the humid broil of another late July afternoon. The one problem with these townhouses was the absence of shaded parking, which meant the car's seat and wheel were almost too hot to touch. She drove down Glen Eden to where it connected with the Raleigh-Durham highway. The senator's regional office was on Hargett, five blocks from the capitol, a ten-minute drive in the Sunday afternoon calm.

The aide was there to greet her at the building's front entrance. "You couldn't be anybody but Mr. Glenwood's new assistant."

"Kirsten Stansted." The phone in her purse began ringing as she stepped into the building's coolness. She decided to ignore it. "I work with Marcus."

"I heard about you, but I didn't believe it until now." He was a pudgy man in the way of many political staffers, bound together with nerves and bad diet and too-long days. "Brent Daniels."

"Marcus sends his regrets, but he is down in Wilmington meeting with his client."

"You just be sure and tell Marcus how much I appreciate him being somewhere else." He ushered her into the large office behind the receptionist's desk. "It's our lucky day, Senator."

The bespectacled man raised his eyes from the papers strewn over his desk. "Now isn't that the truth."

"Kirsten Stansted is Glenwood's right-hand lady, if rumors are to be believed."

"The man is a purebred fool to let you wander around on your own."

"I don't give him any choice in the matter."

The senator tottered over to compress her hand between both of his. "I don't doubt that for a second. You take a coffee? How about a cold drink?"

"I'm fine, thank you."

Each of the senator's steps cast him from side to side, a vessel rocked by time's winds. "Take a seat wherever you'll be most comfortable, Ms. Stansted. I hope you won't mind if we get right on to business. Brent and me, we've got families who don't take kindly to having our Sundays being disturbed. But I wanted to weigh in personally on this matter."

"Senator Jacobs is chairman of the Senate Foreign Relations Committee," Brent added. "He's used his position to press this issue of American children being abducted by foreign parents in custody disputes."

"Germany was an original signatory of the Hague Convention on Children. But their judicial system flouts the regulations at every step. We've been looking for a landmark case to force the Germans' hand."

"This is a draft of the convention." Brent Daniels handed her a bound manuscript. "Germany has become a haven for too many parents who otherwise would never be permitted to retain custody of young children. The German court system refuses to relinquish the children to American parents, even when our courts have come down in their favor."

Kirsten's cell phone chimed again. When she made no move to answer, the senator waited until the ringing halted, then went on, "Word is out, Ms. Stansted. News of this loophole is spreading via the Internet. Citizens of EU countries can reside anywhere in Europe they want. If they marry an American, find their marriage in trouble, and see the American court deciding against them, they grab the kids and flee to Germany."

"Just as has happened with your client," Brent finished.

"We're in the process of enacting punitive legislation against the German government, and we're working to obtain United Nations backing. But we need a high-profile case to demonstrate just how the court system is stacked against us. Then lo and behold, what happens but we hear about Dale Steadman. A top-notch fellow who's got himself in this very plight."

Kirsten's phone began ringing once more. She did her best to ignore it and replied, "I have to tell you, sir, we're just not certain how solid a case Marcus has."

She sketched out what they had discovered. The senator and his aide did not mask their dismay over the news of the fire and the drinking and the local officials' testimony.

The two men exchanged a glance before the senator said, "This is the problem with divorce issues. There are seldom any clear-cut rights and wrongs."

"Sounds like you'd best not become publicly involved until we see the lay of the land," Brent suggested.

"Don't have much choice in the matter."

The aide said to Kirsten, "If you'd be so kind as to keep me informed, my staff will help out any way we can."

"I'll tell Marcus, but right now I don't see . . ." Her cell phone began a fourth ringing.

"Maybe you best see who that is, young lady."

She retrieved the phone, punched the button. "Yes?"

"Kirsten? Ms. Stansted?"

"Yes."

"Oh, thank heavens."

"Who is this?"

"Dale. Dale Steadman." The man choked over his own name. He took a broken breath. "Sorry. Sorry. When I couldn't reach you I feared you were dead as well."

Senator Jacobs leaned forward. "You all right, young lady? You've gone white as moonlight."

CHAPTER

13

MARCUS' WORLD was made up of fractured images, knitted together without the comfort of time's steady flow. Hands lifted and dragged him from the marsh grass. A sun beamed down as voices and shadows came and went in frantic haste. A siren scrambled out of the distance. More hands. The siren blared again, this time closer and constant. A needle like a tiny bone became lodged in his vein. He grew fully awake then, in time to see a man with a worried expression and a stethoscope take his pulse and blood pressure. When Marcus coughed weakly and struggled to rise, the man's gloved palm gently pressed his chest. Marcus stared into the man's eyes and saw just how lucky he had been.

The emergency room doctor treated the burns on his neck and scalp, then pulled several pieces of roasted boat from his back. From a filtered distance the doctor spoke to him about possible ear damage and a minor concussion. A policeman came and asked questions that Marcus did his best to answer. But the man recognized Marcus' state and soon let him be. The doctor, a fussy sort who seemed to enjoy the reflected publicity, gave Marcus a sedative and wheeled him down for a full body scan. Despite the machine's thunderous noise, Marcus was soon asleep.

Fragments of old dreams rose from the coffin of repressed memories. They gathered with images from more recent times and danced to the painkiller's macabre tune. Hours passed, perhaps aeons. He heard Charlie voice the dreaded question yet again: What did his heart say he should do about Kirsten? Then the dream shifted and the boat exploded yet again. Instead of the flash of flames and blackening agony, however, Marcus was battered by loss so potent it flung him back into reality.

Marcus awoke to the sound of that single keening echo. He focused on where Kirsten stood by his bed and reached for her hand. There was no need to ask about Charlie Hayes. Her expression contained all the sad tidings he could bear at that moment.

Deacon stood at the foot of his bed. Dale Steadman hovered by the door, as though uncertain whether he was welcome to the gathering. Marcus lay and waited while the doctor was called. When the doctor ordered them all to leave, Marcus refused to release Kirsten's hand. The act of awakening had only cemented his certainty. He had to let Kirsten go. If he could not do it for himself, he would make it a final atoning memorial to the friend who was no more.

After the doctor pronounced him in need of little more than a night's rest, Marcus again spoke to the police. This took less than a dozen minutes, as there was little to describe beyond a flash and a bang and a dive.

Marcus then directed Kirsten to bring the others back. He asked Dale, "Who blew up the boat?"

"My vote has to go for some of the folks I'm trying to roust over at New Horizons. They're an entrenched group, and don't think highly of what I intend to do."

"Which is?"

"Change things," Dale replied. "Stir things up."

Marcus listened hard as he could, but detected neither guile nor subterfuge nor motive. "You need to meet me Tuesday for court. Eight-thirty sharp. We need to have the judge see with her own eyes just exactly who you are."

"You're flat on your back, near about blown to smithereens," Dale pointed out.

"Either we show up for court Tuesday," Marcus replied, "or your ex gets the kid."

"Didn't I tell you now," Deacon said to the room. "We got us a warrior here for the good and the just."

"If we can find witnesses to refute the testimony against you, the judge will probably issue an *ex partae* order." Marcus reached for the water by his bed. The motion raised a chorus of complaints from his body. He drained the cup, then said, "But Erin Brandt won't be coming back to America. Will she?"

A light gleamed in the dark recesses of Dale's gaze. "Probably not."

"In that case, we need to show the judge documented evidence of your ex-wife receiving the order, then refusing to attend the hearing or return the child." Marcus stretched his back and neck, a test of will as much as muscle. "We'll serve the court papers in London. She will be out of her comfort zone and vulnerable."

"About those references. You need to avoid anyone who's grown fat off the status quo. Which means they'll probably be reluctant to miss a day's work and drive to Raleigh to testify."

Sleep's gentle lyrics drifted with the scent of hospital chemicals. Marcus looked down to the hand he still held. Kirsten's fingers were long and delicate and tipped with nails painted the color of live coral. The thought he might never hold her again filled his chest with fires of eternal regret. But Charlie had been right to ask his dreaded question. There was no choice but to give her what she most desired. Otherwise she would wrest it from him. And in so doing she would sever any chance they had for a future together.

Though it cut him with a force far stronger than the explosion he had just survived, he said, "I need you to go to London to serve the papers on Erin Brandt."

His words embedded themselves gradually. "What?"

"Take tomorrow's first flight. Locate a detective and have him ready to make the handover as soon as the papers arrive. That is, assuming we win the second round in court Tuesday."

"But . . . I can't."

"This is important, Kirsten. Vital. I'll overnight you a copy of the *ex partae* order. Be sure the handover is caught on tape. We may need this evidence in court." When she wrenched her hand free, he did not have the strength to recapture it. "If we have any indication Erin is not going to show up in court, you need to follow her back to Germany. Be ready to supply documented evidence that she isn't complying with the court order."

Kirsten careened off the end of the bed and across the room.

Marcus said, "We both know you need to go."

She searched blindly for a door handle she could not find. Dale finally opened the door and ushered her out.

Deacon stared at the door and murmured, "Lady's got some ghosts screaming at her, sure to goodness."

Her absence was a sudden vacuum. "Somebody needs to get Charlie home."

Deacon's gaze contained such sorrow Marcus had to turn away. "Listen to you. Flat on your back, eyes drifting in the wind, and still you got to worry about all the blessed world."

Strange how the pain could reach him, even though fatigue gummed his words. "If we don't find some witnesses willing to speak on Dale's behalf, we're doomed."

"You just hush and rest now." Deacon's gentle bass sounded in harmony to slumber's symphony. "I'll see if I can't help the gentleman come up with something."

CHAPTER

14

MONDAY MORNING Marcus awoke to find that Charlie's family had already come and gone. He could not decide whether this was a blessing or yet another wound to his lacerated spirit. Dale had driven back to Raleigh with Kirsten, there to see if he could stir up answers. Deacon helped him through the torment of rising and preparing for departure. Marcus called his office, assured Netty that he had all his bits and pieces intact, and pretended he had not hoped for word from Kirsten.

The hospital checkout required over an hour and much of Marcus' strength. The doctor pronounced him as fit as anybody he had ever seen who had just been blown up. He let Marcus go with a smile and a pack of Percodan. Marcus resisted the desire to flee into codeine's sweet embrace, and instead dozed while Deacon drove.

He opened his eyes to find they had stopped by a red-brick church. A mammoth black gentleman with the eyes of a merry inquisitor greeted Deacon with a long and vigorous embrace. He then turned to where Marcus still sat inside the car and extended his hand. "Reverend Cleve Samson. Deacon here says you're the young fellow who lit up Motts Channel yesterday."

"I'm not feeling so young right now."

"I know that's the truth." He showed a pastor's ability to share deepest sorrow with a look, a touch, a very few words. "Charlie Hayes was a saint. His passage leaves a lot of people 'round here feeling much poorer."

"Thank you."

"Deacon tells me you're in need of our help."

"Not me, but a client."

"Any friend of Dale Steadman is a friend of most everybody down this way." He started toward a massive old town car. "Y'all can follow me, the Biggs don't live more'n five blocks from here."

The Biggs residence was down a tree-lined street, a bastion of peace triangulated by the Wrightsville Beach Highway, the hospital, and the ruins of the old port. Deacon parked behind the reverend's Lincoln. Together they followed him up the drive.

A woman in a faded print housedress stood with arms linked beneath her ribs. "Reverend."

"Hello, Ida. I believe you know Deacon Wilbur."

"Nice to see you again, sir. Welcome to my home."

"And this is the gentleman I told you about."

Ida Biggs showed Marcus a face shut tight as a vault. "Y'all best come out of the heat."

The screened veranda ran the entire back end of the house. Ida's husband, a clean-shaven gentleman with the tensile strength of a willow, rose to greet them. "Good to have you come around, Reverend."

"How you keeping, Tyrell?"

"Can't complain." He did not wait for the pastor to introduce them. "Deacon Wilbur, as I live and breathe."

"Mr. Biggs."

"And you must be that lawyer fellow I heard so much about, the one took on New Horizons."

"Marcus Glenwood."

"Always wanted to shake your hand. Yessir, took on the giants of this world with one little stone, ain't that right, Reverend?" Tyrell Biggs was dressed in pleated cotton slacks and a coffee-colored shirt, one shade lighter than his skin. "How about I go fix everybody a glass of lemonade. Ida made some up fresh."

"Lemonade would be fine, sir. Thank you."

"Mr. Glenwood's got some questions he'd like to ask you about Dale Steadman, Ida."

"Don't see as how I can talk comfortable about what's gone on inside somebody else's house."

"That's why we're here, Ida, me and Deacon both. To tell you this ain't just right, it's important. Now sit yourself on down and see if you can help the man help Mr. Steadman."

Marcus eased himself into the padded chair. Nothing hurt in an excruciating manner. But all his aches bonded together, forming a fabric that stretched and tugged with every motion. "Actually, I need to ask you about his former wife as much as I do about Dale himself."

Tyrell called through the house's open door, "It's all about Benjamins with that lady."

His wife sniffed. "No it ain't."

"Yessir, all about those Ben Franklins. All about big money."

"What you talking about?" Something in her tone suggested Ida Biggs was actually glad her husband was speaking, as it released her from what was probably a tight and constant reserve. "You never worked in that home."

"Who's living with you then? Who's watched you talk every day 'bout how hard it was to be in the same house with that lady. Who's heard you fretting day in and day out over the baby being in that lady's care?"

Marcus asked, "How long did you work for Mr. Steadman?"

"A year and some change. Ever since they moved into that house he built her." But her eyes remained upon her husband, who was going around now with five glasses on a metal tray. "Listen to you talk."

"I saw that woman more than I ever wanted to." He handed his wife a glass, then seated himself beside her. "I watched them have words right there on my doorstep."

His wife sipped from her glass. "Mr. Dale is a fine gentleman."

"Did I say anything against that man? No I did not. Not one word. I'm talking about the lady."

"The lady didn't care nothing about money."

"But she cared about her singing, didn't she. She cared about her career. That was her pieces of silver." He leaned back, satisfied. "Tell me I'm not right."

"Go turn on the fan so we can get us some air."

Tyrell set down his glass and rose from his chair. "Her singing was her obsession. Same sin, different currency. Ain't that what you say, Reverend?"

Marcus asked, "You think Erin Brandt kidnapped the child because of her career?"

"She didn't do it out of love, I know that much." Ida Biggs looked straight at him for the first time, and Marcus realized the only reason she was talking to him at all was because of the baby. "One thing I can say for certain about Miz Brandt. She wouldn't know love if it grew fangs and bit her on the backside."

They made two further stops after the visit with Ida Biggs. The meetings proceeded at a country pace, which meant it was almost dark before they finally left Wilmington. Marcus dozed the entire way home. His sleep was never deep enough to dream. Every now and then the mournful note he had heard upon awakening in the hospital drifted through his heart, and he would sense anew the burden of unshed tears.

When Deacon pulled up in front of the house, Marcus opened his door and eased himself upright. He could not help but watch his front door. He knew Kirsten would not be there, but hoped just the same. "Would you come to court with me tomorrow?"

"You still plan on taking that lawyer Caisse to task?"

"You heard what I said to Dale. We don't have any choice. Ida Biggs might be more comfortable on the stand if you were there to greet her."

"Son, I'd rather watch you tear a patch out of that man's hide than sit ringside at a revival." Deacon slapped the car into gear. "I'll pick you up at seven-thirty sharp."

Marcus ate a solitary dinner and stretched out on his bed. But the day had already been too full of sleep. He slipped into his clothes and padded back downstairs. Marcus arrived on the porch just as a concert of wind began singing through his pines. He eased himself down in one of the rockers, testing each joint in turn. There was considerable soreness, particularly around his neck and upper shoulders. But other than a general sense of bearing a body-sized bruise and having come far too close to that last cold breath, he was all right.

The wind's recital was particularly sweet that night. He rocked in cadence to the tossing branches as thunder's profound bass filled the hollows of his chest. It seemed to him that Charlie Hayes walked up and settled into the rocker alongside his own. The sensation was so strong Marcus felt a need to say the words aloud, that he was welcome here always.

Then the first sheet of rain swept in, forming a tight enclosure for all the night's scents. The magnolia blossoms and bougainvillea sang a perfumed lament. The leaves tapped out the rhythm of absent friends.

But it was not merely Charlie's absence that harried him that night. His need to hold Kirsten was a pain that dwarfed his physical discomfort. He ached as well for all she carried. There was no question but that she was judging him through spectacles formed by her past. Marcus sat and rocked and listened to the storm enclose him in his safe little island, and prayed that he could trust her and their love enough to hope she would not only return, but return because she was ready for him. He hoped Charlie Hayes had been right. He hoped he had done the right thing. This time.

CHAPTER

15

K IRSTEN CAUGHT THE MIDDAY FLIGHT to Washington and a late afternoon plane to London. She was plagued the entire journey by
how her life's rules were being tangled and respun in a web-like script
she could not fathom. As she entered Heathrow's Terminal Three, jet
lag hulked in the back of her mind like the onset of a bad cold. She
gathered her bags, passed through customs, and headed for the dis-
count hotel counter. From the sparse high-season choices she selected a
Best Western within walking distance of Paddington Station. On the
express train into London, her jumbled thoughts chopped at the fine-
ness of the sunlit morning with a blade honed from earlier times.

At Paddington she asked directions from an overfriendly porter
and became lost a block from the station entrance. Jet lag and a plague
of almost-familiar images pressed in from all sides. The sunlight was
brighter than she recalled, the weather warmer. London to her mind
was a place of cool nights and misting rain, even in July. By the time
she finally found the proper road, the back of her shirt was clamped
tightly to her skin.

The hotel receptionist was a slender Pakistani with soulful eyes
and a manner that suggested he tried his wiles with every pretty
woman. He pressed the key into her palm, then wrapped his fingers
delicately about her wrist, pinning her into his grip. "Madame is being
upgraded to one of the most newly renovated and air-conditioned
rooms."

Kirsten pretended not to notice either his tone or his clutch. "Can
you tell me where I can find a good detective?"

The receptionist's hand snapped away. "Please?"

"A detective. A large agency would be better. Someone with an international reputation."

"I am certain I do not know." A film descended over the liquid gaze. "Madame must excuse me now. Other guests are soon to be arriving."

Kirsten hefted her own luggage and carried it up the narrow stairs. Her room was an Edwardian box, high-ceilinged and once probably the side parlor to a grand city house. Now it was carpeted in a depressing plaid, painted a shade somewhere between tan and putrid, and lit by the chandelier's three remaining bulbs. Kirsten settled upon the bed, pulled out the proper phone book, and looked up the Royal Opera House. Every motion caused the unsprung mattress to sway like a boat entering harbor. As the phone rang she surveyed the room with tired satisfaction. If any place offered a total disconnection from her unwanted past, it was this.

The phone spoke. "Covent Garden."

"I just wanted to ask about a singer performing tonight."

"The name?"

"Erin Brandt."

The response came too swiftly for it to have been the first time spoken that day. "Ms. Brandt does not accept any calls. But I am happy to relay a message."

"No. No message." She hung up, took a hard breath, then dialed the number for Marcus' office. She endured Netty's recorded message and tersely spelled out her London address. Her hands were shaking as she hunted through her purse for the card from Senator Jacobs' aide. She dialed the senator's Raleigh office and left a detailed message, asking for help in locating a London-based detective agency. As she spelled out her requirements, she found herself fighting a losing skirmish with her steadily descending eyelids.

She was asleep before her head hit the pillow. Familiar dreams rose in what she had hoped would be a sterile room. She danced to a chamber full of strangers, all smiling and waving, all shouting noises that created a screeching cacophonous din. She danced not to a melody, but chaos. The apparitions shouted at her in voices barely below full rage. Though she neither wanted to be there nor understood what they were saying, still she danced, alone and surrounded by enemies disguised with smiles.

The noise in her dream was so loud, when the phone rang she merely absorbed the sound and danced to that as well. Gradually the wordless clatter receded until the ringing was all she could hear, and the dance dimmed to where she had no choice but to open her eyes.

She lifted the receiver, cradled it to her shoulder, and pushed herself upright. "Yes?"

"Madame has a visitor."

"Who—" But the receptionist had already slapped down the phone.

Kirsten slipped into clothes that still smelled of the plane's recycled air. In the doorway she paused and turned back, inspecting the high-ceilinged room with its repainted hints of former grandeur. She saw no hint of her caper with frantic memories save the tousled bed.

She took the stairs in a dull melange of fatigue and dream tendrils. Which made her entrance into the lobby even more eerie.

Afternoon light made a brilliant splash upon the lobby's white-tiled floor. To her squinting gaze, it appeared that a shadow separated itself from its owner and rushed over to find a more suitable host.

Then a face came into view, and eyes looked at her, and a mild yet breathless voice declared, "Beautiful, yes, that I can accept. But not like this. Not like a vision with the eyes of a shattered soul. Do you dance? Do you sing? You have the look of an artist, one whose cry is too great to be held trapped within.'"

"Excuse me?"

A hand reached for her arm and pulled her toward the doorway. "Come, we must inspect you in the full light of day."

The woman's movements were too swift, the tableau too changing, for Kirsten to focus fully. She saw high-heeled suede boots dancing across the sun-splashed floor. They rose to join with rose-silk trousers, and they with a matching high-collared jacket. Hair like a black water-fall poured across the shoulders. The woman was not large. But when she turned back around, and drew in so close Kirsten could see the faint darker flecks within those chestnut eyes, she *commanded*. "Yes. As soon as I saw you moving down the stairs, I knew. We are sisters, you and I. Molded by the same harsh flame."

Her own words sounded feeble, unable to meet the force with which she was being assaulted. "You are Erin Brandt?"

"Of course, of course, you came seeking an enemy. As did I." She had a slight accent, the faintest lilt to her breathless words. As though she were reading them off a score she would later sing. "That was why I came, I had to see for myself. Who have they sent to attack me?"

"I . . . We shouldn't be talking."

"So the world says, does it not?" The woman seemed both young and old, a timeless adolescent trapped in the amber of fame. "But what does your heart say? Does it chant the same incantation as mine, that we meet as sisters held too long apart?"

"How did you find me?"

"That doesn't matter now." Erin stepped away and began scrambling through her purse. "You must come tonight. You know of my performance, yes? Of course, why else would they have sent you." She extracted a silver pen and tiny leather-bound notepad. "Your name, it is Kirsten, yes?"

"Kirsten Stansted."

"So very lovely. Like an aria." Erin tore off the page and pressed it into Kirsten's hand. "Give that to the guard at the backstage entrance to Covent Garden. Be there by a quarter to eight. Someone will greet you and take you to a chair. They say it is sold out, but we must find you a seat somewhere, yes? Of course we must."

The gesture was not enough. Impatiently Erin stuffed the pen and pad back into her purse, freeing her other hand to reach over and grip as well. "Tell me you will come, I beg you. Or say nothing, so that I can at least dream that beyond the lights and the orchestra, there in the dark cloud of strange faces, I will have you to sing to. You to catch my words and know their true meaning. As only a sister can."

Then she turned and fled down the stairs and out to the street, where a uniformed chauffeur rose to hold open the door to a purple Rolls-Royce. Erin cast her a single glance, so strong in appeal Kirsten could feel the slender fingers still pressing and holding.

Kirsten turned from the entrance. The receptionist observed her with the scorn of one who wished to claim he had known this was the situation all along.

CHAPTER

16

MARCUS ARRIVED at the courthouse to discover his case was listed first on Judge Sears' overcrowded Tuesday docket. When Marcus entered the courtroom, Dale Steadman was already there in the back row. Marcus waved him forward. "I've asked Deacon to join us as a sort of unofficial aide. His presence might prove important."

"Whatever you say." Steadman wore a standard-issue gray suit and the grim expression of one entering a war not of his choosing. He pointed to where the court reporter stood by the back doorway. "Do you know him?"

"Omar Dell."

"He seems to have a lot of information on both of us. And a lot of questions."

"Answer him or don't, it's your choice. But if publicity is what your ex-wife seeks to avoid, you might want to consider him a potential ally."

Hamper Caisse bustled into the courtroom an instant before Judge Sears. The judge seated herself and said, "The two of you step up here, please."

When the attorneys were standing before her raised desk, she inquired of Marcus, "Are the stories in the paper true?"

"I'm afraid so, your honor."

She showed Marcus the measured commiseration of a seated judge addressing counsel. "Charlie Hayes was as fine a man as I have ever known."

"He was that."

"Are you all right?"

"I had a close call, no question. I'm bruised and shaken, but otherwise fine."

"Is there any evidence that the explosion has any bearing on this case?"

"None that I know of, your honor."

"What about a tie-in to the recent house fire?"

"My client is seeking to institute some drastic changes at New Horizons, your honor. He personally believes there might be some executives—"

"Your honor, I must protest." Hamper Caisse quietly raged, "Marcus is doing his best to divert the court's attention from what the fire chief himself said on Friday, which was that Dale Steadman was falling down drunk when help arrived. And immediately following the fire he started reconstruction, thus hiding any evidence of foul play."

Judge Sears nodded toward Marcus' table. "Is that your client there?"

"Dale Steadman in the flesh, your honor."

"I see your own table remains empty, Mr. Caisse."

"As your honor well knows, my client is a world-famous opera diva. Her singing commitments hold her in Europe at this time."

"And what is the position your own client holds at present, Marcus?"

"Chairman of the board of New Horizons, Incorporated."

"Sounds like a mighty busy individual to me." She made a note in her case file. "How do you wish to proceed?"

"Your honor, at this time I wish to call Ida Biggs to the stand."

"Just a moment." Before Judge Rachel Sears was a typical morning crush. Lawyers spilled from the courtroom's two side offices. They spoke in muted voices with district attorneys awaiting cases. They scheduled hearings. They leaned over the waist-high partition known as the bench and huddled with clients. They snickered and gossiped among themselves. A pair of translators, one Hispanic and the other Vietnamese, whispered about upcoming cases. Two attorneys spoke in hushed tones with the court recorder, while another waited in the wings, urgently flagging for Judge Sears' attention.

The judge raised her voice and announced, "In case you folks haven't noticed, I'm trying a case here."

The hubbub ground to an astonished halt. Normally a family court judge condoned such maneuverings, for otherwise the caseload would swamp them all. Cases were scheduled ten minutes apart, on the assumption that most of the day's work would be done in this manner. The court built to a twice daily frenzy as the clock approached the midday and afternoon recesses.

"Now I want everybody who is in here to either find a seat or take their business elsewhere." She turned to the bailiff and instructed, "Station one of your team by the rear doors. Anyone who comes in has to stay until I've made a ruling."

"Yes, your honor."

She surveyed the shocked faces and snapped, "You heard me. Grab a seat or take a hike."

As Marcus returned to his seat, his attention was snagged by Deacon Wilbur. The old pastor was seated between the attorney's tables and the railing. Ida and Tyrell Biggs were seated just behind him. But the pastor was paying them no mind. He was too busy blazing Hamper Caisse with a reverend's version of the snake eye. Hamper Caisse ignored Marcus' side of the courtroom entirely, busying himself with something he found of particular fascination within his briefcase.

Judge Sears rearranged the papers in her open file. "In regard to the case between Erin Brandt and Dale Steadman, I have before me two motions. One is from Ms. Brandt and regards a change of custody. The second is from Mr. Steadman and requests an emergency *ex partae* order. Is that correct?"

"Yes, your honor."

"All right, Mr. Glenwood." Judge Sears motioned with her gavel. "You may proceed."

He rose and gestured for Ida Biggs to come forward. The woman was dressed for Sunday meeting in a pink linen dress and black enameled straw hat. She carried a purse big enough to hold a bazooka. She endured the swearing-in process with evident nerves, then seated herself with her purse clenched as a lap shield.

Marcus remained stationed by his table. "You worked as Dale Steadman's housemaid and nanny for over a year, is that right?"

She glanced at Dale, who was intently focused upon nothing. "Yessir, that's correct."

"Can you tell the court what was Mr. Steadman's temperament?"

"Mr. Dale, he's as fine a man as I ever met. It's been an honor working for him." She nodded decisively. "An honor."

Hamper Caisse rose in gaunt and clumsy stages. "Judge, I must object. We're talking to a woman who has every reason to tell the court whatever will ensure her paycheck."

In response, Marcus asked the witness, "Are you still in Mr. Steadman's employment?"

"Nosir."

"He dismissed you?"

"I wanted to stay on, but he wouldn't let me. Said it might be dangerous, since the police couldn't say how the fire got started."

Hamper subsided into his chair without speaking. Judge Sears gave Marcus the nod.

"Tell us about the situation within Mr. Steadman's former marriage."

Ida Biggs took an even tighter grip upon her purse, glanced once more at Dale Steadman, then replied, "They argued back and forth all the time."

"Accusations have been made that Mr. Steadman has physically attacked Erin Brandt."

"Only time I know when Mr. Dale touched the lady, it happened right in the middle of the kitchen while I was fixing the baby's lunch."

"Did Mr. Steadman strike her as has been claimed?"

"She did the grabbing. But he ended up falling on top of her."

"What happened then?"

"Mr. Dale, he pulled himself back up and ran off into the library. The lady went after him. She was swinging something, a pot I think it was."

"So she was the aggressor?"

"Every time I saw, she was the one doing the swinging."

"Do you recall what it was they argued about?"

"Everything under the sun. But Mr. Dale, he never started much of anything unless it was about the child. The rest of the time, he just stood there and let her get all worked up."

"So there was nothing in particular that set her off?"

"Most times, it was how much she hated the place."

"Their home?"

"The house, the town, the heat, the food, the people. You name it, she hated it."

"What about their baby, Celeste?"

The woman's features softened a stroke. "Mr. Dale, he dearly loves that child."

"What about Ms. Brandt?"

"She didn't act like no mother I've ever seen."

Hamper Caisse gave a sonorous blast. "Objection! Generality!"

"Overruled. Proceed."

"How was Ms. Brandt different from what you might have expected?"

"Just the way she looked at that baby. It was strange."

"I'm sorry, Mrs. Biggs. I'm trying to gain a mental picture here. Strange just doesn't do it for me."

"The lady never said a thing. Not to me, not to her husband that I ever heard. She never disabused that baby in any way. She just never did *anything*."

"Excuse me, but could you please try and give me a specific—"

"Why is this not clear to you, sir? If I brought the baby into a room, that lady would get up and walk out. She never changed the child's diapers, not one single solitary time. She wouldn't feed her. She wouldn't dress her. She wouldn't even hold Celeste unless there was somebody who walked over and set the child down in her lap. Then she'd just sit there waiting till she could find somebody to hand the baby to." Ida Biggs kneaded the purse so hard the leather stretched and bunched. "Sweetest child you ever saw in all your born days. Little blond-haired angel was all she was. Just a treasure. I still dream about that baby's smile."

"Your honor, please," Caisse complained. "The child is not on trial here."

"Yes. Sustained. Redirect your witness, Mr. Glenwood."

"Mrs. Biggs, we are gathered here today because Ms. Brandt is fighting to keep this child in her custody."

"Sir, I tell you what's the honest truth. Unless the Lord himself had done touched this lady's heart, she isn't doing what you say she's doing."

"Objection!"

Judge Sears did not release the witness from her gaze. "I'm going to allow this to go a little further."

"But she is, Mrs. Biggs. Ms. Brandt has abducted the child and has brought us all here together today."

"Then she ain't doing it for the baby's sake."

"Your honor, this is absurd!" Hamper was up and pacing now. "How are we to take this woman's unconfirmed testimony against all the evidence I presented on Friday?"

Marcus retreated to his seat. "No further questions, your honor."

"Your witness, Mr. Caisse."

Marcus held his breath. It was a risk, leaving the critical issue unaddressed. But the impact would be far stronger if Hamper did the asking.

Hamper Caisse did not merely step into the trap. He dove in. "All right, Mrs. Biggs! Let's get to the heart of the matter. Tell us about Dale Steadman's drinking!"

"The man liked his bourbon."

"He liked it a *lot*."

"That's true."

Hamper angled his head to ensure the judge was catching this. "Too much from the sounds of things."

"He had himself a glass 'bout every night, that's true."

"A glass? Did you say a glass?"

"Sometimes two."

"Two what, Mrs. Biggs? Two bottles?"

"Nosir. Not Mr. Dale."

"Come on now, Mrs. Biggs. We've had testimony from a variety of sources that directly contradicts your own. We know you like the defendant. But we're after the truth here. Mr. Steadman was a drunkard, wasn't he?"

"Nosir. Not a bit of it."

"I remind you you're under oath, Mrs. Biggs."

"Only time he ever let the drink take control was twice." Ida Biggs kept as tight a grip on her emotions as she did upon her purse. "When that lady left him, and when she came back and stole that child. Mr. Dale's a man with a big heart. That's his only crime. That lady just ripped it right out of his body. And she done it twice."

Hamper cast a molten glance at Marcus, then wheeled about and snapped, "Your honor, there isn't a single solitary thing this woman can tell us of any value. I am not going to waste the court's time with probing what I have already shown to be a pack of self-serving lies."

"The witness may step down."

But Hamper Caisse's words had pinched Ida Biggs' face up tight. "What I told you was the truth."

Judge Sears said, "Please step down, Mrs. Biggs. The court is grateful for your coming all this way."

As she left the stand and passed between the attorneys' tables, Ida Biggs cast another glance at Dale Steadman. This time he returned the look, his expression as bleak as January rain. Whatever she saw there set the woman to humming a deep mournful note as she gathered up her husband and departed from the courtroom.

"Mr. Glenwood?"

"Your honor, at this time I'd like to call Mr. William Pierce to the stand."

The gentleman being led to the front of the courtroom had skin paler than a deep tan. His hair was kinked a reddish gray, and his eyes were an opaque and smoky blue. A lovely young woman with the erect stature of a classical dancer held him by the elbow. She let him set the pace through the partition and up to where the bailiff waited with the Bible. Once he was seated, he whispered something to the young woman, who replied softly and touched his chin, tilting his gaze over to the right. As she returned to her seat, she gave Dale Steadman a grave nod.

Marcus began with, "How long did you work for Mr. Steadman's company?"

"Eleven years and eight months. From the day it opened to the day I retired. Didn't want to stop, but my eyes just went on me."

"You were shop foreman?"

"Started off working in the supply depot. Got promoted five times."

"Tell the court about the factory."

"Mr. Dale, he run himself a tight ship. He was a hard man. He wasn't out there to make folks happy. And he had himself a temper. Yessir, that man could throw himself a rage. But he was fair. And he treated his people right."

"Where was the company located?"

"Down in southeast Wilmington, just a few blocks off the river."

"Was this a nice part of town?"

" 'Bout as bad as you could get, I suppose. Least it was when he started up. Things is improving a little now."

"Because of Mr. Steadman's company?"

"That and some other things."

"But it is safe to say that when Mr. Steadman began his factory, there was no other industry around him."

"Wasn't nothing but ruin and woe down that way. Mr. Dale, he got himself an old school from the city and some money to fix things up. Us early workers used to call it the schoolhouse mill. Some still do, I 'spect. Mr. Dale fixed it up real nice. Took two old falling-down houses and made them his offices. Them places stuck out like new pennies when he was done."

"The court has heard a lot of criticism from other people about Mr. Steadman. Could you tell us any reason you might know for local officials to speak ill about my client?"

"Objection!" Hamper Caisse could scarcely keep from launching himself around the table. "Your honor, this line of questioning needs to be nipped in the bud. Mr. Glenwood is asking this gentleman to make suppositions about people with whom he has had no contact whatsoever."

"You started us down this road, Mr. Caisse. I'm going to allow Mr. Glenwood to carry us along a little further. Overruled."

"Thank you, your honor." Marcus turned back to the elderly gentleman. "Can you please tell the court—"

"I heard you the first time. And there ain't more than a thousand reasons I can imagine. My guess is, most of them folks either run companies themselves or have kin that do. And ain't a one of them that pays their hourly workers a cent more than they have to."

"Objection! There is no possible way this man could have conducted a proper survey of the local business community."

"Overruled. Proceed."

"You say Mr. Steadman overpaid his workers?"

"Nosir. I'm saying he paid a fair wage. 'Bout the time he started up, there was this study they did over to Duke, where Mr. Steadman did his schooling. Said the living wage for a family of four was nine dollars and thirty cents an hour. Less than that, and somebody's gonna have to work more than fifty hours a week or go without something. So Mr. Steadman set that as his minimum wage. Even the janitors got that."

"How can you be certain this was an exception to the local rule?"

The man's shoulders humped in a silent laugh. "On account of how we got almost ten thousand folks 'round there looking for work."

"Objection, your honor, this is clearly a wild exaggeration, and proves just how lame this man's testimony is."

"On the contrary, your honor, I have documents which not only corroborate Mr. Pierce's assertions, but reveal that they underestimate the number of applicants." Marcus marched back to his table and accepted the document Steadman had ready for him. "In the first eleven months of operation, the company received eleven thousand, four hundred applications."

Caisse did not back down. "The witness himself said there was a great deal of poverty and unemployment in the area, your honor."

Marcus continued to read from the document he had asked Steadman to bring with him that morning. "Over half these applicants, your honor, were gainfully employed at the time of their application."

The judge repressed a smile. "Lame, did you say, Mr. Caisse?"

"Your honor—"

"Overruled."

Marcus returned his attention to the witness. "Dale Steadman fired you, did he not?"

"That's right."

"For coming to work intoxicated. But later he took you back."

"That he did. Docked my pay and demoted me, but a year after that he made me foreman."

"Are there any signs he still promotes these types of changes within his companies?"

"Absolutely. Soon as Mr. Dale got his new position, he started working to make them same things policy right through the whole New Horizons company."

Hamper flailed in his seat. "Your honor, this is just ridiculous. How on earth could that man possibly be party to confidential corporate policy?"

Marcus asked, "Would you care to respond, Mr. Pierce?"

"Got me a nephew working as assistant manager over to the schoolhouse mill. A son is accountant to the New Horizons Wilmington import warehouse."

When Hamper had subsided into bitter silence, Marcus continued, "Just one more question, Mr. Pierce. Was there anything else which you can identify that would give the local business community reason to dislike my client?"

"Surely can. Back then, most doctors didn't want to show their face down that side of town. So Mr. Dale set himself up a company clinic. First factory in Wilmington to do anything of the kind."

"These medical services were available to all factory employees?"

"Them and their families."

"Thank you, Mr. Pierce."

But as Marcus was turning toward Hamper Caisse, the foreman added, "Something you said, sir, it needs correcting. The local business people, they didn't dislike Mr. Dale."

"But you just said—"

"They despised him. They spit on the ground where he walked. I seen it happen."

Marcus found himself gripped by how those sightless eyes held steady upon him. "No further questions, your honor."

"Mr. Caisse, your witness."

Hamper Caisse bounded from his chair. "What was Mr. Steadman's response to this supposed attitude?"

The foreman's sightless eyes remained fastened upon Dale. "He didn't say. Not to me. But I suppose he felt pretty much the same way 'bout them."

"Wouldn't it be fairer to say that it was Mr. Steadman's dislike for the local authorities that has colored what you've said on the stand? Better still, wouldn't you say this was in fact your own attitude which you have just described for the court?"

"I don't know what you're going on about."

"No. Of course not." He rustled the pages on his desk to emphasize the point. "You claimed Mr. Steadman had a temper."

" 'Cause he did."

"So you have seen the defendant in a rage."

Another silent laugh. "Not more than two, three times a day."

"Describe what that was like, please."

"Like a bomb going off."

"Like a bomb," Caisse repeated. "What could cause him to react like this?"

"Anybody giving him less than their best, that's what. He paid top dollar and expected the same in return."

"Did he ever attack his employees?"

"With words. Never his fists."

"But you're saying he berated his workers."

"He laid into some of them. Yessir."

"He cursed them."

"He could use some bad words."

"He attacked them with his fists."

"I never said that. And he never did it."

"Not that you saw, in any case. But such a man, with his violent past and his propensity to fly off in unbridled tantrums, isn't it safe to say that he could have become physically violent when not in your sight?"

"What you're claiming just never happened."

"No further questions."

The judge turned to the witness. "You may step down."

"Mr. Dale, he was a good—"

"Please step down, sir."

Angrily the gentleman rose to his feet, muttering, "This ain't right."

As the young woman led him away, the foreman called over, "God bless you, Mr. Dale."

Judge Sears waited until the old man departed to ask, "Do I have all the pertinent evidence to hand at this point?"

Hamper had remained on his feet. "I wish to draw your honor's attention back to what we discussed on Friday. There has been a drastic change to the agreement which he himself drew up with his wife." Hamper extracted his copy of the custody agreement, and waved it for effect. "He wrote it out himself, seated at the dining table with his soon-to-be ex-wife."

Marcus suggested, "You want to add it was done in his own blood? That would heighten your drama."

"That will do, Mr. Glenwood."

"Your honor, I have discussed this at length with my client. He claims never to have seen this document before."

Hamper was ready for that. "We have his signature on a notarized agreement." He waved the sheaf of papers once more. "Is he claiming he was blind drunk then as well?"

Marcus knew this was the direction Hamper would take, as he would have done himself. But the statement needed to go on record. "Not only that, but an agreement which was not even mentioned in the initial proceedings can't possibly be considered either binding on this court or enforceable."

"Not true, your honor," Hamper responded. "The records will

show that there never was a formal custody hearing, merely an uncontested divorce granted in chambers. Anyone in their right mind would know the mother wouldn't dream of such a thing unless there was something like this arrangement on the side."

"Where are your signed affidavits of sworn testimony from this woman?" Marcus shot back. "Better still, where is your client?"

"Unclog your ears, counsel. If you'd been listening, I've already covered that matter. Furthermore, your honor, there is the unresolved issue of jurisdiction. The child is in Germany. This court has no right to make any order binding upon the government of Germany."

"But the child was abducted, your honor. Surely—"

"That may be something for a criminal court to consider, which I very much doubt. But this court has no jurisdiction."

"Not true, your honor. The divorce matter was here. The child was named in the divorce proceedings. That makes for continuing jurisdiction for this court."

"Only if it is in the best interest of the child. Which this is not."

"Thank you, gentlemen." Judge Sears took a long moment to study her own notes, then said, "The original order is valid on its face. It was tried in this court and heard by me. I see no reason at this point to overturn the original court findings. Therefore the original order stands as valid. Mr. Caisse, your motion to set this order aside is denied. Mr. Glenwood, your request for an *ex partae* order, requiring the mother to present herself and the child before this court on Thursday, is hereby issued."

Hamper's face twisted in very real pain. "That presents an intolerable burden to my client, your honor. Her schedule—"

"If her schedule will not permit her to appear before this court, perhaps she is also not able to find the time to properly see to a child." She leaned across the bench. "We are going to have a hearing so that I can listen to live testimony from both sides. Your client has until this Thursday to comply. Is that clear, Mr. Caisse?"

"Yes, your honor."

"It better be." Rachel Sears' face was as unyielding as Marcus could ever recall. "In every single case where I've issued an *ex partae* order, live testimony has revealed that the situation is nothing close to what was represented initially."

Hamper did his best to look affronted. "I have given you nothing but the absolute verified facts of the matter, your honor."

"Save it. You both know the court's standing at this point. I am legally obliged to put the child's welfare before everything else. I therefore expect you both to be here, with your respective clients and the child, at nine o'clock Thursday morning." She applied the gavel with vehemence. "Next case."

CHAPTER

17

ONCE OUTSIDE THE COURTROOM, Marcus planted himself directly in the opposing attorney's path. "I can't believe you started in with those sleight-of-hand tactics."

Hamper Caisse touched the knot of his tie, nodded to a passing attorney, and replied with a casual sneer. "What is this, you don't have a case so you go after me?"

"I've been around this block with you before. You've got a statewide rep for tactics that would make a streetwalker blush."

"You're the one who resorted to shabby tactics in there. You're grabbing at straws and wasting everybody's time."

"What happened to the common courtesy of picking up the phone and informing opposing counsel what you intend? Has backstabbing and deception become your modus operandi?"

"We're not gathered here for a tea dance. I didn't get dressed up so I could ask you to waltz. Your client is a menace. For all I know he's done something horrible to that little girl."

By now every eye in the lobby was upon them. "You know as well as I do there's nothing behind those accusations except your own over-heated imagination."

"That's just the sort of allegation that'll have you begging the review board to let you keep hold of what career you've got left."

"Not to mention those outrageous claims about a custodial agreement." A thought occurred to him then. Marcus decided there was no reason not to probe. "When was the last time you had contact with Sephus Jones?"

There might have been a flicker in those flat gray eyes. "Who?"

Maybe Marcus was just looking too hard. But he continued just the same. "A no 'count chicken thief who works over at the quarry. I wonder if there'd be any mention of the man among your former clients."

"If he's a habitual offender, probably. Since I deal with twelve, maybe thirteen hundred cases a year. Can you even count that high, counselor? Do you even remember what it's like to carry a full caseload?"

"You wouldn't also happen to count among your associates somebody who knows how to forge a corporate check? I'm asking on account of how some things don't add up unless I factor you into the equation."

Hamper slung his briefcase within a hairbreadth of Marcus' nose. "You don't have the first tiny idea of the hornet's nest you got yourself stuck into. I intend to stake your client out in the dirt, strip him bare, and flay him alive! And you're gonna be sprawled in the dirt right there alongside him!"

Marcus remained in the courtroom foyer and endured the solemn condolences of the legal fraternity because he had to. The fact that so many were sincere in what they had to say about Charlie Hayes only made his torment worse. With some relief Marcus spotted Omar Dell hovering on the group's fringe, and excused himself to walk over.

The court reporter wore a form-fitted navy suit with a pale blue chalk-stripe and matching knit silk tie. "Glad to see you able to make it today, counselor."

"You wrote up the story?"

" 'Local Attorney Escapes Assassination Attempt.' By Omar Dell, staff reporter and man on the rise."

"There's no indication the bomb was directed at me. If it was a bomb at all."

"Police think it was. Especially since the explosion happened the week you started another attack on New Horizons." To his credit, Omar failed to show a reporter's objective distance. "I'm very sorry about the loss of your friend. Charlie Hayes was one special man."

"He was that."

"Seeing as how you were one of his closest friends, I expect people want to tell you stories about him, draw him closer in the process. I'd guess that is hard to take sometimes."

"Like munching on glass shards."

"You know I have to ask if you can suggest an attacker's name for the record."

"And you know I can't answer."

Omar pointed to where Hamper Caisse now dealt with a sullen teenage client and a frantic mother. "I'd say that little exchange you just had with opposing counsel would make fair copy, if only I'd understood what was said."

"No comment on that either." Marcus started to excuse himself, then decided to offer the reporter a bone. "You might want to go have a talk with Sephus Jones."

"Spell that first name?"

Out of the corner of his eye, Marcus caught sight of Hamper's head cocking slightly. Most courtroom lawyers picked up the ability to listen to peripheral conversations, a trick that served them well in urgent negotiations. "He works at the rock pit off Blue Ridge Road."

"You think he might have a bearing on the explosion or this case?"

"If he does, I can't tell you how." Marcus sketched out the assault in his front yard, and his supposition that the New Horizons check was a forgery. "Whatever you do, don't mention my name."

Marcus waited for the court papers to be completed, then personally carried them down to the clerk's office for the ruling to be registered and notarized. He entered the central foyer to spot Kedrick Lloyd frowning at him. The crabby Englishman was seated on one of the hard foyer benches alongside a woman far too groomed for this tawdry spot.

Marcus crossed over and offered, "Good afternoon."

The foyer's fluorescents made the aging Brit look even more decrepit than he had in Dale's kitchen. "Spare us the false friendliness, will you?" He waved an aged hand of china and translucent flesh. "Leave us be, that's a good fellow."

The woman beside him had the horsey features of inbred money, and the low voice of one who had endured much. "Kedrick, please."

"Well really. He's only here because he wants me to spend my last few breaths defending Dale in a trial they can't possibly win."

"We're already past that," Marcus replied. "The hearing was today, and the court has issued—"

"And I tell you these legal maneuverings hold all the significance of a leaf in a storm."

An attorney Marcus knew vaguely pushed through the courtroom doors and called over, "Firing squad's armed and ready, Mr. Lloyd."

Kedrick brought himself fully upright. Marcus faced a lion's mane of snow-white hair, a king's bearing, and shoulders that should have carried far more flesh than they did. "You and your ilk are an abominable stain upon the scrolls of human history. Dale approached you in a moment of blind and drunken panic. You, on the other hand, have no excuse save cruel and soulless greed."

Kedrick Lloyd crossed to the waiting attorney with scarcely a limp. Even in his decrepit state, Marcus could see shadows of the man's former strength. At the courtroom's entrance Lloyd turned and added, "Go back to digging worms out of your small-town garden, Mr. Glenwood. Leave these larger matters to people who actually fathom the world's workings."

When the doors sighed shut, Lloyd's wife said, "I keep telling myself, if only he would give in to the pain, admit how close he is to death, he would be so much easier to live with. But Kedrick has never been an easy man."

Marcus took that as an invitation and lowered himself into the seat beside her. It was still warm from Kedrick's presence. He offered a hand. "Marcus Glenwood."

"Evelyn Lloyd." A trace of humor flickered across her wounded features. "My husband had some rather choice things to say about you."

"You're American?"

"From Philadelphia. I met Kedrick at Duke." Her attention slid back to the burnished doors. "The doctors have given him a month to live four times over the past year and a half. That is the kind of fighter my husband is."

"There's no need to explain anything."

Another faint flicker, remnants of a more pleasant time. "Shall we start over?"

"Gladly. I was hoping to ask your husband about Erin Brandt."

"Erin, Erin." She scanned the foyer, seeing none of it. "Kedrick introduced her to Dale."

"So I heard."

"And then flew into a memorable rage when they decided to marry. Kedrick did everything but order Dale not to go ahead with it." She shook her head. "What a vain and stubborn man."

Marcus was uncertain whether she was speaking about her husband or Dale. "Erin Brandt's pictures make her out to be very attractive."

"Erin Brandt can't possibly be captured by photographs. She is the most magnetic creature I have ever come across. I suppose it is what one might call star quality. Even so, I never understood why Kedrick remained so intently focused upon having her sing at the Met."

"Your husband was on the board of the opera house in New York, is that right?"

"He still is. His work for the Met keeps him alive." Her gaze continued its long-distance roving. "Erin Brandt is two persons. The diva is warm and alluring and utterly captivating, with one of the finest voices I have ever heard. When she smiles at you, you cannot help but return the gift."

"And the other?"

"Ah, that is the question, is it not."

"The woman is secretive?"

"I have never met anyone who could say they truly knew Erin Brandt."

Marcus found himself thinking of another lovely woman. One with eyes like an Arctic sunrise, softest indigo and shattered ice. "Maybe Dale came to know the real Erin."

"Perhaps so, Mr. Glenwood. Perhaps that is why she left him."

"If you'll excuse me, I need to prepare these documents for overnight shipment to London."

"We are at the Wyndham another two nights. Come by tomorrow afternoon and I'll tell you a little more about the woman you oppose." She offered a hand long and tapered as a man's. "It is seldom I meet someone able to shrug off one of my husband's broadsides."

Marcus turned away as swiftly as was polite. "Maybe I've just got more pressing matters on my mind."

CHAPTER

18

K IRSTEN FOUND IT STRANGE that she had missed the threat until she came out of the dressing room, since people in the shop had already begun casting glances her way. She had entered the Escada boutique on New Bond Street because she knew the place and liked the dark little number in the window. She figured she'd make a quick in-and-out, grab what she needed, and be gone so fast she could pretend it hadn't really happened. For any moth, however, there was grave risk in flirting with the flame. She opened the dressing room door and aimed for the floor-length mirror on the opposite wall, only to be stopped by a far more ominous reflection.

The framed poster was a blowup of an ad they had run all over Europe. She was standing in heels and a fluffy hotel bathrobe, her hair still wet from the shower, giving a sultry inspection both to the viewer and an array of four Escada dresses and jewels and bags laid out on the bed. The company had made it their trademark ad for three seasons, beyond eternal in the rag trade. Kirsten turned away with the speed of retreating from a white-hot oven. But the salesgirl was there with an old copy of *Vogue* opened to the same page, asking for her autograph. Which drew over the store manager and another salesclerk and one of the patrons, all of them saying how great it was to meet her, where on earth had she been, the girls these days were just empty faces. Which was precisely Kirsten's thought as she stared at herself staring back.

She returned to the hotel and pretended to sleep. But the internal din was resettled now into audible confines. This was not a random series of events. The game was stalking her. She was being drawn back, and to a new level whose appeal was so strong she could feel it grip her middle and twist with exquisite pain.

———————

The early evening traffic was so bad Kirsten finally had the taxi let her off halfway down Piccadilly. The late July evening held an almost autumnal chill, particularly in her new sleeveless number of midnight blue silk. Walking was sweetest anguish. Everything was tainted by earlier memories. She passed swiftly through Leicester Square, skirting the grifters and the crowds. A cluster of Persian boys caught her by the tube stop and chased her with lewd offers. Who's your daddy, they cried repeatedly as she fled. The litany bit deep.

She walked the length of Garrick Street, past the fashionable spots she knew so very well. The Covent Garden market was alive with its nightly theater when she entered, the first-timers agog over the spice-laden air and the multitude of street performers. Kirsten slipped through the knot of autograph hounds waiting by the stage door and gave her name to the very attentive guard. She was buzzed inside, then had to wait while someone was called from upstairs. Over the guard's loudspeaker came the sounds of the orchestra warming up. The preperformance bustle and electric tension squeezed her into the far corner.

"Ms. Stansted?" A bony middle-aged woman with a dancer's stance offered her hand. "Hillary Crampeth. So nice, so nice. Would you care to come this way?"

The guard buzzed them through a second locked door. The hostess led Kirsten past the backstage entrance and hurried up the winding stairs. "We're so delighted to have Ms. Brandt singing tonight. We'd do absolutely anything for her. Naturally we try to anticipate a star's every whim in advance, but when she asked us for a prime seat for tonight's performance, well, it gave us quite a start. Thankfully, sold out never actually means sold out. There are always one or two seats which the house management hold back."

She knocked smartly on a door with a brass plaque proclaiming it to be the director's box, then opened it and said, "Your seat is there on the left. Enjoy the performance. I'll be back to gather you at the inter-mission."

The alcove held the feel of a velvet-lined jewelry case, with a high-ceilinged balcony directly overlooking the stage. Kirsten nodded to the two older couples in formal evening wear, who responded with haughty British curiosity.

The performance opened with a number by the orchestra, chorus, and ballet. Kirsten was so close to the stage she could see the dust fly off the dancers' feet. She observed the cords in the singers' necks tense up with carefully masked effort. She felt their talent and power in her chest.

Erin Brandt appeared to a spontaneous burst of applause. The diva was stunning. The two women to Kirsten's left used the word to death as they applauded her opening aria. Kirsten could think of nothing else which described her. Erin was captivatingly small, certainly not the standard big-boned, lard-encased soprano. She floated, she trilled. She spun her magic and carried the house. Every eye was upon her for every instant she remained upon the stage.

At the intermission the aging hostess was back to lead Kirsten away. She ignored the caustic stares of others who wished for such personal treatment and asked, "How do you find the performance so far?"

"Stunning."

The woman nodded matter-of-fact agreement. "We've arranged for you to have a table in the Vinson Floral Balcony. I hope that's adequate." She did her best not to appear to hurry Kirsten along while slipping easily down the cramped hallway. She pushed through a side door, marched down a private hallway, and entered a massive chamber awash with noise. "This was originally a Victorian floral market attached to the theater. It was then used for storing stage sets before the changeover."

They traversed a balcony-restaurant overlooking a main hall with a seventy-foot domed ceiling. The hostess led Kirsten to a table by the balcony's railing, where an iced bucket and a split of champagne awaited. She signaled to the head waiter, gave Kirsten a tight smile, and departed with "I hope you'll be comfortable."

As the waiter was opening her champagne, a bulbous little man with cat's-eye glasses of electric blue came rushing over. "Ms. Stansted?"

"Yes."

"Reiner Klatz. I am Ms. Brandt's manager." He clipped his heels together and bowed such that his jacket bunched over his belly. "You are most welcome, I am sure."

The man was so familiar she could have drawn him from a hundred different scenarios. "Thank you."

"This hall, it is so very British, is it not? It reminds me of a Victorian train station, all glass and steel and noise and bad air." Klatz found reason for disdain in everything he saw. Another common trait of such hangers-on. "Do you know, they held the final topping out ceremony here when the house's reconstruction was completed. But the week before, they discovered pigeons nesting in the steel railings. How were they to get them out? Of course with all this glass they could not use guns." He gave her a tight smile. "So they brought in sparrow hawks. Very hungry ones. Ingenious, no?"

If there was a message intended for her, she missed it entirely. "Ms. Brandt sings beautifully."

"Of course. Oh, I almost forgot. There's a reception by one of the corporate sponsors after tonight's performance. Ms. Brandt has agreed to make a brief appearance. Naturally you'd be welcome to join her."

"Thank you."

"If you'll excuse me." He bustled away. Kirsten watched him stop at one table after another, hovering like a well-padded moth, but never landing.

The second and third acts were endless and timeless both. Just before Erin began her final aria, she seemed to turn and look directly at Kirsten. The electric quality of her singing intensified to where it left Kirsten breathless. Forget the spotlights, forget even the sun. Erin gestured, and there was such a joy to the movement and the song the audience accepted the invitation and flew with her. Erin gave everything to the crowd, and did so with an abandon that was both ethereal and grippingly erotic.

There came the crescendo and the curtain. The crowd responded with a frenzy. Kirsten could not help but join in—watching them, watching Erin, watching herself.

After the performance she was collected once more by the hostess, who gave her the hasty grimace of one whose night was only gathering steam. "Did you enjoy the performance?"

"Very much."

"I'm so glad. This way please." Down the same hallway, then a jink to the left, and the hostess held open a leather-padded door. Beyond stretched a golden Raphaelite chamber illuminated by a tier of mammoth chandeliers. Thirty-foot-high walls were adorned with Renaissance-style paintings of stage performances. The chamber was aswirl with chatter and jewels and perfect makeup and people who pretended not to observe Kirsten's entry.

Before the hostess could depart, a voice behind them announced, "I'll take it from here, if you don't mind."

The hostess became a fluttering bundle of nerves. "Oh, Ms. Brandt, forgive me, I didn't see—"

But her apology was swept aside by the throng pressing in from all sides. Erin slipped her hand around Kirsten's elbow, smiled a benign acknowledgment to the crowd, then said softly, "There are a few people I must speak to here, darling. Then we'll be off to somewhere more delicious."

Erin released Kirsten and permitted herself to be drawn into the milling throng. People made room for Kirsten, a glass was offered, a few polite words spoken by those to either side. Kirsten was granted entry because the diva clearly wished it. Just one more courtier.

Eventually Erin waved the others aside and said to Kirsten, "There is a horrid little man over by the bar. He's the intendant of the Berlin opera. I must go over and pay homage. Would you mind terribly being my support?"

"All right."

Erin's fairy-like movements granted her a miniature quality. Walking beside her, Kirsten had the impression that the woman never left her toes, never truly connected with the earth at all. Erin asked, "You're not surprised a star must still bother with the unpleasantries and the mundane?"

"I was a model."

"But of course you were, darling." The hand returned to Kirsten's arm. "How else could all this be so perfect?"

The intendant stood beside Reiner Klatz, Erin's manager. He was a toothpick in gray gabardine. A silk foulard tickled the bottom of his silver goatee. He observed their approach as a gourmand would the presentation of his fantasy meal. Erin did not bother to introduce Kirsten. Reiner Klatz's blue-clad gaze never left her. Erin sparkled for the man, then mentioned casually, "I've heard you're doing *Rosenkavalier* next season."

The intendant's gaze traversed Kirsten's form once more. "That is correct."

Erin continued to stroke Kirsten's arm, her hand out where the intendant could observe. "Do you have your Marschallin cast yet? I haven't sung it in four years and I miss it terribly."

"Your last time was in Wien, *neh?*"

"How nice of you to remember," Erin purred.

"The papers gave you rave reviews." He could not force his gaze to settle anywhere for long. "Perhaps we should meet and discuss this."

"Speak with Reiner, why don't you?" She drew Kirsten around. "Come, darling. Our night awaits."

The halls were filled with staff and singers who wanted to exclaim over the diva and her performance. Erin glided through, smiling for all and seeing none. Even the stone-faced guard by the rear door stood to pay her homage and help her with the silk summer mantle. Outside, the purple Rolls was still waiting, a uniformed chauffeur by the open rear door.

"On loan from an admirer who was made positively livid by your arrival," Erin said, sliding in beside Kirsten. When the chauffeur slipped behind the wheel, she ordered, "Take the long way to the Savoy."

"Very good, Madame."

"I love being driven through London in a Rolls. In Germany it looks outrageous. Here it is merely good taste. The house assigns me a car, of course. I couldn't possibly ask for a Rolls, not when I could have a week of five-star luxury in Malaysia for the same price." Erin snuggled deeper, her pleasure so complete it bordered on the obscene. "Isn't this divine?"

Surrounded by Erin's scent and her voice and her eyes, Kirsten decided this was how an alcoholic must feel passing a bar. There was no reward for taking the clean road. No feeling of goodness or rightness. And afterward, the unsatiated desire remained a bare and shrieking nerve. She had never thought of herself as a potential addict until that very moment. "Why Malaysia?"

"The beaches. White sand, coral atolls, perfectly empty. The hotels are very Asian, very discreet, a hundred smiling young men eager to make this a perfect day." Eyes turned obscure by the night studied Kirsten. "Do you have a perfect beach?"

For reasons only half formed, she responded, "Wrightsville."

"Now that wasn't nice." She traced a fingernail along the back of Kirsten's hand. She leaned closer, such that her lips all but flickered over Kirsten's ear. She breathed, "This is your thousand and one nights, sister. The genie is out of the bottle and at your command. Do you really wish to vanquish the spell, and make the magic vanish like smoke?"

She replied overloud, "Yes."

Erin smirked down at Kirsten's hand. She said nothing more, merely continued the soft stroking, until they pulled past Simpson's and entered the Savoy cul-de-sac. When the doorman opened Erin's door, she whispered, "Let's go see what we can find."

CHAPTER

19

S TRIPED MARBLE COLUMNS with gilded caps marched stolidly down the center of the Savoy lobby. The tray ceiling was frescoed in gold leaf and framed ten brass and smoked-glass chandeliers. Kirsten knew because she counted them as she waited. Three steps away, Erin stood surrounded by fans and photographers and chatter. Twice Erin looked her way, imploring her to join in. But Kirsten felt no desire to be a star by proxy. As she watched Erin revel in the diva's role, Kirsten almost wished she could resign herself to falling tonight and never rising again. At least then she would end the terror of being wounded anew by myths of love and hope.

Erin returned then, slipping her arm around Kirsten's waist and smiling as photographers trapped the pair of them in electric epoxy. Another soft grip of her hand, an even softer "Come."

Erin led her to the side hall, away from the lower lounge with its live jazz quartet and smoky elegant din. They entered what was more of an alcove than a restaurant, one named merely "Upstairs." A dozen stools lined the narrow bar, with nine tables set along the windows overlooking the hotel's front entrance. The talk was as muted as the illumination from the Savoy sign over the hotel portal.

Erin stopped by a table where a bottle of champagne already peeked from a glistening bucket. "I only drink champagne and I never smoke. Those are the only traits I covet of the baritones and their breed, how deep-voiced men can have whiskey and cigarillos and still sing. I have tried both and love them too much for a fragilethroated woman." She waved Kirsten into a seat. "Are you always so quiet?"

"Usually."

The look Erin gave her was liquid with tenderness. "You poor fragile beauty. They've robbed you, haven't they?"

"What?"

"Words do nothing for what you've been forced to carry around inside." She leaned across the table, drawing in so close Kirsten could not help but breathe her spiced perfume. "Listen, my sister. I know you. So very, very well."

Erin turned away momentarily, and spoke to the hovering waiter. "Bring us a selection of whatever is freshest and best."

"Of course, Ms. Brandt."

Erin stripped the foil from the champagne bottle and expertly twisted out the cork. "I love doing this, releasing the night's music. Why should I allow a strange man to have this pleasure?"

She poured them both a measure, then raised her fluted glass by the stem. "To sisters bonded by what the world will never understand."

Kirsten listened to the crystal bell and sipped from her glass. She tasted only bubbles.

Erin raised her chin until the faint cleft was accented. The skin of her neck drew tight as an artist's line. She kept this position as she set down her glass. Her dark eyes targeted Kirsten along the bore of her nose. "I know," she murmured. "It's so hard to speak of, all you have inside, all you've been forced to choke off. No words will ever do."

Kirsten drank once more, swallowing tiny fragments of air her lungs could not find.

"How do I know? Because it has happened to me. I said we are sisters, did I not? The world has hurt and cheated and stolen from me as it has from you."

Kirsten looked out the window, down to where the tide of wealth and people passed beneath her. Try as she might, she could not convince herself the night's gaiety was any more real than smiles off a backlit strip of cellotape. She sighed. Perhaps the only way to endure it all was through finding a comfortable lie.

Erin reached across the table and gripped Kirsten's hand with both of her own. "Let me be your voice. Let me sing my arias for both of us.

Let me shout the pain. Then, when we are alone, let us find one another in the intimate sharing of our secret." Fiercely she clenched Kirsten's hand, though her voice remained an enticing murmur. "Shall I tell you what that secret is?"

A shadow appeared and hovered by their table. They looked over together to find a nervous young man in the Savoy's uniform of starched shirt and tails. He handed Erin an engraved calling card. "Excuse me, Ms. Brandt. But the gentleman says it is most urgent."

"Impossible. The man is utterly impossible." Erin tossed her napkin aside. "Forgive me, my dear. This will require two seconds only."

Kirsten tried to lose herself in the champagne and the theater outside her window. But this unbidden space could not have come at a worse time. Now that she was alone, she could not help but acknowledge the inaudible lament. This was not working. Her mental confusion was a serrated blade sawing at the night's façade.

She found herself recalling the high school guidance counselor who had helped her graduate early. Such memories were normally dreaded events, yet this image merely came and spoke and lingered, like a dawn delayed by a passing storm. Once a term she and the counselor had held the same terse conversation, a ritual between two people who were almost but not quite friends. The counselor asked Kirsten if everything was all right. Kirsten always gave the required answer, that she was fine, her home was great, her parents the best. Then the counselor spoke the words that echoed now in the smoke and the chatter and the clink of fine crystal. Know when to ask for aid.

So ask she did. Then and there. Her eyes were wide open, yet she saw nothing save the vague reflection of a lonely young blonde in the window beside her. Kirsten stared into a candlelit gaze of empty confusion and spoke the words. Help me.

So swiftly it could only have been in response, a barrier rose between her and the opulent chamber. The unseen curtain blanketed even sound. Kirsten stared anew at her reflection, this time searching with the honesty of total isolation. Her reflection said nothing. Merely waited.

She knew then what it was she needed to apprehend. Softly she spoke the words, You do not belong here.

Her translucent apparition stood up, and she rose as well. The image guided her out of the restaurant. She walked down the stairs and through the fancy foyer and out the front doors. She thought perhaps she caught sight of the apparition in the window of a departing taxi, moving so swiftly Kirsten had no choice but accept that she was both alone and where she should be. She looked up in time to see Erin return to the table, sit down, drink from her glass, and laugh at something the waiter said. At home in a realm from which Kirsten had been forever expelled.

CHAPTER

20

T HE NIGHT PROGRESSED at the creeping pace of finely tuned torture. Kirsten fought her bed until it could hold her no longer. She dressed and went for a walk. But the night tracked her every move. Defeated, she returned to the stale room with its bleak lighting. There should have been some reward, some offering of peace for turning from Erin's lure. Instead, the ghouls of her past gibbered and shrieked in panicked fury. And right alongside this clamor was the truth she could no longer escape. She longed desperately for Marcus. She craved his voice, his touch, the smell of him. The strengths and the weaknesses, the wounded gaze, the resolve. Yet she feared him as much as she yearned for him. Probably more. She could hear him now, speaking in that soft tone that left her quivering with hunger and terror both.

Her desire for Marcus was an affront to all the rules she had used to rebuild her shattered existence. She survived by never, ever wanting anything this much. Most especially a *man*.

Finally at five in the morning she reached for the phone. Which meant it would be midnight, Rocky Mount time. But that could not be helped.

Deacon Wilbur answered on the second ring. He sounded instantly awake, in the manner of one who had fielded his share of late-night entreaties. He brushed aside her apology. "Where are you, daughter?"

"London. Can I speak with Fay, please?"

There was the rustling and the murmurs, and a longer pause than Kirsten would have expected. Then Fay demanded, "You really in England like my man says?"

She heard another phone click off, and realized the old woman had moved to another part of the house. "Yes. I'm sorry about the hour."

"You forget who you're talking to here. Ain't that long ago, a night without the midnight alarm was so rare we talked about it for days. We still keep the old coffee sitting on the counter." There came the sounds of a door shutting and a microwave fan whirring. "Marcus' granddaddy used to like me to drop half an eggshell into his pot."

"It sounds horrid."

"Adds a certain tang, is all. If the pot's been sitting all day the brew don't grow so bitter. I 'spect after a while, the taste is just natural. You perk every cup up fresh, I suppose."

Kirsten sighed her way down to the floor by her hotel bed. "Usually."

The oven timer pinged. "I'm glad you called, child. I didn't have any right talking to you the way I did."

"We both know that's not true."

"Well now." Fay took a noisy sip. "You're not running scared, are you, honey?"

Kirsten was trapped, not by this woman, but the day. "All my life I've made it work by not caring too much. Not showing too much. Not talking too much."

"Let's see what you got going into this. You lost both your folks, isn't that right?"

"When I was twenty."

"You're a pretty lady. You must've had yourself other men friends along the way."

"I don't even want to talk about them."

"So your trial runs didn't turn out that well." Another sip. "Not too far back, your best friend Gloria went and got herself killed over in China. Now you're living down here in a strange place without any family of your own. And you're looking at life with a man who's carrying his own set of scars." A tight trace of humor colored Fay's words. "I'd say you've got every reason to be scared."

"I've tried my best to run away."

"And it didn't work."

"No."

"You aim on giving life with Marcus a chance?"

"I want it and I don't want it."

"Sounds to me as though you don't think you're good enough for him."

Kirsten dropped her head. This wasn't working. The tumult was just growing worse.

"Don't you go hiding behind that silence of yours. Answer me, child. You figure something's just so wrong and all messed up you can't do right by this man. Is that it?"

"Pretty much."

"Okay. Now we're getting somewhere. You got something inside yourself that makes you feel impure. So you've been trying to convince yourself you don't love him. Which we both know is a lie."

"But it's a comfortable lie."

Fay snorted. "Would be if it worked."

"Yes."

"Honey, people like to think they come into any new relationship all cleaned up. That's just a fable the world wants you to believe, so you've got an excuse to walk away when things don't go right. Child, love is a filthy business. You got your problems, he got his. But love gives you the strength to walk through the messes of life together. Love is a process. You commit yourself to getting in there and working together to make sense out of what life's done to you both."

"I don't know if I can do that. Make it work."

"Of course you don't. I lived with this man of mine for fifty-six years and I *still* don't know how I'm gonna meet tomorrow."

"What does Deacon think about me?"

"You're nothing to that man of mine 'cept one more daughter. And that ain't what we're talking about here."

"What do I tell Marcus?"

"Honey, you tell him what you can."

"What if . . ." She couldn't even finish the sentence.

Fay's voice reached across the void and gripped her. "Believe you me. He knows. That Marcus is a smart young man. He's seen inside you long time ago. He's just been waiting for you to say your piece."

"I don't think I can."

"Then you just go and tell God first." The matter-of-fact tone struck hard as fists. "You're ready to pour out the oil from your alabaster box now. Ain't nobody else will ever know the cost of that oil you're ready to pour on the Master's feet, or how much you done paid for those tears you've been waiting to shed. But he knows. Oh my. Ain't that the blessed truth. And that's all you need to remember, child. He's waiting for you to kneel there and weep for him. He's already done counted every one of these jewels. And they are precious in his sight."

CHAPTER

21

MARCUS SPENT THE MORNING at a remembrance service for Charlie Hayes. There was no way of telling which held more intensity, the mourners' tears or their laughter. By the time he excused himself, he felt internally disfigured by loss. But he had an appointment to keep, as he explained to the family. And the prospect of work offered an illusory means of bottling his grief, at least for a time.

He drove through the Research Triangle Park and exited the highway by the Duke Medical Center. Marcus parked his car and stood in the hotel lot, wishing for a clearer separation between what he had just left and what waited up ahead. An early gloaming had assembled overhead, a harbinger so thick and close the air seemed already wet with the storm still to come. He resigned himself to carrying one more burden with him, and headed inside.

The Wyndham presidential suite was as close to big-city opulence as the region offered. Lightning cut jagged scissor-lines through the cloud cover as Evelyn Lloyd let him in, then returned to the sofa facing the empty fireplace. The suite's parlor had a wraparound view of forest greens and approaching rain. The entertainment center's front doors were open, and an opera poured from unseen speakers. Evelyn Lloyd motioned him into a seat, then signaled for a few moments of silence. She paid the approaching storm no mind.

She used a brief hiatus in the music to inquire, "Do you know opera, Mr. Glenwood?"

"Not at all, and please call me Marcus."

Her voice held a dreamlike quality. "This is one of those essential moments of classical opera. Discovering her lover is dead, Tosca commits suicide by leaping off the battlements of the Castel Sant' Angelo."

Marcus' seat granted him a view of both the woman and the tempest. Lightning danced behind cottony veils, still so distant the sound was muted and constant. From this man-made perch he watched as rain shadows bowed the trees into drenched and windswept submission. The storm offered a soothing balm to his wounded day. There was both harmony and comfort in watching the heavens weep.

When the music ended, Evelyn refocused on him. "In such times, one must take pleasure whenever one can."

"I'm sorry for bothering you."

"Your company is most welcome. There is tea and coffee on the counter. Might I ask you to serve yourself?"

Marcus walked over to the bar and plied the silver thermos set beside the stacked china and the spray of champagne roses. Evelyn continued, "For those of us who love the milieu, an opera star is the most talented artist on earth. They must sing for hours at the level of a full-throated bellow, embracing four thousand listeners with no amplification whatsoever. They must be consummate musicians. They must also act. And they must be linguists, knowing not only the language, but that culture's musical styles."

He took his coffee back over to the suede sofa with its view of the storm that touched neither this woman nor her wealth. "Quite a feat."

She smiled merely with her eyes. "I suppose you prefer banjos plinking against the stars, lanterns for lighting, and peanut shells covering a hard-plank floor."

"Add a dose of Carolina barbecue," Marcus replied, "and you'd be describing my perfect evening."

The storm flailed their window with liquid whips and the noise of a thousand drums. "Singers lead a strange life, moving from the subterranean world of rehearsal and voice-coach chambers to the blinding light of stardom. It engenders a schizophrenic viewpoint. The worst of them take the normal duality of human nature and magnify it all out of proportion. Incredibly pleasant one moment, venomous the next."

"What do you think of Erin Brandt?"

She studied him a long moment, then declared flatly, "A costumed snake with the smile of a seraph. Only those who have been around her for a time and seen her on life's backstage manage a glimpse of her delicate aura of evil."

"But your husband likes her."

"My husband is even more of an opera fanatic than I. The Met's board position originally belonged to my grandfather. My family has been involved with the company since the last century. In the old building we owned one of the boxes in what was referred to as the Diamond Horseshoe. I had allowed the board position to slide. My husband begged me to have it reinstated for himself."

Marcus did not even pretend to understand. "What does this have to do with Erin Brandt?"

"Everything. Kedrick wanted to claim her as his own personal find. But the Met had recently brought in a new intendant, a sort of combined chief conductor and artistic director. The gentleman refused to have anything to do with Erin."

He caught the grim satisfaction. "You don't agree with Kedrick's assessment?"

"I do not care for the woman personally. As far as Kedrick is concerned, personal traits hold no importance here. Erin is a draw. Not merely a star, you see. Someone who could in time virtually guarantee a sold-out performance. The female equivalent of Placido Domingo."

"And the conductor, I'm sorry, I don't recall the word you just used."

"Intendant. His reasons follow the few critics who have not been swept up in the Erin Brandt craze. He feels that she is too young. He claims that her intonations are off and the quality of her sound comes and goes. She works too hard, or so he says, giving her high notes a shrill edge, a fraction off an actual shriek." She shrugged. "His is the professional ear, I suppose."

"I'm still trying to get a feel for her relationship with Dale Steadman."

"Wilier prey than Dale have been duped by a conniving female."

"You're suggesting she went into the marriage planning for it to fail?"

"Those who care for Erin suggest she wanted to give married life a try. See if she could do the family thing and still be sufficiently driven to continue her rise to stardom."

"You don't agree?"

Evelyn escaped the intense scrutiny by rising and moving to the bar. "More coffee?"

"I'm fine, thanks."

"Everything in life affects a singer's voice. Technique can overcome a great deal, but not all. And never for very long."

Marcus rose to join her. "What are you trying to tell me?"

"Erin Brandt is by nature a lyric coloratura soprano. She is quite young to try and bridge the gap between the lighter roles and those of dramatic coloratura."

"Sorry, you've lost me."

"No matter." She made a great procedure of spooning sugar into her tea. "If all goes well with a pregnancy, a soprano's voice can become much rounder and fuller. It adds an entirely new dimension, one that otherwise might not be gained for years. Afterward she sings with far more feeling and depth."

"And if things go wrong?"

"The biggest risk is a C-section, of course. It cuts all the lower breath muscles in half. These lower muscles are a singer's greatest support. Most singers who have a C-section never recover their full range." She sipped her tea and studied the diminishing storm. "Sometimes even the best of pregnancies can destroy a soprano's career. The muscles may never recover their full strength. Or worse still, there may be a long-term hormonal imbalance. If the hormones are off, the vocal chords can swell. The voice becomes raspy, the notes not as clean. It can also generate extra fatigue, which is death for a singer who must hold the spotlight for four or five hours a night."

"It would take a cold and ruthless woman," Marcus said slowly, "to become pregnant for the sake of her voice."

Evelyn was saved from responding by the sound of a key slipping into the electronic lock. Kedrick Lloyd let himself in, coughing lightly in the manner of one drained of all energy. Then he turned and saw them. The shock wrenched him from his exhaustion. "What is the meaning of this!"

"Marcus and I were having a most delightful conversation. Shall I pour you a tea?"

He took a single step toward them. "You permit the enemy into our ranks?"

Evelyn held to her steady calm. "Are you absolutely certain this is how you would care to consume your remaining strength?"

"I assure you, sir," Marcus said. "I'm not Dale's enemy. I'm doing everything I can—"

"Spare me the lies and invectives!" He jabbed his finger at the door. "Get him out of here!"

Evelyn raised her chin a fraction. "Just precisely whom are you ordering about?"

The raised hand formed a trembling fist. Kedrick spun about and stalked to the bedroom. He slammed the door with a thunder louder than that outside the windows.

Evelyn mused to the closed door, "He insists on continuing with his affairs and pretending that all is well. Do you know why we were in court yesterday? Because my husband insists on personally concluding the sale of several hotels down on the coast." She shook her head. "What a vain and idiotic man."

"He's probably just trying to see to your welfare."

A bitter humor stretched her features. "I doubt that very much, since he used my money to acquire them in the first place."

As she walked him to the door, Marcus said, "I still don't understand why Erin took the child."

"I am certain you will uncover the truth, if it is there to be found. But one thing I can tell you with utter certitude. Erin Brandt's reasons do not even approach love." She offered him a cool hand and a carefully controlled smile. "I will bid you farewell. The doctors are arranging for Kedrick to receive further treatments from our New York oncologist. He is only scheduled to return in four months' time. Which, given his present state, I very much doubt will occur."

CHAPTER

22

THE NICEST THING ABOUT the American Embassy was how summertime trees made it impossible to view the entire monstrosity at once. Three sides of Grosvenor Square were formed of symmetrical Georgian facades, which only made the embassy more conspicuous. The building was one gigantic blunder, from the cracked stairs and vault-like entrance doors to the eagle on the roof, which a postwar British contractor had pointed in the wrong direction. Kirsten helped an elderly couple wrestle open the bombproof door, gave her name to the Marine trapped at attention inside his glass coffin, and entered the vast marble lobby.

She seated herself by a central pool that did not work. Dead presidents glared down from their high perches, clearly dissatisfied with her presence. She shut her eyes, weary from lack of sleep and the ceaseless torment. Her mind returned to the previous night with such vividness she was surrounded by Erin's spicy perfume. Once again she stared at the candlelit reflection of her own lost and empty gaze. She felt convicted, a woman undone by her own hand. Either she returned to lies that she had already rejected as unsatisfactory, or do the unthinkable and trust Marcus. As footsteps approached across the marble tiles, she heard herself whisper the same words again. Help me.

"Ms. Stansted?"

"Yes."

"Adam Ross." He offered her a hand as cold as the lobby. "Assistant political attaché. This way, please."

He waited until they were safely inside the elevator to continue, "The ambassador was woken up this morning by a call from Senator Jacobs himself. Jacobs said you needed a detective."

"That's correct."

"Jacobs also said we were to treat any further request as though it came from him personally. If you'll excuse me for saying, that's some impressive clout."

"Apparently I've become involved in a pet project of his."

"A staffer by the name of Brent Daniels also left a message for you." He consulted his notes. "The lady in question has booked a flight back to Düsseldorf this afternoon."

"Excuse me?"

The attaché repeated his message. "He indicated this left you with very little time to make a connection."

"Did he tell you how he got this information?"

"I've told you all I know."

"Can you get a message back to him?"

"Absolutely."

"Could you ask him for a family court lawyer and another detective, this time in Germany? Would you also book me a flight to Düsseldorf and a hotel in the city center?"

"No problem. This way, please." The upstairs foyer was carpeted and painted a muted gray. At their entry a stocky man in a crumpled navy suit rose to his feet. "Kirsten Stansted, Chris Faber. Mr. Faber was formerly a detective-lieutenant with Scotland Yard."

"Ma'am."

"You can use the conference room at the end of the hall, if you like."

"That won't be necessary." She took a pair of steps away from the staffer. The detective followed, moving in close enough to catch her whisper. Swiftly Kirsten outlined what she required. The detective listened with the dead-eyed calm of one who had heard and seen it all many times before.

When she was finished, he said, "I'll meet you at the Savoy Hotel's main entrance in two hours."

"Thank you."

The hovering staffer had his secretary walk the detective out, then asked Kirsten, "That's it?"

"I do have one further matter I could use some help with."

"Anything."

"I was wondering," Kirsten said, "if you know of anyone in the embassy who is fanatical about opera."

He registered her request with a single slow blink. Then, "Actually, I do."

Fifteen minutes later the staffer ushered Kirsten into the basement cafeteria, and over to where a gray-haired couple were seated. "Kirsten Stansted, meet Elizabeth and Richard Powell. Elizabeth is one of our administrative aides. Richard is retired military, now working with embassy security."

The woman was both kindly and authoritative. "You have a question about opera?"

"Made every premiere at Covent Garden last season," her husband interjected. "Great season."

"Richard and Elizabeth love to test our patience after every performance." The staffer smiled tightly. "I'll leave you to it, then."

"Actually," Kirsten said, "I'm interested in one particular singer."

"Have a seat, why don't you." The man was bulldog in appearance with a gravelly bark. "Take a coffee?"

"No, thank you. I wanted to ask you about Erin Brandt."

Both their faces brightened. "A brilliant singer. One of the best."

Elizabeth asked, "How well do you know opera?"

"Hardly at all."

"So why are you interested in Erin Brandt?"

Kirsten replied delicately, "It pertains to research I'm doing for Senator Jacobs."

They looked at one another, then his wife said, "Zurich."

"Absolutely."

"Excuse me?"

The husband said, "Her first foray into the limelight was at the Zurich opera house. She was nineteen and a student under the great Adrienne Salzer."

"You have to understand," his wife added, "that it is extremely rare for a young would-be soprano to be given a chance at a starring role. The opera powers assume that her voice would require further development. Sopranos of Erin's age are rarely even permitted to audition at a major house. Which makes what we're about to tell you all the more remarkable."

Kirsten asked, "You know Ms. Brandt well?"

"Oh, we've never met. Well, Elizabeth bumped into her once in the Savoy elevator. But our introduction to Erin Brandt is part of operatic lore. Ms. Brandt was in the audience that night in Zurich, you see. Then what happens but the lead singer collapsed backstage."

"Bad cramps, so we heard," his wife interjected. "*La Traviata*. Some say it's Verdi's finest opera. Violetta is a courtesan. She falls in love. And dies. It's a classic Italian fable."

Her husband continued, "The director of the opera house was actually onstage, about to apologize and say there was no time to bring in a replacement, so the evening's performance would be canceled. Then it happened. Erin Brandt walked up to the conductor with her teacher, who is known and respected throughout the entire operatic world."

His wife took up the story. "The conductor, Mrs. Salzer, and Erin Brandt went backstage and met with the director. He then returned in front of the curtain and said there was a student of the same voice coach who had prepared that night's star for the role. Ms. Brandt had sat in on all the rehearsals and been walked through the opera by the house's artistic director, as a favor to her teacher. The conductor had heard her sing, and was willing to use her for the night's starring role."

"Naturally, none of us were very enthusiastic about the change," her husband continued. "We had been treating this evening's performance as the highlight of our Swiss vacation. It didn't matter whether she could sing. It would be a *student*. One who had never been on the stage before, much less performed this particular role."

"They delayed the opening curtain a full forty-five minutes, which did nothing for the audience's frame of mind." His wife's face was alight with the thrill of remembering. "When Erin Brandt came onstage, my goodness, it seemed as though a child was playing in her mother's clothes. The seamstress had done her best, but the costume just swallowed her. She had to use both hands to lift the skirt every time she moved."

"Which only made it more amazing," her husband added, sharing his wife's thrill.

"We could actually see the people in front of us squirm, like the entire audience wanted to draw farther back. We were ready to bolt, I don't mind telling you."

"And then she began to sing."

"Magic," the husband reminisced. "We were captivated from her very first note."

Kirsten asked, "She was good?"

"Magnificent," the man said. "Extraordinary. Utterly wondrous."

His wife continued, "The first act concludes with 'Sempre libera,' one of the most challenging arias in a soprano's repertoire. At the end of the aria there is an E-flat above high C. The myth is that Verdi wrote it into the original score, then decided it was an impossible challenge and took it out."

"Not only does it arrive after a very taxing aria, but the singer then has two full hours left to sing," the husband explained.

"The audience was so spellbound by that point, I'm certain they would have forgiven her if she had tripped over that atrocious costume and fallen flat on her face."

"But she didn't," her husband recalled, smiling into the past.

The wife drew closer to Kirsten. "She hit that note and held it forever. She held it so long we could see the conductor's baton begin to tremble. The audience began to cry their bravos while she was still singing."

"The Swiss are never what you would call demonstrative," her husband said, still smiling. "But that night they gave her a standing ovation. Right there, while she was still holding the note, they rose to their feet and cried out their applause. The man next to me was weeping."

"She drew them up like she had cast a spell," the wife said. "I stood because I had to, the people in front of me were on their feet and I could not bear to lose sight of that beautiful, beautiful woman."

"Callas reborn into a fairy's body," the husband said. "That is what the Zurich papers declared the next day. The new Anna Moffo. The find of the century. We kept all the reviews."

"Callas never had her voice," the wife sniffed.

"They were referring to her stage presence," he replied, with the patience of one who had covered that same ground many times before. "Erin Brandt is a consummate actress as well as a great singer."

"The night has taken on mythical proportions," the wife said. "I know people who weren't even on the continent who claim to have seen the performance."

Kirsten glanced at her watch and rose to her feet. "Thank you for your time."

CHAPTER

23

THE DETECTIVE was there waiting when Kirsten's taxi pulled into the Savoy alcove. He did not approach, did not really even look her way. But she felt a need to check things out once more. She walked over and pointed to his briefcase. "Is that it?"

His tone suggested he had fielded the question a thousand times before. "The trigger's in the handle, miss. The coverage is excellent. Absolutely spot on. Used it several hundred times and never had reason to complain."

"All right." She took the revolving doors into the lobby and walked straight to the room telephone poised on the front desk. When the operator came on, she said, "Ms. Brandt's suite, please."

The phone clicked, rang once, then a man responded with "Yes, what is it?"

Kirsten recognized the voice of the well-padded manager who wore his suit like a sausage skin. "This is Kirsten Stansted."

She knew the little man was tempted to hang up on her. But he ticked off the words "Stay there on the line."

As she waited for Erin, Kirsten checked her shoulder bag for the FedEx envelope that had arrived from Marcus that morning. She then surveyed her own inner space, finding satisfaction in this new determination. She had spent her entire life avoiding the hidden side of people. Pretending she could escape ever noticing it, so long as she held to counterfeit blindness. But it had gotten her nowhere she wanted to go. It was time, as they said, for a change.

The dulcet voice declared, "Tell me I'm not dreaming, sister."

"This is Kirsten. I'm downstairs."

"Well, of course you are. I spent my entire night hoping this might happen."

"I'd really like to have a minute of your time."

"A minute? Darling, come up and let's find us a few hours." The low chuckle finally broke free. "I assume you've come to realize just how awful you were to me last night. And how wrong you were to leave."

"There's been a change of heart. Definitely."

"Then your apology is accepted. Give me three minutes to free up my afternoon and put on something more in taste to the occasion."

"I'd rather you come downstairs."

"Nonsense. Three minutes. Suite four two six."

When Kirsten hung up the phone and started for the rear elevators, the detective rose from his chair, picked up his briefcase, and fell in behind her. Several other people crowded into the cage with them. The detective did not say a word.

The fourth-floor doors opened to reveal Erin's manager with his angry gaze peering at her through electric blue spectacles. "I have had to cancel an interview with the *Daily Telegraph*!"

The detective slipped by her and started down the corridor away from them.

Reiner Klatz stepped into the elevator, still venting fumes. "Do you have any idea how long it took to set that up?" He wagged a finger at her as the doors closed. "You are bad for my business!"

She waited until the elevator doors closed to reply, "I hope so."

The detective returned, treading with catlike grace. "Room?"

"Four two six."

"To your right. Make sure she comes outside."

She watched him disappear around the next corner, then started down the hall. The suite had one of the old-style brass doorbells she had to pull. An instant later the door opened to reveal Erin dressed in heels and a floor-length silk dressing gown of periwinkle blue. "You are just as beautiful in the morning as you are at night." She pushed the door wide. "But those clothes are far too stern."

Kirsten took a step away. "I'm not certain I want to do this."

"But of course, darling. That's what makes you so positively irresistible." She used one hand to sweep back her hair. "Now come in and have a glass of champagne, then you can struggle as hard as you like."

"No, really." One step more and she was touching the opposite wall. She risked a single glance down the hall, was dismayed to find it utterly empty. "I shouldn't."

"Oh, this is absurd." Erin checked the hall in both directions, then stepped out far enough to grab her arm. "You know precisely what it is you want."

"If only." Kirsten wrenched her arm free, reached into her shoulder bag, and stuffed the papers into Erin's outstretched hand. "You have now been served."

Erin stared down at the mass of pages. "What is this?"

"A court order. You are hereby ordered to appear in Wake County District Court and relinquish the child Celeste Steadman to Judge Rachel Sears."

In the space of two frantic heartbeats, Erin Brandt aged a decade. "You tricked me."

"Yes."

A movement out of the corner of her eye whipped Erin about. Kirsten was amazed to find the detective standing in the middle of the hallway, the briefcase by his feet.

Erin's head spun back, her hair a cinnamon wash over her face. "This is your bodyguard?"

"I don't want any trouble."

"Trouble?" The laugh was as wild as the look in Erin's eyes. She flashed an operatic gesture down the hall. "You think this muscle-bound beast can save you?"

"I am doing this for the child."

"What an utterly provincial and wretched little sentiment!" She was shrieking now, the force of her voice striking Kirsten like claws. *"Nothing* can save you, do you hear what I'm saying?"

Without seeming to move at all, the detective was now between them. Erin struck at him with her fists. *"Get away from me!"*

She might as well have beat against a stone wall. The detective suggested calmly, "Perhaps we should be going, miss."

"Yes."

Erin reached for Kirsten, but was blocked by the detective. "That's right! Run while you still can!"

Kirsten edged down the side wall, unwilling to turn her back on such wrath. "Run back to that stinking hole of a town! You think I can't reach you there? You think you're *safe?"*

Erin did not seek to move around the detective so much as to use him as a prop. She flayed at the air between them, then took the court order and shredded it. "You pitiful little creature, you're *nothing*. You've spent your life running from anything that might even *resemble* pleasure! You're a worm in human form, and you're soon to be squashed. I'll see to that *personally*!"

The detective kept his arms outstretched and gently nudged Erin back toward the door. She jerked her head toward the ceiling, spilled her hair back over her shoulders, then spun about and marched into her suite. The door slammed.

The detective hefted his briefcase and offered, "I'd say that went rather well, wouldn't you?"

CHAPTER

24

T HE SCHWANENSPIEGEL was a place out of time. Flanked by a trio of
five-lane city thoroughfares in the heart of Düsseldorf rested an
eighteenth-century marvel. Beyond the walking paths ringing the twin
lakes and their thick veil of summertime trees, the city flew at its furious pace. German drivers drilled their Mercedes and Porsches and
Audis toward the Kö, while to the south rose the mammoth Rhein
Knee Bridge and the even more awesome satellite tower with its
revolving restaurant atop the hundred-and-forty-meter-high needle.
But here it was possible to turn one's back on the rumbling traffic and
the city's pressures, and almost believe in the myth of historic tranquil-
lity. The old Landtag, or state parliament, anchored the park's far end,
flanked by Venetian bridges and monitored by hundreds of swans.
It was the perfect place for a diva to live. Even on the days when
Reiner detested Erin Brandt the most, he could not fault her choice of
residence.

Lining the lakes were twenty-one precise little houses, whose
inhabitants liked to pretend they were utterly untouched by any contemporary offal. This one street was the single segment of all central
Düsseldorf which had been completely unscathed by the British
bombers. The houses were fabulously expensive. Erin's house was one
of only five that had never been chopped into apartments or office
warrens. She probably had no idea how much it cost, or what it was
worth today. Reiner knew because he had bought and paid for it. Erin
Brandt had enormous difficulty paying for her own coffee. She took
the act of bringing out her credit card as an affront. Just as Erin didn't

drive, even though she owned a Mercedes SL 500 which Reiner was required to keep pristine. Erin Brandt felt she deserved a palace on the Schwanenspiegel. And whatever she wanted, she received. That was one of the unshakable axioms of Erin Brandt's world.

Which made the current state of affairs all the more baffling.

Even before Reiner fitted his key in the antique oak front door with its carvings of vines and figs, even before he rang the bell, he heard. As he entered, the sound of an infant's mewling filled the marble-tiled foyer. The baby's whimperings were everywhere. The stabbing little sounds endangered what was already going to be a massively difficult day.

Reiner shut the door overloud and called out, "Erin?"

"In here, darling."

He slid open the double doors and entered her parlor with its two-hundred-and-fifty-thousand-dollar antique Steinway. "Where is Goscha?"

Erin lifted her hand from stroking the young man's neck and waved toward the floor overhead. Goscha was her Polish housekeeper, and had been with Erin for as long as Reiner had known her, which that morning seemed like several lifetimes and counting. "Why are you so late?"

"Your investigators were delayed with their reports."

"Do they have something?"

Reiner merely waited.

Erin uncoiled from the Parisian fainting couch which occupied the central position beneath the front bay windows. She drew the young man up with a caress to his cheek. The lad was quite handsome in a raw and unfinished manner. He was also utterly bewitched by Erin. "You do understand, don't you, darling. I'd love to spend the entire day in your delicious company, but all the pressures I face just now."

She endured his lingering kisses of farewell. To Reiner's trained eye, the young man was not long for this parlor. Reiner never bothered to even ask their names unless they lasted more than a week. Which, since Erin's return from the dreaded Swampville, had happened with less and less frequency. Erin had always shown a voracious appetite toward virtually every pleasure. But since her return to Düsseldorf, her cravings had been alarming.

The situation in London was a perfect case in point.

"Well?"

Reiner seated himself on the polished piano bench. "She has decided to follow you."

"Kirsten?" Erin swiveled around to face the bay windows. The lakes shimmered in uncommonly strong July sunshine. Even the swans looked smug this morning. "She is here?"

"She is on her way." Reiner pointed out to where the city loomed beyond the lakes' fringes. "Your minions reported that she has booked herself into that ghastly hotel by the Kö."

As if to punctuate his news, the baby began squalling in earnest. He demanded, "What is the matter with that child?"

Erin responded as she normally did, which was to pretend the baby did not exist. "Does she know where I am?"

"One can only assume so."

"What about my trip to New York? Does she know about that too?"

"Erin, you cannot possibly be serious about traveling to America. Not now. Not with all—"

"Answer my question!"

Her screech was so loud it momentarily silenced even the child. Then the baby began screaming back. Erin pounced up and marched to the doors, sliding them back so hard they hammered the side walls and accordioned back toward her. "*Goscha!*"

The Polish woman was not even Reiner's age, yet appeared closer in years to his mother. In many respects she reminded Reiner of his wife, a silent specter who was far more comfortable with life's back rooms. Goscha padded down the stairs, her silver-blond hair bundled into the tight knot she always wore, her limp sweater and housedress some color that always seemed scarcely able to pull itself from drabbest gray. Like her voice. "Madame?"

"That screaming must stop!"

"I fear she has a cold."

"Then call the doctor! Take her to the hospital! Whip her until she understands! Do whatever you must! But *make her stop!*"

Goscha's one unfailing habit was absolute obedience. Her means of avoiding life's confrontations was to anticipate Erin's every need and serve them in advance. It was rare even to hear her speak, much less speak *back*. But this morning, Reiner was drawn to his feet by the impossible happening. The woman showed such fury it drew her features back into a slit-eyed snarl. Even Erin was forced to retreat toward the study's safety.

Goscha lashed out, "Celeste is a *baby*. A *beautiful* child."

Erin drew the doors shut against Goscha's glare. She then declared, "Something must be done."

Reiner studied her face, and realized the impossible was happening. Erin Brandt was afraid. Which only strengthened his plea. "You can't go to New York. You heard the attorney's warning. There is every likelihood that you will be ordered to appear in the Raleigh court. If they learn that you are traveling to America, they can issue an arrest warrant."

She did not even seem to hear. She stood frozen to the spot, seeing nothing.

Reiner found himself thinking back to their earliest days together. He had been managing a few other sopranos, good voices and fair actresses, but none of whom would ever make the world's top ranks. That evening Erin had been singing a lesser role in *Turandot* in Vienna, where the oldest of his ladies had the lead. To have *any* role at Erin's age at the Vienna house was a coup, and he went as much to see what the fuss was about as to attend his own star's performance.

Before the performance he found himself listening to the conversation around him. Which was something he never did. But tonight every voice he heard was about Erin Brandt. They were not here to see a new production by perhaps the finest opera company in the world. They were here to see *her*.

Reiner Klatz found himself completely spellbound. Erin sang the role of Liù, a slave girl from another country, and should have merely polished the star's luster. Erin's voice was exactly what Reiner would have predicted—underdeveloped and somewhat thin, the standard weaknesses of every young soprano. Yet every time Erin entered the stage, the audience waited breathlessly for her next note. In the last act, the diva broke with stage instructions and marched angrily to the stage's far corner. Still everyone's eyes remained focused upon the real star. And when Liù died and Erin was carried offstage, the night dimmed somewhat and the performance turned pallid.

The next day Reiner made an appointment to meet this astonishing young woman. He was thrilled to discover that her allure in person was even stronger than upon the stage. She entranced him such that, when this too young singer with almost no record asked him to manage her career, Reiner Klatz had felt *honored*. Only his wife remained untouched by Erin Brandt's spell. His wife was not a person to have many opinions about anything, which was one of the reasons why she made such an excellent wardrobe mistress. She did exactly what was expected of her, and never revealed an opinion contrary to the artistic director's. But she despised Erin Brandt. The worst argument Reiner could recall ever having with his wife had been over his decision to take Erin on.

Reiner now watched as Erin crossed to the small locked corner cabinet. This in itself was astonishing. The first time he had seen the cabinet had been the day he had arrived with her contract. She had been residing in a tiny walk-up flat on the outskirts of Cologne. Reiner had spotted a photograph within the cabinet and asked about the stolid, formal, utterly Germanic family staring coldly at the camera. Erin had responded with cold viciousness, ordering him never to ask about her past. Why she even kept this locked cabinet, he did not know. But it had followed her from that cramped apartment to Koblenz where she had her first standing contract, then Brussels, then Munich, and finally here. Always locked, never mentioned. Yet here she was, extracting a key from a mock Fabergé egg and opening the cabinet.

"Erin?"

She plucked a diary of some kind from the top shelf. The volume was so worn she had to hold the pages in place. She leafed through a series of letters bundled in the front. She found what she was looking for, unfolded the yellowed page, and reached for the phone. When someone answered, Erin switched to French and said, "I wish to speak to Sister Agnes, please."

Whatever it was she heard, it was enough for Erin to spill the diary in a heap of tattered pages at her feet. "You can't be serious." Then, "No, no, forgive me, that was not what I meant at all. It's just, well the news is so unexpected."

Erin hesitated a moment, then decided, "No, please do not tell the Mother Superior anything. I want this to be a surprise for her as well."

She hung up the phone, and resumed her blind stare out the front bay windows.

"Erin, you must permit me to call New York and cancel—"

She turned to him and revealed a smile that would only have confirmed his wife's worst fears. "Go and bring the car around," she ordered. "Then come back for the baby."

From the safety of his Mercedes Reiner witnessed a remarkable departure scene, something that truly belonged upon the stage. The Polish housekeeper was transformed into a dreadful maniac by the realization that Erin was going off with her own baby. Goscha followed Erin down the front stairs of their jewel-box home, wailing and shrieking so loud the baby had no choice but to scream in reflected fear. Erin marched with determined fury toward the car while the housekeeper played the diva herself, gripping the wrought-iron railing and clawing the air and shrieking her grief to a cloud-flecked sky.

The journey south held to a travesty of calm. By the time they passed Neuss on Düsseldorf's southern border, the baby had cried itself to sleep. Erin fed Reiner instructions in terse little bites. But underneath, the diva raged as Reiner had seldom seen.

Reiner felt his heart wrenched by the baby's occasional whimpers. His own father had remained a closet Nazi all his life, his mother a hapless Rheinlander hausfrau who relied on her husband for all strength and every opinion. One of the things Reiner liked most about his own wife was her fervent desire never to have children. Yet there was no mistaking the gentle pull this child exerted. Only Erin remained obstinately aloof.

South of Bonn, Erin instructed him to exit off the A61 and head west toward nowhere. Reiner cast her a quick glance and said, "Are you sure?"

Erin said nothing. She had aged twenty years that morning, and carried her silence with the determined grimness of one being fitted for a future shroud.

"I have lived in the Rheinland-Palatinate all my life," Reiner said, steering his way up into the forest and the sky. "And I have successfully managed to avoid ever entering the Eifel."

"Then you were very lucky indeed."

"You lived here?"

"Nine measureless, miserable years."

Between the Mosel and Ahr rivers, stretching from Koblenz westward to the four-country juncture of Luxembourg, Germany, Holland, and Belgium, lay the Eifel. Time-softened hills rose and fell in forested waves, drawing the visitor into a hoary land which mocked Germany's high-impact industrial might. From Aachen southward the region was little visited, save for morel hunters and local hikers. Even the road signs, such as they were, were inscribed in the old cursive script. But Erin's directions remained bitterly constant.

"Why did your parents choose to live here?"

"Did I say my family? Did I mention them at all?"

"Erin, softly please, the baby."

"My mother never came here. Not one time." She was silent so long Reiner assumed it was all he would learn of her past. Which was already more than she had ever said before. "My mother was a true Prussian blueblood. My father was Belgian. They divorced before I was born. I never met him. He was rich, an industrialist. Textiles, I believe she once said. When he left, she kept the money, which was all she wanted from him. She hated me."

"I doubt very much—"

"She loathed the sight of me." Erin used both hands to sweep her hair back, tilting her head in the gesture he had come to know so well, dismissing everything about the world she did not find to her liking. "Summers we moved to Antibes. Every September when my mother returned to Germany I was sent off to a horrible school in the middle of a forest. The driver brought me down. He never spoke. I hated him. I hated every one of them, my mother and all her little playmates. But I hated the convent most of all."

A few kilometers past the Belgian border, they entered a valley with a lake at either end. The middle portion was well-tended pasture, with horses gamboling in the knee-high grass. Wildflowers shimmered in an earthbound rainbow ballet under the light summer breeze. The air was fresh and full of country smells. The road was rough and poorly kept. The tires scrambled around a tight corner and entered through a high stone wall. Beyond, the tree-lined drive seemed endless. Erin's hands were gripped fiercely in her lap as they halted before a second stone wall. Somewhere in the distance a church bell rang a doleful welcome or dismissal, he could not tell which.

"A convent," Reiner murmured. "So the rumors are true."

Erin was already climbing from the car. "Come with me," she said curtly. "Bring the child."

They crossed a curved stone bridge over a stillwater moat. Birdsong sounded loud and raucous. The wind was a mysterious undertone that only accented the quiet.

Reiner felt pressured from all sides by the city's absence. "Horrid," he declared. "Utterly hideous."

Erin remained upon the stone bridge, staring eastward to where the high wall bowed inward to permit a tiny garden. Watched over by a pair of moat-fed willows were three flower-bedecked graves. "You can't imagine."

"Why are we here, Erin?"

She marched past him to where a bellpull dangled. She wrenched it down, once, twice, three times, pulling so hard the cord almost touched the earth. From within the bell sounded strident.

A narrow portal set within the massive front doors opened to reveal an elderly nun in formal black habit. "Yes?"

"We are here to see the Mother Superior."

"Do you have an appointment?"

"The Mother Superior," Erin declared, "will see us."

Something in her tone did not sit well with the nun. "Your name?"

"Erin Brandt."

"One moment."

But before the nun could shut the door, Erin was already pushing through. "We will wait inside."

"But you are not—"

"Will you tell the Mother Superior we are here? Or shall I?"

Within the compound, the silence was only more intense. The nuns Reiner could see moved without disturbing the serenity, as though they had already been swallowed and lost. He wanted to shout, rage, scream, burn. Anything to add a bit of comforting chaos.

By the time the sister returned, Reiner's skin felt attacked by a million roaches, all crawling and scrambling with a shared urge to flee. The nun gave him a look that suggested she knew exactly what he was thinking, but all she said was, "This way."

"I know precisely," Erin announced, striding rapidly away from the nun, "where the Mother Superior's offices are located."

The nun released Erin with a huffed indignation, leaving Reiner to catch up alone. They passed through an inner portal and entered a much larger courtyard filled with colorful playground equipment. "A school," Reiner said.

"A prison." Erin turned into a passage so ancient the outer walls were thicker than Reiner was tall. "A scourge." She hammered her heels into each stone stair, so that they echoed with her words. "A pestilence. A misery. A torture. A place of hatred and pain and fear."

"Only for some," announced a quiet voice at the top of the winding stairwell. "Only for a very few."

"You felt the exact same way." Erin would have barreled right through the sister, had she not stepped away.

"Only for a time."

"For years." Erin marched into the office occupying the stone-lined corner. "How often were we whipped together?"

"Too often." The Mother Superior held the door for Reiner and gave the baby a startled glance. "And not often enough."

"Just exactly the sort of miserable response I would expect from someone who joined the enemy."

"Sit down, Erin."

"I will not be here that long."

"Sit. Please."

She crouched into the seat, her backside barely scraping the wood's edge. Her hands formed claws around the carved armrests as she watched the Mother Superior step behind her desk. "I need your help."

"You are looking well." The few strands of hair escaping from beneath the nun's habit were almost transparent, as though the silence had sufficient force to wash away all color, all pretense of freedom. Her voice held the eerie quality of being able to speak without ruffling the stillness. "I have heard you are doing great things."

"Someone is after my baby," Erin continued grimly. "I need you to look after her."

Agnes looked at Reiner for the first time. Her gaze was as excruciating as the rest of this place. "Your husband?"

"My manager."

"Ah. Of course." She dismissed him. "You know we do not care for infants."

"She is a child. You take children. She is merely a bit younger than most."

"This is not possible."

Reiner watched with the experience of years. He knew Erin had come expecting these words. And was prepared.

She leaned forward and said in the musical tone that marked Erin at her most dangerous. "It was nice to see how well the cemetery remains tended."

The Mother Superior's eyes were gray in the manner of a cloudless sky the hour before dawn, so clear Reiner could look and see nothing but the hated stillness of this place. "The parents still come. Three of their next generation are with us now."

"How utterly calamitous," Erin spat back, "that not even they could learn the mistake of their ways."

Agnes started to reply, then changed her mind. "I will help you," she decided. "But not for the reasons you think."

"Of course not."

"How long do you need us to care for your child?"

"Not long. A week. Perhaps two. Then all this will be settled and behind us."

Agnes walked around her desk and reached for the child. Reiner's relief at turning Celeste over must have been evident, for the nun shot him a severe look. Nothing escaped her. Nothing. "How old is she?"

"Sixteen months."

"Her name?"

"Celeste."

"She is a beautiful child."

Erin rose from her chair. "I will pay you, of course."

"You will do no such thing. When did the child last eat?"

Erin faltered for the first time since entering. She glanced at Reiner, who could only shrug. Agnes observed this as well, and hardened. "Two weeks, Erin. Any longer and I will be forced to ask questions of my own."

CHAPTER

25

J UST BEFORE KIRSTEN'S last visit, the Düsseldorf airport had caught
fire and been largely destroyed. She passed through the new soaring steel-and-glass structure with a threatening sense of entering enemy
territory.

In her previous existence, Kirsten had made the pilgrimage to
Düsseldorf twice each year. The *Igedo* was the largest fashion event in
northern Europe. For five days Düsseldorf's hotels and restaurants and
limo companies and nightclubs and cafés were dominated by the rich
and beautiful and impeccably dressed. Cruise boats from as far away
as Sicily were moored along the Rhein docks, serving as additional
hotels and reception venues. A model with Escada or Ferragamo or
Hermès or Jil Sander was queen for a week. The entire city became a
runway for the newest and latest. Porsches and Ferraris outnumbered
Opels. The moneyed crowd from all over Germany, Scandinavia,
Holland, Luxembourg, Belgium, and Eastern Europe came to be part
of the spectacle.

She took a taxi to the antiseptic European-style commercial hotel
where the London embassy had booked her a room. Once checked in,
Kirsten walked the seven blocks to the American Consulate, which
through downsizing had relocated from its massive building on the Rhein
to a series of rooms above a bank. Kirsten sat in the office of an assistant
commercial consul who made no attempt to hide her curiosity. The sealed
windows were inch-thick glass embedded in steel frames. A building of
dark gray brick rose directly opposite, close enough to touch. The air
conditioner's soft sigh only heightened the claustrophobic closeness.

Kirsten waited the woman out, giving nothing in response to her questions.

On the way back to the hotel, she used a pay phone to call the detective. She wanted to meet this man in person. The consulate had obviously alerted him, for he was ready to roll as soon as he heard her name.

Back at the hotel, she called the German lawyer and explained enough to justify the woman shifting her schedule around. As soon as she cut the connection, the front desk rang through to say the detective was downstairs.

In the instant between hanging up and reaching for her purse, the phone rang once more. Kirsten hesitated a long moment, for no one save the consul knew she was here. "Yes?"

A woman demanded, "You are Kirsten Stansted?"

"Who is this?"

"You have friends in high places." The American voice sounded grated through wire mesh. "There's a service tonight at the International Church of Düsseldorf." She spelled out the address.

"Why don't you just come here?"

"Because you're being followed. Obviously somebody else thinks you're important."

"Did Senator Jacobs' office tell you I was coming?"

"Seven o'clock, Ms. Stansted. Be on time."

Downstairs, the detective proved to be extremely German but otherwise cut from the same mold as his British counterpart—former cop, prematurely gray, overdosed eyes, stone voice. An utter professional. He heard her out with scarcely a blink, then only said, "I will require four additional staff. And a retainer, since you are not local."

"I'll call as soon as America wakes up to confirm, but for the moment go ahead."

As he rose to leave, she added, "I've just heard I'm being followed."

"We can check on this also. Do you wish for a bodyguard?"

"Only if it's for real. What should I do in the meantime?"

"Wherever you go, before anything else," he instantly replied, "find the rear exit."

It was a lovely cool day, so Kirsten decided to walk to the restaurant where she had agreed to meet the German lawyer. She took Graf Adolf Strasse to Berliner Allee, passing high-rise thrones for the mighty

German alliance. She turned right onto Schadowstrasse, and passed an invisible barrier. Suddenly all the signs were in Japanese, the majority of faces stylishly alien. People greeted one another with oriental bows and voices that sang amid the thundering din of a workaday world.

She entered the restaurant through a series of three doors—sliding glass, then reed, then a portal framed with hand-carved beams. Beyond that opened a world of soft colors and honeyed wood and sparkling fountains and glowing lanterns and bowing ladies in silk robes. Kirsten crossed a tiny stone bridge and entered a tatami-square chamber with sliding shoji screens.

A blond heavyset woman demanded, "Ms. Stansted? I'm Maggie Heller."

"Nice to meet you." Kirsten lowered herself onto a cushion. "You're American?"

"German to the core. But I did my doctorate at NYU, then clerked there for a year. Loved the place too much to stay any longer. It was either get out or change allegiances." She waited while the waitress made a ballet of slipping out of her wooden clogs, kneeling by the table, and offering them hot towels and tea. "I've ordered for us. Hope that's okay. I'm due back at court in thirty-five minutes."

"It's fine."

Another waitress arrived bearing two lacquered lunch trays of sushi, miso soup, ginger chicken, and rice. Heller's opening was casually brutal. "Your client stands very little chance of recovering his child. Shall I tell you why?"

"All right."

"There are several main problems. The first is that German family court does not have the right to enforce its own judgments. Unlike America, our legal system is not set up to be coercive. We can't send in the federal marshals like you can. But that's just the start. Our federal government doesn't have the right to act as *amicus curiae*. Do you know what that means?"

"A friend of the court."

"Right. In America, if the government feels a lower court has issued a flawed ruling, it can enter suit in federal court, seeking a new judgment. But over here, the Nazis used the courts as a tool to persecute and destroy. So now civil liberties are tightly protected. Not only that, but many small-town judges are convinced from the outset these half-German children will grow up better in Germany."

"You've handled a lot of these cases."

"Too many, and the numbers are steadily mounting. I tell the left-behind parent the same thing every time. The German court system is rigged against you. There is a standing rule in our family court system. If the child has been relocated for more than six months, it is too damaging to force another move."

"So all they need to do is create delays."

"Exactly. Plus there is a clause in the Hague Convention, section thirteen it's called, with a loophole big enough to drive a thousand children through. It says the whole agreement can be tossed out if the court finds what it considers to be 'exceptional circumstances.' In these local judges' eyes, choosing between raising a child in Germany versus America is all the exception they need."

"None of this changes why I needed to meet you today." Swiftly Kirsten outlined what she was after.

When she was finished, Heller demanded, "Did you come up with this yourself?"

"Yes."

"Are you a lawyer?"

"I did a year at Georgetown law, then quit."

"This has the makings of a very good brief. Excellent, in fact." She made a process of detaching herself from the table and cushion. "It is very un-German to bring the press in like this."

"Is that a problem?"

"For some of my colleagues, perhaps. But I personally like the idea of trying some American tactics." Heller stood upon stubby legs, a tough little woman who relished the prospect of coming battle. "I currently represent thirty left-behind parents. It is one thing to talk about isolating myself from the trauma, and another thing entirely to succeed. Do you know where the courthouse is?"

"I'll find it."

"Four-thirty. Family court is on the third floor." She seemed reluctant to release Kirsten's hand. "You're still young. I would urge you to reconsider your professional direction."

The meeting with the PR agent was even briefer. The young man was tight and thin and struggling desperately with poor English. "All this can I do. Is no problem."

Kirsten could not tell whether it was bravado or German professionalism. "You're sure?"

"You want to make conflict with Erin Brandt, yes? You have a story. You need me to make public. All is most good."

"You don't seem surprised."

"Erin Brandt, she is diva. But she is also, how you say, *hochgefährlich*. Dangerous. Yes. And with enemies. You know her manager, Herr Klatz?"

"A fat little man with strange glasses."

"Is so." He reached for his phone. "This will be good action. I will enjoy."

Kirsten found it good to walk and pretend to forward motion under her own steam. All around her the city bloomed in cool profusion. Tree-lined parks adorned many crossroads, with canals and lakes breaking the monotony of overprecise roads. Only the meandering Rhein defied the German's desire to straighten every curve and carve every angle with brutal accuracy.

The detective met her in the plaza fronting the Carsch-Haus, at the Altstadt's border. They sat on the stone bank which curved around a central bandstand of slate and bronze. Gas street lamps stood in the old Baroque fashion, their wrought-iron limbs sprouting leaves of crystal plate.

The detective greeted her with "I can confirm that you are being followed."

"Now?"

"Try to look without looking." He opened a file in his lap and pointed to Erin's publicity photo. "A man in a gray leather jacket, standing by the escalator leading to the subway. A lady with a peacock's shawl by the far right shop window, the one with the mirror in the background."

"I see them."

"Steinhauser is the group. Germany's largest detective agency. Very reputable."

"This is reassuring?"

"Steinhauser is not the sort of group who will attack you. It also means whoever is behind this is extremely well financed, and taking you very seriously."

She caught the tone. "You don't think Erin Brandt is paying them?"

"Steinhauser specializes in corporate espionage, kidnap ransoms, high-profile personal security, international crime rings. Several governments subcontract their services." He stabbed the picture as though he wished to hammer the woman herself. "Someone living in this area who seeks to have you followed would go to a local specialist."

"Can you find out who is paying them?"

"Impossible." Definite in the German manner. "If we had weeks, perhaps. But days? No chance."

"What else do you have?"

"Erin Brandt has made a vocation of hiding her past. She was born in Cologne. Her mother is German, her father from Brussels. She was educated privately, probably outside the country, as there is no record of her schooling. She began her voice studies in Zurich when she was seventeen. I have summarized her career since then."

Kirsten made a pretense of studying the sheet. "Are they watching us?"

"The woman only. The man has probably gone to call in."

Kirsten folded the page and stowed it in her purse. "Where is she now?"

"Ms. Brandt apparently left her house before we stationed our men. We have checked the airports, and there is no record of her flying out. Her manager and his car are also gone. Which suggests they have traveled somewhere locally. As soon as she returns, we will know." He shut the file. "There is still the matter of our retainer."

"I have another meeting now. When that's over I'll make the call." Kirsten rose to her feet. "Make sure Erin is aware you are staking her out."

"Your instructions were perfectly clear, Ms. Stansted. Rattle her cage, is that not what you Americans say?" He eyed the female watcher. "We will do so. With pleasure."

The Düsseldorf state courthouse was a Weimar manor occupying an entire city block on the Rheingasse, a thoroughfare rimming the city's western border. The ground floor was built of granite blocks a meter square. Higher floors were ringed by pillared balconies and overtall French doors. The courthouse struck a highly dignified pose, dwarfing any fleeting human ambition or desire to thwart the proper course of German law.

The PR agent proved as good as his fractured word. Four journalists and two photographers watched her entry with skeptical gazes. The agent introduced them by the papers they represented, "*Rheinlander Presse, Frankfurter Allgemeine Zeitung, Süddeutsche Zeitung.* Is good for three hours, yes?"

"It's excellent." She addressed the gathering. "Do any of you speak English?" When most responded with reluctant nods, she said, "I am very grateful for your coming on such short notice."

The sole woman demanded, "You have something new on Erin Brandt?"

Kirsten pointed to where the attorney descended the central staircase. "I'll let her answer that."

The palace's marble-tiled foyer had been desecrated by the insertion of a sentry station and a bulletproof glass wall. Maggie Heller spoke at length to the guard, who permitted them entry with evident reluctance.

Maggie Heller, on the other hand, was struggling with an overload of suppressed excitement. Her black legal robes fell to her ankles and added an august dignity to her stodgy frame. "An excellent turnout, Ms. Stansted."

Kirsten pointed to the hovering press agent. "It was all his doing."

The lawyer led them back to where the staircase wound its way around an antique brass-caged elevator. The mosaic tiled walls were adorned with generations of stern-faced portraits. "This should make for a decent backdrop."

Kirsten tried to hang back and have the photographers focus on the berobed woman. But Heller would have none of it. The best Kirsten could do was to position herself two steps lower. The journalists gathered at the base of the stairway. Other attorneys and clients began clustering beyond them. Heller said, "I will speak to them in German, to ensure accuracy, yes?"

"Fire away."

Kirsten assumed she knew what was being said because they had discussed it over lunch. What she had not anticipated was the fire Heller brought to the occasion. Her passion echoed through the high-ceilinged chamber, galvanizing even this cynical little group. The journalists drew out pads and pens and scribbled away, while the photographers bounced around, searching for the best angle. To heighten the drama, Heller drew a sheaf of papers from an inside pocket, unfolded them so that the official seal at the bottom right corner was visible, and held them up between herself and Kirsten.

As the photographers caught them in impermanent flashes, Heller switched to English and related, "I have informed the press that we are entering suit without delay. I will start with a *Schriftsatz*, an initial motion accusing Erin Brandt of child abduction." She turned back to the cameras and continued in irate English, "My brief will anticipate the flaws within the German legal system. Each parental abduction case becomes an inspection of all the bad things within American society—guns in schools, terrorist threats, drugs, and so forth. The defense attorney will link himself to the judge, saying how *we* know Germany is a better place for this child. *We* know it would be bad to uproot the child a second time. *We* know the child is better here, in this good and orderly land."

Her rage was so forceful she crumpled the pages as she shook them for the cameras. "Together the defense attorney and the judge will do their best to overlook what has *really* happened. That the mother abandoned both child and husband, and disappeared for *months*. That she returned and kidnapped the baby, and now has refused to appear before the American judge as ordered."

Heller then turned and gave Kirsten a hard-eyed smile. "Your turn."

It would have been better to discuss this first with Marcus. But there was a momentum building, and she had to go with what her gut was saying. Which was, "Because the pattern of German courts is well known, we are also instituting an action in the European Court of Human Rights. Not against Erin Brandt. Against the entire German family court system. For their abject failure to protect the rights of this kidnapped little girl."

She might as well have doused the reporters with gasoline and set them alight. The chamber became filled with the baying of journalistic hounds. Heller had to shout the words "That is enough for now. My office will have more information for you tomorrow."

As the PR agent took that as his cue and began shepherding his charges outside, Heller steered Kirsten around and guided her up the stairs. "Leave them panting for more, isn't that what you Americans always say?"

CHAPTER

26

THURSDAY MORNING Judge Sears opened the court proceedings with "I fail to see either the mother or the child here this morning, Mr. Caisse."

"Extenuating circumstances make it impossible for her to arrive on such short notice, your honor." He rifled through his briefcase to avoid meeting Judge Sears' eye. "I have letters from the German opera house and several high officials begging the court's understanding on this matter."

She accepted the papers and perused them briefly. "Mr. Glenwood, do you care to respond?"

"Your honor, we ask that the court issue an order of contempt against Ms. Brandt."

"You have the relative papers?"

"Filed this morning, your honor." Marcus lifted two notarized copies from his briefcase. He handed one to Hamper Caisse and another to the judge. When he returned to his table, he could not help but cast a mournful glance at the open case. Beneath his files lay the videotape received that morning from Kirsten. No note had been attached. When he called her London hotel he had learned that she had checked out the previous day. No word as to where she might now be.

"You anticipated this event, then."

"Up to now, all we've had is a series of smoke and mirrors, your honor. It was fairly safe to assume that anyone willing to lie so freely would continue to defy this court." Marcus pulled a second sheaf of papers from his case. "We ask that attached to the contempt order, the court assign costs to both Ms. Brandt and her attorney."

She gave the papers careful inspection. This was a critical issue, for it would effectively hold Hamper Caisse liable for all of Marcus' costs in the event that Hamper's client did not appear. Court costs were shared between client and lawyer only when the court believed the attorney was involved in subverting justice, but did not have sufficient hard evidence to open criminal proceedings.

"Mr. Caisse?"

"Your honor, I am here as directed."

"But your client is not present."

"As I explained, she could not appear on such short notice."

"Have you had any communication with your client?"

"Any discussion between client and counsel is confidential, as this court knows."

"I am hereby asserting my judicial authority. The principal issue before this court is the welfare of this abducted child."

"The child was not abducted, your honor. Far from it."

"Then why is your client not here to attest to this fact personally?" Judge Sears leaned forward. "The court is hereby ordering you to disclose any information related to the whereabouts of this child."

"With respect, your honor, I must refuse."

Marcus tensed. Hamper's calm obstinance did not bode well.

"Mr. Caisse, you seem awfully relaxed for someone who is only two steps from being held in felonious contempt along with his client."

"Your honor, I feel this court may be missing something of grave importance here. But I wanted to wait for opposing counsel to finish cantering around the courtroom on his high horse before we got down to business."

"Proceed."

"Your honor, it has come to my attention that opposing counsel has had direct contact with my client, and without my being present."

Judge Sears gaped at Marcus. "You went to Germany?"

"London, your honor," Hamper corrected. "And it wasn't Marcus. It was his fiancée."

"Is this true?"

"Not only is it true, but the woman is still there! I heard from my client earlier today that this woman has actually followed her back to Germany." Hamper Caisse slipped pages from his briefcase, dropped one set into Marcus' lap, then carried the others to Judge Sears. "Hot off the press, your honor. Faxed to me this very morning."

Beneath the London *Times* logo and yesterday's date was a society photograph. Kirsten stood beside a smiling dark-haired Erin Brandt. The look on Kirsten's face knotted Marcus' gut far more than the fact that she was with Erin. Or how Hamper knew more about Kirsten's whereabouts than he did himself.

"Well?"

Marcus wrenched his gaze away from the photograph. "I asked her to go over for me, your honor, and find a private detective to serve the papers."

"I can't understand what possibly caused you to take such a course of action."

"Well, I most certainly understand!" Hamper Caisse commanded the stage's center point. "Opposing counsel doesn't trust his own client! Mr. Glenwood here decided to send his own fiancée over on this sneaky, underhanded mission to try and find out just exactly what is going on! Just look at that picture, your honor! Does Mr. Glenwood's lady friend look disgusted with what she's found out? Of course not! She's seen the truth! And the truth is, Dale Steadman is a liar and a fraud. He's not fit to be in the same room with that poor child, much less hold sole guardianship!"

"That's enough. I am required to recuse Mr. Glenwood only if his being a witness to actions could be prejudicial either to the case or his own client."

"But his fiancée was over there acting on his behalf, your honor! He's dancing too close to the flame here!" He almost shouted with adrenaline glee. "It's completely improper for him to have had this sort of communication with my client! Most especially when I was four thousand miles away, and without giving me proper notification. For all I know, he has used his fiancée to obtain factual information which has a direct bearing on the outcome of this case."

"Mr. Glenwood, would you care to respond?"

But Hamper's tirade was not so easily stemmed. "Your honor, Mr. Glenwood is no longer in a position where he *can* respond. He is unable to act objectively with respect to his client. He and his fiancée clearly have access to information that I need to examine in order to defend my own client's position."

"Mr. Caisse—"

He raised his voice to override the judge. "I therefore ask that he be sanctioned for this highly improper conduct. Furthermore, I ask that he be removed from this case, and that you instruct the plaintiff to seek other counsel."

Judge Sears had no choice but to ask Hamper the question she had sought to avoid. "Do you intend to call him as a witness?"

"I feel compelled to, your honor. In matters of such a sensitive nature, we've got to scrutinize everything with great care. Only he can testify to the substance of the conversation with my client."

"Only my fiancée," Marcus corrected.

"Which is the same thing, your honor."

Judge Sears' gaze held more caustic reproach than Marcus could bear without flinching. "Have you spoken with your fiancée about this matter?"

"I knew nothing about this at all, your honor."

Hamper interjected, "May I remind the court that Mr. Glenwood is not under oath."

Judge Sears chose to ignore him. "You have had no contact with her at all?"

"Only through the mail." Marcus lifted the package. "Apparently she has videotaped her contact with Ms. Brandt."

"What?"

"I assumed Erin Brandt would not be returning today. So I wanted a reputable detective to photograph the document handover, with someone from my staff there to ensure it was delivered intact. Obviously she misunderstood, and assumed she should make the contact personally."

"So what you have there is a tape of the documents being delivered?"

"I assume so. It arrived just as I was leaving this morning."

"You have not seen it?"

"No chance yet, your honor."

"Court is adjourned for twenty minutes. You gentlemen join me in my chambers. Mr. Steadman, perhaps it would be a good idea if you joined us as well."

———

Judge Sears waited until she was midway down the side corridor to lash out at Marcus. "How *dare* you put me in such a position!"

"I am deeply sorry, your honor. Kirsten overstepped the proper bounds."

"By about four thousand miles." She had to tilt her head until her hair spilled over the robes, but Marcus still had the distinct impression of being the smaller of the pair. "Why didn't you instruct her more properly?"

"When she left, I was still in the Wilmington hospital, recovering from the boat blast."

Hamper stepped to the plate. "That is no excuse, your honor."

"I agree." Pliers could not have tightened her face any further. "This way." As she passed the court recorder's desk, she added, "Join us, please."

The judge's office was a bare-walled alcove whose single dirty window overlooked the parking garage next door. She seated herself behind the desk and said, "Be seated, gentlemen. Mr. Steadman, do you wish to continue with Mr. Glenwood as counsel?"

"Absolutely, your honor."

"I am inclined to recuse him from this case."

"I'd ask that you not do that. If he's made any mistake here, it's for caring too much."

She reached across the desk. "Give me the tape, please."

"Your honor, I have to object—"

"Save it until after we've seen what we have here, Mr. Caisse."

The videotape began with the elevator doors opening onto an irate little man compressed into an overtight suit. The camera was held at knee level, and was shot through a wide-angle lens that made the little man appear even broader. Dale snorted at the image, but said nothing. The scene was shot in colorless accuracy, the sound quality excellent save for a rustle matched to each of the man's steps. Marcus realized the camera had to be fitted into a case held by the unseen man's side.

"Your honor, I must protest—"

"Either be quiet or leave my chambers, Mr. Caisse."

The man took them on a quick little tour of empty hallways. Kirsten appeared and disappeared so fast Marcus had time only for a single lancing instant of concern. She spoke a number and gave the camera a tensely frightened glance before disappearing.

Voices sounded in the distance, and the man began hurrying. He rounded a corner, another, moving so swiftly now the camera bounced like a ship in heavy seas. Then two women came into view. He thunked the camera down onto the floor. Legs blocked their view for a moment, but not the sound of Erin's rising ire.

Then the man came into clear view, standing purposefully to one side, allowing them to observe Erin Brandt come completely undone. Marcus tried to focus upon this first glimpse of his adversary in action. But time and again his gaze was drawn back to Kirsten. He was hammered by the conviction that she was lost to him.

After they had watched Erin's impromptu performance, they all required several minutes to gather themselves. Dale Steadman sat and stared at the screen long after it went blank, his features pinched with bitter regret.

Hamper spoke first. "All this is very self-serving, your honor. Glenwood has concocted a most elaborate sham."

"It looked pretty authentic to me," Judge Sears countered.

"We have no idea what preceded this exchange. I should have the right to elicit information from Glenwood on the witness stand. Information which I believe he sent his fiancée over to obtain. Right now, all we've got is his claim that they did not discuss anything of bearing on this case. A statement made completely off the record and not under oath."

Judge Sears turned to Marcus and said, "You've been around the block enough to know this is the kind of stunt that gets lawyers in serious trouble."

"Yes, your honor."

"Didn't you spend some time serving on the disciplinary committee of the state bar?"

"Three years."

"Then you know this was highly improper."

"As I stated, your honor, the intention was for her to hire a private detective and stay well away from Ms. Brandt."

"You know what this sounds like to me?" She hiked her sleeves back and planted her elbows on her desk. "It sounds like you've got a client with a lot of money and clout, who convinced you that this was a good idea."

"That's not the situation here. At all."

"The client does not run the case, Marcus. The law does. To have it any other way is a weakness on the attorney's behalf that damages both the client's interests and the law's credibility."

"I can only repeat, your honor, that was not what happened."

She then turned to Hamper. "How long have you known about this?"

"Since yesterday, your honor. My client called to inform me."

"Did you file the motion in writing to have Mr. Glenwood recused from this case?"

"No, your honor."

"In other words, you've been sitting on information which you knew full well needed to be filed in advance with this court. You wanted to come in and drop another bombshell. Just like when you sought to have a custody hearing without either Mr. Steadman or his counsel present."

Hamper started on a high-pitched whine. "Your honor, I must protest this—"

"Save it. I'm not in the mood." She planted her hands on the desk and pushed herself upright. "Let the record show that the request to recuse Mr. Glenwood has been denied. Marcus, I want a detailed explanation of everything that was discussed between your fiancée and Hamper's client. In writing."

"Yes, your honor."

"Tomorrow."

"First thing, your honor."

"I am hereby charging Erin Brandt with felonious contempt." Her upraised hand halted Caisse before he could begin. "Be careful, else I include you. A warrant will be issued for her arrest. If she cares to change her mind and appear before this court, *without delay*, I will consider rescinding this order."

Judge Sears rose from her desk, marched to her door, plucked it open, then turned back to add, "These walls are awful bare, Marcus. Even so, I'd hate to nail your hide up there for decoration. Are we clear on this point?"

Marcus ushered Dale Steadman from the judge's chambers. Hamper shoved his way between them, rudely impatient to move on to the next fray. Dale gave no sign he even felt the lawyer's passage. He had not spoken at all since his ex-wife had appeared on the screen.

Omar Dell moved up to Marcus' other side. "I need to have a minute, counselor."

To his other side, Dale remained in lockdown mode. Marcus said, "Now is not the time."

"Sorry. Deadlines say otherwise."

"I am telling you to back off."

"Easy now. I just want to pass on something." He stepped in closer. "The lead you gave me. Sephus Jones. He's vanished into thin air."

"When?"

"The quarry boss claims it was the very same morning you and Hamper had the set-to in this hallway."

Marcus tried to make room in his mental jumble. He tracked Hamper's progress down the hallway, and said to no one in particular, "I get the impression that man is working on something more than our declared agenda."

"Hamper Caisse is just another courtroom junkie. Whoever heard of any junkie with a conscience?"

But there was more at work here. Marcus was certain of that. He was fighting a case to retrieve a missing baby girl. If Caisse was involved with Sephus Jones and the bogus New Horizons check, he had another agenda entirely. Even so, the day's events and Kirsten's absence bore down like a ton of stones loaded onto his chest. It was hard to draw a decent breath, much less come up with a solution.

When Omar saw he was gaining nothing more from Marcus, he said, "I need to ask your client something that you've got to hear."

Dale Steadman showed only blind resignation. Even the court-house reporter used the soft tread of one approaching the recently bereaved. "Mr. Steadman, I'm sorry to bother you, sir."

Dale blinked slowly, drawing himself into the here and now. "You want to ask about my being fired."

Once again, the day proved remarkably adept at blindsiding Marcus. "Say what?"

"They canned me this morning."

"I got the skinny from an inside contact," Omar confirmed. "New Horizons is issuing a statement this afternoon. They claim they have no choice but to terminate Mr. Steadman's position as chairman."

"This was inevitable," Dale replied.

"I'll tell you what it is," Marcus fumed. "It's typical."

"The New Horizons spokesperson repeated the recent character assault brought out in court. Seemed positively delighted to do so. Didn't show a bit of interest in the testimony that ran counter to Hamper Caisse's witnesses. She claimed they simply can't afford more adverse publicity."

When Dale resumed his blank inspection of the distance, Marcus said, "That's nothing more than a perfect excuse. My guess is, they've already started rolling back Dale's changes. The increased wages tied to higher productivity, the new doctors and factory clinics, the child care centers, they'll be gone before you know it."

Omar flipped to a blank page in his notebook. "Can I quote you?"

"Be my guest. New Horizons will return to their same old tactics. Only now they'll trumpet how these new ideas brought them nothing but more bad news."

"Do you think they're behind this little girl's abduction?"

"You know I can't answer that."

"Mr. Steadman, do you have any—"

"Don't respond, Dale." Marcus resisted the urge to shove the reporter aside. "We're leaving now."

CHAPTER

27

WHEN MARCUS did not pick up his phone, Kirsten listened to the answering machine's message, waited through three tight breaths, then hung up and dialed Dale Steadman. He answered before the first ring was halfway finished. "Mr. Steadman, this is Kirsten Stansted."

"Where are you?"

"Düsseldorf."

"Have you seen Erin?"

"Not since my arrival. But she's here."

"I watched the video of you serving her with the court papers."

It had not even occurred to her that he might be present. "I'm very sorry about that."

"Don't be. The judge watched it too. It made all the difference, believe me."

"I needed to check with you about a couple of things, please."

"Sure. Do you like opera?"

"What I've heard, which isn't a lot."

"I always figured myself for a bluegrass sort of guy. The year after I busted my shoulder, I was doing rehab at a sports clinic outside Boston. My trainer and her husband were real opera fanatics. I got tickets to the Met and flew us down for the weekend. Figured if she could put up with me groaning and sweating on the table for six hours a day, I could sit through three hours of people hollering words I couldn't understand."

She refused to offer what he wanted, which was an invitation to delve further into reminiscences and regret. "The reason I'm calling, I'm facing some unexpected expenses here in Germany."

"Spend whatever it takes."

"I can fax you an itemized breakdown."

"Don't bother. I'll be a moving target for a while. I actually thought your call was going to be the New Horizons board rep telling me I've been canned."

She didn't want the man's trust. Nor did she want to feel more sympathy and shared sorrow than she already did. But the emotions welled up unbidden. "I'm so sorry."

"The way I see it, they knew about my drinking and they made it their business to find out about my marital problems."

"You're saying that was why you were hired?"

"They wanted somebody they could yank up the flagpole, wave in front of the press, and say, Look at what we're doing. We've hired ourselves a reformer. But when I started putting into place things they didn't like, they could cut the rope and say it was on account of my personal difficulties. I was a patsy from the get-go."

"Could you please fax me an authorization to give the detectives a retainer?"

"No problem." He made note of the number, then added, "Marcus is lucky to have you."

That was definitely a course she had no intention of taking. "I was wondering if you could also fax me a photograph of Celeste."

"I suppose so."

"I'd like to have something to show around."

"Give me five minutes." A pause, then, "This is hard on you too, isn't it."

"A large black and white picture would probably come through more clearly," she replied, then hung up the phone. Kirsten sat on the edge of the bed, staring at her hands. She glanced at her watch, rose, reached for her purse, headed for the door.

Downstairs she waited as the fax pulsed through the machine. The receptionist took one look and beamed back at the smiling baby. "What a lovely child! Is she yours?"

Kirsten accepted the fax and headed out the door. "For the moment."

———

It was the hour before sunset as the taxi drove Kirsten through a middle-class residential quarter. Neat apartment blocks stood tightly abreast. Trees and a meager strip of green formed a rivulet down either side of the central trolley tracks. The buildings were of a regimental order, all six or seven stories, all freshly painted, all double-glazed and politely ornamented. They broke ranks only to permit in the side streets and more battalions of close-ranked buildings. When a trolley rattled down the street, the residential cavern trapped the sound and kept it there forever.

Her taxi rounded a corner, took a second sharp turning, and suddenly entered a world of cathedral greens. The forest was so ancient all Kirsten saw were vast spaces and living pillars. The taxi driver took deep breaths through his open window and pointed to the ancient growth. Kirsten nodded her understanding. She had entered the city's lungs.

From the outside, the church was singularly unimpressive. All she could see when she rose from the taxi was the wall of a forest hut. A thick coat of gold-green moss bound the structure to the forest floor. Once inside, she found that three of the sanctuary walls were glass. As she took her seat, the wind flung a fistful of apple blossoms at the glass, as though the trees sought to join the congregation.

The service was a standard midweek rite, intended primarily for fellowship. Kirsten sat and listened to her own internal discourse. She was not yet able to examine her flaws and come to terms with all her emotional baggage. But she had an instinctive understanding of Erin Brandt. Their motif was the same; to appear to be someone else, to form a wall no one could breach.

Until now.

After the service, people flowed good-naturedly into the adjoining kitchen-dining area. The covered dishes emitted a rainbow of odors— curries and chilies and cumin and spices she could not identify. Kirsten remained standing by her chair and observed the casual intermingling of Europeans and Asians and Arabs and Africans, the diversity a living condemnation of most American churches.

The couple waited until the congregation had dispersed to approach. Only one other person remained seated up by the nave, a gray-haired matron who appeared to study Kirsten even with head bowed and eyes diverted.

The younger woman demanded, "You're taking on Erin Brandt?"

"I represent an attorney acting on behalf of her former husband."

She had the weak countenance of many redheads, as though the effort of inserting such brilliance into her hair had drained her features of strength and clarity. "I sing with the opera. My husband is one of the lead dancers with the *Stadtsballet*."

The young man was slender and muscled and held himself with taut grace. He asked his wife, "Does she look like a lawyer to you?"

"And just exactly what is a lawyer supposed to look like?" The woman did not turn around. "Male?"

"This is your career we've got on the line here. *Our* careers."

"Where else would be safer? Tell me that and we'll go there."

"You heard them the same as I. This case is high profile. People are watching."

Kirsten asked, "Who has been talking about me?"

"I can't tell you that." She seemed irate with her own need to talk. "Look. If there was a support group for left-behind parents, we couldn't ever discuss it, you understand?"

The young man continued to glare at his wife. "The German government takes a very hard look at any resident foreigner who makes trouble."

"This isn't just a problem for Americans. It's a dilemma facing people from nations right around the globe. And it's getting steadily worse. Word is out."

Kirsten asked, "What can you tell me about Erin Brandt?"

"Almost nothing. She got her start singing in a convent choir. I know that much."

"It could be a lie," her husband muttered.

"I don't think so. She was too angry with herself for telling me."

The gray-haired woman on the front row remained intently focused upon the hands in her lap. Kirsten asked, "When was this?"

"Not long after she returned to her position as resident diva. Erin was furious after she said it. So angry she frightened me. Like I was suddenly a threat."

"Because she had spoken to you?"

"Because I *listened*. Erin knew I'd been paying attention."

"But why was this important?"

"I don't know. But it was. To her, it was something vital."

The gray-haired woman rose from her seat and turned their way, revealing features cast into permanent resignation. The couple said nothing as she slipped into the pew in front of Kirsten. She spoke in German with heavily accented weariness. The singer translated, "You have succeeded in worrying Erin Brandt."

"May I ask who you are?"

The couple exchanged glances with the woman before the singer responded. "Goscha is Ms. Brandt's housekeeper."

"Goscha." Kirsten turned so she faced the woman directly. "Can you tell me how the baby is doing?"

The woman made a careless gesture of clearing away sudden tears. The singer translated, "Erin and her manager took the baby away this morning. She has no idea where to."

Kirsten touched the woman's sweatered arm. "Was Celeste all right this morning?"

The woman struggled to respond directly. "Is beautiful child. Please, you are forgiving my English, yes?"

"Of course."

"Celeste is little angel."

"Why did they take her away?"

The woman switched back to German, which the singer translated, "Erin is preparing to travel again."

"When?"

"Tomorrow. She has agreed to sing at a gala function."

"Where?"

The housekeeper replied with a gift bearer's determination. "New York."

Kirsten joined the crowd drifting into the forest and the night. The path back to the main forest road was poorly lit and furrowed from recent rains. Women in high heels pitched like drunken ballerinas and grabbed at whoever was closest. The atmosphere was gay and soft as the air, good friends reluctant to leave the dusky respite. The trees were blue-gray shadows etched against the fading summer light. An orchestra of birdsong made a mockery of the autobahn's distant thunder.

Kirsten felt an urgent need to talk with Marcus. Yet the flush of pleasure over sharing these events also raised the specter of panic and flight. Which saddened her, thinking that perhaps this would remain a part of her forever, an addictive craving for the needle of isolation.

A hand gripped her arm. For an instant she thought it was another parishioner offering support over the rocky path. Then the thumb searched out the soft point in her elbow, and punched down like a stake going for blood.

The pain was a white flash against the backdrop of falling night, so severe she had to gasp first, before the scream could be formed. Another hand was there and ready, this one gloved and closing over her throat and dragging her back the three paces into the first line of trees.

A man breathed into her ear, "Sometimes there ain't nothing as real as pain. Tell me I'm right."

Kirsten struggled for a purchase against the hand over her throat. The man lifted her up slightly so that her toes scrabbled across the leaves. Her nostrils became filled with the man's stench. The odor was as strong as his grip, a revolting combination of old sweat and cheap cologne.

"Know what I think? Pain's like a flower. You get inside deep enough, you find it just keeps on opening up." His voice was muffled by cloth. "One level to the next. On and on. And you can't decide which is worse. Living with the pain you know, or worrying about how bad it's gonna get."

The man slackened his grip on both her elbow and her throat. The dual agonies were replaced by a single throbbing ache that coursed through her entire upper body, melded together by sheer terror.

"Now you just calm down and listen hard. Either that or I'm gonna introduce you to the next level. Nod that you're paying attention to what I'm saying."

The distant road flashed with the brilliance of a car pulling away. Another car started and turned on its lights. A spectral glow lit their tiny corner, the tree trunks turning silver on one side and black on the other. The man was so strong he could hold her full weight by the gloved hand gripping the bones of her lower jaw.

Kirsten clenched both her hands to the wrist and forearm and took as much of her weight as she could. She might as well have been holding a roof brace. She nodded.

"Okay, here's the deal. You made yourself busy asking questions and causing problems. Nod that you're still listening. See how easy it is? Now nod again, and show me you're gonna be leaving tomorrow. Good. Nod once more. We've got us a promise, right? You're nodding 'cause you don't ever want to know what kinda pain I can cause you if I want."

The next car illuminated their monochrome grove. The man's second hand released her elbow and flashed a blade before her eyes. "Some pains, they stay around for what seems like forever." He moved the blade back and forth, like a barber ready to probe and shave. "They're there every time you look at yourself in the mirror. You think maybe I oughtta show you what I mean, make sure you don't ever forget our little talk?"

A woman's voice called from down the path, "Ms. Stansted?"

The man froze.

Footsteps scrunched back down the gravel walk, and the singer called out, "Kirsten?"

The man held the blade up before Kirsten's eyes, a warning.

Footsteps came farther back down the path. "Are you there?"

Kirsten lifted both feet off the ground, nauseated by the man's stink and that flashing blade. But the fear of having the singer move away and leave her there alone was far greater. She cocked her ankles so as to sharpen the edge of her heels, and drove them like dual spikes into his ankle.

The man grunted softly, the sound scalding her ear. The blade wavered slightly. She ducked her chin down as far as it would go. Her senses were filled with the man's oily stench. She fought down a rising gorge and opened her mouth so wide she heard her bones grind against the pressure of his grip.

"Kirsten? Are you—"

She wedged her chin down, fitting her mouth about the width of his wrist. Then she bit down with every shred of force in her entire body.

The man bellowed.

Somewhere out in the distance, a woman screamed in response.

Kirsten hung on to his arm like a leech. She beat her elbows back against the solid rock of his chest and hammered down with her heels a second time. And ground her teeth deeper.

Something sliced her at the hairline, not a strike so much as a flash of light deep inside her skull. There were more shouts now, and she was pounding his leg and ankle and biting so hard she felt nothing else, heard nothing, not even the muffled screams choking her own throat.

There was the sound of people rushing into the trees. The man ripped his arm free and flung her to the earth.

"She's over here!"

Kirsten fell to all fours. Hands reached down for her, then backed off as she squeezed her body like a fist in the effort to be sick, to rid herself of the stench and all that had just happened.

"She's bleeding! Somebody get a towel!"

A hand touched the point below her ear where she could sense the wetness, and there came a searing pain. But with it was the relief of knowing it was over.

As she rose from the earth, Kirsten grabbed several leaves and stuffed them into her own mouth. The sweet earthy grit did much to cleanse away the taste of that man.

CHAPTER

2 8

"KIRSTEN, I DON'T LIKE THIS. Not at all."

It was approaching midnight, two hours since the police had driven her back to the hotel. But the residual fear would not let her be still. Kirsten cradled the phone with her shoulder and continued to pack. "Could we move beyond this, please? Erin is going to New York. I intend to follow her."

"The woman had someone attack you tonight and—"

"Marcus, I didn't tell you about this so you could use it like a club. I told you because I felt you should know what happened."

When Marcus had answered the phone and heard her voice, he had sounded so delighted, so open, so *eager*. Kirsten had retreated instinctively, watching herself cut him off and hating the weakness. But she was powerless to do otherwise. Even so, to hear him respond with his own curt professional tone hurt far worse than her neck's throbbing.

"I don't understand why you're so determined."

Kirsten pressed down the clothes into her suitcase, punching them in time to her words. "What has hiding brought except misery and lies upon lies?"

"Are we talking about the case here?"

She did say what she was thinking, that her own internal fight was so tightly interwoven now, she could not halt one without retreating from the other. "This is important, Marcus."

His capitulation came in the form of a sigh. "You're sure you're all right?"

She straightened and traced the bandage covering the nine stitches running along the base of her skull. Although the doctor had shaved her hairline slightly higher, the hair's trailing edge remained long enough to cover the scar. The local anesthetic was beginning to wear off, and the residual fear throbbed with her pain. "Just tell me what to do."

"All right. First off, you'll need to go to the Manhattan offices of the INS. Speak with their staff attorney and request that they issue a detaining order against Erin. The child has U.S. citizenship, she's been abducted, the mother has failed to appear as the court instructed. INS should be willing to help. Do you know where Erin is staying?"

"I'll try to find out."

"Don't go there yourself, Kirsten."

"Is that all you want me to do?"

"Call me with your hotel. I'll have the name of a local attorney. Give him the casework I fax you and the INS detaining order if you can get one. He should take all this to the district court and request the local police take Erin into custody. Am I talking too fast?"

"No. Go on."

"The attorney will request the court's assistance based on the Full Faith and Credit Clause of the U.S. Constitution. This says that each state agrees to recognize and enforce the rulings of other states' courts. The judge will do what's called domesticating the judgment, which means the local sheriff is then required to enforce the order."

"All right. I've got that."

The silence was cut by a series of staccato pulses, as though the distance was magnified by their quarrel. Marcus said quietly, "This is not what I had been hoping we'd be talking about."

Kirsten was clenched by a sudden desire to reveal her feelings, to confess her *need* for this man. "I have to go."

She slammed down the phone with the force of all the rage she felt against herself. She sat there for what seemed like hours, warring with her own burning urge to lift the receiver and call him back, the only outer sign her tight gasping breaths.

When the phone rang, she jerked her hand away from the sudden heat. But it was only the detective. "I am in the lobby," he barked. "You will please come down?"

———

The German detective was so furious he stalked the empty hotel bar like a gray-suited beast. "This is not how it is done."

Kirsten touched the bandage. She had decided not to take any painkillers. The cut throbbed with exquisite precision. "You don't believe me?"

"Of course I accept this. But not coming from a company like Steinhauser. Even if they were not behind the attack, they should have seen it and stopped it." He glared at her as though it was her fault the codes had been broken. "This is not cowboy land. We do not carry guns at our hips. We do not draw and shoot the first chance we get. We do not attack our suspects in dark corners."

Kirsten felt the night's grainy quality deep in her bones. "You'll put a bodyguard on me?"

"Of course. But it is too late now, yes?"

"I hope so."

"Describe this man again, please."

"I didn't see anything except his sleeve and two gloved hands." And the knife. She shuddered at the taste and the scent of him. "He wore a heavy coat of some rough weave. He was much taller than me, and very strong. He sounded American."

He showed doubt. "It is unlikely that a German woman would bring in talent from outside the country."

"American," Kirsten insisted. "And he wore the most awful cologne I've ever smelled."

He made careful notes. "You did well, Ms. Stansted."

She stood and reached for her purse, then winced as the motion pulled upon her cut. "I need to get some sleep."

"And tomorrow?"

"I'm booked on a midday flight to New York. But first I want to have a word with Erin Brandt." She traced her hand along the bandage, wishing there were some way other than drugs to take the edge off the pain. "And I want you to make sure she is good and ready when I get there. Her and that insect of a manager."

The detective took careful measure of her. "Tell me what you want doing."

CHAPTER

29

THE MORNING'S PAPERS were flung about Erin Brandt's front parlor. A very private tornado had entered this room and torn the calm to shreds. Reiner watched Erin stride to the front window once again. This was what his career had come to. Twenty-nine years of clawing his way to the top, axing the competition, and kowtowing to a multitude of egos, so that he could sit in Erin Brandt's front parlor and watch her come undone.

"Why are they staking out my house?"

The previous night he had finally done the unthinkable and confessed to his wife that she had been right all along. Taking on Erin Brandt had been the worst mistake of his entire career. He had said this not to grant his wife immense satisfaction, which it most certainly had. He needed answers. He was at the end of his rope, dangling over a precipice, millimeters away from the fall that would send his career crashing upon the rocks. His wife had no answer save a scream very much like the one he was hearing now.

"I asked you a question!"

"They have staked out my house as well."

"Did I ask for information about your health and well-being?" Erin struck the window so hard it was a wonder the glass did not break. "I want to know what you are going to do about that man!"

He walked over to join her by the window, wondering how many other fingers had itched to wring that alabaster neck. "Is that him there?"

"Are you intent on being perversely dense this morning? How

many hulking strangers do you see outside my door? Of course that's him!" She stamped her foot. "I want him *gone!*"

Reiner returned to the sofa, distancing himself from the impending cyclone. "Erin, I forbid you to go to New York."

She tore her attention away from the window. "What?"

Reiner gave himself time for a long look. He took in the imperious chin, the power that defied her diminutive form. The regal bearing that translated so forcefully to the stage. He had gained much from this connection. But lost far more. Gradually his other top singers had grown resentful of playing second fiddle to Erin's star. For three years now Erin had been his only client. A disastrous state of affairs. "You can't possibly go to New York."

"Can't I."

"You've lost your case in North Carolina. They can *arrest* you. The lawyer said traveling to America at this point would be insane."

She treaded across the Chinese silk carpet, alighted upon the sofa next to him, and took his hand. "Shall I tell you what is insane?"

Reiner fought against the urge to rip his hand away. He knew that soft, melodious voice. It was the viper's hiss. "Please, Erin, I'm thinking only of your welfare."

"Oh, I know all too well how you look after me." She stroked the veins running down the back of his hand. "For example, I know about the secret accounts."

"I . . . What?"

She took hold of the flesh between his thumb and forefinger and pressed delicately. "The accounts, dear Reiner. The ones where you slip in the extra five percent of my earnings. Above the ten percent written into our contract."

She gripped more tightly now, searching for a hold on his racing pulse. "Not to mention the percentage you add to everything you acquire for me. This house, for example. How much was your secret take on this? A hundred thousand?" She used her fingernails to clench the sensitive flesh. "Two? Four?"

"Erin, please, you're hurting—"

"Now I shall tell you what you are going to do." As she gave her instructions, she continued to tighten her pincher hold, until he could feel her talons actually join together. "Is that all clear?"

He gasped, "Perfectly."

"I'm so glad." She released him and rose to her feet. "Now if you'll excuse me, I must go see to my packing. Goscha has been of no help whatsoever since the child departed."

Reiner stared at his hand. The raw quarter moons bled softly and ached as though he had been branded. His gut churned so that the words emerged as a plaintive moan. "Why did you bring the child back at all?"

"That is not your concern." She swept open the doors like a queen taking her leave. "Your concern is making safe my journey to New York."

―――――――

Kirsten exited the hotel in the company of an extremely vigilant detective. Traffic thundered and the trolleys clanged metallic music as they walked toward the river. Overhead the sky had darkened to a gunmetal hue. The city's muted pastels and prismatic grays were now matched on all sides. A chilly yet harmonious order hemmed in this very German world. Only the trees and flowers shouted defiant accolades to a summer now lost.

The Schwanenspiegel lakes and their whimsical bridges were as colorless as the sky. When they approached the line of houses on the lakes' other side, the detective pointed her toward a jewel box of a house in powder-puff blue. A cupola adorned the upper floor, opening into double French doors and a tiny balcony painted a very feminine ivory.

As they started across the street, the detective made a sharp drumming sound deep in his throat and veered off to their right. Kirsten hesitated, feeling very exposed. The detective aimed straight toward a watcher who had suddenly appeared beside a Mercedes van. The observer was caught off guard, and momentarily debated the wisdom of flight. But the detective was too swift. He gripped the man by his lapels and roared an extremely German invective.

A woman Kirsten had not noticed before raced across the bridge they had just crossed and tried to move in between the two men, both of whom were now shouting. Kirsten's detective shoved the woman so hard she bounced off the Mercedes and sprawled on the pavement. She scrambled to her feet and added her own shrill cries.

A voice behind Kirsten demanded, "How *dare* you show your face at my house."

She turned to confront an irate Erin Brandt. Her manager hovered in the background, three suitcases at his feet. Kirsten told them both, "I just wanted to make sure you realized your attack didn't succeed."

Erin showed bitter amusement. "My attack? Darling, you vastly overestimate your importance."

Kirsten switched her attention to the manager. From behind his electric blue spectacles, gray eyes shot venom her way. "Your lackey, then. It doesn't matter. You both failed."

"Oh, so someone else is after you? How utterly comforting." Erin fingered the diamond pendant draped about her neck. "Is this a gift, how you manage to create enemies in every new town? Does the grass also wilt beneath your tread?"

Kirsten gestured at the suitcases. "When is your flight to New York?"

The manager sucked in his breath, but Erin merely smirked her response. "You and your meddling lawyer are in for a great astonishment."

Reiner protested softly. "Erin."

The diva ignored him. "You think me helpless? You assume you can waltz into my world and attack me at will?" She noticed the bandage on Kirsten's neck, and lifted her smile until she revealed small perfect teeth. "You think I am without friends? Without power?"

"Erin, enough."

"You have been neutralized, my dear. Phone your darling little lawyer. Hear what he has to say." She glanced over to where the three detectives were exchanging a few parting words. "While you're at it, call off your toothless dogs."

As they started away, Kirsten called after them, "Where did you hide the child?"

Erin hesitated, but was drawn forward by a hiss from her manager. Kirsten raised her voice. "I'll find her, you know."

The diva was kept from turning back by the manager reaching over and gripping her arm.

Kirsten watched the pair slip into a new Mercedes sedan and drive away.

The detective appeared at her elbow. "We should move away from here."

"Just a minute."

He reached for her. "It is far too exposed."

She shook her arm free. "Wait."

The minutes ticked by, until Kirsten thought she might have been mistaken. Finally Erin's front door clicked open and a fearful gray head peeked through. "The madame, she is gone?"

"Yes."

Apprehensively Goscha crept outside. She began rubbing the brass banister with a cleaning rag and spoke without looking directly at Kirsten. "She has said nothing more about the child."

Kirsten made no move to approach any closer. "Where is she staying in New York?"

"The Plaza. Always the Plaza."

Kirsten turned to the detective. "Give me one of your cards." She took it and started toward the front steps. Goscha watched with fearful eyes but did not retreat. Kirsten slipped the card into her apron pocket. "If you find out anything more, call this man."

CHAPTER

3 0

T HE DETECTIVE DROVE HER to the airport. He accompanied her to the check-in counter, a gray-suited appendage attached to her left shoulder. As she checked her bag and received her boarding pass, he draped one casual hand upon the counter and leaned in close. The professional bodyguard doing his best, even if it was a day late.

She turned from the counter and offered her hand. "Thank you for everything."

His grip was cool, small, and tungsten hard. "I should have been there last night."

There was nothing to be gained by agreeing. "You will fax me any further information?"

"There is little to go on, unless the housekeeper discovers where they took the baby."

Kirsten headed for the customs barrier. The airport's ultramodern interior was softened by a brilliant sunset. The clouds had parted sufficiently for all the colors of heaven to escape, reflected inside the hall by marble and steel. Kirsten passed one of the multifloored openings that transformed the airport's upper tiers into giant balconies. Only when she smelled the downstairs restaurants did she realize she had eaten nothing since the previous evening.

The airport elevators were glass pillars that appeared to support the upper tiers. She watched a flock of pigeons wheel above the sweeping expanse of glass overhead, then stepped into the elevator.

And smelled the man.

It was the same odor as the previous night, a repulsive blend of body odor and oily spice, like a hair pomade from the last century. Kirsten gripped the steel balustrade. The glass cage trapped her utterly.

The descent took long enough for a thousand gasping breaths. As the lower floor arrived, Kirsten unclenched her grip on the railing enough to turn and scout in all directions. The restaurant alcove was off to her left. Arrivals and baggage claim to her right. Directly ahead were the rental car and limo booths. People strolled and chatted. She saw no one who might be the menace in tweed. Yet he was here. There was no doubt whatsoever.

She exited the elevator sensing two forces at direct conflict within herself. She wanted to flee, to turn away from the terrors and the trouble, just as she had done all her life. To look for the safe corner, to hide and never show herself to whatever new evil was stalking her. But there was a new sensation as well. One that defied the fear and the stalker both.

A pair of middle-aged gentlemen were walking toward her, dressed in high German fashion, giving her the eye. For once she did not turn away from them either. Instead she flashed her most winning smile and said, "This is just an amazing place, isn't it."

They both showed surprised delight. The taller one said, "You are American?"

"I most certainly am." She sidled in close beside him. "I used to model here, but I haven't been back since they opened this place."

The other man inquired, "*Eine Modelle?*"

"*Natürlich.*" The younger man said to Kirsten, "My friend, he speaks no English, I am happy to say. Please, you will take a glass of *Sekt?*"

"I would love one." She allowed herself to be guided over and seated at the long restaurant bar, one man to either side. She smiled at their comments, spoke a few words, and scouted.

She was about to rise and head back upstairs when she spotted him.

The man wore a bulky navy jacket. One far too heavy for the cool German afternoon. A baseball cap was pulled down so far as to mask his entire face. He leaned over the third-tier balcony and stared straight down at her. When she looked up, he drew back. But not fast enough.

Kirsten rose from her seat, flashing the smile perfected before a thousand cameras. "This has been just lovely."

"But you have not touched your *Sekt*."

She slid the glass over in front of the man who spoke no English. "Why don't we let your friend finish it, and you walk me to the departure lounge?"

"By all means." The man insisted on toting her carry-on, which left her with a hand free, which she draped over his elbow. The man moved in closer than the detective and announced, "I am Joachim."

"Kirsten."

"You will be returning often?"

"You never can tell." She found herself unable to step back inside the elevator, even with the man standing beside her. "How about if we take the escalator?"

By then the man would have trekked the Gobi for her. "Whichever is slower."

She spotted the watcher again midway up the stairs, a swiftly moving blur in blue. There was still nothing to be seen of his face. He kept his hands in his pockets and his shoulders hunched such that nothing was visible save the tip of his nose and the brim of his cap. Though he did not glance her way she felt his eyes drift over her, leaving blisters and clammy skin. He was one tier lower now, directly above the customs barrier, walking from left to right. Just another stranger on the move.

She realized the man beside her had halted in his monologue and was looking at her, waiting for a response. She said the first word that came into her head. "Certainly."

He gave an utterly boyish grin. "Most excellent."

When they stepped off the escalator, he shifted her carry-on to his other shoulder, and found great delight in how she refused to release his arm. "Please, you will take my card and you will call me the minute you know when you are next coming to Düsseldorf."

"We better hurry, I've just heard them call my flight."

"This is as far as I can go, I fear. Only ticketed passengers can cross through customs." He gave a stiff-backed bow and kissed her hand. "Such a pleasure you cannot imagine."

She took back her hand and her carry-on, gave her passport to the customs official, then returned the man's wave. Her last glimpse was of the stalker, slipping past on her own floor now, not even looking her way. She carried his odor to the plane.

CHAPTER

31

THE FRIDAY MORNING PAPER had Omar Dell's byline on the front page. His article took a very hard stance against Dale Steadman's firing and the company's immediate rollback of Dale's changes. Marcus stopped reading when he came to his own name. He dressed and headed out just as Deacon's paint-spattered truck pulled into the drive. Today he managed a wave, nothing more.

Dale's corporate apartment was located outside the neighboring village of Louisburg. His was an end unit with views over windswept lakes. Two dozen baby goslings scattered at Marcus' approach, moving like ungainly fluffballs while their nannies raised long necks and marked his passage.

Steadman met him at the door with a pair of folded shirts in one hand and no sign of welcome. "I was packing."

"Need a hand?"

"No, and I'm still sober. Which is why you stopped by, isn't it?" But he stepped away from the door, permitting Marcus entry. The apartment was large and sunlit and sterile. Dale returned to the trio of half-packed cases sprawled over the sofas. "Coffee's old but hot."

"I'm fine, thanks." Marcus shut the door behind him. "Actually, I'm on my way to court to formally request a warrant be served when Erin arrives in New York."

"Last night I received a call from Erin's manager. The concert is Tuesday night. She's agreed to come down Monday after the final rehearsal. But only if we don't hassle her."

"She's coming to North Carolina?"

Dale caught Marcus' skepticism. "You told me yourself, this case won't bring Celeste home."

"An arrest warrant is our best way of pressuring her." He realized Dale was not listening. "At least let me go ahead and file the paperwork."

"Do I need to come with you?"

"Not really. This is a formality handled in the judge's chambers."

"I'll skip it then." Dale dumped the shirts, then stood with hands dangling. "What do a pair of guys do when they don't drink?"

Marcus glanced at his watch. Just gone eight and the guy was thirsty. "They talk."

Steadman disappeared into the bedroom. He was gone so long Marcus finally rose and walked over. A cabinet drawer had been upended onto the bed. Dale stood over the pile, staring down at a framed picture. Marcus did not need to see what he inspected. There was a new corrugation to Dale's features, a settling into lines of such intensity Marcus felt the pain in his own gut. "You know about my own kids."

Steadman dropped the photograph facedown onto the bed, gave a single nod.

"It took me almost two years to unpack their photograph. You don't have to tell me a thing if you don't want to. But if you need to talk, I'm ready to listen."

The pain emerged further, creasing his features, wracking his voice. "Marcus, tell me what I'm supposed to do."

"One step at a time. It's the only thing that's ever worked for me." The man's loss was a fiercely bonding current. "Why don't you finish up here, and let's meet up for dinner at the Angus Barn. That sound okay?"

As he let himself out the front door, Dale was still standing there, staring at the back of the photograph.

———

When Marcus knocked on the door of Rachel Sears' chambers, the diminutive judge looked up and showed him genuine distaste. "What is it now?"

"I'm sorry, your honor. I just thought—"

A voice behind him called out, "You can't possibly be trying an end run around me and my client."

Marcus turned to find Hamper Caisse striding toward him. The lanky attorney declared, "You're gonna have to go a lot further than this to catch me napping."

Judge Sears aimed her ire at Hamper. "Would you happen to know where your client is today, Mr. Caisse?"

"I would indeed, your honor. On her way to New York." He cocked a thumb at Marcus. "Which is why he's sniffing around your chambers, hoping for a bone."

"I just wanted a slot on your sheet this morning to request a subpoena," Marcus corrected. "But I'll save the rest for court."

"No, you absolutely will not. Under no circumstances am I going to permit you two to wreak havoc with my schedule twice in one week." She raised her voice another notch. "Martha!"

A laconic voice called back, "She's gone down for your mail."

"See if you can borrow a court reporter from somewhere, please." She directed them into the seats opposite her desk. "Two minutes, Marcus. Two."

"Your honor, I learned yesterday evening that Erin Brandt is traveling to America. I wanted to request that you issue a warrant for her arrest. You have already found her in contempt." He spread his hands. "This should be a formality. I intend to serve the order in a New York court and request that they arrest her. That's it."

"Seems straightforward enough. Mr. Caisse?"

"There's *nothing* straightforward about this, your honor. Next week she sings in the gala charity event to aid children with cancer. My client was asked at the last minute to take the place of a star who's fallen ill. This is a function to which she is not only giving her time and her talents, but she is paying her way over. And she has agreed, your honor, to come down to North Carolina first thing Monday."

Marcus protested, "Your honor, I seriously doubt that this woman is ever going to show."

"May I remind you who we're talking about here. This is Erin Brandt's own child, your honor. Obviously it means the world to her."

"She," Marcus corrected.

"What?"

"The child. She's a little girl by the name of Celeste. Not an it."

Hamper dismissed him with an angry wave. "This is just the sort of tantrum you had to censure him over yesterday, your honor. You see what I have to deal with here?"

Judge Sears demanded, "You're telling me your client is actually going to show up this time?"

"She's not going to walk into this courthouse, your honor. She's going to run in. I'll stake my reputation on this."

"Your reputation," Marcus repeated.

"I spoke with her before she boarded the plane for New York, your honor. She's given me her word. And now I'm giving you my word. Come Monday, Erin Brandt will be here."

The ring was muffled by the clothes he had piled on the side table. Dale scrambled and unearthed the phone on the fifth ring. "Hello?"

"Is this Dale Steadman?"

"That's right."

"Mr. Steadman, this is Cheryl Sampers at Lincoln Center. How are you today?"

The woman was pure New York art world—brisk, pressing, and with a nasal Bryn Mawr superiority. "Fine."

"I was asked to call and pass on a message from Ms. Erin Brandt."

"Why isn't she capable of phoning me herself?"

The woman did not care for his tone. "I didn't speak with her personally, but I imagine it's because they're running late. The rehearsals were held up because of some work they had to do on the stage. Ms. Brandt asks if you can come up to New York."

"You've got to be kidding."

"That's what the message says. I was to call and ask if you could please fly to New York today. On the next available flight. Ms. Brandt needs to speak with you urgently, but will be unable to make the journey to North Carolina because of changes to the rehearsals. And she's been invited to sing next week in Paris so she can't come down after the benefit."

"Of course not."

"Ms. Brandt went to the trouble to check on the flight schedule. There's a plane leaving in about an hour and she asks if you can possibly make it. If so, I'm to arrange for a limo to pick you up at the airport and bring you straight here."

Dale knew Marcus would forbid him to do this. The whole thing stank of Erin's maneuverings. But the court case would not bring his baby home. He could see it on everyone's faces, smell it in the air. They were all just going through the motions, dancing to a legal tune that satisfied no one.

"Sir? Mr. Steadman?"

Dale felt burdened by years of unexpected blows. "Give me the travel details."

When the phone rang, Kirsten had no idea where she was, or why the noise would not stop. Or why, when she began fumbling, the phone was on the wrong side of the bed. "Yes?"

"Hi."

When Kirsten rolled over in bed, it felt as though her brain spun in the other direction. "Marcus?"

"You were asleep. I'm sorry."

"What time is it?"

"Almost five."

She could not get her mind to work. Everything was dark, save for a perpendicular line of light at one end of the room and a horizontal one at the other. "Which five is that?"

"Five o'clock Friday afternoon." His voice held a hint of laughter now. "You sound absolutely delightful when you're sleepy."

"I feel like I was in a coma." Kirsten slid her feet to the floor. "How did you get this number?"

"You called me."

"I did?"

"When you got in. You said you were very tired."

"I don't remember a thing."

"Did you have a rough flight?"

"Crowded. A baby cried the whole way. Just a minute." She walked to the window and swept back the curtains. Her room was low down within the city's caverns, so her only sunlight was reflected off the building opposite. Traffic noise invaded with the light. As she walked back over she recalled that she had dreamed of sirens and horns all night. "I'm back."

"Should I call you later?"

"No. I need to get started."

"Actually, you don't. I've just come back from court. Her lawyer claims Erin has promised to come down Monday."

"To Raleigh?"

"That's what she said."

She needed to be awake for this. She scrubbed her head, willing the blood to start flowing to her brain again. "She won't come."

"No. I don't think she will."

"It's wrong to stop this. We've got momentum. She's worried." When Marcus said nothing, she added, "I know all about keeping secrets from the world. You never bother to hide strengths."

"What are you saying?"

"You hide weaknesses. You hide things you're terrified might be discovered."

Again he was silent. Only this time she realized what it was she had said. It turned her voice feeble as she finished, "I think I should keep looking."

But Marcus was not ready to let it go. "I'll never press you, Kirsten."

"You do, though. You push me harder than anything has in my entire life."

As usual, he understood her all too well. "I'll never stop loving you. Never."

It was not the words which finally awoke her, but the burning. Her eyes, her chest, her throat, the pit of her stomach, all were caught by a web of constricting flames. "I don't think we should stop pressing her, Marcus."

He released a long breath. "I'll speak with Dale tonight and see if he'll agree to let you keep nosing around."

CHAPTER

3 2

D ALE WAITED UNTIL the plane was descending into New York's La
Guardia airport to call Marcus' office, which as hoped was
unmanned. He left a terse message and hung up, glad to avoid that
encounter.

Inside La Guardia's baggage claim, Dale ID'd the driver with his
name on the sign, let him take his bag, and headed straight for the limo
stand by the southeast entrance. Five minutes into the journey, he was
already impatient to depart. Despite all the time he had spent in New
York, he had never carved out a sense of identity here. Dale had partially adapted by segmenting the place and focusing upon a parcel
small enough to claim as his own. People said the upper east side possessed a more neighborhood feel. His initial forays had suggested nothing but cafés and frou-frou boutiques and young people talking nasal
English so fast he could not understand them. His own patch ran from
Saks in the south to Lincoln Center in the north and the river to the
west. Even crossing 65th Street on his morning jogs in Central Park left
him feeling as though he had entered the unknown.

His thoughts flickered with the sunlight lancing between the compressed buildings. He recalled the night Erin had told him she was
pregnant. His response had been automatic; why not marry and make
a second home in Wilmington? Dale could not say which of her assents
had astonished him more.

Almost immediately had come signs that things would not work
out. Her insistence on a secret ceremony at the city registry had been
bitterly disappointing. He had wanted the world to know of his joy;

she had sought no publicity at all. Then there had come the planning of their home. On the good days she would sit in his lap or curl up at his feet while he described his plans for her music room and the adjoining thousand-square-foot bayside parlor. The two chambers were interconnected by massive hand-carved sliding doors, in hopes she would give at-home performances. The walls that were not glass had paneling of African rosewood, the same wood used throughout the Met's auditorium and reputedly the finest acoustic material in the world. Handworked baffles decorated the seventeen-foot-high ceilings. A Bösendorfer grand dominated the music room, with a professional sound system climbing the back wall. Only the finest was good enough for Erin. This was to be her palatial retreat from the rigors of stardom's road. Yet whenever he tried to share his dream with Erin, she showed a complaisant surprise over his passion. Are you always so focused, so driven, she asked time and again. As though only in such moments did she even bother to notice.

Then Celeste had been born. And his world had been canted on its axis by the discovery that he could love anything more than Erin.

The day they had come home from the hospital, there had been a vital sign so poignant not even Dale in his stupefying overdose of ardor could ignore it. The hospital had refused to release either mother or child until the baby had been named and registered on the birth certificate. Erin had been seated in her wheelchair, still weak from the sixteen-hour delivery. She had turned her face away from his quiet entreaties to help name their child. So Dale had told the hospital staffer to write down the name Celeste, for his two stars.

Now, as the limo turned off Columbus onto the raised Lincoln Center drive, Dale sought to convince himself that it was a sign of age and faulty memory that he could never recall hearing Erin refer to her daughter by name.

Lincoln Center contained seven buildings housing twelve theaters, making it the largest artistic complex in the world. From where he exited the limo, the Met rose directly beyond the plaza's central fountain, with the City Opera to his left and Avery Fisher Hall to his right. In the right rear corner, beyond the smaller building housing the two nonorchestral theaters, stood the footbridge spanning the subterranean cavern of 65th Street. On its other side rose the Juilliard School of Music and two further halls for small symphonic and chamber concerts. Workers were busy hauling up a new banner that stretched

the entire way across the front of Avery Fisher Hall, proclaiming that
Erin Brandt would star in the benefit concert for the children's cancer
hospital that Tuesday.

To Dale's mind, Lincoln Center represented the nadir of postmod-
ern architecture—designed with too much flair, refashioned by committee, underfinanced with city money. In the daylight the resulting
structural breaches and architectural mistakes were all too evident. At
night, however, the tall glass walls gave off their magnetic glow. The
chandeliers radiated like giant diamond pendants. A train of limos
pulled into the long drive off Broadway and emitted a constant stream
of fine garb and gab. The central fountain splashed a rainbow, the jewels glinted and shone, the excitement was a feast shared by all. Everything worked to extend the performance's magic beyond the stage.

Dale debated momentarily whether to try the stage entrance. Security at Lincoln Center was notoriously tight. Even in their best times
Erin had regularly forgotten to leave his name with the guard. But if
possible he would prefer not to have any public discussion with Erin.
She played to whichever audience was around. It was in her genes.

Dale paused long enough for a glance at the Met, his favorite
opera house in all the world. Through the front wall of pillared glass
he could make out the two Chagall hangings and the starburst chandeliers of Bohemian crystal. For months after Erin ran away to Paris, he
had tried to convince himself that things would have been different
had she only received the invitation she deserved. But the afternoon
light was too great, the summer heat too oppressive, and his interior
baggage too heavy to cart around such lies any longer.

He walked parallel to where Columbus and Broadway joined just
north of the center, then turned left and descended 65th Street's gentle
slope. He recognized the huge black guard doing sentry duty outside
the stage entrance, but could not remember his name. There was
clearly some recognition on the guard's part, for he nodded a greeting
and held open the door.

The white guard stationed behind the security desk looked planted
permanently in his seat, there so long his entire body had been pulled
down by gravity to puddle around his chair. "Help you?"

"I'm here to see Erin Brandt. But I don't know if she's signed
for me."

"Name?"

"Dale Steadman."

"Steadman. Sure, you're down. Ms. Brandt must've had them call you in from upstairs." He ticked the name off the sheet. "I have to have somebody show you up."

"No problem." Dale pointed to the loudspeaker from which he could hear his former wife singing. "Are they running late?"

"By almost two hours."

"Makes for a long day."

The guard shrugged. "We go time-and-a-half in exactly eleven minutes."

Dale waited while the guard signaled for an escort, then followed a harried young woman through the backstage maze. Formerly known as Philharmonic Hall, Avery Fisher Hall had been the first building to open and was by far the coldest and least imposing of the Lincoln Center structures. Low ceilings and massive pillars transformed the lobbies into a series of tight marble-lined cages. The foyer's soundburst sculpture had no real space from which it could be appreciated, and so looked more like bronze blades threatening to plummet at any moment.

The hall itself was functionally excellent yet aesthetically horrendous. The four levels and twenty-eight hundred seats had originally been decked out in royal blue plush, which looked fabulous but held the acoustic quality of a sealed coffin. Avery Fisher, the founder of Fisher Electronics, had redesigned the hall and paid for it himself. Like his world-famous speaker systems, the result was a minimum of fancy and a maximum of functionality.

Not even the New York Philharmonic, the oldest symphony orchestra in the United States, nor its roster of famous conductors which included Zubin Mehta, Kurt Masur, and Leonard Bernstein, could overcome the fact that Avery Fisher Hall resembled nothing so much as the interior of a kettledrum.

The backstage was a tangle of settings and wires and lighting. Entrance stage right was made between the chief pulley system for the fire curtain and the principal video monitors. As soon as he heard the first note, Dale understood how Erin could never have refused this chance to return. They were performing Puccini's *La Bohème*, a vastly popular work that had become Erin's signature piece since the pregnancy. The stage of Avery Fisher Hall was definitely not the Met. But it was still a vital part of Lincoln Center. She was coming in to save a gala charity event. The publicity would be enormous. It was one giant step closer to her goal.

The hall contained no orchestra pit, which meant she would be giving a concert performance—no theatrical backdrop, the singers and orchestra onstage together, the crowd there for the music alone. Dale arrived stage right just as Erin concluded the Abandonment aria in the third act. Her back was to him, and she sang to an almost empty hall. A group of children were assembled stage left. Most were in wheelchairs. Many bore the shaved heads and haunted features of recent chemo. Still more children filled the auditorium's first few rows. The aria was a tragic crescendo of potent sentimentality, and Erin sang with the alluring force that was all her own. Several of the children's faces were stained with tears. A pair of photographers moved about the aisles. It was a traumatic blow for Dale, seeing these hollow-faced children captivated by her spell.

At the aria's conclusion, the children broke into spontaneous applause. The conductor waited them out, then began reviewing last-minute changes with Erin and the musicians. Erin smiled for the children before turning toward the conductor. And spotted Dale.

She showed a bewilderment that under different circumstances would have been truly comic. "What are you doing here?"

"You called me."

"I most certainly did not."

"Your assistant, then."

Her incredulity gradually became a flush of genuine anger. "That is ridiculous."

"Then how do you explain my having a backstage pass waiting for me?"

"I don't need to explain anything!" All eyes were upon her as she crossed the stage toward him. "I told you I would come down Monday."

"And I was waiting at home for you to get there. Until your staffer called and said it was urgent I drop everything and fly up."

"This is absurd!"

"Oh, wait, let me guess." He knew his voice was rising, but no longer cared. "This is just another of your classic maneuvers."

Fire flashed within those dark eyes. She hissed at him, "Stop making a scene!"

"It won't work this time. I've spent years enduring your tantrums and your tactics. But not now. Not over Celeste." He jabbed his finger at her, wishing with all his might for the freedom to drive it right through the place where, in any normal person, a heart would be beating. "You've lied every step of the way. Everything I've done has been for the sake of Celeste. But you've done nothing except use our baby girl like a pawn. It's enough, Erin. It's too much. It's over."

"This isn't the time or the place!"

"Yes it is! You're going to answer me now!"

"Answer you? You want me to answer you?" Her control slipped away. The observers no longer mattered, the fury would not be denied. In the space of two heartbeats she aged twenty years. "You want the world to hear how you're the one responsible for all this?"

"Forget what I told Reiner. The deal is off. My lawyer is going to have you arrested."

"Arrest *me?*" Her shrieking laughter filled the entire stage. "Am I the one who got so blind drunk he set his own house on fire and almost murdered his own wife and child?"

"That's not true and you know it."

"I wouldn't have had to do any of this if you weren't a drunk and a brute! There's only one person to blame for all this. You've threatened me and you've bullied me and now I'm the one saying it's over!"

"This isn't about you, Erin! It's about—"

"No! It's about *you!*" She backed a step away. "You're just trying to get at me again! You want to destroy me, and I won't let it happen!"

He took a step toward her, saw the triumph flare in her features, and knew he'd been duped.

She confirmed it by lifting her voice even louder now, singing for the rafters and the farthest tier. "Keep away! Don't hurt me again!"

He froze, trapped by the realization he had become just another prop for her to use and destroy. "You know I've never laid a hand on you. Never."

"You don't control me anymore! *I'm* in control now. The days when you could abuse me are gone!" She stomped to where two gaping stagehands held open the rear doors, then spun about and shrilled, "You need counseling! You need serious help and you need it *now!*"

As she took her exit to awestruck acclaim, he shouted, "I want my baby girl!"

She could never let her supporting cast have the final note. "You country fool!" Her disembodied laughter shrieked overhead. "Whose child did you say?"

CHAPTER

3 3

For Kirsten, New York was a desert of the soul. Memories of earlier times rose unbidden, taunting her with the hollow knowledge of circular mistakes. She slept as much as she could, only to wake from dreams of gaily laughing skulls and streets filled with death dances and shrill dirges. She dressed and walked to Seventh Avenue and had an afternoon breakfast at the Stage Deli. She walked down Madison and up Fifth, staring at shops with the names of her former world. Passersby showed the viper's habit of seeking prey even while gorged.

She walked until she was hopefully tired enough to sleep once more. She returned to the hotel and decided to try Marcus first on his home phone. To her surprise, Fay answered the phone. "How you keeping, honey?"

"Fine. Where's Marcus?"

"Off doing man things, I 'spect. Where are you?"

"New York. Isn't it a little late for you to be over cleaning?"

"Deacon felt like one or the other of us ought to keep an eye on him and the place."

"What's the matter?"

"Nothing, so far as we know. But things are heating up, that's for certain."

"Is Marcus in danger?"

"Honey, there's danger in breathing. But 'round here he's safe as anybody can be. We've got a lotsa years behind us, learning how to deal with folks wanting to mess up our neighborhood. Now what about you?"

"I'm still here."

She huffed softly. "Child, what I said the other day, it wasn't 'cause I wanted answers. I just wanted to know if you were asking these questions yourself."

"I am now. I can't stop." Once more, the air seemed to compress about her. "Just tell Marcus I called."

The Angus Barn was a bastion of Old Raleigh, stationed off Highway 70 in what once had been rolling pastureland. Now the only remaining old forest belonged to Umstead Park. To its south encroached industrial parkland and the Raleigh-Durham Airport. North and east and west was just more residential sprawl. When it was first built, the Angus Barn was as close as Raleigh came to big-city cuisine, with steaks known statewide for quality and size. Nowadays its patrons sought a semi-clubby atmosphere where families let kids run about the plank flooring, the adults visited from table to table, and locals pretended their little hometown had never grown into the stranger it now was.

As Marcus stood in the doorway waiting for Dale, he spotted Rachel Sears leading a very young rendition of herself out of the restaurant. The diminutive judge was dressed in cream and lavender. "Debbie, can you say hello to Mr. Glenwood?"

While the child possessed her mother's intense gaze, her eyes were still unafflicted. "Are you another lousy lawyer?"

"Debbie, shush."

"I sure am."

"Mommy doesn't like you."

"Marcus is one of the good ones, honey." The judge's glance became scathing. "Most of the time."

"I can't tell you how sorry I am."

"Shame on you." She held to a musical tone for her daughter's sake. "Putting me in a position where I had to search for some way not to give in to that man."

"I know."

She lifted her daughter up to where Debbie's face nestled in close to her own. "Are you meeting someone?"

"Dale Steadman. He's late."

"It wouldn't be proper for me to wait around and greet him." She waved to where her husband was extricating himself from a table full of good old boys on a steak and scotch binge. She swept her hair back in a practiced manner, and seemed perplexed as to what to say. "I hope you have a nice evening."

Marcus nodded a hello to her husband and decided he had no choice but to venture a single comment. "Something tells me we're not seeing the full story in this case."

She took her husband's arm, then showed Marcus the first hint of approval since their confrontation. "Maybe that's why I'm glad you're still on the job."

Marcus stepped to the porch's far end, drew out his cell phone, and checked for messages. There were none. He then called his home, intending to do the same. Fay answered his phone with "Glenwood residence."

"Have you been there all day?"

"The boys spelled me for a while. Why didn't you let Deacon come with you, you had somewhere to go after dark?"

"Go home, Fay. I'm fine. The house will be fine."

"Time you understood something, Marcus. You can't handle all things life sends your way alone."

"I realize that."

"Nosir, you do not. You shape the words with your mouth all right. But you don't swallow them down. You don't want anybody to hear you say the words, I need something."

"Has anybody called?"

"Kirsten did a while back. And you ain't getting off so easy. You ever think maybe you ought to let her hear you say those words?"

"She knows I need her."

"Sure she does. But you still got to let her hear you say it yourself. Know why? Cause till that happens, you'll always be able to class her wisdom as a little something extra, 'stead of making all the difference in the world."

He turned from a jolly crowd entering the restaurant. "Nobody else called?"

Fay gave a dissatisfied harrumph over his response. "Your business phone rang a while back. But I didn't bother with it."

"Thank you, Fay. Now please go home."

She hung up on him. Marcus cradled the phone to his chest, staring out at the muggy dusk. Traffic roared up and down the Durham highway, oblivious to the fact that the old black woman had managed to rock his world yet again.

He dialed his office phone and coded in the voice mail instructions. He listened to Dale announce his arrival in New York, then hung up. His hands dropped to his side. He stared at the sunset-drenched horizon, and said quietly, "Something is very wrong here."

CHAPTER

34

NORMALLY ERIN FED OFF TENSION. Early in her career she had learned to channel all energy, particularly the negative and disharmonious, into a greater brilliance upon the stage. It was a secret seldom mentioned and never shared, that lights and the camera's eye feasted upon whatever created a greater craving in the viewer. For Erin, calamity was merely more fuel for the fire. But this only worked when she was in control.

She made an utter mess of removing her makeup. Nor could she call someone else. The makeup woman was a typical New York hag, all greedy eyes and gossiping tongue, who would dearly love to know Erin could not stop her hands from shaking or her chest from heaving tight little gasps. The gown's cloth hooks drove her borderline insane before she finally gripped the two top edges and ripped them all out. Erin swiped away the worst of the smeared eyeliner, then donned her Yves St. Laurent day dress and her Hermès overwrap and heels. She checked her reflection and gave her lips another quick jab, brushed some fury out of her hair, and faced the door as she would an adversary.

"I am a star," she quietly declared. And she knew it was so.

The backstage area was a rat's warren, ill designed and windowless. All the Lincoln Center nonpublic areas were a horror. Water seeped down cracked walls and puddled around live wires. Wallpaper draped like last year's marquees. The buildings showed their crumbling flaws nowhere so well as backstage.

Where the dressing rooms joined with the main hall leading to the guard and the stage exit, Erin faltered. What if Dale was still waiting for her outside the main stage door? There in front of the fans waiting to beg for a moment of the diva's time, with the photographers and the tourists and the reporters, all eager to see the disastrous second act— she couldn't face him. Not like that.

Eyes were on her now, she could feel them like snakes coiling to strike. Thankfully, she had taken time to charm the young guard manning the stage-door booth. Erin flipped the silk shawl higher upon her frame like a countess arranging her cloak. The guard watched her with the careful gaze of one who knew Erin Brandt had her moods, and that he should speak only when she addressed him first. Then he noticed her smile and rose to his feet. It was good to know the magic worked, even in her present wounded state.

"Ms. Brandt, how are you today?"

She recalled his name at the last possible moment. "Greg, you're looking positively delicious."

He grinned and hitched the heavy gun belt all the guards wore. Greg's smile broadened to where he showed every stained tooth. "Thanks, ma'am."

"And that Southern gallantry, why, I don't know if I can control my baser instincts." She leaned over the panel so that he could catch a whiff of her perfume, a concoction made specially for her by an Oriental spice merchant off the Rue St. Honoré. "Would you do me a great kindness?"

"Anything, Ms. Brandt."

"I don't feel able to meet the public today."

He was already raising his walkie-talkie to his lips. "Jimmy, you think you could step inside for a sec?"

Avery Fisher Hall's stage door opened directly onto 65th Street. For dress rehearsals and major performances, a guard the size of an industrial refrigerator was stationed outside. Jimmy had to bend over to make it through the door. "What you need?"

"Ms. Brandt wants a hand to the side door. You mind taking over here for a second?"

"No problem." All the guards came to know the quirks and fancies of the major stars. Erin Brandt had a rep for showing little patience to the fans and would-be singers who collected around the back entrance. "You got a car coming today, ma'am?"

She hesitated. This was something Reiner would have seen to. But Reiner was still in Germany. "I'm not sure."

"No problem. I saw a couple of limos cruising out front, I'll call one around."

She could have kissed the man. Really. "Thank you so much."

Greg shifted his bulk out of the tight guard chamber and walked to the steel side door. He used his guard's passkey to unlock the door, and held it open. "Right this way, Ms. Brandt."

Greg scuttled ahead to the end of a drab concrete hallway and opened the second connecting door. This joined to the hall's side entrance. Greg then held open one of the glass doors connecting to the underground parking lot. The lane made a tight U around the bank of backstage service elevators and exited just before where 65th Street met Columbus Avenue. On this late July afternoon, the hot air held an astringent stench. Erin could not help but glance over to the Met's main stage entrance. She felt her features draw back in bitter wrath. *That* was where she should be. It should be *her* full-length photograph staring loftily down from the long hall leading to the guard's station. This should be *her* era.

Her bitter reverie was interrupted by someone calling, "Ms. Brandt?"

The driver was a stranger, not uncommon in a city where the limo listings took over ten pages of the phone book. He was standing along-side a new-style town car, which she particularly detested. "Yes?"

He opened the rear door. "I was sent to collect you."

The guard took a step forward. "Do I know you, man?"

The driver was an odd-looking character, even for this town of bestial abnormalities. His red hair descended in a gradual slant to almost meet his eyebrows, leaving the impression that his frontal lobe had been compressed into apelike proportions. He raised both hands, bunching his dark coat around shoulders like knotted melons. "I just go where I'm ordered. My call sheet says this car's been laid on for a Ms. Brandt."

Suddenly all she wanted was away. "It's all right, Greg."

"Jimmy was gonna call somebody around from the front."

Which would be just another stranger, and one she would have to pay herself. Another item on her much-loathed list. "This man is already here. I may as well go now." And if she waited Dale might find her and make another scene.

Greg hovered alongside until she was in the wash of air-conditioned air. This was New York. Lincoln Center guards were uniformed, alert, and everywhere. Which was why she was not particularly worried about the redheaded man shifting himself behind the wheel. Even when she caught a whiff of his scent, which was atrocious. "Who sent you?"

"City Services, ma'am."

"I meant who ordered you to pick me up."

He halted by the exit onto 65th and checked his clipboard. "All I got here is the place, the name, and the time."

"Never mind." She relaxed into the black leather seat, and was instantly enveloped by the smell of cold ashes. Another reason why she hated these American limos. Cigarette smoke clung to them for centuries. And the man's odor really was too much. He smelled like one of those grease-laden men who populated the waterfront bars back in Wilmington, blind to any turn the world might have taken since rockers all wore white socks. "Take me to the Plaza."

But the driver continued one block farther toward the park, then halted by an entrance to another parking garage.

"Where . . ."

Her unformed question was answered by the rear door pulling open. An all too familiar face leaned over and said, "Going my way?"

"Not you. And especially not now."

"This won't take long." He slipped into the seat beside her. "Drive."

She slid as far from him as she could. "You really are detestable. If you had any idea how difficult a day I've had, you wouldn't dare disturb me."

"*Your* day is difficult?" His laugh had deteriorated more than any other external component. He still managed to hold on to his looks and his power and his rage. She had always found his wrath most appealing, particularly when she could harness and exploit it. But his laugh sounded like something unearthed from a very old grave. "My dear, this is just too rich."

Instead of turning onto Central Park West, the driver powered through the light and entered the park on the 65th Street transverse. Erin demanded, "Driver, stop this car."

In reply, he took the turn onto West Park Drive so hard the car rose up like a boat in heavy seas. Turning *away* from the Plaza and safety.

"Driver!"

"Save it, my dear." The man beside her propped his briefcase in his lap and flipped the catches. "He cares for you about as much as I do. Which of late is hardly at all."

The knife he drew out was long as a scimitar. She would have screamed, but all she could feed into her lungs were ashes and fear.

"I don't suppose you'd care to tell me where you've stowed the little darling."

She could not take her eyes from the blade. "You're insane."

"No, I thought not. My mistake to have waited on you this long." He laughed in a most peculiar manner, the phlegm-filled chuckle of one delighting in the morgue. "Never you mind. I shall find her. Of that you can be absolutely certain."

Erin aimed a high-heeled kick at his face. He batted it away and laughed again. When she tried a second kick, he shoved the blade into her thigh and snarled, "Come now, surely you can do better than that."

The pain was hardly as shocking as the sight of her blood and the ragged tear running from her right knee up into the bunched and crimson silk. She heard a small child's voice protest, "You've hurt me."

"Have I indeed." He jammed the blade through her middle, the thrust so savage she became pinned to the seat. Erin looked down to see her own life staining her dress and the haft and his hand.

He required both hands to heave the knife free. Her flesh gave way with a rude sucking sound.

Then the pain struck, a brutal incandescence that sent her writhing out of the seat and onto the limo's floor.

"Think of it this way." He leaned over her, the knife poised for yet another blow. "At least you shall miss the diva's inevitable decline."

CHAPTER

35

MARISHA'S FEET ACHED TERRIBLY. This was nothing new. Her feet and ankles hurt all the time. The doctor she visited last year said the bones were beginning to separate and she needed to lose weight and put both legs in casts for three months. The cartilage and ligaments needed to heal before they split completely, he had told Marisha, and at her age this would take time. She had thanked him and paid the nurse the seventy-five dollars and left. She might as well have given the money to her daughter. When the girl had been nine Marisha had carried her from Kiev to Prague and then on to the refugee camp in Vienna. Which of course was why her feet still hurt her today, the fact that they had walked the entire nine hundred miles. Only now her baby was seventeen and they no longer spoke to one another. For this she risked the border dogs and the wire and the guns? For her daughter to sleep until three and paint all the portions of her body that were not pierced and bring home stray dogs with spiked hair and sneers and the laughter of maniacs? If she had the journey to do over again, she would have remained in Lodz. Better to have starved or been beaten to death by the neo-Communists than see what has become of her precious baby girl.

Her feet did not bother her as much as the heat. The temperature had to be above forty degrees Celsius. She heard the newscaster speak of a hundred-plus Fahrenheit, but the numbers meant nothing to her. As did so much of this harsh new world and its blaring noise and idiotic habits. Violence and drugs and sex everywhere. No respect for the proper order of things. The Ukraine's neo-Communist leaders who had stolen power after the Soviet downfall were almost better. At least they tried to justify what they did. Here in America it was take and snort and eat and steal and grab and beat. They even ate their own language, spitting out the half-mangled remnants.

But none of that mattered now.

She had spent money this day like water. And why not? What difference did it make if they were cast into the street next month? She had dreamed of this moment for eight long years. Ever since the refugee camp in Austria, when the language class she was attending had distributed tattered copies of *Hello!* magazine. There on the cover was the diva Erin Brandt. Of course Marisha knew her diva's voice already. Her parents had been opera fanatics. Good people of passion and order. All the elements Marisha had been unable to pass on to her daughter. But today not even that mattered.

Marisha had followed Erin Brandt's career ever since her arrival in America. Nine scrapbooks contained every item she had ever come across. She had learned to use the library's computer so that she could track Erin's career in different countries. She had made friends with neighbors who could translate for her. Her daughter sneered at her interest and called it a sick obsession. But her neighbors were kind and helpful and understanding. It was just such a neighbor that read her the article about how Erin Brandt had been brought in at the last moment to sing.

In her excitement to meet Erin Brandt face to face, Marisha had not given thought to the heat. The flowers she carried for the star were wilting. There was little chance Erin Brandt would arrive for hours yet. Marisha decided to move into the shade. She left the Fisher Hall stage door and entered the doughnut-shaped tunnel beneath Lincoln Center Plaza. She walked with the swaying gait of a vessel fighting vicious crosscurrents. At nine o'clock in the morning, no one was about save a pair of guards lounging inside the air-conditioned basement foyer. They watched her limping progress with somnolent gazes. She mounted the curb as she did the stairs of the restaurant where she cleaned, heaving herself up. One of the guards leaning against the glass doorway said something and the other laughed. She could feel their careless gazes and knew they mocked her in the way of all barbarians. She walked farther into the cavernous parking area, expecting them to come outside and call her back. But it was too hot for them to move, and what damage could a fat old woman with an armful of flowers do?

Then she spotted the shipping crate.

The crate was three feet high and perhaps eight feet long and rested back behind the first Dumpster. The top and sides were stamped with the words "Property of New York Metropolitan Opera House." The odors were fiercer here, trapped by the windless morning. But the heat was less oppressive in the shade, and she was used to bad smells. She eased herself down onto the crate, and sighed with relief as the weight came off her aching feet.

She huffed with frustration when the lid fell off the front. It probably meant nothing, since the crate was resting here by the refuse bins. Marisha debated whether just to sit there awhile longer, but there was the risk that some bored guard would use it as an excuse to move her back into the light and the heat. Gingerly she set down her bouquet and eased herself off the crate.

She groaned as she leaned down for the lid, then groaned a second time when she saw what was inside.

Erin Brandt's face was far too serene for anything other than gentle repose. But the diva's frock was pushed up high upon her thighs and her cloak was bundled about her shoulders. And the crate's interior walls were stained with shadows that glistened in the dim lighting.

One hand was cast up and over the diva's head, reaching out to Marisha in wretched appeal.

Marisha permitted herself only a pair of sobbing moans. Even in this first instant she knew what was required. The world could not be permitted to gape at the diva in such an unkempt state.

She leaned into the crate and adjusted the dress. Marisha settled the diva's hands upon her chest, then draped the cloak over the sodden dress. Marisha fought to stifle her sobs. There would be time enough to weep when she had performed this service.

She pushed herself erect and reached for her bouquet. Marisha cast aside the wrappings and scattered flowers all over the corpse.

She remained there a moment longer, surveying her handiwork. Then she leaned over and kissed the diva's brow.

Marisha hobbled back toward the sunlight and the harsh exterior

world, blinded now by more than sunlight. She stopped by the glass
doors and wiped her face clean. One more task, then she could give
herself over to mourning.

She waited until the guard unlocked the glass door and pushed it
open. Then she announced, "An angel has fallen."

CHAPTER

36

Darren's patrol car was parked outside Marcus' house when he returned from his Saturday morning run. The deputy kept his distance as he completed a walk around Marcus' house, probably because he knew Marcus would have had something to say about the special treatment. Darren climbed back into his car and drove off without a word, leaving Marcus swamped by a gratitude that shamed him.

He showered and breakfasted and spent a comfortable fifteen minutes by his back porch, surveying the day in his mind. That afternoon he wanted to make a start clearing some of the rubbish and growth that stretched from the first line of trees back to a gravel path bordering his property.

The sound of squealing tires and a honking horn barely managed to dent the pattern of his thoughts. Somebody began shouting out front, but he was not quite ready to give up on the day's goodness just yet.

Then Deacon Wilbur came flying around the corner, legs churning and hands waving. "You gone completely deaf?" He raced over and made a desperate grab. "Come on, we've got to be moving!"

"What's the matter?"

"No time, no time!" He flung Marcus at the passenger door of his paint-spattered truck, climbed behind the wheel, and laid rubber the entire way back down the drive. The truck was a good thirty years old and took the dip where the drive met the road like an elephant on a ski jump. Marcus barely managed a saving clench on the dash and ceiling. The gears ground angrily before Deacon managed to find first.

"Take it easy!"

"You just hush up and let me concentrate!" Deacon's nose almost smacked the windshield when they crested the rise at the end of Marcus' road. Two boys playing kickball were so dumbfounded by the truck's flying appearance they scarcely made it out of the way. A trio of happy dogs shouted them down the street and through a four-wheel skid around the corner. Marcus kept a grim hold and decided his questions could wait.

The truck's original color was time-washed to a monochrome gray. When Deacon hit the highway headed east the speedometer needle maxed out at a quivering seventy-five. The engine roared as though it was ready to leap out from under the hood and eat them both whole.

Outside of town they raced over a hilltop and spotted a sheriff's car flying up from the opposite direction. Marcus felt pure relief over being saved from careening death, until Deacon began honking his horn and blinking his lights. The sheriff's car whoomed by them, made a controlled skidding turn, and raced up to where Deacon was shouldering the truck onto the verge.

The old preacher only started wheezing as he tottered toward Amos Culpepper. The sheriff called, "You gonna make it, Deacon?"

"Thought for a minute there I was sixteen again." The pastor huffed his way onto the rear fender and fanned himself with his shirttail. "Hateful thing to see a body age."

"Hop on in." Amos pointed Marcus into the passenger seat. When they were seated he cut on the siren, whoomed over to the passing lane, and cast Marcus an adrenaline grin. "Didn't wake up this morning expecting a high-velocity touch-and-go, did you?"

"What's going on?"

Amos shouted over the alarm and roaring engine, "This is strictly a good old boy kinda deal, you understand what I'm saying?"

"I shouldn't mention this to anybody," Marcus interpreted.

"Not unless you want me to lose my job." He shot a quick thumb back to where Deacon was gradually recovering. "That gentleman there must've heard about it from goodness only knows where. He told you. Then you called me and officially requested my help, which is why I'm involved at all."

"Right."

Amos shot by a truck going seventy as though the rig was hauled over and parked. "Good buddy of mine down on the Wilmington force called me with a strictly unofficial heads-up. Seems an NYPD boyo called him from the airport, asking could he supply Dale Steadman's home address. Your client must like his privacy, since he registered his home under a corporate name."

Having a professional behind the wheel was offset by the fact that their speed now topped a hundred and fifteen miles an hour. Marcus winced as they almost played bumper cars with an SUV whose rear window was completely blocked with children's toys. "A New York policeman?"

"Manhattan detective. An Italian-sounding name, you know the kind, enough vowels for a whole family." Amos released his double grip on the wheel long enough to fish in his pocket. "Hang on, I wrote the name down here."

Marcus read, "Lieutenant Aureolietti."

"My buddy knew about Dale Steadman running the company up here and all the legal goings-on. Told me the detective's got himself an arrest warrant."

"What's the charge?"

Amos granted him a lightning glance. "Murder one."

———

Near the Greenville airport's turnoff, Amos used the radio for a series of barked messages. As the engine was still bellowing and the tires screeching and siren screaming and the world was whipping by at something near ninety, Amos might as well have spoken in Martian. Which was why, when they pulled through the airport's emergency-access entrance and wheeled over to where a helicopter was already spinning up, Marcus was caught completely by surprise.

Amos cut off the engine and siren. "I sure hope you got a whole pile of the ready with you. Either that or a heat-resistant credit card."

Marcus was glad to find he had the strength to stand unaided. "I can't thank you enough."

"Always a pleasure to do the local community a service." Amos offered his hand. "Go out there and save the world, Marcus. It's what you're good at."

As they approached the revving chopper, Deacon grinned so broadly he revealed the gold embedded in his back teeth. "Always did want to have me a ride in one of them things!"

Amos hustled them over to the rear door, helped Deacon climb inside, then gave the pilot a thumbs-up.

Deacon's eyes grew steadily rounder as the blades began thundering overhead. When the pilot reared back on the stick, Marcus felt as though he had left his stomach back on the landing pad.

Deacon whooped as the ground shot away. "Great jumpin' Jehoshaphat!" He plastered his face to the side window. "Now this here is flying!"

Once he was fairly certain the pilot was not going to plow a furrow down someone's tobacco field, Marcus forced his brain into gear. Only one idea came to mind, and that one held no satisfaction whatsoever. But try as he might, he could come up with nothing better. With the miles sweeping by in great swatches of cloud and pine and summer-green fields, Marcus touched the pilot's shoulder and motioned that he needed to say something.

The pilot pulled a plasticine map with a red circle drawn over a point along the coastline off the copilot's seat and gestured Marcus to come forward. The pilot handed him a headset with built-in mike and plugged it into the console. When Marcus had fitted on the padded earpieces, the pilot asked, "What's up?"

"I need to make a call and my cell phone is back at the house."

"Number?"

"No idea. Can you connect me to information?"

The pilot switched over the radio controls and said, "HR 438 to Wilmington airfield."

"Tower here. Go, HR 438."

"Emergency request for phone patch."

"Number?"

"Request help with number. Can search?"

"Affirmative. Name?"

Marcus was ready. "Judge Garland Perry, in Wilmington."

"Office or residence?"

"Private residence. On Fourth Street."

"Hold one."

The pilot used the interim to point ahead. Through the sun-drenched bubble Marcus made out the first glint of sea-blue. Not long now.

There were a series of clicks, then, "Call ready. Go ahead, HR 438. Tower out."

The judge's irate voice shouted, "What in blazes is going on here?"

"Judge Perry, this is Marcus Glenwood."

"Who?"

"Marcus Glenwood, your honor. I met you on your doorstep last weekend in regard to the Dale Steadman case."

The judge's ire heightened. "Is it your habit, sir, to disturb officers of the court during the little free time they have?"

"No sir. But this—"

"I was on the phone to my daughter. In *Geneva*. All of a sudden I've got sixteen dozen different operators climbing into our private conversation! And because you, sir, have the gall to declare another national emergency!"

"Not national, sir. But an emergency just the same."

"What in tarnation is all that racket?"

"I'm inside a helicopter, sir."

"What?"

Marcus swiveled in his seat so he didn't have to observe the pilot's grin. "Your honor, I've just learned that a New York detective has appeared at the Wilmington airport with the intent of arresting a local citizen."

There was a longish pause as the judge switched into official gear. "You mean he's set to arraign him for an extradition hearing."

Legal jurisprudence required an arrest warrant from another state be served to a local judge. The judge would then issue a second warrant for extradition, assuming the evidence was sound. But big-city cops were notorious for considering the court system a foe. "You'd think so, wouldn't you. But my guess is he plans to slap the cuffs on our gentleman and take him back."

"Without a hearing?"

"Sometimes they do that, judge. They march in, pick the guy up, then claim later that our man consented to the move." *Our* man. Making it a local issue. "Then it's my client's word against the detective's."

"Now why would he wish to rile the local court with such an outrageous act?"

"Holding an extradition hearing means I get to see his evidence, as your honor well knows. He may not want to reveal all his cards at this point."

"I assume," Judge Perry said, "the man in question is the client we spoke of earlier."

The pilot pointed to a tiny island attached to the mainland by a wooden bridge. The cream-colored stone and steeply pitched slate roof gleamed with the myth of moneyed perfection. Marcus nodded affirmative and said, "Dale Steadman. Yes sir. I am still acting as his counsel."

"I do not like this. Not one bit." He chewed over his options as the pilot started a swooping descent. "But I like the alternative even less. You know where the courthouse is located?"

"I'll find it."

"Ninety minutes."

The detective was a bulldog with a mustache. His leather jacket was emblazoned with the NYPD seal, the zipper open to reveal the gun on his belt beside his badge. Dale was stretched out on his own front lawn, his face in the dirt by the rotunda's central fountain. The detective was in the process of fitting cuffs onto Dale's wrists as Marcus leapt from the still descending helicopter. He shouted over the rotor's din, "Let go of my client!"

The detective played at not hearing him, taking his time with the manacles, then hauling Dale to his feet at the very last moment. "Something on your mind?"

"I am Marcus Glenwood."

The detective played at unconcern, though his face was pinched from the sudden reversal to his plans. "This is supposed to mean something?"

"Dale Steadman is my client."

Dale shook his head to clear the grass from his forehead. "I didn't kill her, Marcus. I was in New York but I didn't do this thing."

"Let's hold that thought for a minute." Marcus nudged Steadman to one side so as to focus tightly upon the detective. "Aureolietti, do I have that right? Swell job you did, informing us of your intentions."

The detective gave Marcus the sort of flat-panned inspection he would offer a stain on the road. He glanced at where Deacon stood, the silent sentinel. He shrugged his acceptance of the new situation, attorney and witness and no way to continue with headlong intent. "Your man here consented to being transported north."

Dale waited until the chopper rose and departed to protest, "How was I supposed to say a word with my face pressed in the dirt?"

Marcus asked, "What exactly are we talking about here?"

"What the warrant says. Murder in the first." He handed over the folded sheaf of papers, then unwrapped two pieces of gum and stuffed them in his mouth. "Mind if we get a move on here? I got a plane to catch."

"I'm not bound to anybody's schedule but my client's. How did you get my client's name?"

"What is this, twenty questions? We got his name from the two hundred witnesses who place him at the scene of the crime." He substituted his finger for a gun. "Which is why I'm down here to pick your boy up and carry him back."

"I tell you I didn't do it."

Marcus stepped between them without lifting his gaze from the warrant. "What puts him at the scene, a gun, a knife? I don't see anything like that stated here."

"Then you're not reading what's written. Your client and the victim got into it before an audience of hundreds. She left. He followed. He did her."

"So the murder itself did not actually take place in front of these eyewitnesses of yours?"

"The dispute did. The threatening did."

"You're saying my client actually threatened the victim with bodily harm?"

"Absolutely. Your boy here stalked her and threatened her. Left her so scared she ran screaming from the scene, yelling about how he's not going to abuse her ever again." The detective gave Dale his mobile grin. "Sound familiar?"

"My client has no criminal record of any kind."

"You look like a smart guy. You know crimes of passion are almost always a one-off."

"Are you aware my client is involved in a custody dispute with the

victim? A dispute caused by the victim abducting their baby daughter
and carrying her off to Germany?" Marcus weaved slightly, intent
upon keeping himself at the center of the detective's roving gaze. "Why
would my client kill the one person who could bring his daughter
back?"

"Don't know, don't care." He glanced at his watch. "We done
here?"

Marcus flipped through the pages, searching for the required
ammo to keep Dale Steadman firmly planted on Carolina soil. "I still
don't find anything about the murder weapon." He flipped through
the pages once more. "Do you have the gun?"

"The victim was stabbed eleven times, the kind of frenzy
you'd expect from a guy who'd lost his little girl. Ain't that right,
sport?"

When Dale Steadman shifted to one side, Marcus halted him with
"He's looking for a reason to charge you with resisting arrest."

But the detective found pleasure in what Marcus could not see.
"Some of the stab wounds were so deep they went right through the
body and punched the limo's seat."

"I didn't—"

"Don't say another word," Marcus snapped.

The detective lifted his chin, a tight little come-on. He said to
Steadman, "My mother's seen this lady sing maybe a dozen times,
sport. Called her the empress of the stage. She's gonna weep real tears
when she hears what you've done. Gonna be a pleasure telling her I
watched you shake and bake."

"Let's get back to business here." Marcus swung back to the affidavit's first page. Controlling the tempo with all his might. "So there's
no knife. What about the limo driver. Is he listed here?"

"We're on that."

"And the limo number, you managed to note that, didn't you?"

"You're the one holding the affidavit. Have a look at page three."

"I'm just trying to get the information about this case straight in
my own mind. What you're telling me is, you don't have the murder weapon. You have no eyewitnesses to the incident itself. And for
all you know the limo driver has immigrated to Kazakhstan."

"You're playing attorney for the defense with the wrong party. I
got enough probable cause for a judge to issue the warrant. Far as I'm

concerned, we got our man. There was a fight, there was a killing. They happened in close proximity. We believe he's responsible and the judge agrees. We straight on this? I'm asking on account of you being in my way."

"Fine." It was Marcus' turn to check his watch. "The *local* judge should be about ready to begin our extradition hearing."

Dark eyes burned him where he stood. "All this time, you been setting me up?"

Marcus let a little of his own rage show. "Absolutely."

Marcus drove them to the courthouse in Dale's Esplanade. The detective sat in the backseat with Dale beside him. Aureolietti slipped on mirror shades and practiced his sullen routine. Dale sat with cuffed hands in his lap, giving directions in a voice as bleak as his gaze.

The Wilmington courthouse fronted Water Street. Big blocks of granite formed a four-story bracket with a fountain in its middle. Half-cut pillars and tall sash windows were embedded into the building's face. Deacon remained with the car as they made their way inside.

The judge's third-floor offices were large and furnished with a woman's taste for Southern plaids and warm colors. The office smelled vaguely of weekend cleansers and tobacco. Judge Perry was in the process of packing his pipe as they entered. "I'd ask if anybody minded my smoking, but I don't care one way or the other." He pointed at Dale. "Why is this man cuffed?"

"He's under arrest, judge."

"And you are?"

"Lieutenant John Aureolietti, NYPD."

"Since when do New York detectives have license to operate in my jurisdiction?"

The detective looked ready to argue, then thought better of the issue and unlocked the manacles. Dale continued to bear the tragic expression of a man ready to gnaw off his own limb. His clothes were grass-stained, his knees caked, his forehead smudged. Marcus guided him into a seat by the side wall, then waited for the judge to point them into chairs opposite him. Judge Perry asked, "I assume you have a warrant?"

"Right here."

The judge reached across his desk, unfolded the document, and took time lighting his pipe as he read. He asked Marcus, "You have seen this?"

"Only briefly, your honor. Standing on Mr. Steadman's front lawn."

He slid the papers across his desk. "All right, Lieutenant. Now perhaps you can explain why you intended to waltz in and out of here without so much as a by-your-leave to the local courts."

Aureolietti shifted in his seat. "Look, the guy did her in."

"Did he now."

"Open and shut. Broad daylight, the perp assaults her verbally in front of two hundred wits, then kills her on the way out." He shrugged. "What's to figure?"

Marcus skimmed the papers a final time. Arrest warrants followed a standard two-part pattern. The first portion was a fill-in-the-box form—what type of warrant, what charge, who, address, and so forth. The second portion was the affidavit, which spelled out the probable cause. On most occasions, state-to-state extradition hearings were mere formalities, which was why some police officers failed to jump through the hoops. They were in a hurry, they had other cases piled on their desk, and the last thing they needed was to hang around just so another judge could sign on the dotted line. Generally a local judge required something serious to overturn what another judge had ruled as compelling evidence.

And this Marcus could not find.

Until it struck him.

He looked up to find Judge Perry watching him. "Mr. Glenwood, you have something to say?"

Marcus turned to the detective. "You've supplied us with a copy of the original document."

"So?"

"So this photocopy doesn't bear the clerk's seal."

The judge sat up straighter. "Let me see that."

The detective looked pained. "What's the problem here? We got a serious criminal who's a flight risk. He's already skipped the state where the crime took place."

"Your honor, a document from another jurisdiction that is not under seal is not authenticated."

"It was the weekend, the clerk of courts was off, and I was in a hurry," the detective protested. "Whose side are we on here?"

"On the side of the law, sir." Judge Perry eyed the detective over the brow of his horn-rimmed spectacles. "Let me see if I can give you a different take on this situation. You knew full well you didn't have all your ducks in a row. So you figured on slipping down here before anybody had the first idea what was going on, grabbing your man, and handing us a fait accompli."

"Come on, judge, give me a break here."

"I am fully aware of the full faith and credit clause of our Constitution and the extradition laws between our states." He used the wet end of his pipe to still the detective's protest. "But this is a serious charge. Due process requires at the minimum that you have your paperwork in order. I am not going to allow you to drag this man's reputation through the dirt by publicly hauling him up I-95. Not on this. When you and your friends in New York comply with the law, I will reconsider this matter."

"So where does that leave me?"

The pipe swiveled over to aim at the door. "Unless you have some other matter to bring before this court, you are free to go."

"What, this is your basic introduction to Southern-style justice?" The detective stalked to the door. "Or maybe I missed the family resemblance, a little backwoods connection. All you guys drawn from the same stink."

Marcus realized Dale was not going to stand on his own, so went over to help the man. "Thank you very much, your honor."

"Make no mistake, sir. I dislike this whole affair almost as much as I dislike you dragging me into it. But I despise being maltreated by a no 'count trash-talking big-city policeman." He fished in his vest pocket and drew out a flat gold-plated lighter. "Who's been handling this dispute so far?"

"Judge Rachel Sears."

"I know her well. There's the matter of a missing child, do I recall that correctly?"

Marcus could feel Dale flinch the entire length of his frame. "A baby girl. Abducted by the mother."

"All right. Come Monday I'm going to remand this entire matter over to Judge Sears' court." He flicked the gas flame and puffed until the pipe was drawing clean. "If you truly want to show your appreciation for demolishing my weekend, sir, you will never darken my door again."

CHAPTER

3 7

D ALE OFFERED TO DRIVE them back to Rocky Mount, claiming it was the least he could do. Deacon and Marcus exchanged glances over the man's bowed head, both of them hearing the hollow tone of one lost to all but his own wretchedness. Marcus excused himself and walked over to the bank of phones on the courthouse's brick wall. He obtained the number for the *Raleigh News and Observer* and asked for Omar Dell's voice mail.

To his surprise, the young man himself answered the phone. Marcus asked, "What's a court reporter doing in the office on a Saturday afternoon?"

"The editor lets me come in weekends and work on side issues. Man on the move's gotta go the extra mile." Omar's voice gradually heightened in pitch. "You're phoning me with something, right? This ain't no weekend social call, see how your favorite hack is spending his time."

"I've just gotten out of an arraignment hearing. Dale Steadman has been charged with murder one."

"Wait!" There was the sound of a drawer being violently torn open. "All right. I'm ready!"

Marcus sketched out what had taken place. "That's all I know so far."

The court reporter responded to the news with his own cry of delight. "Didn't I say this was gonna happen? The man makes it his job to light up the sky!"

"I just felt like I owed you."

"This is the kind of payback I like!"

"I assume I don't have to state the obvious."

"Course not. Sorry, I didn't catch your name. Who is this I'm talking to?"

Marcus hung up the phone and walked outside to where the pair waited in the Esplanade. "Let's go."

It was dark by the time they dropped off Deacon and drove to Marcus' home. The silent ride had seemed endless. Dale's morose state had defied all attempts at conversation and planning. Marcus climbed out of the car, stretched, and offered, "Why don't you come in and stay the night?"

Dale did not turn from his grim inspection of the night ahead.

"It's too late for you to drive back to Wilmington, Dale."

"Shut the door."

Marcus knew the tone and the intention all too well. "Friend, that voice you're hearing is only speaking lies."

In reply, Dale slapped the Esplanade into gear and gunned the engine. Marcus stepped back as the SUV shot forward. His door slammed shut with the sound of a gavel pounding nails into the grim and uncaring dark.

Marcus ate a weary dinner standing by the kitchen sink. The wall phone was there at eye level, waiting for him to end his futile debate. He called Kirsten's hotel and left a message for her to get in touch. Then he stood cradling the phone and knowing he had to make the call.

Thankfully it was Darren who answered at the sheriff's office. The young man understood enough not to bother him with senseless questions.

Marcus washed his dinner dishes, then cut off the air conditioner and moved about the house, opening the windows. The night filtered through the screens, humid and earthy with the flavors of late summer. Marcus stepped onto his front porch and settled into one of the rockers. Heat lightning flickered against the horizon, a visual accompaniment to the crickets' serenade. A nightbird shrilled a soprano's high call, answered by a dog barking several doors down. He rocked in time to the night rhythms, exhausted from the day, yet knowing if he went to bed he would not sleep. There was nothing to do but wait.

About two hours later, Marcus was drawn to his feet by a patrol car pulling into his drive. Darren Wilbur slid his bulk from behind the wheel and waved Marcus over.

"F-Found the man leaning on the w-wall outside the Deadline Bar and G-Grill." Darren reached down and hefted Dale by an utterly limp arm. "Staring at his c-car like he c-couldn't make up his m-mind."

Marcus moved to Dale's other side. Up close the man smelled of sour mash and other people's smoke. "If you're going to be sick, I'd rather you do it out here."

Dale struggled to raise his head and draw Marcus into focus. "Don't be angry with me."

Even with the two of them helping, Dale made hard going of the front stairs. Marcus used his foot to push open the screen door. "Let's take him straight upstairs."

"S-stand aside." Darren gripped Dale so hard the air huffed from his lungs, and hustled up the steps.

"First door on the right."

Darren pushed into the guest bedroom and eased the man down. Dale's fumbling would have cast the side table and lamp to the floor, had Marcus not been there to catch them. Dale's gaze roved with the unwilling fervor of lost control. "So afraid."

"The bathroom is through the door straight ahead of you." Marcus positioned the trash can by the side of the bed, then laid a towel by Dale's head. "Don't worry. Their case is full of holes."

Confusion writhed across his features. "What're you talking about?"

"Prison. This afternoon. New York. Remember?"

Dale laughed with drunken contempt. "Couldn't care less about all that."

Marcus stared down at the rumpled man.

"Where is my baby, Marcus?"

He motioned Darren toward the door. "Sleep it off. We'll talk tomorrow."

As he flipped off the light and closed the door, a voice crushed by a mountain of pain moaned, "Where is my daughter?"

Sleep, night's intimate companion, bid Marcus a jarring farewell. He dressed and stood in the upstairs hallway, listening to the house. A sonorous snoring came from the guest bedroom. Marcus tread quietly down the stairs, grateful for the isolation.

He made a coffee and took his mug and the cordless phone out onto his front porch. His thoughts shifted in time to the pungent predawn breeze. Strands of honeysuckle and bougainvillea climbed trellises to either side of the porch, offering aromatic alms to the day ahead. The previous autumn he had planted a stand of fruit trees beside his office, replacing the huge elm burned by New Horizons lackeys sent to destroy his home. The day was so young and the sky so clear the saplings and neighboring pines stood as Chinese etchings upon a gold-embossed sky. Between him and the road, magnolia blossoms cupped the first glimmer of light in scented white hands.

The night's final dream lingered like half-heard whispers. He had been seated in this very same spot, rocking away and watching his little corner of the world. Fay had appeared and spoken to him. In the dream he could not make out her words, but he heard the wisdom of hard-fought years and knew the woman's message. He waited through his second cup, then dialed the New York hotel's number from memory.

Kirsten answered with the soft breathiness of one still asleep.

"It's me."

"Marcus, hi." The voice was so intimate he tasted the words as he would love's caress. "I was at dinner when you called. When I got back I was so sleepy I just fell into bed. I've still got on half my clothes."

He forced himself to push that thought away. "It's early, but I couldn't wait. We've got to talk."

"Why, what's wrong?"

"Kirsten, I need your help."

There was a moment's pause, then, "Wait just a second."

The first birds of dawn chirped a welcome as he waited. She returned equipped with a totally different tone. "All right, I'm back."

He took it slow, giving her the full details. Walking her through the three court appearances, the way opposing counsel had constantly stayed ahead of him, the news yesterday, the journey, the confrontations. Then, because it had tasted so good the first time, he finished as he had started. "I know I'm missing something. I just can't seem to see this clearly."

"Someone else is involved here."

Fifteen minutes on the phone and she had the answer. Marcus found it difficult not to scoff. "Kirsten, who on earth could possibly have such a strong interest in this baby they'd go to all this trouble?"

"That's our problem." She remained as soft-spoken as always, but there was no doubt to her response. "We've been hitting our heads on a question we can't answer. Let's look at it another way."

He stared at the gathering light. "What other way is there?"

"We need to discover," Kirsten answered, "who else could be pulling Hamper Caisse's string."

"But what would they want?"

"That's exactly the issue we have to work out."

The impulse to play the lawyer and pick away at her certainty was so potent it forced him out of his chair and across the dew-flecked lawn. "You're saying we look first for motive, then the person."

"Erin had a secret. We know that much. We've assumed it was nothing more than a desire to avoid bad publicity. What if it was something else?"

"I'm not sure I follow you."

"We've got to start looking for answers where she cared the most." She pondered a moment. "I need an introduction at the Met. That was her obsession, right? It's as good a place to start as any. But I need a contact."

He shrugged in silent bafflement to reasoning he could not fathom. "Let me make a call."

CHAPTER

38

REINER KLATZ was a man undone. He sat locked inside Erin Brandt's front room. Goscha the maid was upstairs somewhere, packing Erin's belongings. Her wailing drifted through the ceiling overhead as though Erin's specter had already arrived to take up ghoulish residence. Newspapers were spread about the table and sofa and floor in devastating array. The tabloids had used police photographs for their front covers. They and the headlines were fists that beat him almost senseless.

Erin's word, her mood, her every thought had been so tightly woven into the fabric of his day that he now had neither direction nor purpose. His mind hunted like a frantic little animal for the familiar, finding empty solace in meaningless memories.

He recalled the thrill he had felt at discovering Erin's pure sound was not based upon perfect pitch, which was a source of false pride for many divas. Instead, Erin had the much rarer quality of perfect *relative* pitch. Perfect pitch meant the ability to remember a note and hit it perfectly, first time, every time. But some of the world's greatest orchestras held to the centuries-old tradition of tuning a quarter note low or high. This meant the diva was forced to perform in what was for her slightly off-pitch. Erin, on the other hand, took her pitch from the oboe used to tune the instruments. Right first time, every time. So rare a quality it was seldom even discussed.

His mind scampered further, recalling her pattern before every performance. She liked to arrive at the concert hall very early and give the music a final study. Dinner prior to an evening performance was an apple and a few sips of champagne. An iced bucket was always there in her dressing room. Always. She rarely drank more than a single glass, but she insisted on a full bottle. She considered such touches her due. Her voice coach arrived then and together they did a major warm-up. Then she was fitted into the opera's first costume, assisted only by one trusted dresser, for it was during this period that she also moved into character. Then the final warm-up, another few sips of champagne, and up to the stage. No calming exercises for Erin. This was time for energy and excitement. Reiner sat and recalled what it was like to move along-side Erin Brandt as she headed for the stage. Her focus was so tight that the rest of the world faded into meaningless shadows. She saw nothing, heard nothing, felt nothing. Her world was ahead of her, her life, her entire existence. The only reality she ever cared about waited just beyond where the stage manager stood and smiled the welcome she did not see, his hand timed to open the curtain on the conductor's down-beat. Then she could step forward, and drink in the lights and the music and the adoration. Then she knew the rapture of being worshiped.

Goscha's shriek ripped through his reverie. Reiner winced at the impact of returning to the here and now, with the photographs and the headlines shrilling that his life was over. Stabbed eleven times. Brutal murder. They might as well have plunged the knife into him, he was that dead.

The housemaid's cries were directly overhead now. But it was more than her proximity that heightened the noise. She was in the baby's room. Reiner stared up at the ceiling with dawning realization. Goscha was not weeping over her deceased mistress. She cried for that cursed child.

Even this heightened caterwauling could not drive him out. Where was he to go? Certainly not down his beloved Kö, where the grey-hounds slavered for his blood and the world was ready to watch his death throes. And not home. His wife was waiting for him there. The world might see her as the compliant one, the silent seamstress ready to do anyone's bidding. But Reiner knew this wraith had teeth. She had gnawed on him relentlessly since the news arrived. How he was brought low now, how he should never have mixed himself up with that singer. As he had fled their expensive riverside flat, the one they would now be forced to vacate since his sole source of income lay full of gaping wounds, his wife had shrilled that he had earned his place in the grave beside Erin Brandt.

Definitely he could not go home.

The wailing overhead gradually lessened. The Polish maid seemed content now to moan a single word. Over and over she repeated the baby's name. Celeste. Celeste. Reiner folded his head into his hands, inwardly moaning along with Goscha.

Then he realized what he was saying.

He stood and walked to the window. Goscha's moans were no longer a vexation. They pushed him forward. Of course. There was indeed a way out of this. A perfect way.

The phone rang just as he was reaching for it. Reiner stared in confusion. The ringing continued. Tentatively he picked up the receiver. He stared at it a moment longer before placing it to his ear. "Yes?"

"Tell me you haven't done anything yet."

Reiner sighed. Of course this man would have anticipated everything. Of course. And in that moment, for the very first time, things began to grow clear. "No," Reiner replied. "Not yet."

"Good. Very good." The voice held the quality of a dagger wrapped in a silk scarf. "Now I will tell you precisely what is going to happen. But first I need to know, does your wife speak English?"

"Yes." For once, Reiner was able to anticipate the man's thinking. At least partially. "But she won't help us."

"That," the man replied, "is where you are most assuredly wrong."

CHAPTER

3 9

MARCUS GAVE IT as long as he could, then took a coffee and two aspirin upstairs and knocked on the guestroom door. Dale had risen during the night and managed to undress himself. The burly man peered up at him with the furrowed brow of one striving to keep the lid of his head from splitting open.

"I have to be going," Marcus told him. He knew from experience the last thing Dale wanted was questions as to his well-being. "But first I need to ask you something. And you need to answer. So do whatever it takes to wake up."

The man pushed himself to a seated position, swayed and almost went down the other way, then rose to his feet. When Marcus moved to offer support, Dale halted him with an upraised hand. He disappeared into the bathroom, returned, took the aspirin with a slug of coffee, sighed, drained the cup. He croaked, "Go where?"

"Church. You ready to listen?"

Unwilling to nod and risk dislodging his head, he made do with a wave. Go.

"Is there anybody else you can think of who might have a motive to make a run for your daughter?"

Dale's head came up far too swiftly. He applied a palm to his temple to stop the world from swimming. "What?"

"Anybody who might be trying to get to you through your daughter," Marcus repeated. "Think, man. This could be very important." Or an utter waste of time. But there was nothing to be gained by expressing his doubts just then.

When Dale answered by staring at his empty mug, Marcus took it from him, went downstairs, and returned with another dose. "What about New Horizons?"

Dale drained half the mug before responding. "What's the gain? They've already sunk my career."

"Do you have other enemies who'd see this as a way to retaliate?"

"Not me." He drained the mug. "But Erin does."

"Of course."

"Even so, stealing a child wouldn't be their way. They'd go after what would hurt her the most. Her career."

"Would they kill her?"

"Maybe. Opera's like every other art form, too many talented people hunting too few spots. It breeds a special form of viciousness. Why are you asking?"

"You mean, other than the fact that I've got to clear you of a murder charge?" Marcus glanced at his watch. "I need to be rolling. You're welcome to come along if you like."

Dale gestured at the pile of grass-stained clothes he'd worn since the arrest. "Got something that'd fit me?"

The man outweighed him by forty pounds. "Sweats only," Marcus replied. "But I seriously doubt anybody will mind."

―――――――

The day was quiet and drenched with eight o'clock sun. Dale endured the ride in stoic silence. When they pulled into the church parking lot and Dale remained where he was, Marcus wondered if he had made a mistake, bringing this broken man to a black country church. Then he realized Dale's gaze rested upon the hillside, where the New Horizons headquarters glinted like a polarized tombstone to his own career.

"You okay with all this?"

"I was just thinking," Dale said. "How hard it is to be so wrong about love."

Marcus kept his engine running and the car cool. Now that they were here, he felt no urge to move inside. "Do something for me, will you? Think back to the last time you saw Erin. I mean, before New York."

"When she took Celeste."

"Tell me about that night."

Dale looked at him. "Why?"

He understood the man's desire to avoid the pain of inspecting a running sore. "Kirsten has the feeling maybe there's an ulterior motive at work. Something we've missed up to now."

Dale turned back to the front windshield. "Erin called and said she was over for another PBS special."

"You mean, back in the States."

"She wanted to come down and talk. How could I refuse her? She hadn't seen her baby in months. We met for dinner. The worst in a long line of bad moves."

"You did the only thing you could, Dale."

"She played her charm card. Again. I let myself get taken in. Again."

"What did you talk about?"

"The usual. Her career. Mine. She wanted to know about the burglary."

"The what?"

"A couple of guys broke into the house. Didn't I tell you about this?"

Something niggled at his mind, but Marcus could not bring the pieces together. "It was a week or so before she came down?"

"Five days, maybe six. I caught them in the act. Clocked them with a lamp. Made the papers." He shrugged. No big deal in the grand scheme. "Erin and I had your normal catch-up kind of talk."

"What happened after dinner?"

"She drove me home. Like usual when I'd been drinking." He rubbed his face, pushing the glasses up to his forehead, revealing the white splotches on his temples and the weary creases and the eyes of one already convicted and condemned. "Another major mistake."

"You passed out?"

"Apparently. I don't remember. One minute I was on the sofa in the back room, the next I was in bed and the house was on fire."

"Do you normally lose consciousness when you drink?"

"No. Not usually."

"Ever?"

"What are you saying?"

"I'm just searching, Dale. Do you frequently pass out?"

"Not ever that I recall."

"What about forgetting events?"

"You're suggesting Erin drugged me?"

Marcus cut the motor and opened his door. "I don't know, Dale. I wish I did."

Outside the car the heat hung thick as fog. Dale wore an old pair of Marcus' running shoes without socks, a golf shirt, and sweatpants that on Marcus sagged almost to his knees. The simple exertion of crossing the parking lot left Dale sweating so hard the back of his shirt was plastered to his skin. "Are you all right?"

Dale waited until they had stepped inside the air-conditioned coolness to reply, "I don't know how much more of this I can take."

Marcus did not have the heart to warn him of just how long a murder investigation and trial could require. He offered Dale his keys. "Go on home if you like, I'll grab a ride with someone later."

Dale accepted the keys but staggered toward the sanctuary. A pair of ushers stood by the doors. As soon as Marcus introduced him, the ushers were vying over which hand Dale would shake first. Others were called out from the sanctuary, where the choir and music director were busy warming up the crowd. People saw the gathering by the rear doors and moved close. Dale's name was passed around. More smiles and hands extended toward the confused man.

When Marcus finally managed to pry him loose, Dale asked, "What was that all about?"

"A lot of families here live off New Horizons paychecks. I should have warned you."

"But I've been fired."

"They know what you tried to do in there. It means a lot."

The music and the shouting and the applause did not seem to bother Dale nearly as much as the welcome. When the minister invited the congregation to offer one another Sabbath greetings, Dale shrank inside his own skin. People gave no sign of minding either his manner or his dress. They didn't turn from him until the next chorus began.

Marcus noticed Omar Dell only after the service ended. The young man wore a collage of dark gray—gabardine suit, slightly darker shirt, finely patterned tie. He worked his way smoothly toward Marcus, doing the easy greetings of one known and liked by many. When he finally stood before Marcus he said, "I'd heard about you hanging with the home crowd." He motioned to where Dale was trying his best to reach the outer doors. "But how come you didn't take him someplace tamer, you know, so he could mellow with the vanillas for Jesus crew?"

"Now is not the time or the place, Omar."

"That's where you're wrong." Omar steered them over to the side aisle. "This is what you might call a very private heads-up."

"Call my office tomorrow."

"You just hold tight and listen. I'm doing this as a favor to a mutual friend." He moved in closer still. "Yesterday evening, papers were filed by Health and Human Services, requesting an emergency hearing first thing Monday morning."

"What about?"

"They aim on declaring Dale Steadman an unfit parent."

Marcus backed against the wall, but was unable to find a handhold. "That's insane."

Omar grinned, satisfied with the impact of his news. "Makes you wonder, don't it."

"Dale doesn't even have possession of the child."

"Sounds to me like people in the know are trying for another of these end runs around you and your client." Omar shifted so that he was right in Marcus' line of sight. "Now you got to promise me, you come up with another headline, you call me first."

Marcus pushed past the reporter. "I have to find Dale."

Dale had thought getting outside would bring safety. But the heat formed a thunderous din in his head, worse even than the church's echoes. He held to a steady gait across the parking lot, though it would have been more comfortable to fall to all fours and crawl. It was not the drinking that left him so devastated. Or at least, not that alone. The church's welcome had been crippling, a smiling condemnation of everything he had failed to achieve at New Horizons. As if he needed another reminder.

His cell phone pinged as he was opening the passenger door. He had carried it with him constantly since the night. Another symbol of futile hope. Dale waited until he had started the engine and turned the a/c on full before answering. "What now?"

A heavily accented woman's voice said, "I am calling for a mutual friend."

The words were enough to push him into high gear. Forget the heat and the hangover and the gripping misery of compounded defeat. "What?"

"Someone connected to you by the one who is now gone." She spoke with the dull rote of one reading from a page. "Do you understand?"

"Yes."

"This party, they now have the child."

"Where are you?"

"Never mind. She is hidden. Make any move, take any action at all, and the child will never be found. Speak one word and all will be lost to you. The party says, they have nothing else to lose."

"What do you want?"

"Five million dollars."

"All right."

"Five million dollars," the woman repeated. "Or the child disappears."

"I said I'd pay you." Marcus appeared at the side door. Dale reached over and hammered down the door lock so hard he ripped the skin. He pressed his palm into the sweatpants to stem the blood. "What do you want me to do?"

"You will stay in North Carolina. They will have you watched. Believe me. They will know."

Dale turned away from Marcus' stare. "I understand."

"The blond one. The troublemaker. You know who I mean?"

"Kirsten Stansted."

"She will be the go-between."

"Give me five days."

"You have forty-eight hours."

"I can't get the money—"

The line was dead. Dale cupped the phone to his chest. Took three deep breaths. Then reached over and unlocked the door.

Marcus clambered inside. "What is going on here?"

"Something's come up." Dale struggled to bring his heart back under control. "I have to get back to Wilmington."

"Did you hear about HHS?"

"What?"

"Health and Human Services. They're lodging a complaint against you." Marcus pointed at the phone. "Is that what this was all about?"

"Just drive, okay?"

Marcus remained as he was. "It's vital that you show up for the hearing with Judge Sears tomorrow morning." When Dale did not respond, he asked again, "What's going on?"

Dale could not bring himself to meet his attorney's eye. "Maybe a miracle."

CHAPTER

40

MARCUS DID NOT CALL BACK until late that afternoon, which meant Kirsten had yet another day for circular condemnation. Not that talking with him helped anything. Every conversation with Marcus became a struggle with herself. And they were growing worse, not better.

She wanted him so bad the hunger seared her chest and turned her bones to kindling for her heart's flames. For years she had assumed her earlier experience had cauterized all desire, all hope for ever knowing a normal relationship. No question about it. She was terrified of this man.

Now here he was again. Hurriedly Marcus described how it had taken him almost a dozen calls to arrange a meeting with Evelyn Lloyd. Kirsten was to meet her the next morning for the introduction inside the Met. Then he raced through other things he needed her to check on. But his impatience was evident. Hurriedly he concluded that portion, then began spelling out the latest developments. As though only now could they be sorted out, here while she was listening. "Dale agreed to the ransom amount without a quibble. He's gone down to sell his house and his boat. Apparently a local agent has made a cash offer for the house, the boat, the works."

"Five million dollars," she repeated, thinking this was not what she wanted to be talking about. The awareness of where she wanted this conversation to go left her cheeks flaming. No matter they were in the middle of a murder-one case, not to mention a kidnapping and a ransom situation where she was to act as go-between. Her breath seared her nostrils with internal heat.

"It's going to wipe Dale out, putting this amount together at short notice. Suggesting we get the police involved almost got me fired. Ditto for trying to talk them down. All he can see is, this is the only chance he has of getting his child back."

"Marcus, we've got to talk."

"What do you call what we're doing now?"

"No, I mean . . ." She could not believe this was happening. But the hunger gnawed away at everything. She wanted to talk about what she wanted. Which was him. She wanted to *know* this man. She wanted to brand him with her love. Her impatience to move forward ate at the barriers she had spent years building, the silence and the reserve and the distance and the reasons why she could never love any man.

"Kirsten?"

There was only one way this was going to work. She didn't know how she knew, but she knew it was not just true, but *real*. She had to talk. She had to tell him why she battled so against him, and even more, against herself. "Marcus, I have to tell you something."

He caught the change. "Honey, what's the matter?"

She wanted to curse him. To rage at him like she should at all men for their macho ways and their ability to hurt and crush and blind. But she couldn't. Past wounds were no longer enough to bind her. The words rushed out like lava. "Everything I told you about myself is a lie. But that's not for now. I don't know if I can ever . . ."

She stopped to pant, squeezing the receiver so hard her ear felt mashed to a pulp. "I was raped."

He moaned in the manner of one who did not know he had even breathed, much less spoken.

"I was seventeen. There were three of them. I was drugged. It was on a boat. But that doesn't matter. After that I went a little crazy. Not right then. Later. But I did. I tried a lot of things, Marcus. None of them worked. Every time I was . . . with a man, all I saw was the smoke. And the stars." She knew that would make no sense to him. But the further she went, the less she could say for whom she spoke. "So I stopped caring. I stopped feeling. I stopped everything. It was better that way. Safer. And it worked. Then you came along. And it doesn't work anymore. I can't stand this, Marcus. I can't *stand* it. I can't keep myself trapped away. I can't . . ."

She slammed the phone down. Rose to her feet. Walked from the bed to the window to the door and back. Passing the mirror over the desk she caught sight of herself.

She was amazed to find her face drenched with tears.

The phone rang. She stared at it. The phone rang seven times. Then stopped. Kirsten could not unlock her chest. Her need for air was a burning fury, almost as strong as her desire to hear him speak to her. About love and healing and comfort and sharing. The phone started ringing again. If she could make her chest move she could reach for the phone. The phone stopped once more.

The silence. Not breathing, not really even thinking. Not letting anybody touch her in this sterile little cocoon. Trading one tight little cage for another. Going through life with no change. Nothing moving, especially not inside herself. Flying all over the globe, going through the motions of having a life. But held by the safety of empty silence. Just like now.

She did not lower herself so much as crash to the floor. Crawled across to the bed. Knelt there waiting. When the phone rang again, she made the grab before the first ring was through, not giving herself time to enter lockdown again.

Marcus started speaking. He said the words. She felt them cascade over her but she could not actually hear what he said. All she could make out was the tone, the message of concern and love and acceptance. It broke her entirely.

CHAPTER

41

When Marcus entered the courtroom early Monday, Hamper Caisse was seated in the first public row. Hamper gave a little double take at Marcus' appearance. Marcus was too preoccupied to take much pleasure in turning the tables. The conversations with Kirsten and her revelations had left him utterly drained. He had also spent futile hours trying to track down Dale. Under any other circumstances, he would already be headed to Wilmington.

Judge Rachel Sears offered Marcus a tight smile of approval as he set his briefcase upon the table. "Are we alone this morning, Mr. Glenwood?"

"Apparently so, your honor." Marcus turned to inspect his new foe. Opposing counsel's table was occupied by a Health and Human Services lawyer. This one was white and male and had a slick nervous sheen to his skin. He wore a button-down Oxford blue shirt with a stained wool tie. Normally the HHS attorneys were the least prepared of all local counsel. They generally worked between fifty and seventy active cases at any one time. Their paperwork was notoriously shoddy. Family court judges usually granted them enormous leeway. If an HHS attorney requested a stay, that was generally enough for the court to require a medical assessment. Where children were concerned, most judges preferred to err on the side of extreme caution.

The HHS attorney opened with "Your honor, we have learned over the weekend that Erin Brandt has died. We are here to request that her child immediately be made a ward of the court."

Marcus demanded, "Let's get this straight. You're pointing the finger at my client? *You* are? Or Hamper Caisse?"

The HHS guy kept his gaze locked on the judge. "Your honor, we have reason to believe that Dale Steadman has proven himself to be an unfit father. The father is under indictment for the murder of his former spouse. Plus there are numerous other issues that raise warning flags." He fumbled with his own case and drew out three bound portfolios. "We have prepared a brief outlining our concerns." He plunked a copy on Marcus' table and walked forward with another.

The judge eyed his work with consternation. She flipped through the pages. She looked at him. "What is your caseload at this time?"

He struggled with the knot of his tie. "Hard to say, your honor."

"Ballpark figure."

"Around three hundred. Of which about fifty are active."

"Three hundred cases." She rifled through the pages. "How many staff?"

"Just me and my secretary."

"And you put together a brief that runs to," Judge Sears checked the top of the last page. "Two hundred and twelve pages?"

"We are aware that the child is about to come home, your honor."

"Is that so? And just exactly how did you learn this?"

Marcus could hear the guy swallow from across the room. "It stands to reason, judge. The mother is dead, the child has nowhere else to go. We are asking that the baby be made a ward—"

"Hold that thought. First I want to get a fix on what's brought us to this point." She crossed her robed arms over the closed brief. "In all my time on the bench I've never seen anyone from HHS come in here so prepared. Normally I have to be satisfied if you've bothered to interview the neighbors to either side. When did you have time to prepare these documents?"

"Yesterday." He swiped at his hair. "As I said, your honor, we are deeply concerned about this boy's well-being."

Judge Sears slowly repeated, "This boy."

The lawyer almost turned to where Hamper had taken a choke hold on the railing. He caught himself just in time. "Did I say that? Sorry, your honor. I meant the girl."

"Are you sure? What is the child's name?" She halted his motion with a tightly aimed gavel. "Don't you open that brief, sir. Anybody who's gone to all this trouble over a weekend is bound to at least know how the child is called."

The lawyer was caught flat-footed. Judge Sears let the silence hang a moment, then said, "You may open your brief if need be."

The young man almost dove for the pages. "Celeste, your honor. Celeste Steadman, no middle name. Sorry, it just slipped my mind there."

Judge Sears shot Marcus a silent heads-up, then asked the young attorney, "I assume you have included the child's birth certificate?"

"Ah . . ." The attorney's search of the pages became more frantic. Hamper looked ready to explode from his seat.

"That's all right." Sears at her mildest. "No doubt you have a copy in your files."

When the attorney's search through his briefcase came up with nothing more than sweat and bumbling fingers, Hamper Caisse sifted through his own papers, then reached forward and rammed it into the HHS lawyer's outstretched hand. The HHS attorney spun about and announced, "Here it is, your honor."

Marcus was already rising to his feet. "Your honor, I feel it is in the court's interest to know what else Mr. Caisse has in his briefcase."

Hamper gave his best imitation of a man severely electrocuted. "What?"

Sears gave him a tiny nod of approval as Marcus continued, "If Mr. Caisse has an attorney-client relationship here, he has to assert it. Otherwise, he's just a witness. If he's a witness, I want to call him to the stand."

Hamper bolted to his feet. "Judge, I protest! There's nothing more sinister here than a lawyer who's been hooked up with this case for weeks now, worried about this child."

Sears aimed the gavel at his face. "What I see is an individual on the wrong side of the bar addressing this court."

"But—"

"Either sit yourself down and be quiet, or come up before me here and declare yourself!"

When Hamper reluctantly forced himself back down, Marcus announced, "Your honor, I ask that you issue a bench subpoena. Mr. Caisse must not be permitted to leave the courtroom until the subpoena is served."

A bench subpoena would act as a search warrant on Hamper's person and his briefcase, granting the court power to seize any documents deemed pertinent to the case. Another brief nod told Marcus he had handed Judge Sears the ammo she required. "Step forward, Mr. Caisse."

Hamper was loath to move. "Do I need to have the bailiff assist you?"

When Hamper stood before the judge's podium, Judge Sears used both hands to pull her hair back in a gesture of tight animosity. "All right, give. What's your role in this petition?"

"Interested third party, your honor."

She turned to Marcus, inviting his response. "I'm here about the child, your honor. Everything else is secondary. Including whatever tricks opposing counsel is up to now."

"Your honor, I object in the strongest possible terms!"

Marcus continued to address the judge. "This child is a United States citizen. She has the right to grow up here among her people. Right now she's lost to us. First her mother abducted her. Then she hid her away somewhere. She obviously was planning something. I want to know what. I want to know *why*."

"Wait a second now," Caisse sneered. "You're not suggesting Erin Brandt had a hand in her own demise."

"How are we to know *what* happened so long as the facts remain hidden?" Marcus stabbed the air between them. "Whatever Hamper has secreted away, I feel the court has a right to know!"

"Spare us the histrionics," Hamper shot back.

"Mr. Caisse, do you know where the child is?"

"No, your honor, I do not."

"Do I need to put you under oath?"

"It would not change my response one whit, your honor. I'm telling you the dead solid truth here."

"In that case, I hereby am issuing forthwith a subpoena to search your briefcase. I wish to see if you are withholding any documents of vital concern." She waved to where the deputy sat in the empty jury box. "Bailiff."

Hamper used both arms to hug the case to his chest. "You can't do that!"

"You're about to witness," she declared grimly, "just how wrong you are."

Hamper danced a step away from the approaching deputy. "Your honor, this is proprietary information!"

Marcus protested, "But your client is *dead*."

"We're still seeing to her interests!" He slackened his hold on the case long enough to a jab a finger at Marcus. "That man is representing an abuser and a murderer! Dale Steadman can't be granted the chance to hurt this poor little child!"

"Fine." Judge Sears started to rise from her chair. "In that case, the bailiff will escort you to my chambers, I will issue a protective order on everything I find, and then you will show me whatever you have *in camera*."

This meant only the judge would review whatever he was holding. But Hamper merely looked more trapped. "Your honor, I declare attorney-client privilege."

"You're now representing a *different* client?"

"That is correct."

"Is your client before this court?"

"Not at this time."

"Does your client have a valid interest in this case?"

Hamper was growing increasingly agitated. "He feels a desperate concern for this child."

"That is not a satisfactory answer in my book." Her desire to get right in his face was so strong she perched herself on tiptoe and gavel. "I want to know who your client is."

Clearly this was the question Hamper feared. "My client has instructed me not to reveal his identity. I did not come down here intending to make an appearance in this court."

"But you did."

"Under duress, your honor. Under duress. Given the circumstances, this court must agree I should have a chance to confer with my client before answering your question."

Hamper had her, and they both knew it. Judge Sears reddened until her freckles all but disappeared. "You were playing that poor HHS lawyer like a puppet. You had everything but your hand up the back of his jacket. Now tell me what your client's interest is in this case!"

"Judge, I can't do that."

"Then someone in this court is going to jail!"

Hamper deposited his briefcase at his feet, so as to use both hands to swipe at his face. "Your honor, my client's instructions were very precise. He told me to assist this young attorney with the brief related to Celeste Steadman. He told me to appear in court. And he told me not to reveal his identity. That is all I can say."

"Then I am ordering you to speak with your client and gain authorization. Otherwise, come tomorrow I'll be sentencing you to ninety days in jail. If he wants to be heard by this court, he will be heard on the record. If you act in this court, you will do so with full disclosure of your client's and your motives." She smiled at his stricken expression. "Cheer up, Mr. Caisse. You should find ample acquaintances among the prison community."

"Your honor—"

She banged her gavel. "Next case."

CHAPTER

4 2

"WHY DID YOU WANT TO MEET with my husband, Ms. Stansted?" Kirsten was seated opposite Evelyn Lloyd in the city apartment equivalent of a palace. The parlor was oval-shaped and flanked by bas-relief onyx pillars. Along one side resided museum-quality art. Along the other, seven French doors opened onto a terrace larger than Kirsten's entire townhouse. Down below, the cars streaking along rain-washed Central Park West sounded like shredders working on tissue paper. The open patio doors formed billowing parachutes from silk drapes. The light was muted to pastel patterns. The floor was a mosaic of blue marble and old wood. The ceiling was twenty feet high and sculpted around a pair of crystal chandeliers.

Kirsten replied, "I'm not sure I can answer that."

"Try."

"Erin Brandt was last seen alive at Lincoln Center. I'd like an insider's glimpse of the place, just to see if there's something we might find."

Evelyn Lloyd cocked her head. "You think you might discover something missed by the local police?"

"We're working on different purposes, Mrs. Lloyd." A silent housemaid drifted past the open door. "My first concern is locating the child."

Evelyn Lloyd was dressed in daywear of ivory crepe de chine. "You realize my husband has cancer."

"Yes. I'm very sorry."

"You are also aware that we could not have children."

The French parlor clock ticked down elegant seconds as Kirsten balanced a bone china cup on her knees. "No. I had not heard that."

"It was a blow to my husband, I don't mind saying. We were married almost eight years before the doctors finally stopped pretending they could spend my fortune and give us what Kedrick longed for above all else. An heir."

Kirsten set her cup on the table between them. She directed her eyes to her hands. Not to avoid Evelyn's gaze, but rather to focus more intently upon what was being said. "*Your* fortune."

"Kedrick came into our marriage with little more than a title, a crumbling palace in Wiltshire, and the vast ego of ancient power voided by time."

Kirsten tasted the air, hunting for what she was missing, what Evelyn wished her to hear. A woman of this moneyed clan did not share such confidences. It was not done. Ever. Particularly with a stranger. "It must have been hard, not being able to give him what he wanted."

"Far harder for my husband," Evelyn responded, rising to her feet. "As it happens, Kedrick is at the Met now. Let me call and tell him you are on your way over."

She had no choice but to gather her remaining questions and be led from the room. "Thank you."

At the door, Evelyn Lloyd offered her a cool hand and the words "Erin Brandt had the gift of drawing the audience over to her side, even when they didn't want to come. Even when she was the villain of the piece. It made her a star, but it also made every other woman in the world her enemy."

Kirsten kept hold of the long-fingered hand. "Why every woman?"

"Did I say that? Forgive me. I meant every singer." She opened the door. "Thank you so much for stopping by."

Kirsten was coming down the apartment house's front stairs when she was struck by the stench. The all-too-familiar mixture of body odor and bad cologne pushed her away from the street and back inside.

The uniformed doorman lounged just inside the second set of doors. "Can you please call me a cab?"

The blank stare said she was not paying his salary. "Lady, there's a hundred of them going by every minute."

Kirsten fished in her purse and came up with a ten. "I'd really be grateful. I think I'm being followed."

The doorman pushed himself off the wall and sauntered outside. A whistle, a wave, and the man was holding the door open for her. She powered forward, slipped the note into his waiting palm, and tumbled inside. The doorman paused long enough to grin and ask, "Old flames die hard, don't they."

"What?"

"The stalker. He's after one more bite from the apple, right?" The doorman's gaze swept down her frame. "Can't blame a guy for trying."

Kirsten ripped the cab door from his hands and said through the plastic divider, "Go, please."

"Where to?"

"Just go."

Only when they had pulled away and lost themselves in the sullen stream of city traffic did the gasping hit her. The sweats. The feeling of just how close she had come. Her purse became a vault with a tricky lock she had to struggle over. The cell phone almost defeated her. But she finally managed the number and said as soon as Marcus came on, "He's here."

"Who?"

"The guy who attacked me in Düsseldorf."

"You saw him?"

"Smelled." Despite the morning and the fact that she was coming to trust this man, she could not halt the sudden suspicion. That he would patronize her. Play down her fears and her imagination. Tell her something disparaging, like how she needed to put the past behind her, something utterly natural and completely despised. "I smelled him."

"Where are you, Kirsten?"

"A cab. I'm okay."

"Tell me how he smelled."

"Body odor and some old guy's cologne. Like Old Spice but different." It sounded lame to her own ears. "I'll never forget that smell. He was wearing this heavy coat when he grabbed me, and when I bit his arm it felt like I had swallowed a gallon of the stuff."

"English Leather."

"What?"

"The cologne he was wearing. English Leather. You never told me you bit him."

"Bit and kicked both." But her mind was clutched by what she had just heard. "How do you know the smell?"

"Because I've been a fool. Everybody's been half expecting an attack against me. Fay and Netty are camped out at the house, Darren sweeps by four or five times a day, Deacon baby-sits me. And all the while, I wasn't the threat. It wasn't just Düsseldorf, and it wasn't just Erin."

"Who are they?"

"I only know one name. Sephus Jones. The guy must bathe in that stuff."

She leaned her head against the glass. "When did you see him?"

"Never mind. Go back to the hotel. Forget all the other things you were going to do."

"I can't do that."

"Kirsten—"

"No, Marcus. You can tell me to be careful. You can tell me to limit myself to the absolute essentials. But we're in the middle of something big, and the clock is ticking. I can't hide myself away and pretend the world is going to be all right without us."

He acquiesced by not objecting further. A pair of breaths, then, "Who could be behind this?"

The name came to her, but not a reason. "Let me call you back."

Kirsten cut the connection, leaned forward, and tapped on the glass. "Please take me back to where you picked me up."

The doorman called upstairs, then directed her to the penthouse's private elevator. Evelyn Lloyd herself stood in the doorway, coiling her pearls around two fingers. "That was quick."

Kirsten realized the woman was not going to invite her inside. "Mrs. Lloyd, I need to ask you something that is going to be difficult for us both."

"More difficult than watching my husband expire from cancer?"

Again there was the sense of hearing one thing, but being told another. "What kind of cancer does your husband have?"

She showed a slight widening of the eyes. "What a remarkable query to draw you back off the street."

Kirsten waited.

"My husband has chronic myeloid leukemia, or CML. I am told it is quite rare." A brittle smile. "For once, Kedrick was not pleased with exclusivity."

"Could you think of any possible reason," Kirsten asked softly, "why your husband would wish to do Dale Steadman harm?"

"What an utterly remarkable thought." The pearls twirled more swiftly. "Dale is Kedrick's best friend. He saved Dale's business when he was ready to go under." A minute hesitation, little more than a silent press for emphasis. "Of course, there was an ulterior motive. I decided Kedrick would be happier if he had his own income, rather than simply living from my funds. So everything he did in North Carolina was his own. When Dale sold his business, Kedrick made a rather tidy profit, and reinvested that sum in a group of hotels."

Evelyn dropped her hand to her side, terminating the conversation. "That is all, I assume."

"Yes. Thank you."

But as Kirsten pressed the button and the elevator door swept open, the woman added, "A harsh thing, is it not. Being forced to ask a woman about her own husband."

"I'm very sorry, Mrs. Lloyd."

"Don't be. Handling a spouse's death and departure generates discretion, but never a dishonest blindness."

Kirsten pressed the button to keep the elevator doors open. "Excuse me?"

"Leukemia is actually a family of diseases. They affect blood cell production in the bone marrow. About two years ago Kedrick started becoming increasingly tired. This left him more furious than worried. Kedrick has no patience with anything that hints at mortal weakness, including his own body. Then he was struck by one of those horrid bicycle messengers, and the blow was enough to rupture his spleen, which had become weakened by the disease. Then the doctors discovered both the cancer and the fact that Kedrick has a very rare type of blood."

Kirsten started to step from the elevator, then decided to remain exactly where she was. No notes taken, no indication made that what Evelyn was saying was anything more than two women sharing the news of a stricken husband.

"He's lived this long on blood transfusions and fury and his passion for the Met. Finding the blood initially was virtually impossible. So Kedrick set up his own private blood bank and began acquiring on the open market, which needless to say was horrendously expensive. He's had a ridiculous amount of horrid things done to him. They attached him to what is known as a Hickman line, a sort of semipermanent intravenous system, and pumped in gallons of chemo. Twice he's had bone marrow from banks, but both times he rejected them. The second time he almost died." Evelyn Lloyd spoke with the detachment of one who had learned to live with diamond-hard composure. "What if I were to hire your Mr. Glenwood to represent my husband?"

"Does he require representation?"

"Determining that," she replied, "would be the attorney's first task, would it not?"

"I'm sorry." Kirsten spoke very carefully. "But there could be a risk of conflict with the interests of another client."

Her hands stilled. "Ah. Yes. I was afraid of that."

Kirsten lifted her finger from the button. Their eyes remained locked in silent communion until the door slid shut.

"Marcus, it's me."

"Are you at your hotel?"

"No. I went back to see Evelyn Lloyd."

"Why?"

"Just wait and listen. I need you to do something for me."

"Kirsten, if the attacker was there before, there's every chance—"

"Marcus, this is important."

He caught the tone. "All right. What . . ."

"Kedrick Lloyd owns some North Carolina hotels."

"Owned."

"What?"

"He's sold them."

"How do you know?"

"His wife told me. Why?"

Kirsten tried to force her mind through the tangle. "Could you take a look at the sale documents?"

He showed her a rare impatience. "In case you haven't noticed, I'm handling some other pressing matters right now."

"This could be important. Vital."

"What am I looking for?"

"I wish I knew."

"You're not making sense."

"I know. But I have this feeling that Evelyn Lloyd just handed me something important, if only I can figure out what it is."

"The sale will be a matter of public record. Let me make a couple of calls. Where will you be in the meantime?"

There was no reason the answer should worry her as it did. "The Met."

———————

The call from Marcus came while she was still in the Met's basement-level reception area, waiting for someone to escort her to Kedrick Lloyd's office. "I'd like to congratulate you, but I'm too freaked right now."

"What did you find?"

"We struck gold. Or you did." Tension crackled like a storm of interference. "I spoke with a contact in the office of public records. Know who handled the legal proceedings?"

She knew the answer from his tone of voice. "The same man you've been fighting every step of the way."

"His name is Hamper Caisse. Know what this means?"

"We've found the connection."

"But not the motive."

The Met's reception area was a windowless cave down a narrow concrete hallway from the parking garage. The walls were adorned with wall-size posters of divas starring in this season's performances. She felt the sudden flood of temptation to fling the investigation and the case and the worries to the wind. "I miss you, Marcus."

He had to pause and swallow. "I feel like a yo-yo, swinging back and forth between what I want and what my mind is telling me I've got to do."

"I know," she whispered, "just exactly what you mean."

A pair of shared breaths, then he asked, "Tell me you want me to come up."

So much. "We can't walk away from this."

"I would, though."

"Marcus, do you think we can work things out?"

"I'm not looking for perfection, Kirsten. I passed the point of thinking I deserved that a long time ago."

"What are you saying?"

"Whatever you can give, whenever you're ready. How does that sound to you?"

She bit her lip against the hunger. Then, "Do something for me."

"Anything."

"Run through the way all this started. What you haven't told me before. I have the feeling what we're looking for is right in front of us."

"I've covered pretty much everything important."

"The small things. The details."

He expelled a long breath, pushing away what they both wanted to talk about. Then, "You were there for the first meeting with Dale. After that . . ."

"What?"

"I just thought of something." Sharper now. Focused. "Sephus Jones."

"The man who attacked me?"

"Yes. This might be the key."

A young woman appeared from the back hallway, and was pointed over by the guard. "Ms. Stansted?"

She said into the phone, "I have to go, Marcus."

"Come home."

"Soon."

"Now."

She gave the young woman a one-moment signal. "You know I can't."

"This is turning very dangerous, Kirsten. What could be more important than staying safe?"

"Finding the child. I'll call you as soon as I can." She shut off the phone and rose to her feet. "Sorry."

"Mr. Lloyd will see you now."

CHAPTER

43

DEACON AND FAY WILBUR'S HOME was located two miles east of the church, out in an area that was one step away from pure country. Marcus climbed from his car and passed under an oak canopy so tall there was no real shadow, just a gentle veil of verdant green.

The Wilbur home was a single-floor brick ranch whose side porch was almost as large as the house itself. Fay had lined the painted concrete slab with tubs of hydrangeas and hibiscus, the flowers so tall now they formed a solid wall encircling their outdoor parlor. The roof had been extended over the patio, then broadened to where the edges almost met the highest blooms. Overhead four ceiling fans spun gentle circles. Fay had linked woven reed mats to form a tatami-style flooring. Even in late July, the room held to cool and serene shadows.

Marcus found Yolanda seated by the cast-iron table, a schoolbook opened in front of her. Her older baby played at her feet. The young mother's eyes widened when she realized who he was. But before fear could push her away, Fay opened the screen door and said, "Marcus Glenwood, I've got a bone to pick with you."

"Afternoon, Fay. How are you doing, Yolanda?"

"She's getting along just fine. Ain't you, honey. Got herself into summer school, teacher says she's never seen a smarter lady." Fay emerged carrying Yolanda's younger child on her hip. "Listen up,

Marcus. It's been years since I've gotten you over here for Sunday dinner. You don't like my cooking anymore?"

"It was three weeks ago and you know it."

"That can't be right."

"I don't want to be a bother, Fay."

"Listen to you. Like another mouth at my dinner table's ever been a bother." She turned to Yolanda and said, "Honey, this child needs feeding. I'm gonna go heat him up a bottle."

Marcus pulled another chair to the table. "Fay, do you ever sit down?"

"Got all the time I'll ever need for sitting, once I find my place at heaven's table. You want I should bring you a lemonade?"

"No thank you."

"How 'bout you, Yolanda, you thirsty?"

"No thank you, Miz Fay."

Fay waved a hand at the child by the table. "Honey, why don't you come inside with me, let these grown-ups have a word. I think maybe I could scare you up an oatmeal cookie."

When they were alone, Marcus asked once more, "How're you doing, Yolanda?"

She frowned at the schoolbook. "This stuff sure is hard."

"I need to ask you something about what you told me the day we brought you back from Raleigh." He gave her a chance to object, then said, "You told me Hamper Caisse came around from time to time."

"Unh huh." Her face remained pointed straight at her schoolbook.

"Did you ever see another white man? Red hair swept straight back, pale gray eyes, almost no forehead at all, jailhouse tattoos across his knuckles."

The half-hidden face creased with a grimace far older than her years. "Terrible bad smell."

Marcus fought to keep his voice calm. "You don't remember ever hearing a name, do you?"

"Of the red-haired man?"

"Yes."

The young face scrunched up tighter. "Sephus?"

Marcus could not completely mask his excitement. "Did you ever happen to see him with the attorney who represented your former landlord?"

Fear hitched her voice up an octave. "You ain't gonna make me say something in court?"

"Nobody can ever force you to testify against your will, Yolanda. I won't let them. Think carefully now. This is important."

She gave a fraction of a nod. "That lawyer fellow, he used to call Sephus his walkaround man."

CHAPTER

44

T HE ONE NICE ELEMENT to Kedrick Lloyd's office was its window. Framed posters from previous galas only partly hid the water-stained walls. The ceiling bowed slightly above Kedrick's desk. The carpet was time-grayed and stained. The furnishings were functional and cheerless.

Kedrick Lloyd was a cadaver in tailored summer blue. His lion's mane of silver hair framed a face that had been sucked dry of all juices, all muscle, all tone. His skin slumped such that the edges of his eyes and mouth folded into constant disapproval. He did not rise at Kirsten's entry. "Illness has a few benefits, Ms. Stansted. One is the opportunity to do away with many senseless courtesies."

He was obviously expecting her to take offense, which is why Kirsten gave no indication she had even heard. As she crossed the carpet toward him, there was a knock on the door behind her. "A moment, Kedrick?"

"Sorry, Maestro, I have a visitor."

Nonetheless the heavyset gentleman slipped inside. "A second, then. I am rehearsing the full orchestra. Stanley phoned me during our break. He needs to have a word with you about our new *Tosca*. He told me the most disturbing news." He flashed a smile. "There, you see? A second and no more. All conductors must learn to count time with great precision." He slipped out.

"Unlike the Met's former leaders, this intendant has quite a rare appreciation for people's schedules. Most particularly my own." Kedrick Lloyd pointed her into a chair. "Evelyn insisted I give you a few minutes. The clock is now ticking."

She elected to be equally blunt. "Could you tell me why you objected to Dale Steadman marrying Erin Brandt?"

His only indication of surprise was a lifting of his eyebrows. "A strange sort of question, seeing as how the parties are now divorced and one of them also happens to be dead."

"But the problems related to their union remain."

"Oh, very well. Steadman has far too much trust in human nature. I saw it as my duty to try and correct that fatal flaw." He shrugged. "I failed."

"You call him overly trustworthy, yet you bankrolled him out of a tight spot."

"Dale is a fool only in his selection of mates. Whatever else he might enter into, he would win."

They were dancing, really. A step up, a step back. Watching and gauging and neither speaking of what was just below the surface. "You warned Dale away from Ms. Brandt, or tried to. Yet you repeatedly pressed the Met to hire her."

"Really, Ms. Stansted. This should be obvious. I was proposing the Met take on a talented singer. Not join her in unholy union. Our senior conductor disagreed. Erin was not invited. End of story."

"There was no other reason?"

A vague shifting of the currents behind his gaze. "What are you suggesting?"

Kirsten danced away by lowering her gaze. She asked the next question to the hands in her lap. "What about the child?"

A longish pause was by far the clearest answer he had given thus far. "What about her?"

Before she could decide how to respond, the phone rang. She lifted her gaze to find him inspecting her, head cocked to one side, eyes squinted in tight disdain. Finally he reached for the phone. "Lloyd." A moment, then, "You wish to know what I do with my time these days, Ms. Stansted? Behold. This is the budget director for our new production of *Tosca*." He punched the speaker button and declared, "You have thirty seconds, Stanley. I have a visitor."

"It's star chamber time," the sharply accented New Yorker declared. "They're going for the jugular."

"From the maestro's agitation, I take it this means they're after your budget again."

"Last spring they whittled a quarter million extra for the first production by that woman with the name like a poisonous creeping vine. Now they're back for the rest."

"I'm sure I can find you another hundred thousand or so from somewhere."

"It's not enough, big guy. Not this time. Word is she's after another half a mil."

Kedrick could not hide the shock. "You can't possibly be serious."

"They're sucking me dry, I tell you. I've got sets that haven't been redone since trench warfare was in vogue. Last rehearsal the soprano broke through the top stair, did a balancing act long enough to hit an F above high C, then crashed to the floor."

"This is utterly unacceptable," Kedrick snapped. "We have put off new *Tosca* sets far too long already."

"You're telling me. Imagine if it'd been Placido under her. We'd have made headlines all over the globe. Diva makes Domingo marmalade. But they're so far behind schedule, only some serious money will bandage the wound."

Kedrick checked his calendar. "They're seven weeks from opening!"

"Tell me."

"All right. You want me to call the director. What do you want me to say?"

"The truth."

"Yes, yes, yes. But what bits of the truth?"

"The truth I can't say."

"In other words, you want me to play the butcher's boy." Another silence. "I had always thought my swan song would leave them in tears, but of a rather different sort."

"You'll do it?"

"Of course, dear boy. Have I ever let you down?" Lloyd hit the disconnect, then immediately buzzed his secretary. "Get me Barry Schonfeld."

"I'm not certain he's in the building, Mr. Kedrick."

"I didn't ask for his whereabouts. I said get him!" He hammered the disconnect, swiveled his chair to the window, and sat feasting upon his upper lip. As he waited, he said idly, "Popular operas like *Tosca* bring in the dollars. New radical pieces keep a house on the artistic and critical map. The problem is, you get directors and artistic designers who have won their stripes doing Hollywood sets or theatrical

numbers with twice our budget and half our stage dimensions. Every
new production is a tournament between the artistic director and the
budget committee. When it moves into rehearsals, the conductor's ego
is added to this potent mix. It's a wonder we don't see bloodletting
more often."

"You truly live for this," Kirsten observed.

He turned and stared at her, clearly wondering what she had
heard. Then his secretary buzzed through with "I have Mr. Schonfeld
on line three."

"Thank you." His hand hovered over the receiver, beset by indeci-
sion, before hitting hit the speaker button. "Barry, I have been asked to
insert your nether regions into the fryer."

A laconic voice replied, "Everything's under control, Kedrick."

"Quite the contrary, from what I hear."

"Don't tell me Stanley's gotten to you with his woe and agony routine."

"I could build a house in the Hamptons for what your set is cost-
ing. Not to mention the fact that your designer is six weeks late and a
mil over budget. Why? Because you contracted the same designer who
demolished our budget last year!"

"You have a point. I'll take a personal look at how we allocate this
overspend."

"Allocate? *Allocate?*" Kedrick's ire lifted him from the chair.
"You're seven weeks from your opening night! Fire the woman! Sue
her! Burn her at the stake!"

A horrified silence. Then, "This is Louella Rhyther you're talking
about. She's the most famous set designer in LA."

"She won't be when this goes down! She'll be toast!"

"She wants another week."

"Of *course* she does. The closer we come to our final deadline the
more we'll be willing to throw money at her problem!"

A sudden case of nerves oozed from the speaker. "Apparently she
was slowed down by a severely sprained ankle."

"Oh. Dropped her wallet, did she?"

"She's splendid, Kedrick. The best."

"I find her an absolute shambolic mess, if you must know. To have
you say otherwise leaves me questioning your own abilities."

"What is that supposed to mean?"

"Well, the board can hardly be expected to maintain a strong rapport with a director whose judgment they question."

There was an audible gulp. "I'll handle it."

"You really must be fierce with her about this deadline. And if she balks even by a half hour . . ."

"Yes?"

"Fire her. Or I shall personally fire *you*." He punched the button and declared, "No doubt our famous new director will now give birth to a nine-pound ulcer."

Kirsten rose to her feet. The smoke and mirrors were complete about this man. She would gain nothing more here. "Thank you for your time."

"Go home, Ms. Stansted. That's my advice to you. Marry your nice little lawyer friend, raise some beautiful children, forget there is a big world out there beyond the confines of what you find comfortable." He smirked a superior farewell. "Leave these other matters to those of us who understand how the world truly works."

CHAPTER

45

I T WAS NOT UNTIL MARCUS was turning into his drive that he finally managed to get an answer at one of the man's numbers. "Dale? It's Marcus."

"I can't talk now."

"This is important. Vital."

"Oh, and this isn't? You think selling my house for a million less than it cost me to build is fun? Or maybe how I'm cashing out my entire portfolio and losing almost as much as I'm getting?"

"Dale, listen to me."

"No, Marcus. The time for listening is over. Kedrick was right. The case was hopeless from the start. There's only one way to get my baby girl back and that's what I'm doing."

"You're right."

"You're not talking me around, I'm going ahead with this . . ." Marcus' words finally sank home. "What?"

"The case was a nowhere job to begin with. All it did was bring them close enough to the brink for us to have this shot." Marcus gave it a moment, then said, "Are you with me now?"

"Yes. But we have to hurry. I'm waiting to hear from the mystery buyer's bank."

"All right. I want you to think back to the break-in."

"You mean, the one here at the house?"

"Tell me everything you remember."

"Now is not the time."

"Believe me, it's never been more the time. Please."

"It was just your basic burglary. They were here when I got in."

"Here where?"

"In the house. Where else? You think I'd hammer them because they were walking across my backyard?"

"So you found them in the house. Where exactly?"

"On the landing leading to Celeste's bedroom."

"That's it." That was the point he had half remembered.

"It's the same stairs that lead up to the master bedroom. The safe's bolted to the floor in my closet. Where else would they be?"

There was nothing to be gained by sharing suspicions. "I'm coming down."

"To Wilmington?"

"Yes. Keep your mobile switched on. I may have something important." Marcus hung up before Dale could argue.

———————

Marcus did not want to be going to Wilmington. His heart was already covering the distance to New York. Every time he spoke with Kirsten, the draw was stronger. He had not known such a sense of impatience since he was sixteen and just another hyperhormonal high school jock with nothing more than football and Carolina cheerleaders on the mind. The connection was so potent he could feel it radiating like a carnal scent, flavoring the office atmosphere.

He dialed the judge's office in Wilmington. "Judge Perry, this is Marcus Glenwood."

"I thought we had us an arrangement. You weren't to ever bother me again."

"Things change."

"I've got me five minutes between two felony trials, and that's the best you can do?"

"I need an introduction to the Wilmington district attorney."

"I am astonished to hear I am the best reference you can find to our local constabulary."

"The one and only."

"Sir, your confidence in me is utterly unfounded." When Marcus did not rise to the bait, he added, "In case you have missed it, I do not like you. Nor do I think much of your tactics."

"Which tactic would that be?" Marcus lashed back. "The one that says every individual convicted of a felony in this land has the Constitutional right to legal representation?"

There was a silence from the phone. Netty's head poked in around the door. Even his secretary realized it was not sensible to be yelling at a sitting judge.

But Marcus was too far gone to care. "Wait, no, it must be my *other* tactic you're thinking of. The one where I have a man arrive on my doorstep and beg for help. This after all your local lawyers proved too cowed by Wilmington power brokers to realize the man is innocent of everything except wanting back his baby girl."

"The DA's name is Wilma Blain," the judge replied. "You two should get on like a house on fire."

Marcus slammed down the phone. He spoke to Netty before she could comment on his actions or state of mind. "Get the Wilmington prosecutor's office on the line for me."

She started for the door, then asked, "You doing all right?"

Marcus hefted his mug. His coffee was stone cold. "I'm worried about Kirsten."

"You're nothing but a bundle of nerves and frets." She walked over to the desk and took the mug from his hand. "More caffeine is the last thing in this world you need."

A few moments later, Netty called from the other room. "DA's office on line two."

"Marcus Glenwood for Wilma Blain, please."

A half minute of seventies retro-rock, then, "This is Blain."

"Marcus Glenwood. I'm an attorney operating out of Rocky Mount, mostly in the Raleigh—"

"I know who you are." The woman's voice was almost as deep as a man's, and sounded both black and rapid-fire intelligent. "We might be working out of a sleepy backwater town, but we're wide awake in this office."

"I have come across something related to a case I'm involved in that might interest you."

"Who referred you to me?"

"Garland Perry."

"Judge Perry gave you my name?" She sounded genuinely surprised.

"He did."

"Are you sure he was on the proper medication at the time? I've never gotten a thing from that man but a full-on runaround."

"This matter is urgent, no matter what Judge Perry might think."

"Ain't they all."

"Do you happen to recall a break-in at Dale Steadman's residence, I'm not sure exactly when it would have been—"

"Seven weeks, give or take a day." All business now.

"You're familiar with the case?"

"You might say so. Tell me something, counselor. This have anything to do with the missing child?"

"Possibly."

"What about the still pending investigation into the demise of Charlie Hayes?"

Angry sorrow ground down his voice. "I sincerely hope so."

"Not to mention the murder-one beef that brought the big-city detective barging around?"

"You don't miss much."

"This is a small town with mostly small-town problems. Happens I like it that way. And you didn't answer my question."

"The answer is," Marcus replied, "I'm calling to hopefully find out that very same thing."

"Well, now. That's an answer I like."

"Why is that?"

"Happens the two gents are still locked up next door."

"What?"

"Garland Perry was off fishing the day they came for arraignment. We got us a hotshot district judge, young fellow who was a state prosecutor in an earlier life. This judge was willing to listen when I pointed out the pair had a mess of prior felonies and seven parole violations between them. He invited them to remain our guests until the trial."

Marcus was already up and moving. "You think I could come down and have a word?"

CHAPTER

4 6

KEDRICK LLOYD'S SECRETARY was not in the cramped outer office when Kirsten departed. She slipped into the hallway and decided to wander.

But around the first corner she was halted by a voice from behind. "Can I help you?"

Kirsten turned to face a young man in tank top and linen drawstring pants and sneakers. A sweater was bundled around his neck. His smile was lustrous, his poise dancer-perfect. "I was hoping to meet the senior conductor."

"Are you supposed to be back here?"

"I'm meeting with Kedrick Lloyd."

His flirtatious attitude vanished. "Right. Sorry, with all these security scares we're supposed to be extra careful."

"It's fine."

"The orchestra has just finished rehearsals, so you'll probably find the maestro up toward the stage somewhere."

She followed the hall up a flight of stairs and around a corner. She stepped to one side as a stream of people poured through the stage door. Up ahead she spotted the maestro reading over the shoulders of three women. The ladies held thick scores with both hands. Violin cases stood at their feet. The conductor had on a herringbone flannel shirt and fitted Cerrutti jeans, and displayed the swept-back hair of a dedicated Romeo. He wiped his face with a thick hand towel as he studied the music.

"Do you still have a fermata after the second beat?"

"It was taken out, Maestro."

"Fine, fine, just so long as I know." He had an odd mixture of accents, Italian and something heavier, a liquid German or Eastern European. "Let's hold to the rigid beat throughout, then. I'll inform her majesty at the dress rehearsal that she is not permitted to breathe through the entire aria." He smiled them on their way.

Only when he faced her was his age evident. And the strain of the rehearsal. "Yes?"

"I was wondering if I might ask you a question, Maestro."

"Did I not see you upstairs in Kedrick's office?"

"That is correct."

"And he sent you down?"

Kirsten was unable to hide behind a lie. "He probably would be furious to discover us talking."

That brought out a smile. "Well then. Perhaps I can find a moment."

"I'm trying to obtain some information about a singer."

"Dirt, you mean." When she did not contradict him, he inquired, "Are you a journalist?"

"I work for a lawyer. We are involved in a very serious court case."

"Another singer is in trouble with the law?" He shook his head in sorrow. "There is nothing magical about the Met for those of us fortunate enough to work here. Our job is to create magic for those out front. We work the backstage magic machine. One of my predecessors used to ride home by subway after every performance. He had a limo paid for and waiting outside, but he went by subway. Why? Because he felt it was important to remind himself just how mundane and ordinary his backstage world truly was." He had a most attractive smile. "Myself, I would prefer a note card attached to the door of the limo."

She realized he was coming on to her, and smiled in reply. "Positioned just above the champagne bucket."

"You like champagne. Excellent. A sign of good breeding and fine moments to come." He gave her a moment to continue the flirtation, then shrugged his acceptance of her distance. Another time. "So. Which singer is of interest to you?"

"Erin Brandt."

His good humor vanished. "But Ms. Brandt is most decidedly dead."

"That is correct."

"Still her problems go on?"

"I'm afraid so. And a very good man risks losing everything."

He inspected her. "Do I want to know more?"

"Probably not, Maestro."

"*Bene*." He glanced in both directions, then drew her over to one side. "We are not having this discussion."

"I understand."

"We would not be talking at all, except for the fact that Ms. Brandt is now lost to us all." He scouted the hall once more. "You know I came from the Zurich opera house, did you not?"

"No."

"Indeed. And from your expression I see you have heard the story of Erin Brandt's debut. Yes. I was intendant there before coming to the Met. Erin made her debut at a performance that I conducted."

"How did she sing?"

"Magnificently. Erin Brandt's singing was never the issue. Nor her acting. It was the *person* I refused to work with."

"Can you give me something more precise?"

"Not for the record. You understand? I have nothing for you if you wish to make notes or write something public."

"I am working on background information for a court case, Maestro. Nothing more."

"Then with you I will share my secret. The diva scheduled to perform that night, she was a friend. A very, very good friend. You understand?"

"Perfectly."

"She also had a cast bronze stomach. She had many problems. Her voice, her age, her hearing, her legs, her circulation, her . . . Never become involved with a singer, my dear. They are a most taxing group of ladies. But her stomach was never a problem. Never, never, never. Do you understand?"

"You think Erin poisoned her?"

"Not poison. My friend recovered. She was very ill for three days, then it was gone." He wagged his finger between them. "And you will remember what I said, yes?"

She offered her hand. "It was very nice not meeting you, Maestro."

He bowed over her hand, not quite drawing it to his lips. "You really must come by and introduce yourself some other time, signorina. I am certain I would be delighted to make your acquaintance."

CHAPTER

47

T HE DA CAUGHT MARCUS on his cell phone just as he was turning onto I-95. "Wilma Blain, counselor. You someplace where you can give me your full attention?"

Marcus tucked himself behind a lumbering Freightliner doing an easy sixty. "Fire away."

"I've done some checking." The tiny phone turned her voice flat as cold iron. "The fellow who represented the accused at the arraignment is still listed as their attorney."

The lawyer would have to be notified of Marcus' arrival, as he was required to be present for all questioning by the authorities. "Do you know him well enough to get him down on short notice?"

"Can't say. Seeing as how they're represented by a courtroom rat from up Raleigh way."

Marcus braked sharply, causing the SUV on his tail to swerve and honk and shout something he could not be bothered to hear. "Not Hamper Caisse."

"On the money. The fact he's still involved brings two critical questions to mind."

"You want to know why two lowlifes involved in a simple B&E are being handled by a guy from Raleigh. And you want to know why Hamper agreed to take the case."

"I like the way your mind works, counselor. A courthouse rat like Caisse wouldn't dream of spending a day down here for an arraignment, followed by visits to his clients, then a week for a trial."

A courthouse rat was a lawyer whose real office was the district court's front patio, since all courthouse rats smoked like chimneys and used butt time to prep their clients. Their hours coincided with the metal-detector guards'—first to enter, last to leave. "Hamper has been down for visits with this pair since the arraignment?"

"Interesting question. Know what I did after I learned Hamper was still listed as handling this mess?"

Marcus found his chest tightening. "You checked the prison visitors' log."

"You're not looking for a job, are you?"

"I'd never be able to keep up with you, ma'am."

She laughed. "Apparently Hamper Caisse is beating a path between Raleigh and the coast. You man's been down here eight times in the past six weeks. What's more, Hamper's only seen one of the guys six of those times."

"Are you sure about that?"

"Your mental lightbulbs just went off. I can hear it happening. Just popping on everywhere."

"You're enjoying this."

"You kidding? I've got me two bad guys with sheets long enough to wrap them up like shrouds. You don't think I'd like to find something to bury them?"

"Calling Hamper directly won't work," Marcus said. Courthouse rats had mobile phone usage down to an exact science. They never answered their calls. Never. They checked messages, thus giving themselves an out when cornered. "And it might be Halloween before he actually visits his office again."

"So?"

"Call Judge Rachel Sears. Family court. Third floor of the district courthouse. Tell her exactly what we're facing here. Then see if she'll *order* Hamper to meet us in Wilmington."

"I am liking this conversation," the DA said, "more and more."

"Ask her to do so with a minimum amount of nicety. We want this guy to show up parboiled," Marcus suggested. "Oh, and one more thing. Ask Judge Sears if she would not tell Hamper it's me. We might be able to use that as leverage."

"I get the impression you already know why this Raleigh hotshot is taking the trouble to drive down and handle the case of two punks on a burglary charge."

"I don't know, but I can guess."

"Guess away."

"It wasn't robbery."

"I'm listening."

"And they're not his client."

"Then who is?"

"That is exactly," Marcus replied, "what I want to ask them myself."

CHAPTER

48

FINDING A DOCTOR who would meet with Kirsten at short notice required going back to the hotel and asking the receptionist for help. When she said she wanted to meet urgently with an oncologist, the concierge looked bereaved. An hour later, she was seated in the swank outer office of a Park Avenue specialist. The nurse was polite but firm in requesting an up-front payment. The doctor's waiting area was done in suede and steel, with a pink coral coffee table and framed Picasso etchings. A half hour later Kirsten was seated in his office—same artwork, more valuable antique furniture. Nothing to suggest it was a doctor's office except for the books on the shelves behind his rosewood desk. That and the vague clinical odor from somewhere farther along the dreaded corridors.

"Ms. Stansted?" He was young-old and tall in the way of men who bowed over slightly to accommodate themselves to a shorter world. "Jay Walsh. I understand this is something of an emergency."

"I'm actually here for information," she said. "About a friend's condition."

"An acquaintance."

"That's right."

"Is this acquaintance a patient of mine?"

"I hope not."

He slid into his high-backed leather chair. "And you are?"

"Working on a legal case."

"I don't do court work, Ms. Stansted."

"This is a preliminary interview for background information only."

He had the lean look of a dedicated athlete. But no healthy regime could erase the smeared strain of watching patients die. "Your friend has cancer?"

"He does."

"What form?"

"Leukemia. CML."

He had the good grace to grimace. "I assume he has gone through the traditional treatments."

"Yes."

"And they have not been successful." It was not a question.

"No."

"Do you know his blood type?"

"Only that it is rare."

"Has he had bone marrow transplants?"

"Twice. They failed."

"Does he have a living blood relative?"

"No. Why is that such a problem?"

"For reasons that still are not absolutely clear, marrow from a blood relative is far less subject to rejection."

She read the unspoken from his expression. "But there are problems."

"Putting it into the patient is not difficult. It is not inserted into the marrow, but rather into the blood. Eventually, if previous treatments have eradicated all the diseased marrow, this new substance will take over production of white blood cells and replenish the bones with new healthy marrow." He struck his leg with a tight fist. "But drawing the marrow from living bone is a very difficult procedure, and not without risk. The needle has to have a bore large enough to extract a substance with the consistency of cold molasses. We must thrust this probe right through the arm or leg, and punch deep into the bone."

She spoke with extreme care. "What if the only blood relative is an infant?"

"How old?"

"Sixteen months."

"Is that what your case is about?"

"I'm sorry, I don't understand."

"This is an ongoing issue. Personally, I wouldn't subject an infant to this for love or money. We have no idea what effect this procedure might have on a child's development. What if it retarded growth in that limb?"

"But another doctor might be willing?"

"Nobody I'd associate with." His voice and features had both turned to flint. "Are we done here?"

"What if the patient does not have a blood relative?"

"Then I would urge you to begin making arrangements."

Kirsten rose to her feet. "Thank you for your time."

But the doctor was not finished. "Without further delay."

Kirsten called Marcus from the doctor's waiting room. Or tried to. But he was either out of range or had his mobile shut off. She left a terse message, her words strained through the awareness of patients pretending not to listen. Their features bore the same shadows as the doctor's. Suddenly she could think of nothing nicer than being out and away.

She walked down Park Avenue taking deep draughts of the city's air. She tasted the diesel fumes like the elixir of life. She relished the sirens and the horns and the jostling crowds and the muggy overcast heat. Question: What would a vain and blindly conceited man do, given the fact that his life depended upon it? Answer: Anything and everything he could.

When the phone cheeped at her, she felt such a rush over the prospect of talking to Marcus again it embarrassed her. Kirsten walked down a side street and up a trio of stone stairs, then turned toward the wall in an effort to find as much privacy as midday uptown Manhattan could provide. "Marcus?"

"Ms. Stansted?"

"Yes?"

"This is Kurt Luft. Calling you from Düsseldorf."

The fact that there could be only one reason for the German detective to call her did nothing to cut away her disappointment. "Yes, Mr. Luft."

"I have been contacted by the former housemaid to Ms. Erin Brandt. She is a very stubborn woman, Ms. Stansted. Very difficult."

"What did she say?"

"Nothing. She refuses to speak unless she can personally deliver the message." The detective sounded genuinely irate at the disorderly process. "Wait, I am putting her on the line."

There was a scratching hiss, then, "You are here now, yes?"

"Goscha? How are you? How is the child?"

"The baby, ah, ah, the baby. Please, you must help her."

"But the money isn't ready yet, Goscha. Do you understand about the money?"

"I am overhearing conversations. Bad things are happening, and right now. You must come."

"Goscha, who is behind the kidnapping?"

"This also I am wondering. I hear Reiner Klatz speak to his wife. You know Klatz?"

"Erin Brandt's manager."

"They say ten million dollars is coming."

Kirsten inspected the cracked stone wall in front of her face, searching for understanding. "They told Dale five. I'm sure of it."

"Ten million. Herr Klatz, he says something about new instructions. Please, you are helping now, yes?"

CHAPTER

4 9

THE WILMINGTON district attorney's office was attached to the police station and city lockup. All were built of the same Carolina brick, with slit windows and an air of grim functionality. The DA's appearance was a perfect fit to her voice—big-boned and heavy, a shiny black force that cleared everything from her path. She greeted Marcus with, "Hamper Caisse would not be doing a trial of two would-be robbers down in Wilmington. How many cases does he have running at any one time, thirty?"

"More."

"Call it thirty cases to stay conservative. Even for a DUI he'd be clearing five hundred dollars a pop. Bound to have five or six cases on a decent day."

"Somebody else is pulling Hamper's strings," Marcus agreed. "Did you call the Raleigh courthouse?"

"Just like you suggested. Judge Sears is a fine lady, by the way. Sends you her regards. She heard me out, then brought Hamper into chambers and put me on the speaker phone." She had a brilliant smile. "I tell you what, that made my day. He hit a high note. Several of them, in fact."

"Is he coming?"

Wilma Blain ushered him down the hall and into her office. "Made a lot of noise about how we had to put this off. So me and Sears, we struck Hamper with a double whammy. Sears ordered him down, just like we hoped." She pointed Marcus into a chair. "I told him we were opening the case again, starting from scratch, seeing what else we could hit these guys with. Man didn't even let me finish. Soon as he realized this was a happening thing, he was up and headed for the door."

"A happening thing." Marcus returned the grin. "How did I ever miss working with you up to now?"

"Shoot, you're too busy chasing dragons from what I hear. Got your guns loaded with high-velocity heat-seekers."

"I'm just another Carolina country lawyer."

"You can go sell that one down the street." She settled into her chair. "I hear Charlie Hayes was a friend of yours."

"That's right."

"Says a lot for you. He was a good man."

"Yes."

"I'm sorry. Don't know what else I can say except we aim on tracking down the killers and putting them away. You can take that to the bank." She gave him a full-on inspection. "Straight up, now. Did Dale Steadman murder his wife?"

"No. Absolutely not."

"Dale Steadman held two fund-raisers for me at that Disney castle he built. Went out of his way to help me when most of the wealthy citizens of this good town would just as soon have shown me the back of their hand."

"If I was his judge and not his lawyer, I'd be telling you the same thing. Dale Steadman is innocent of everything except loving his child."

"I believe you." She tightened her gaze. "Ain't that a shocker? A DA admitting such a thing to a defense attorney."

"It's the nicest compliment I've had in a long while."

"Okay. Enough of the talk-talk. Here's what we got." She opened the files. "Local boy, James Walker, aka all sorts of silly old names, most recently going by the highly original guise of Studley."

"Studley Walker. I can see him already."

"Boy's so smart he thinks Cheerios are doughnut seeds. Been arrested a grand total of nineteen times, not bad for somebody still making a grab for twenty-five." She stabbed the second file. "Skyler Cummins. Altogether different ballgame. You run across him before?"

"No."

"You must not do much criminal work. He's from Durham originally, then Raleigh by way of Chicago. Extortion, assault, battery, armed robbery. Two stints of hard time."

"A bad one."

"You'll see." She closed the files. "So let's hear your impression."

"Two-bit was approached by the heavy."

"Looks that way to me as well."

"Heavy is the only one who knows who's behind this. Which means we have to turn him."

"I want to work on Studley first. One thing we might use. When I spoke to our chief jailer about the visitor's log, he mentioned James Walker had words with him a few days back. The begging kind. Like he'd be willing to do something if it meant getting him away from his present digs. At the time, the jailer didn't give it much thought, seeing as how we were dealing with a simple B&E." She motioned to the coffeepot. When Marcus shook his head, she asked, "So how do you want to play this one out?"

"This is your turf."

Wilma Blain shook her head. "I like your style, counselor. Help me out here."

"I like the fact he's already approached the jailer. A lot."

"Our man James may not be the brightest penny in the roll. But he's managed to smell out something's not right with this picture."

"Or he's been threatened."

"That thought crossed my mind as well."

"So have the jailer bring him over, and on the way let it slip about these visits Hamper made to the other man."

"I'm with you."

"The jailer might even mention how talking to you without his lawyer present isn't possible unless he first dismisses Hamper." Defense counsel was required by law to be present whenever a representative of the opposition wished to speak with the accused, unless of course the accused fired his counsel. "Bring the guy out here. Hold your meeting in a courthouse chamber. No manacles. Leave the guard outside the door."

"You mean, when he talks to us."

"Do you have a room with one-way glass?"

She showed surprise for the very first time. "You want to hide yourself away?"

"Only," Marcus replied, "until we spring our trap."

———————

"Reiner Klatz."

"Reiner, this is Kirsten Stansted."

There was an astonished silence. "You are finding me even at ten thousand meters?"

"What?"

"Never mind. I had hoped for the pleasure of never hearing from you again."

"The feeling is mutual, Reiner. Now tell me about the other offer."

A pause. "Please?"

"The other offer, Reiner. The one not coming from Dale Steadman."

A muffled curse sent Kirsten bounding off the bed and shooting for the corner of the hotel room where she had stowed her empty suitcase. "Ten million, do I have that right?"

"Goscha," he muttered. "It could only be."

"Focus, Reiner. It's either answers or the police. Take your pick."

"No police!" The man moved to high falsetto and stayed there. "I am told the baby will die!"

"Who's talking with you, Reiner?"

"I know nothing! Nothing! First I am slave to Erin Brandt, now to mystery men who have her child! I am an *opera manager!*"

"Slow down, Reiner. Tell me what you know."

"Did you not hear me? I know nothing at all! I receive a call from people, bad people. They say they have the child. They tell me you will be coming with money."

"Then what about—"

"You just *wait*! Then I receive *another* call."

"Same people?"

"Who am I to know? They are not giving me answers to anything! They say forget you and forget Dale's money. Now there will be *other* money."

"From where?"

"They tell me asking questions will only cause pain and death, you understand? All I am told is, I am to travel to Wilmington to receive the money. They have sent for me a private plane. I will be the go-between for the child."

"But if Dale isn't to pay then why—"

"Please, you are to ask no more questions. You are to call me never again. You are to go away and never reveal yourself to me. Are we clear on these matters? Good. For the first time since this horror began, I have a gladness."

CHANPTER

50

J AMES STUDLEY WALKER wore a pompadour two inches tall. From
behind the one-way glass, Marcus watched him saunter into the
room rubbing his wrists where the manacles had just been removed.
The blond pompadour looked waxed. He carried cigarettes rolled
into his right sleeve and a foot-long comb in the back pocket of his
prison coveralls. No tattoos, no earrings, no jailyard jewelry. James
was a redneck hood, pure and simple. Marcus checked his sheet.
James' last attempt at the straight life had lasted sixteen months and
seen him pass through eleven different jobs, all construction. He
had been arrested while still on parole. Bar fight. James Studley
Walker had used a bar stool and steel-toed boots to dance all over five
other men.

The first words out of his mouth were "I'm not stupid."

"I'm glad to hear that, James. Because I don't have a second to
waste on stupid men." Wilma Blain gestured across the scarred table.
"Take a seat, why don't you."

"Is it true what the guard said?"

"What's that?"

"How the lawyer's been down to see the other guy and not me."

"Six times, James."

"That can't be right."

She lifted the broad register, set it on the table between them,
opened to the relevant pages, and swiveled it around. "This is the official prison logbook. You know the routine. Everybody signs in and
out. Have a look where I've marked. See that name? Hamper Caisse.

And see the next column here? Who he's here to visit. Skyler Cummins. No mention of you, now, is there?"

"I don't believe this."

"Six times, James. Count 'em." She leafed through the pages, pointing to the highlighted entries. She let him brood for a moment. "Tell me what he said to you, James."

"Who?"

"Come on now. Work with me here. The attorney who's forgotten all about you. The one you just told the jailer you've decided to fire. That is correct, isn't it?"

"The dude's left me here to rot!"

"Just what I said." She slipped a sheaf of papers from her briefcase and set it on the open logbook. "This is a formal statement that states you are hereby dismissing your defense attorney. Put your John Henry down by the cross there." She waited for him to sign, then flipped the page. "And this says you are talking to me of your own volition, and have elected not to have any legal representation present at this time."

She stowed the pages away, shut the logbook, and drew a tape recorder from her case. The same one that had been running since James walked in the door. "You don't mind if I tape this conversation, do you, James? It'll save me having to repeat all the questions later for the record."

"The guy never even offered to bond me out!"

"He couldn't, James. The judge denied you bail. Now, see how I'm playing it straight with you? I could have given you the runaround, agreed with you just to make it seem like I was on your side. But I didn't. Because I'm looking to receive the same from you, James. The straight skinny." She folded her hands upon the table. "So tell me what happened."

"We went in to do this deal, okay?"

"You were hired to break into Dale Steadman's residence."

"Right." He unfurled his sleeve, pulled out a cigarette, waited while she lit it for him, dragged deep. "I handled the locks and the security system."

"No big deal."

"Your basic snatch and grab, only we came in by boat. Which at the time seemed kinda cool. But once we were inside, the guy wouldn't let me touch a thing."

"Skyler Cummins, the other inside man."

"Right. The guy told me once we were finished, he'd give me money. He was looking for something particular and didn't want anything else touched. Only I never got paid." A heavy drag. "So I didn't do a thing."

"James, you're forgetting one thing here."

"What."

"You were caught on the premises after breaking into this guy's house."

"So they're gonna give me ten months for taking a walk?"

"Remember the list of priors, James. Try three to five."

"This is nuts."

"Hard time, James. You know how they treat repeat offenders in this state."

He slung one arm over the back of his chair and smoked. Patches of sweat began spreading across his back. "So are you gonna help me out here or what?"

"That depends on you, James." She remained an utterly calm presence, her eyes as flat as her voice. "My guess is, you know what was going down here."

James just sat and smoked and sweated.

"You said it yourself. You're nobody's fool. You know this wasn't a straight B&E. You know something bigger was going down." She leaned in close. "Now tell me what Hamper Caisse said to you the first time you met up with him."

"The guy came in, said he was a bigshot attorney from Raleigh sent down to take care of me."

"Take care how?"

"Exactly what I said. The guy just tells me to sit tight. Says I don't know what I've gotten into, like it was my fault."

"You're saying he threatened you?"

"Pretty much. Told me not to talk to anybody, inside or out, and he'd be back. Does that make sense to you? I mean, a lawyer's supposed to get me *out*, not tell me to hang around inside."

"So why did you stick with him until now?" She sat and waited with him for a while, then said very quietly, "Somebody got to you, didn't they."

"The other guy."

"Skyler Cummins."

"Told me if I said a word to anybody, I was gonna get shanked."

His shirt was plastered wet and shiny to his frame. "Which is exactly what's gonna happen if you put me back in the cage."

"Like I said, James. That depends on you."

"I don't know what I'm into here and I don't care. I've had all I'm gonna take of somebody else playing me like a fool."

She inspected his face, tight now, peeling the skin back with the force of her gaze. "You're telling me you don't know who was behind all this?"

"They never mentioned a name to me. Not once."

"But you know what they were after."

He responded by mashing his cigarette to a pulp in the ashtray.

"Come on, James. Work with me here. You know it. I know it. I want to hear you say it." Her voice was a gritty whisper. "Tell me what the other guy was going to take."

"He never said."

"But you know."

"Sure. Okay. It was the kid."

"Celeste Steadman. He was there to kidnap Dale Steadman's baby girl."

"It had to be, right? I mean, what else could it be?"

"Just one more question, James. Tell me about the other man."

"The boat guy?" He shrugged. "Didn't even get his name."

"Skyler brought him along as well?"

"No idea. The driver didn't say a single word the whole time."

"He dumped you in the pinch, James. There's no need to protect him."

"I'm telling you I don't know a thing."

"So describe the man."

"Hard-time guy. Red hair. Crazy grin. Awful smell."

"If he didn't speak, how do you know he was a repeat felon?"

Marcus was tightly attached to the window, close enough to see James display his own bare knuckles. "Guy carried some real jailhouse art."

"On his hands?"

"Body art everywhere. But some older stuff on his knuckles you know had to be done inside."

Wilma Blain leaned back. "Okay, James. You've been very helpful here."

"So you're not gonna put me back in the lockup, right?"

She clicked off the tape player and slid it back into her briefcase.

"You'll be transferred to another prison and registered under an assumed name until we need you to appear in court."

"I didn't sign up to be a stooge."

"Not a stooge, James." She rose, walked over, knocked on the door, then stepped back as the guard entered. As the guard refitted the manacles, she gave him a grim smile. "Think of it as your one shining hour."

CHAPTER

51

MARCUS' PHONE RANG just as he was exiting the cramped glass-walled room.

Dale Steadman demanded, "Where are you?"

"The DA's office. Dale, I think we may have found the missing link."

He might as well not have spoken. "Coastal Citizens Bank. First and Harbor. I need you to come now."

"Dale, I've got the DA here with me, and we've—"

"Get over here now!"

Marcus let the dead phone fall from his ear, slightly embarrassed by the way he had been publicly treated. The DA met his gaze with the hard warmth of one who had been there before. "Client?"

"I think," Marcus replied, "Dale Steadman is about five minutes away from coming totally undone."

"Take your time. We can't move on Skyler until our mister rat gets down from Raleigh anyway."

"The third man James mentioned. I have a name for you."

She crossed her arms. "Man, you're just full of surprises."

"Sephus Jones. He's got a record long as Skyler's."

"You know this gentleman?"

"Met him. Once. He's attacked my fiancée. Twice."

She pointed him toward the door. "You go see to your business. We can hear the rest when you get back."

Dale waited for Marcus in a bank built to resemble a Grecian tomb fronting Wilmington's waterside. The bank manager was bug-eyed at the size of the banker's check he had on his otherwise empty desk. Marcus could see the zeros all the way across the office as the manager's assistant ushered him inside. He did not need to count them. He knew the amount and he knew what it meant.

"You've sold your house?"

Dale replied with the raspy baritone of a man whose voice was only the outermost sign of interior shredding. "How soon can Kirsten be ready to go?"

Marcus waved sharply at the banker, halting him from rising. "Dale, you have got to hear me out."

"No, Marcus. I'm the one who's talking here. You're listening, you're doing. You got that?"

"But—"

"Question one." He paused to slide the arm of his jacket across his forehead and then sweep the crook of his elbow down over his face. "Is anything you've got to say going to bring my baby girl back to me *now*?"

"Maybe."

Dale sent his fist crashing down upon the desk. The banker backed up a notch. "Maybe isn't an option! Yes or no. Is my baby coming home because of what you have found?"

"I can't guarantee you that. But—"

"No buts! No maybes, no tomorrows!" Dale kept his gaze leveled at the corner of the office, a grim focus as tight as the menacing crouch to his shoulders. He cocked his head at the check on the desk. The motion corded his neck muscles. "That's everything I own, Marcus. Everything I've spent a lifetime putting together."

"We've managed to speak with one of the burglars you caught."

"That is ancient history."

The fact that Dale heard him at all pushed Marcus forward. "They were after Celeste, Dale. They were paid to kidnap your child. It's all tied in somehow. Erin's return, Hamper Caisse, the trial, the attack on Kirsten, everything."

Still he refused to lift his gaze. "So they won."

"All we need is a little—"

"All *we* need? All we *need*?" Dale shook his head, a bull struggling to contain a red-flag rage. "Will you and Kirsten do this thing or not?"

"I think you're making a terrible mistake."

"That's me. Dale Steadman, master of the perpetual blunder. Yes or no."

"Yes, Dale. If you insist, I will act upon your behalf."

The banker was so ready he could not get his hands to move fast enough, or keep the tremolo from his voice. "If you'll just sign here for the receipt of this check, Mr. Glenwood. Thank you. May I see some identification that bears your signature? Fine. You understand that this is a banker's check, and once you have signed this release, it is as good as cash."

Marcus signed the triplicate forms, accepted back his driver's license, then slipped the envelope and the check into his pocket. Five million dollars. He turned back to where Dale's gaze bore a hole in the far corner and settled his hand upon Dale's shoulder. Beneath the jacket was nothing save stone.

When he returned to the DA's office, Hamper Caisse had still not arrived. Marcus placed the check in Wilma Blain's evidence safe and went for a walk. Two blocks on and he was lost within an east Carolina realm. Pines and hardy scrubwoods formed uniform walls at either side of the road, a comforting enclosure that invited a peace and slower pace. Two blocks farther and he entered a neighborhood of time-washed houses and empty lots turned to neighborhood truck gardens. Dogs panted and watched his passage from shaded porches, reluctant to enter the heat. The sun filtered through the overhead limbs and turned the road into a shimmering silver-black river. Heat blistered the air.

He knew he should apply his mind to the pressures at hand. But the afternoon held room for little more than the sound of his footsteps and the unspoken bonding to this place and time. There was nothing that explained why even a day drenched in summer humidity could sparkle and shine, save for the fact that he belonged here. He was determined to accomplish the impossible in this contemporary world of fickle allegiances. Here he would stay, here he would breathe his last. There was only one more thing he would ask from life, or so it seemed at the time. One final wish, and he would ask nothing further. He stared into the heavens and let the sun heighten his single consuming desire to have a white-haired beauty walk this lane with him.

Which was why, when his phone rang and he heard Kirsten's voice on the other end, the first words out of his mouth were "Marry me."

"What?"

He stepped beneath a live oak and gripped the nearest branch with his free hand. "I'm surrounded by a billion pressures, and all I can think about is us. I love you so much it hurts to breathe. Marry me, Kirsten."

"Marcus . . ." A pause, then, "Wait, wait, I have to sit down."

Which is exactly what he did. Dressed in his business suit and sweating through his shirt and jacket both, he dropped down to the dusty curb. A dog meandered over and sniffed at him. There was some hound in the curious canine face, but no aggression. Which was good. Right then Marcus doubted he could have risen to flee a slavering Doberman.

When Kirsten spoke again, she had somehow managed to shed half her age, for it was a little girl's voice which said, "Being away from you this time has become agony. But a wonderful pain just the same. Do you have any idea what I'm talking about?"

"Oh yes."

"I am full of contradictions and contrary ways, Marcus. There is much about me that is very ugly. I am trapped by cages I have spent all my life constructing."

"Does my love hold any hope of helping you? Does needing you so much . . ." He stopped, caught by the need to gasp. "Kirsten, I will spend a lifetime helping you be who you want to be."

"This is one of your most remarkable traits," she said. "Knowing which words carry the most exquisite agony."

He waited, surrounded by golden light and a distant car's murmur and the sound of his four-footed companion panting in nervous communion.

"All right."

"What?"

"Yes, Marcus. I will marry you."

The drenching relief left him unable to form a single word save "What?"

He could hear her smile. "You don't believe me?"

"Kirsten . . ." His heart hammered so hard he knew his voice shook. "I never thought I'd hear you say those words."

"I want to ask you to do something, Marcus."

There was no reason for tears now. Or finding his vision clouding over until he could see nothing save a blur of time. "Anything."

"I want you to ask me in person."

"Today."

"In Wilmington."

"What?"

"I have to come down."

"Why? I mean, I want you to, but we have things to do."

"I know. That's why I'm coming. I'm checking out now. I'll call you back in a while from the airport and tell you what's happening. Right now I just want to put our work to one side and sit here. Just for a minute. Do you understand?"

CHAPTER

52

HE SAT AT A CORNER TABLE of Level Five, a bar on the fifth floor of the old Masonic temple, now an upscale office complex. Across the street was another of those fire-baked-brick buildings. He could stare over the ledge at the dresses in the shop window. The elegant plastic dolls held their hands up to him, looking so fine he wouldn't mind making time with one. Wilmington was a new place for him. The first time he'd ever been down was to rent the boat on the deal that went so totally wrong. Back then, he'd done his drinking at the Ice House, the last of the old waterfront dives. Sephus sipped at his twelve-year-old single malt and grinned at how wrong that deal had gone. Wrong as in flying him to Germany, first time he'd ever been farther afield than the gambling cruisers where he'd worked until they caught him ripping off passengers' rooms. So wrong they'd also sent him to New York. Now that was one fine place. He could see himself spending a few days there, getting to know the local color, having himself a time. Once this deal was done and the money was cooking in his back pocket, he'd be on his way.

"Sir?" The sweet young dolly was probably a college student, she had that look. Chestnut hair in a ponytail, not a trace of makeup, perfect teeth, shining skin. "Would you like another scotch?"

Sephus leaned both elbows on the table, moving in as close as close could be. "Tell you what, dolly. How about you letting me have a taste of something I bet's a whole lot sweeter'n what I got in this here glass."

She caught a good strong whiff of him. It backed her up. No

surprise there. Her eyes skimmed down the fine duds he'd picked up in the Big Apple, landing on the jailhouse art on his knuckles. Sephus grinned up at her. "You like? Here, lemme show you something." He undid one sleeve, rolled it back far enough to show the crimson lady dancing upon the daggers, the woman with snakes for hair and eyes of blue fire. "I got pictures on places you don't even know how to name."

The sweet young face hardened several notches. "Don't bet on it, buster."

Sephus watched her spin that ponytail in an arc and stalk away. That was the problem with your basic modern woman. No interest in living up to a guy's fantasies.

As he pulled his sleeve back down, his eye was caught by a newer, moon-shaped scar. The white imprint where she had bitten him cut directly across the crimson woman's neck, slick as a knife. Sephus Jones buttoned the sleeve and thought how sweet it was going to be, meeting up with that particular blond-haired fantasy again.

A pair of secretaries in their evening grab-me gear started to go for the table closest to him. The nearer one caught a whiff and did the backtracking. Sephus smiled and waved them away. He'd been wearing the signature scent so long he rarely even gave it any thought. It was something he'd started on in the third of his juvenile joints. Looking for a way to stand out, basically. Make a stand in a place where they did all they could to grind the boys down to nameless sameness. He'd stolen a bottle of the stuff when mopping down the guards' shower room. Gotten a beating for it, then a scrub-down with wire brushes and two weeks solitary when he doused himself from head to toe. But they never found the bottle. He took to hiding away at shower times, waiting until he had trouble walking around in his own stinking skin, then applying the bottle like varnish. Which gained him some serious pain from the guards. Sephus raised his sleeve, took a slow drag. Twenty-three years and seven prisons later, those early beatings were still closer than yesterday. Which was why he kept to the habit. Far as he was concerned, the odor was as close as he could come to pure rage.

"Excuse me, sir." The bartender hovering by his table was a college football heavy, all shoulders and clear eyes and about as dangerous as a TV commercial. "I'm going to have to ask you to leave."

Sephus swiveled his chair about. Propped one steel-toed boot on the table. Cradled his drink with both hands. Showed the guy just how worried he was. "Let me guess. Tight end. No, no, you swinging with the dolly there, it's got to be king of the field. Am I right?"

"The drink's on the house, sir. Please go."

"See, I'm interested on account of how you plan on playing once I do a number on both your knees."

The guy started to shift back, but eyes were on him now. "I don't want any trouble."

"Then you're messing with the wrong table." Sephus pointed with his chin to where the waitress was using the corner of the bar as a shield. "Scuttle on back over there and have your dolly bring me another round."

The man he was here to meet chose that moment to scurry over and glare down at him. "This is the way you keep to a low profile? Shame!"

Sephus inspected this fat little German sausage squeezed into twill. And those glasses. And that accent. "Man, you were made to make me grin."

"This is no smiling matter!" Reiner Klatz spun about and poked a finger into the quarterback's chest. "You please go now."

"Not until this gentleman has left the premises."

"Yes, of course. He is going with me. You leave, he leaves. So simple."

Sephus drained his glass, rose to his feet, and faced the quarterback. Just looked at him. Showed him what was there. Sephus Jones had a way with looks. Anybody did, they wanted to come out of the places he'd been in one piece. Just showed him a trace of the secrets. Usually he'd think one tight thought, just enough to ram the rage in hard. Like how he'd managed the guards' beatings because they weren't so bad, not really, compared to what he'd been through at home. Like that.

The quarterback was scared. But he stood his ground. Sephus had to give him that.

"No, no, this is too wrong." The fat little German squeezed in between them and shoved Sephus back. "We are please to be going now."

"Okay, Adolf. Anything you say." He gave the dolly a smile and a wave, then said to the quarterback, "See you around."

CHAPTER

53

Wilma Blain brought him a fresh coffee while they waited for Skyler Cummins to be brought up from the cells. "Everything all right?"

No way was he going to add more smoke by talking about Dale. Or taint the sparkling memory by mentioning his conversation with Kirsten. "Fine."

"How are you enjoying our little show?"

"You played James well."

"It's what I do."

"Where's the subject?"

"Waiting in the interview room."

Blain accompanied Marcus back to his tight little chamber. Together they inspected the prisoner through the one-way glass. Skyler Cummins was every inch the heavy. He had what Marcus classed as a biker's build—two hundred pounds of muscle coated by another hundred pounds of flab. Fighter's hands, broken nose, scar rising from his gray-brown beard. Another old wound ran around his neck, clipped off the bottom third of his right ear, then disappeared into his shoulder-length hair. Custom snarl.

Blain held the file so that Marcus could read over her shoulder. Skyler's age was put at thirty-eight. His sheet was twelve pages long. "I believe we'll leave the manacles on this one."

"Maybe have the guard hang around as well."

"We'll see." She flipped through the arrest warrant. "Says here our

Mr. Steadman clocked them both using just a lamp and his fists. Remind me never to get Dale mad."

The deputy popped his head in. "Hamper Caisse just arrived."

"He well cooked?"

The deputy grinned. "Snorting and breathing fire."

"Show the man in." Wilma pointed at Marcus. "You see anything out of the ordinary, call out the guards."

"Don't worry."

As she closed him into the observation room, Marcus observed a furious Hamper Caisse come striding into the chamber on the glass's other side. Hamper wore one of his custom courtroom suits and the expression of a man sorely put out. He glared at the prisoner. "What are you doing here?"

"Me?" Skyler Cummins rattled as he wheeled around to face his attorney. He was rigged in what sheriffs classed as traveling gear—yellow one-piece prison coverall, gray socks, plastic slip-on sandals. His cuffs and ankle bracelets were chained to his canvas belt. "Who's the one they got tied up like a crazy man?"

The guard opened the door a second time, and Wilma Blain entered the room. "Stay close," she told the deputy.

"With you all the way." The deputy shut the door, then unlatched the faceplate and planted himself before the wire-mesh window.

Hamper Caisse offered Blain a furious sneer. "So you've finally decided to deal?"

"Oh, you thought this visit was for plea bargaining? I do apologize." She crossed to the table's other side, seated herself, then pointed to the chairs opposite her. "Have a seat, Mr. Cummins."

The prisoner and his lawyer both remained standing. Wilma held Skyler's gaze and kept her tone easy. "I'm sure the deputy would be happy to help you find your chair, sir."

Skyler moved with the ease of long practice, cocking his leg and seating himself without using his manacled hands. And without unlocking his gaze. Wilma held the moment awhile, then said to Hamper, "I asked you down to inform you of new evidence that's come to light. Thought you both would like to hear it straight from me before we go public."

Hamper Caisse slipped into the other chair and told his client, "She's bluffing."

"Let's get one thing straight up front, gentlemen. This was not a burglary. And we're no longer treating it as such."

"You don't have a thing on my guys."

Wilma actually laughed. "That's a wild pitch, even for you."

"What are you talking about? My guys—"

"Were caught inside Dale Steadman's house."

"My guys were brought in here under false pretenses. They didn't steal a thing. The burglary charges won't hold in court and you know it."

"The original charges were B&E. Not burglary. They stick. We've just decided to up the ante a little to attempted kidnapping."

"I want a moment to confer privately with my clients."

"Oh, you want me to show in your *other* client?" She smirked for Skyler's benefit. "Wait now, what am I saying. You don't *have* another client."

That stilled them both.

Wilma took quiet relish in playing her trump. "James Walker has fired you, Hamper."

It was Skyler who responded first. "What?"

"That's right. And he's turning state's evidence." She plucked the page from her briefcase. "There in black and white. See right there at the bottom? Our man Studley's signature."

"This is sheer travesty," Hamper declared. "She's winding you up."

"Like a clock, Mr. Cummins. With this rap sheet of yours, going down again means you're looking at a whole new career path."

"Don't listen to her. It's total rubbish, what she's saying."

Skyler rounded on his attorney. "What are you talking about, man? I know the score here."

"And I'm the one who's going to get you out!"

"Yeah? So how come I didn't even make bail?"

Wilma Blain's calm voice acted like a goad. "Listen to your jail-house lawyer buddies, Mr. Cummins. They know a lifer in the making. You're going to get to know them *real* well."

Hamper shrilled at her, "You shut up!" To Skyler, "She's paid to scare you."

"What for? I'm already locked up!" Skyler addressed Wilma straight on. "You got something to say to me?"

"What are you talking to her for?" Hamper flipped his chair over as he bolted to his feet. "She's the DA!"

Wilma replied to Skyler, "I think I might have something here that might interest you."

The prisoner demanded, "You want to deal?"

"If we can do business here and now, absolutely."

Hamper shouted, "I forbid this!"

They both ignored him. Wilma continued, "Basically, you've got two choices. I can have your charges reduced to misdemeanor, and you serve a year—"

"No time."

"No chance, Mr. Cummins. We know what happened. But we don't have the backer's name and we don't know who the third guy was. You get me? We know this was a capital offense in the making. Right now, we can lay the whole thing at your feet. If that happens, they'll carry you out of Central Prison in a box."

Gradually the yellow suit darkened with sweat. "And I'm telling you. No time."

Hamper shrieked, "I *demand* to speak to my client privately!"

Wilma gave no sign she heard Hamper at all. "I don't bluff, Mr. Cummins. And I don't deal in fables. You keep up that line, we lay the whole case on you. I'll retire to go play with my grandkids and you'll still be inside, weeding your little garden patch and trying to remember what your last beer tasted like." She smiled once more. "Forty years ago."

"So?"

"So today we've got us a sale. From life down to twelve months. All I want is the guy who hired you to steal that baby."

Hamper inserted himself into the discussion by hammering both fists on the table. "Quit talking directly to my client!"

Only the manacles kept Skyler from making a grab for Hamper's throat. "I'm not doing life for nobody!"

"Don't you understand what's happening here? She's trying to flip you!" To Wilma. "We need a week to think over your offer."

"Why?" From Skyler. "So you can get me shanked?"

Hamper wheeled about and waved at the deputy through the face-plate. "Open this door!"

"Doesn't his behavior strike you as a little strange, Mr. Cummins?" Wilma hurried her words to get it said before the guard unlocked the door. "Why is he so intent upon keeping you as his charge here? I'd suggest that it's because *you're not his client!*"

The door shuddered open. Hamper declared, "My client and I are outta here."

Wilma asked Skyler, "Mr. Cummins, do you wish to return to your cell? Because if you leave this room, my deal is off the table."

"You won't get life!" This from Hamper. "We can go to the parole board!"

"What, in twenty years?" Skyler remained where he was. "That's it? A couple of names and I'm done?"

"From your lips to my tape player." Wilma planted her recorder on the table. "I want to hear you say why you were there, and who hired you."

Hamper was sweating harder than the prisoner. "You know how much is at stake here?"

"Yeah," Skyler replied, not even glancing his way. "The rest of my days."

Hamper leaned back over the table and covered the tape recorder with both hands. "Don't forget the money."

Wilma showed surprise for the first time that day. "Excuse me?"

"In case you've forgotten, man, I haven't seen a dime. You're the one walking around in your thousand-dollar suit. I'm in here looking at life."

Wilma again. "Did you say money?"

"I ain't going down for nobody." Skyler's manacles rattled as he tried to take aim at Hamper. "You're fired, man."

"You can't do that."

"Point of law, counselor. He can." Wilma withdrew another sheaf of pages from her briefcase. "Mr. Cummins, would you care to use my pen?"

He had to lift himself from the chair to hunch over the pages. Hamper had turned an ashen shade. "You're finished, Skyler. Finito."

Wilma looked at the attorney. "Would you mind lifting your hand from my machine and repeating those words about money for the record?"

Skyler finished signing and planted himself back in the chair. "You're not Mafia, man. Matter of fact, you're nothing but history."

"Mr. Cummins, are you declaring this man is no longer your attorney?"

"Absolutely."

Wilma lifted the pages and waved them like a battle flag. "Coun-

selor, I suggest you use what little free time you have left to find yourself a good lawyer."

Marcus took that as his cue.

The last thing Marcus saw through the one-way glass was Hamper
righting his chair and replanting himself. He used both hands to clamp
himself down tight. "Until this man has new counsel, I insist on
remaining to protect his rights."

"No problem there." Wilma Blain cheerily waved Marcus past the
guard and into the interview room. "Matter of fact, I've got someone
right here who will be happy to advise your *former* client."

Hamper Caisse had a difficult time recognizing Marcus. Awareness came in stages—who he was, why he was there, how Hamper had
been set up all along. Marcus saw the last realization come in a flash of
panic-stricken rage. From sweating lawyer to cornered feral beast in
the blink of an eye.

Hamper catapulted over his chair and launched himself into
Marcus.

Marcus dropped his jaw to his collarbone to keep Hamper's
hands from locking around his throat. He launched a series of pent-
up blows, going in low and hard. Hamper grunted when Marcus
found the soft flab beneath his ribs. But Hamper's fingers kept weasel-
ing in, seeking a lock on his neck. Marcus saw the fear in Hamper's
gaze, the wild rage. And matched it with his own. A portion of his
brain took note of Wilma shouting for more guards and the deputy
grunting and cursing as he sought to unwind Hamper's arms. Hamper
screamed and blew spittle in his face. The prisoner had himself a good
laugh over a bad man going down. When Hamper's thumb came
within reach, Marcus bit into the fleshy portion of his palm. Hamper's scream hit a new note. Marcus put everything he had into three
more punches, two into the man's flabby gut and a strong right jab
directly at the heart.

The fight left Hamper in a whoosh of putrid breath. Marcus spat
out the sweaty mouthful and backed away. A second guard shoved
himself into the overcrowded room. Black limbs the size of a pro
wrestler's pinned Hamper to a massive chest while the first guard
cuffed him. Hamper struggled futilely and rasped, "I'll *kill* you."

"Deputy, why don't you show our new guest to his suite."

Hamper sought to hold himself in the room with a foot on the
doorframe. "You're dead, Glenwood."

"Oh, I think your killing days are over." Wilma waved them off. "Charge him with assault. I'll be back directly to see what else we can cook up."

The prisoner gave Marcus a yellowed grin. "You're a lawyer?"

"Yes." His jacket was ripped down one sleeve. Marcus took it off and used it to wipe his face. "Unless the DA wants to weigh in otherwise."

"Not me, counselor." Wilma looked almost as happy as the prisoner. "Now that I've seen that left of yours at work, I'd best keep you on my side."

The prisoner turned to Wilma and declared, "I like this dude's style."

"I can serve only as a temporary adviser," Marcus warned. "Potential conflict of interest means I can't represent you."

"That makes it in my book." Wilma waited until the kicking and screaming diminished down the hallway. "Counselor, why don't you join us for round two?"

CHAPTER

54

Working through Skyler Cummins' account took the better part of two hours. Marcus left the building utterly drained. Sometime while he was inside the day had passed into twilight. He glanced at his watch. Six-thirty. The day seemed far older. Ancient, in fact. Full of dirty secrets and stained motives and plans that cared little over who got mauled in the process. He turned on his phone and dialed Dale's numbers. No answer. Yet another worrisome development.

His phone rang just as he was shoving it back into his pocket. When he answered, Kirsten breathlessly announced, "I caught the only nonstop from La Guardia to Wilmington. Can you believe it? I made it by a hair."

"When do you get in?"

She caught his tone. "Tell me what's the matter."

"This," he replied, "has been a really long day."

"But a good one."

"Yes. I suppose so."

"And it's about to get even better."

He clenched his eyes shut. Fatigue pummeled him with bruising force. "Kirsten, I'm pretty certain I know who was behind the kidnapping."

"So do I."

"But I don't know why."

"I do." She lowered her voice to a whisper and told him about her meetings with Evelyn Lloyd and the oncologist.

Marcus rubbed his face hard, striving to force blood through his sluggish brain. "I have to go to the DA with this."

"You can't."

"Kirsten—"

"Just listen to me, okay?" Swiftly she related the call from Goscha, and the conversation with Reiner.

"Dale doesn't have ten million dollars."

"I know."

"Putting together the five has wiped him out."

"The second offer did not come from Dale. I'm certain of that much."

"Then why is Reiner coming to Wilmington?"

A pause, then, "Do you have any idea who bought Dale's house?"

"He said it was kept anonymous. My money's on Kedrick Lloyd."

"It's a bitter thought, but I think you're right."

A silver Explorer with dark-tinted windows cruised slowly by. "I can't keep this from the authorities."

"Reiner said if we bring in the police, they'd kill the child."

"The DA has to know." And Dale. He would have to tell the man what was happening. If Dale could be found. "Wilma Blain is a good woman, Kirsten. I think we can trust her."

A pause. "All right. But be careful."

"Give me your flight details."

"No, Marcus. I'm a big girl. If you're so busy I'll make my own way into town."

He was in no state to argue. He turned his back to where the Explorer had pulled up and parked on the darkened street away from the station. "This is not how I wanted the day to play out."

"The day," she breathed, "is not over yet."

He clicked off the phone, but could not bring himself to rise from his station on the wall. He punched in Dale's mobile number. One more try, then he would go speak to Wilma Blain.

Marcus could not tell what was more surprising, the fact that Dale answered or the sound of footsteps scraping up behind him. "Dale?"

It was the last word he spoke for a very long while.

CHAPTER

5 5

THE WILMINGTON AIRPORT was a scene straight from the fifties. Kirsten deplaned via roll-up stairs and walked across the tarmac to the main building. She searched for Marcus, knowing he was probably tied up with Dale but disappointed just the same that he was not here. She did not want to work on the case. Not tonight. First she wanted some serious face time with this man. See if the reality held a candle to the fantasies. She had to smile. It was probably good for everybody concerned that their first meeting not be here in public.

She called Marcus at the Hertz counter, but he was not answering his phone. Rental contract in hand, Kirsten stepped out into the dwindling daylight. Two weeks away and she had already forgotten the intensity of a Carolina summer dusk. She took a deep breath. She could actually smell the sea.

The Hertz spaces were at the back of the airport's miniature parking lot. By the time she found her car, the night's velvet cloak was gathering more tightly. The first stars appeared, tiny beacons to all the secrets she kept sealed in her heart. For now.

A silver Explorer cruised along the bank of rental cars. The windows were opaque, as though the night had been painted across the glass. The lights were off. The Explorer continued slipping up quietly toward her, a rude intrusion into the warm stream of things to come.

Then the door opened. "Hello there, dolly." The overly taut features formed a rictus grin as he moved toward her. "Don't that sound like a song to you?"

She did not need to smell him to flee.

But she had not taken two steps before the fist gripped her hair and plucked her back so sharply her feet kept going right out from under her. The pain of her hair being pulled out by its roots was a brilliant light behind her eyelids.

Sephus Jones did not try to break her fall. Instead, he fell with her, or at least his arm did. The fist in her hair directed her head toward the fender of her rental car. She partly caught her weight with one hand, but the fist in her hair was pulling hard now, and her skull struck the metal with such force she lost consciousness.

The next moment she lay sprawled out on the pavement, her head shrieking the pain and fear her mouth could not seem to form.

Sephus' grinning face looked monstrous from this position, his slender stripe of a forehead creased with foul humor. "Oh, good. I was hoping you'd come around for the show."

She knew she should be screaming. But the jolt to her skull robbed her of breath, much less a good yell.

Then he picked her up by her hair.

He clamped his free hand over her mouth and dragged her bodily into the Explorer's backseat. He tossed her inside, slipped in beside her, and said, "If you gotta do it, man, now would be a good time."

She could not name the bizarre little beast who appeared in her streaming vision. But she knew the electric blue glasses. He did not look at her, not really. Instead he took aim for her arm. Kirsten felt a pinprick, then heard him say, "It is done."

"What a waste." The fist in her hair shook her hard. The Explorer slipped into gear and drove off. Then the hand over her mouth rose such that the man's wrist hovered before her eyes. In the glare of passing streetlights she saw a puckered white scar. "See what you did to my body art? I had all sorts of plans for us, dolly. The slow kind."

"Enough with the talking." Reiner. That was his name. Reiner Klatz. Strange how the name appeared at the same time that the pain in her head began to recede. Stranger still how her thoughts all began slowing down. Reiner's voice slipped further away as he said, "We are approaching the exit. Hide her in the back as well."

Sephus Jones released her, now that she could no longer feel the grip he had kept on her scalp. She heard a rustling, then from the end of a very long tunnel came the words "Yeah, she oughtta like that."

Hands lifted and slid and dropped her down into the space behind the seat. "You two already know each other, so I won't bother with the intros."

The last thing she saw was Marcus' face. He looked so troubled in his sleep. Like a bad nightmare had caught them both. She wanted to lift her hand and gentle it away. But her limbs would not work. Then the veil of night was cast over them both, and she could hold herself there no longer.

CHAPTER

5 6

VOICES DRIFTED THROUGH Marcus' fog of pain. Voices and the sound of a rhythmic clanking. "This don't make any sense at all."

"I have orders. We both do."

Something pounded in time to his thudding heart. The pain was enough to compress tears from the corners of his closed eyes.

"Listen, Adolf. This is America. The land of the free, okay? Here we make our own rules."

"The man giving orders also has the money!"

The metallic clangor halted. Marcus heard the footsteps grind through the sand around his head. He was on the beach. Then he heard the other sound. Waves. Impossibly close.

"All I'm saying, you don't stake them out, man. A bullet, a knife, you watch the end, you walk away. Job well done."

"Yes. Fine. This job, your way, it is more important than being paid, yes?"

The clanking started anew. Only this time Marcus was aware enough to feel it resonate down his right hand. "You got a point there, Adolf."

"My name is Reiner!"

"Whatever." The pounding stopped. Marcus felt his right hand being hefted as the man pulled on the ropes.

Then his consciousness returned fully. With it came new pains. Four of them. He was staked spread-eagled in the sand. His wrists and ankles were tied impossibly tight. His arms were extended beyond their full reach, to either side of his head. His legs were splayed so far apart he felt the threat of being split down his middle. He could actually feel the blood pulsing down his arms and legs, only to break upon the ropes like hot waves against knotted dikes.

The man named Sephus Jones gripped him by the chin and squeezed so hard Marcus could feel his jaw being dislodged. "Open your eyes, sport. That's it. Remember me?"

A bizarre little man stood to his right. The moon was rising behind him, casting silver shadows over his sandy legs and arms. The man reached into his pocket. "We must hurry."

"You're the one running to somebody else's clock, man." Sephus Jones shook Marcus' head. "Don't you pass out on me, you hear? The boss man says you gotta stay awake for this performance, else he docks my pay."

The fat little man stepped forward, and Marcus realized he was still wearing a tie. And a vest. He squatted in the sand by Marcus' head, drawing so close Marcus could see he was speaking into a mobile phone.

"This is Reiner. All is as you instructed." He listened a moment, then said to Sephus, "Make him look."

The man holding his chin could not stop grinning. "And people say I'm the sicko."

Sephus twisted Marcus' head to the left. His grip was a probe of titanium and fury. Marcus groaned at the pain, and then again at the sight that awaited him.

Kirsten lay beside him. Her legs and wrists were tied together and then staked. She was utterly immobile. Marcus blinked fiercely, trying to see if she was breathing.

Then he focused beyond her, and saw the sea.

"All right," the little man said. "Let him go."

Sephus remained over him a moment longer, savoring the pain he saw in Marcus' gaze. "Looks to me like you and your dolly made the wrong dude mad."

The hand compressed his jaw further still, until he could feel the ligaments plucked out taut and screaming. Then it was gone. One moment pain white as desert light, the next and the little man was there. Looking down at him through ridiculous blue spectacles. "There is someone here who wants a word." He mashed the phone to Marcus' ear.

The languid voice started in, "For a time I was genuinely morose over missing this final performance of yours."

Marcus worked his mouth. Open and shut. A breath in and out. Sorting through the pains and the fears. "Kedrick Lloyd."

"Ah, excellent. You are both awake and aware. I am so glad. Everything seems to be working to my design. Behold my grandest creation, a symphony of sight and sound and operatic tragedy. You will watch your intrusive young woman perish, then expire yourself. Is it not marvelous?"

"Don't do this."

"You know, I understand Beethoven's plight for the very first time, how it must have felt when the poor deaf man could not hear his own creations being performed. Bitterly frustrating, yet at the same time the void holds a certain savor. Were I there, I would most certainly discover some imperfection. Humans are defined by their failings, particularly when it comes to creative effort. But from this distance, I can close my eyes and see the flawless unfolding of my revenge."

"The DA knows."

"Of course she does. But my lawyers, that is, my *new* lawyers, will confound her feeble testimony. Who will a jury believe, a third-rate courtroom turncoat or the ailing board member of the New York Metropolitan Opera? No, my dear boy, there is a grand distance between what is known and what is provable."

"Your men blew up the boat and killed Charlie Hayes."

"Most regrettable, that. But knowing as I do what the poor man faced, I take comfort from the fact that he might well have thanked me."

"What about the baby?"

"Have you learned nothing? Your meddling over the child is what landed you and your paramour in this predicament. But never mind. I shall savor this night as I have few things in the past year of madness and agony. Tonight, even the tide charts work to my favor. Adieu, Marcus Glenwood. Do try and stay awake for the entire performance."

CHAPTER

57

M ARCUS STARTED AWAKE. Something had drawn him from the semiconscious state of thudding agony and the distant wash of waves. He had difficulty opening his eyes, which frightened him into full alertness. He straightened his head and understood. His temple was leaking blood, and it had matted with the sand and caked against his eyelid. He twisted his facial muscles and blinked hard and finally pried his right eyelid free.

"Stars."

The word was so soft, Marcus had difficulty separating it from the pounding in his skull. He turned his head fully to the left. "Kirsten?"

"Marcus." She did not turn her head to meet his gaze. Instead, her eyes stared straight up at the sky. "It is you, isn't it?"

"Yes."

"I see the stars, but where is the smoke?"

"Kirsten, try your bonds."

"You didn't need to do it this way."

"Try and focus. Please. This is . . ." A wind too feeble to touch them pierced the clouds. Moonlight illuminated a face pale as the sand upon which she lay. She was blinking very fast. Each blink pressed out another tear. "Kirsten, we're going to get out of this."

"Where are the others?"

His hands were wet from where he had torn the skin off his wrists, trying to work free of his bonds before passing out. No matter how hard he pulled and struggled, there was no give to the stakes. He could feel the grit crusted to the fold of his eye and his mouth. "Kirsten, look at me."

"There have to be others." She blinked and spilled more rivulets. "Will they hurt me again?"

The voice was not hers. Nor the expression. Nor the eyes. "Kirsten, please, darling, wake up."

Her face rolled toward him. Her eyes attacked him. Deep as pits and luminous with old pain. "You're Marcus."

"That's right, darling. And I love you."

"But you weren't there."

"No. I wasn't."

The tears slipped out to gather on her nose and drip like slow pain. "Why are you here now?"

He tried to keep his voice steady. "Kirsten, look at my hands. Lift your head. That's right. No, up there. There, you see?"

She squinted hard. "You're tied up."

"Darling, listen to me. This is now. Do you understand? The men are not here."

She rolled onto her back, offering herself to the night. "But I see the stars, Marcus. Look, and the smoke. Are they coming back now?"

"Kirsten. No, don't go to sleep. Darling, you have to wake up!"

But she was gone from him. Marcus lifted himself as high as he could. And shouted to the dark. "Help! *Anybody!*"

He screamed again, on and on, until he felt something tear inside his head.

———————

When he woke up, the pain was so intense he thought all the crashing came from his brain. Slowly Marcus sifted through the agony and realized the noise was mostly the ocean. He needed even longer to recognize that the ocean had moved.

Then he came fully awake as the next wave lapped over his left arm and leg.

He turned his head. The sky had cleared while he had been out. The moonlight was strong enough for him to see the next wave as silver-white. Kirsten's face was drenched and her hair sodden. The retreating water swept entirely over her body. "Kirsten!"

Her face was utterly immobile. The moonlight turned her pale as a bound specter. He shouted her name again. A third time. He stopped as another wave rose and crashed. The sight frightened him more than his immobile fingers. More than how Kirsten's chest did not seem to be moving.

The next wave looked huge. It rushed up toward him, covering his left limbs and sloshing over his chest. The water on his arm and leg felt lukewarm. But he could not feel anything in his hand or his foot. He twisted his neck so he could see his hand and tried to move his fingers. They remained locked into a half-curled position.

Marcus shut his eyes as the water rushed up and over him. This time the current was strong enough to fling the water across his chest and up the length of his right arm. He lifted his head from the stream and felt the froth flow back and away. The wet sand made a scrunching sound as he lowered his head and turned back to Kirsten.

A strand of seaweed was now wrapped across her cheek and one eye. The sight was obscene. And deathly still.

"*WAKE UP!*"

The effort of his scream clenched his entire body, pulling his limbs in tight. He dropped down, filled his lungs, clenched himself up tight, and screamed again.

Kirsten did not move.

But the stake holding his left arm did.

Marcus arched his entire body in an effort to swivel his head up so that he could see the stake. Then down, another panting breath, then back in the other direction. Yes. The left-hand stake was definitely canted more sharply than the right. He turned back, which was good, because he caught sight of an even bigger wave. One that crashed almost directly on top of Kirsten and broke over him so hard he choked. He gasped and fought for breath as the wave receded, blinking away the sting in his eyes.

Kirsten was still not moving.

He struggled against the stake, pressing himself far beyond the borders of pain. He did not care if he broke his arm, his shoulder, his back. He shouted out the pain that ripped through his shoulder and elbow. Down for a few moaning breaths, then he turned his head away as the next wave crashed. Not because of the water. Because he couldn't bear to see it wash over her.

But this time, when the water receded, he felt the stake tremble.

His fingers were unable to feel the rope, much less clutch it.

Marcus heaved and bellowed. Panted and groaned. He held his breath through another wave. Heaved again.

Slowly, with the sucking sound of being pulled from a living wound, the stake came free.

He curled away from the next wave. The water only made his joints and bones ache more. Where he had torn the skin around his ankles and wrists, the salty wash felt like hot acid.

His fingers refused to make a fist. He curled his left hand limply around the stake and punched his arm down into the sand by his side. Again. He lifted his hand up to his face, then clenched his eyes against the next wave. Blinking away the salt sting, he saw the stake's blunt end was now caught into the ropes at his wrist. He turned and reached and jammed the stake into the sand by his right arm's pinion. He dug and groaned and coughed through two waves, pulling as hard as he could all the time.

His right arm came free.

He sat up. His fingers were thick as sausages and utterly numb. He clamped the pair of staves together between his palms and attacked the sand by his left foot. With his feet spread-eagled it was a gymnast's trick to reach it at all. His groin hurt worse than his wrists from the strain.

His left foot pulled free.

The stave holding his right foot seemed to take the longest of all. Now he could not stop himself from looking over and staring at Kirsten's immobile form. Each new wave formed a foamy moonlight shroud. Marcus ripped out the final stave.

He crawled over to Kirsten and flicked the seaweed from her face. "Please, sweetheart, open your eyes." He dropped his face close to hers, then to the chest, praying for a sign, a breath, a heartbeat. All he heard was the next wave.

He crawled to her hands. He heaved and roared and plucked the stave free. Down to her feet. Again.

He moved to her left side, so that his back took the next wave's force instead of her head. He dug his numb hands under her and wept anew at the realization that he did not have the strength to lift her.

"Kirsten, help me, please." He bent over her face, used the flesh of his palms to pry back her jaw. He fitted his lips to hers. She tasted of salt and impossible cold. He breathed. He held his mouth pinned there as the next wave crashed over them. Release. Breathed again. A third time. Another wave. And he knew they had to move.

He pushed and rolled her because there was nothing else to be done. The weight of her was an impossible task. He lifted and yelled and heaved and shoved her a yard farther up. Again. Over and over until they were both completely covered with sand and debris.

He did not know how long he continued with the gasping, weeping effort. Aeons. But he did not stop until the sand which formed their outermost cover was utterly dry, a frosting that shimmered in the moonlight. He remained on his knees above her, swaying slightly. Mouthing her name. Begging her to wake up.

She groaned.

The sound was so soft he could scarcely believe it at all. Then she shifted slightly, and took a deeper breath. Shuddered. Groaned again.

Only then did he realize his head was throbbing worse than his arms. The pain seemed to sweep up all at once, a wave so strong it could divorce itself from the sea and still be capable of crashing him to the beach, thrusting him down, then plucking him away.

CHAPTER

58

H E AWOKE with a cry of pain. Everything hurt him. Even opening his eyes was a gritty torment.

The sun was a vexatious flame, magnified by the ocean to torch the entire eastern sea. A tugging pulled at his stretched and torn shoulder. He cried out again.

"Your hands."

The words were more shivered than spoken. He blinked against the sand and salt caking his face. Kirsten was seated by his side. She held his left arm in both hands, and she gnawed at the knot with her teeth. Her entire frame shook with almost constant tremors. But she worked the knot like a ferret.

"So cold."

But it's blistering hot, he wanted to say. Yet when he could not make his mouth form the words, he decided it really didn't matter. She was there, she was awake. Her hair was matted and bloody, her face powdered by white sand like a broken Kabuki doll. Her eyes were red and watering, her limbs and body filthy with dried mud and seaweed. But fully there.

"I was dreaming," she said.

I know, Marcus wanted to say. But he found it difficult even to nod.

"It was awful." A more violent tremor ran through her. She paused at working on his knot long enough to stare directly into the sun. Her face looked sugar-frosted. Gradually the tremors subsided. She looked back at him. A single tear tracked its way unnoticed across her sandy pallor. Her voice rasped with thirst and wear. "You were there, Marcus. In my dream. You made the bad ones go away."

She went back to work on his knot. Seabirds scissored across the gold-blue sky. Their caws threatened to split his skull. The waves worked his brain like liquid drills. Even the sun's heat was noisy.

She spat out a length of rope. "There."

The pain in his fingers was so unexpectedly fierce he reared his head back and howled.

She gripped the hand to her chest and pummeled the swollen dig-its. "Marcus, oh Marcus."

He wanted to beg her to stop. But before he could manage the words, he heard his name called again. In the distance. A faint halloo-ing almost lost to the waves and the rising wind.

Kirsten rose then, staggering and falling back to her knees. "Here!"

"Marcus!"

Dale was the first over the dunes. Followed by a pair of patrolmen, one of whom stopped long enough to call and shout back behind them.

Kirsten was crying as Dale raced over. "His hand."

Dale stared at them. The stricken look he shared with the on-coming policemen was enough to make Marcus hurt even worse.

This time Kirsten shrieked the words. "Cut the ropes!"

Dale dropped to the sand beside them. "Give me a knife."

She was sobbing so hard now she could not make the words. She made do by pushing Dale's hands away from her and toward Marcus. As he cut Marcus' three remaining bonds, Dale kept glancing over at her, sitting there beside him, her powdered face streaked and mottled, her own bound hands and feet of no concern whatsoever.

When the bond was cut to his right hand, Marcus had no choice but to give himself over to the shrilly piercing agony. He would have begged Dale not to open two more wounds at his ankles, but he could make no audible plea. Then it was too late.

When he managed to refocus, he saw that a policeman had dropped to the sand beside Kirsten and sawed off her own bonds. Marcus crawled the distance between them on his elbows and knees. She met him with an embrace even the agony of his joints could not diminish. Her sand-encrusted lips scraped across his face. He felt the pressure of her fingertips on the wound to his forehead. Not even this pain mattered. Not then.

In the distance there was a faint halloo. Dale called back, "Over here!"

More footsteps and huffing breaths signaled the arrival of others. The first words out of Wilma Blain's mouth were "Bring this pair a drink of water."

Only then did one of his other pains separate enough for Marcus to give it a name. He groaned beneath the sudden weight of his thirst. Kirsten trembled in his arms and whimpered.

Wilma Blain's voice rose to where she sent the seagulls soaring and calling their alarm. "*Now!*"

CHAPTER

59

K IRSTEN LET MARCUS DRIFT while they were poked and prodded by the medical team. At Wilma Blain's command, they had been settled into the most secure corner of the Wilmington hospital's ER unit. When they asked where she hurt, Kirsten had to smile. Her face felt as though it would crack beneath its shell of sunbaked salt and sand. Everywhere, she wanted to say, but that would only slow them down further. And the clock was marching on.

The police strutted along the corridor, their radios crackling. Just beyond the cubicle's curtain Wilma Blain talked on her mobile phone. She waited while the nurse swabbed Marcus' forehead and the doctor injected a local anesthetic and began stitching. The doctor snipped away the unused thread and dropped his utensils into the metal pan. He inspected his handiwork, then turned to Marcus' hands and feet. The pain was obviously diminishing, or perhaps it was merely that his fatigue offered a comfort all its own. Whatever the reason, Marcus watched the doctor's actions with the detached disinterest of an onlooker.

"Can you make a fist for me, Mr. Glenwood? Excellent. Let's try this hand. Good. Does that hurt? Yes, I suppose it must." The doctor moved down to Marcus' legs, thumped the filthy pant's leg with his little hammer, nodded at the response. He lifted one foot and ran the hammer's handle up from the heel and across the arch. The doctor's pale features and scraggly goatee only accented his youth. "Curl your toes for me. Good. Well, there's no evidence of severe atrophy so far as I can tell from a cursory examination."

He dropped his hammer into the pan and said, "I'll just go see if they've got the scanner free. We'll want to have a look inside, make sure they didn't scramble you with that blow."

Marcus did not speak until they were alone. "I don't know what to do anymore."

It was all the impetus she required. Understanding what Marcus needed and giving it to him was such a rush. She had never known anything like this before. The concept itself jarred against all she had known, all she saw herself as being.

None of those gathered outside knew it yet, but she was about to take control.

Kirsten pushed herself up from the gurney, then had to stop and wait for the dizziness to pass. She kept her hand on the railing as she rounded the cabinet and pushed through the dividing curtain.

Everybody in the lobby stopped and stared—police, the DA, nurses, patients, visitors, the works. Everyone save Dale. The big man sat in the far corner, hunched over his hands. His agony was ignored by all.

She called over, "Dale."

He started, dragged from a nightmare he assumed was hidden from all but himself.

She tried to offer him a smile. It was the least she could do for the man who had just saved their lives. "It's time."

Her fatigue struck more fiercely once she had showered and dressed in clothes from the hospital's Goodwill closet. She felt divorced both from her surroundings and herself. Time swept past, leaving her stranded. Then the weariness diminished to where she could pull things back into shape once more.

She was in the middle of talking to Dale and the DA, explaining what they needed, when everything just seemed to shift. The next thing she knew, she was in a police car with Marcus, the siren wailing and the light positioned on the dashboard blinking at her. Calling for her to focus. Only she could not remember how much she had said, or how to fit all the strands together.

But when they arrived at the airport, a two-prop Cessna was there waiting. The pilot was a young buccaneer equipped with aviator shades and mustache and jacket and grin. Marcus had obviously taken the doctor's offer of painkillers, because his eyes were dilated and his bearing unsteady as he sat and waited for people to help him rise to his feet.

When Dale pried himself from the car that rolled up behind them, Kirsten walked over. "You can't come."

Perhaps she had already said the words before and forgotten. Or perhaps it was merely that he trusted her enough to do whatever she required. "All right."

"You need to be at home in case they call," she lied. For an instant she even forgot why it was vital that he not be with them, she was that tired. "We'll phone as soon as we know something. You have Marcus' mobile number?"

"Yes."

"One question." Though her tongue drifted lazily over the words, she managed to ask, "Why did you come looking for us?"

"You already asked me that."

"Tell me again."

"I got an anonymous call."

She rested a hand on his arm, wishing there were some way to draw strength from him. "Did anything about the voice seem familiar?"

"She had a cloth or something over the receiver."

A woman. Kirsten nodded. "Do you remember anything about the way she spoke, anything odd?"

"Only that she was very precise. You were in danger. I would find you somewhere around a stretch of very empty beach."

Wilma Blain moved up alongside them. "There's only one beach around Wilmington where you can be fairly sure you won't find other people. The two islands opposite Monkey Junction are nature preserves."

"Folks boat over sometimes for picnics, but it stays pretty isolated," Dale said.

"We didn't want to move out on this," the DA admitted. "But your man here just wouldn't let go."

Kirsten started to bid the DA a firm farewell, but Wilma Blain halted her with "Don't you even start on me. I'm going and that's that."

Kirsten had no strength to argue. "Could you please give Marcus a hand?"

The DA and a policeman both had to help Marcus reach the plane's rear seat. His hands still looked tortured and swollen. His feet were hidden in oversized sneakers now, but the way he shuffled made it apparent he could not feel the pavement. The pilot was too much a macho player to find any grace in helping an apparent invalid. He leaned against a wing stanchion and gave Kirsten the careful eye. She ignored him until they had Marcus safely stowed away. She knew the pilot's next move would be to make some smooth offer for her to take the seat next to him, have a chance to see what it was like to do it at fifteen thousand feet. She caught him with a glare so hard he swallowed the grin and the words both. Then she pushed her way past Wilma Blain and took the seat beside Marcus.

The Cessna was designed to carry three times their number. Once they powered up and took off, Kirsten fitted a blanket around Marcus. Though she could not hear him, she saw his mouth shape the words, I can't do this.

She patted his arm. Said back, Don't worry. Then she moved to the next row and stretched out as best she could.

Wilma Blain watched her with a grindingly intense gaze. "Want to tell me what's going on?"

"I can't. Not yet."

"You're going to have to, sister. And sooner rather than later." When Kirsten merely settled lower into the seat, Wilma went on, "We've got APB's out for Sephus Jones and the German fellow."

"Reiner Klatz. My guess is, he's already left the country."

Wilma accepted the news with a careful nod and asked, "Then I've got another question for you. Who's calling the shots here?"

Kirsten did not awaken until Wilma Blain shook her shoulder. The Cessna's motors were off. They were stationed on a sun-drenched tarmac. The pilot was gone. Wilma handed her a coffee and said, "Decided to let you sleep as long as I could."

The plane was empty save for them. "Where is Marcus?"

She pointed over her shoulder. "He made a call for a friend to come drive us around. I figured there wasn't any need to wake you before our ride got here. You ready to go?"

"Getting there." She sipped from the Styrofoam cup and willed herself to full alert status. "Thank you for the coffee."

Wilma Blain remained where she was, blocking the exit with her bulk. "I'm repeating my earlier question," she said. "Who is singing the tune we're all dancing to?"

"I'm on your side, Ms. Blain."

"Maybe so. But my concern is, do you know enough to keep us to the legal straight and narrow?"

"You'll tell me if I don't."

"You can count on that."

Kirsten set the cup aside. Swept back her hair. Took a breath of the steamy air. Knew she was as awake from this little confab as the day was going to permit. "All right. I'm ready."

The section of the airport reserved for private planes was empty save for the car up ahead. A group of pilots and mechanics lolled in the shadows of a distant hangar. Otherwise all the noise came from the commercial jets landing and taking off on the other side of the highway. The shimmering asphalt was an oven set on full broil. Kirsten shielded her eyes, but could not make out the figure behind the wheel. Wilma Blain pointed her to the front passenger seat, then climbed into the rear beside Marcus before she could object.

Deacon Wilbur smiled at her arrival. "How you doing, child?"

She resisted the urge to wrap her arms around that corded neck. "It's so good to see you."

"Before we get started," Wilma interrupted, "I got some questions that need answering. Such as, why do I have a banker's check sitting in my office safe for five million dollars?"

Kirsten swiveled around. A single glance was enough to assure her that Marcus was not answering anything. He watched her with a gaze fogged by painkillers and exhaustion.

"While you're at it, maybe you could also clear up why you didn't want Dale Steadman along on this little jaunt."

"I don't know about the check."

Marcus licked his lips, and muttered, "I do."

"I'm hoping the rest of the answers will be confirmed at our first stop," Kirsten continued.

"And just where might that be?"

Kirsten directed her answer to Deacon. "The Raleigh offices of Senator John Jacobs."

The DA crossed her arms. "I guess I don't have any trouble with that. Long as you talk along the way."

The explanations took them down I-40, along Ridge Road, onto the Downtown Boulevard and the five blocks down Hargett Street to the underground parking lot's entrance. Wilma did not say a word the entire time. Nor did her gaze move from Kirsten's face, not even when Marcus attempted his own drifting additions.

Kirsten waited until Wilma was helping Marcus hobble across the parking lot and into the downtown building housing Senator Jacobs' regional offices. Then she told Deacon, "I need to thank you."

"What for, daughter?"

She reached over and settled her hand upon his own. His palm was hard as dry leather. "Everything."

He peeled away the present with his gaze and stared into her recent past. "This has been a testing time for you."

Kirsten swallowed down the heat of weary sorrow. She made do with a nod.

"I been through some tough things in this life. Believe you me. And when they've bent me and broken me and sent me crashing down onto my knees, I've found God waiting there, ready to make me strong."

She squeezed his hand, then released it. "I better go."

"The good Lord wasn't drawn to us on account of how righteous we are. You hear me, child? He didn't come down to this earth because we were good. Or whole. Or strong. He came because we *needed* him."

———————

Marcus could see their state reflected in the receptionist's expression. Kirsten was dressed in a stained denim skirt and torn black workout shoes with laces of different colors. Her top was an East Carolina warm-up jersey that almost swallowed her. Her hair, dried to the consistency of winter straw by the night and the day, was flung about her head like a frayed halo. She walked straight to the receptionist and declared, "We are here to see Brent Daniels."

"Do you have an appointment?"

"No."

Her gaze shifted from Kirsten to Marcus to Wilma and back again. "I'm sorry, but Mr. Daniels' schedule is very tight this week."

"Just the same." She brushed the strands from her forehead, and the gesture revealed her fragile state. "Perhaps Mr. Daniels might find a couple of minutes for us."

"I don't think—"

"Tell him we are here with the Wilmington DA, and are on our way to the district court to give evidence in a murder trial. A trial that will have a direct bearing on Mr. Daniels and Senator Jacobs."

The silence lasted long enough for two heads to pop out of neighboring offices. The receptionist lifted the phone. "Who did you say you were?"

"Kirsten Stansted." She walked back over and seated herself between Marcus and Wilma. When attention turned away from them, Kirsten said to the DA, "I need your help."

"Is that a fact."

"All I want is for you to go along with me on this."

Wilma tightened down. Gaze, arms, perch on the seat. "Go along."

"If I step over the line, jump on me. But until then, back me up. Please."

Wilma Blain was in no mood to promise a thing. Kirsten turned to Marcus and tried to soften. "You still with us?"

"Barely."

"You could go wait—"

"No."

She nodded. Started to take his hand. Retreated. Sighed softly. Then straightened. Being hard and strong for them both. Which was good.

The senator's chief local aide came scooting around the corner and skidded to a halt at the sight of them. "Ms. Stansted? I'm sorry, I wasn't expecting—"

"Five minutes," Kirsten said, pushing herself to her feet. "Now."

Marcus made it down the hall with Kirsten on one side and Wilma on the other. His feet throbbed in harmony to the rest of him. He wore a band of white for a skullcap, an apostate's dunnage for all the wrongs of a long and bitter era. He entered the senior aide's office and let them settle him into a chair, content to have Kirsten think on his behalf. Kirsten's determined assurance was a balm to his badly scattered brain. He found a strange comfort in the need and remedy both.

Brent Daniels was a chubby bundle of nerves, unable to halt his little dance behind the high-backed executive chair. "I can't say it was a great move out there, scaring my receptionist with accusations of tie-ins to a murder investigation."

"I need some answers."

He tried hard for a smile. "We're not in the Q&A business here."

Kirsten waved a careless hand to the chair on Marcus' other side. "Wilma Blain is the Wilmington DA, up here on the case involving the murder of Erin Brandt. You remember her."

"So?"

"So we want to know how you learned about the abduction of Celeste Steadman."

"Easy enough. That was headline news."

Marcus spoke for the first time. "Dale Steadman's firing was. The article only gave a single sentence to the abduction and Dale's recent divorce."

"We're paid to give careful attention to the local press. That's the nature of politics."

"Then here's another one," Kirsten said. "How did you come to know about Erin Brandt being outside Germany? And here's another. The London embassy staffer said you had called him to report that Erin Brandt was departing London early to return to Düsseldorf. Who was feeding you this information?"

Brent Daniels began beating a nervous drumbeat on the back of his seat. Clearly this was the question he had been dreading. "I'm totally unable to respond."

"Then I'll make some points for you. All you have to do is let me know if I'm moving in the right direction." She hurried along, not granting him a chance to object. "You were contacted by someone from outside the senator's constituency. A woman by the name of Evelyn Lloyd. She offered to make a huge donation to the senator's war chest. She had some serious connections with the Washington crowd, and knew precisely how to channel the funds so they would go directly from her account to yours."

The hammering of his hands gradually halted along with his breathing. He even stopped blinking. He stood and he stared. On Marcus' other side, Wilma Blain leaned forward and gave Kirsten a squinty-eyed inspection.

"Evelyn Lloyd told you that she shared your aims. She was deeply concerned over the abduction of American children and their illegal transport to Germany. She wanted to see it stop." Kirsten gave him a moment to respond. "How am I doing so far?"

The aide said nothing.

"Perhaps you would rather we subpoena the senator and formally request his presence in a court of law."

The surprise was not merely in the threat, but the fact that it came from Wilma Blain. The aide looked pinned by his own fear to the rear wall of his office. "No."

"Then answer the lady's question."

Kirsten held the DA's gaze for a long moment, drawing strength from the act.

"I can't."

"No problem." Wilma made as if to rise. "Maybe you better call the senator and let him know we'll be serving a subpoena on him and you both this very afternoon."

"Wait, no, that can't happen."

"Can and will, sir. Can and will. Unless, of course, you care to respond."

Brent Daniels pulled out his chair. Lowered himself by the arms. Took the motions in the careful stages of the ailing and defeated. "It wasn't like Ms. Lloyd was coming to us with something out of left field."

"You were already involved in the action," Kirsten offered.

"Absolutely. This was a cause close to the senator's heart."

"So she was seen as an ally," Kirsten continued. "Then she returned with news about what you thought would be the high-profile case you'd been searching after. Something so big it would attract the international press, and maybe even stimulate the German parliament to take action."

Wilma Blain let out a low chuckle, almost a hum. She leaned back in her chair and gave Kirsten a look of pure approval.

"Only this case blew up in your faces."

"Did it ever," the aide muttered.

"You and the senator took great pride in the fact that you had remained in the background, doing little more than making a few calls that could easily be denied."

Brent Daniels stared at her. "How did you know?"

"I didn't." She moved to help Wilma Blain lift Marcus from his seat. "Until now."

Once they were back in the car, Kirsten said to the DA, "Could you call Judge Sears and ask if we might stop by?"

This time Wilma did not hesitate. When she was done, Kirsten reached across the seatback and asked, "Can I use your phone?"

Kirsten obtained the number from New York directory assistance. The phone was answered on the first ring. "Evelyn Lloyd, please."

"Whom should I say is calling?"

Kirsten recognized the precisely superior tone. "You know exactly who this is."

A fragment of hesitation, then, "I beg your pardon?"

"First of all, I want to thank you."

"What on earth for?"

"Saving our lives. Secondly, I want to check some facts."

"I am still waiting," Evelyn Lloyd replied, "to learn whom I am addressing."

"You knew something was wrong when you learned about Kedrick selling his hotels. He had to have something serious going on for him to want that much money at this point in his life." When Evelyn did not respond, Kirsten added, "Did you know he's purchased Dale's house with the remaining funds?"

"Young lady, I thoroughly detest this insinuating tone of yours."

"My guess is you've tracked his every step," Kirsten continued. "The only problem was, it simply isn't done in your circle."

"What isn't?"

"Going after your own husband."

The woman on the other end was silent so long Kirsten feared she had hung up. Then Evelyn said, "Obviously you are addressing the wrong person. But whoever it is that has acted in such a manner, I would say they had an uncommon appreciation of the cold sweet taste of careful revenge."

"I'm not looking to blame anyone," Kirsten said. "I just want to find the child."

This time the pause was even longer. "Not here."

Then the phone went dead.

CHAPTER

60

EVELYN LLOYD TOOK GREAT CARE with her dress and makeup. Everything she selected bore the invisible stains of memories made bitter by lies and deception. The gown was a Dior one-off, designed for the first reception they had given after completing the renovations of Kedrick's family castle in Wiltshire. The work had taken three years and almost four million of her dollars. They had brought in woodworkers from the Garonne region of central France, the only place they could find people still skilled in the Jacobean style of paneling. The step-in fireplace was carved from massive blocks of white Grecian marble, sculpted as close to the original sketches as they could manage in this day and age.

Her diamond-and-emerald necklace had also been a gift from Kedrick—acquired with her funds, of course. They had celebrated their ninth wedding anniversary with a weekend getaway to Paris. They had taken a suite at the Ritz and walked across the Place Vendôme to the same jewelers who had served Kedrick's great-great-grandfather, back in the family's heyday. That same weekend had been Kedrick's first occasion to hear Erin Brandt sing. The young diva had lit up the Paris Opera House with a brilliance that had outshone even these fabulous gems. Evelyn fastened the necklace into place, grimacing at the bitter irony of such tainted and poisoned joy.

She gave her makeup a careful check, then crossed the foyer to Kedrick's office. The servants all had been given the afternoon off. The apartment was uncommonly still. The only sound came from Kedrick's sound system. She recognized the muted strains of Tchaikovsky's tragic opera *Eugene Onegin*. Even here was a note of fatal correctness.

Evelyn pushed open the doors and entered the stage.

Her husband was seated behind his massive stinkwood desk. His cell phone lay open and waiting upon the leather blotter. His hair was a scattered sheath of winter wheat. His face looked ravaged with strain. He cast her a glance, then started to look away. Then it gradually registered. She stood with regal dignity, both hands holding the handles to the double doors. "Yes?"

"I came to inform you," she said, "that this particular script will not play out as you intended."

He sought to gather himself, but failed. "I beg your pardon?"

She started to walk over and turn off the music, but decided it suited the occasion more than silence. The final act was building now. Onegin was about to confront the utter depravity of his misdeeds. "Let me guess. You and your minions can't locate the child."

Awareness dawned within that burning gaze. "What are you saying?"

"You couldn't possibly think that I would let you get away with all this. My only regret is that I did not think you capable of murder. But then, I have always sought to believe the best in you. Even when you have constantly sought to prove me wrong."

"My dear, you are not making—"

"The authorities are seeking your Mr. Jones and that strange little German fellow as we speak." She rose up to her full height, wishing there was some sense of satisfaction to be found in this moment. Some vindication. "And both Marcus Glenwood and Kirsten Stansted are alive."

He took the news as he would a blow to the heart. "What?"

"I failed to protect Ms. Brandt, though heaven knows she deserved her fate as much as anyone. But as for these two, my guess is they are now sharing their suspicions with the proper authorities."

The rage she had always known was there gradually fueled the ravaged features. "Then there is nothing to keep me from exacting my final revenge upon you."

"Revenge for what, Kedrick? Remaining blind to your deceit for far too long?" Evelyn stepped back enough to call into the foyer, "Come here, please."

The muscled young detective stepped in alongside her. Evelyn watched her husband descend into the dust of defeat. She then pointed to the sound system. In this production Onegin confessed to his life of misdeeds, then shot himself in the temple. "Perhaps you should consider the wisdom of your one and only love."

CHAPTER

61

JUDGE RACHEL SEARS pointed Kirsten into the seat directly in front of her desk. They were in Sears' private office on the district courthouse's ninth floor. Photographs of her husband and child were situated on her desk and the two window ledges. The sofa upon which Marcus sat was beige leather. The feminine tone was matched by the three chairs and the Indian carpet and the desert scenes on her walls. Kirsten tried to keep from paying Marcus any attention, but it was hard. He looked increasingly pale, as though his strength continued to seep from some undetected wound. She wanted him back in bed, resting and comfortable. She wanted the same for herself. But not yet.

Judge Sears had the gaze of too many hard days compressed into too little time. She did not shout. She did not need to. Her presence was commanding, even here in her personal space with the judge's robes hung on the back of her door. "You want to tell me what has happened here?"

"I don't know," Kirsten replied. "But I can guess."

Wilma Blain was seated beside the court stenographer over by the window. Kirsten was alone in her front-and-center position, taking the full brunt of Sears' gaze. "Erin Brandt and Kedrick Lloyd had a long-term affair. Kedrick was spellbound by her. Erin was Erin."

Judge Sears had the ability to bark at scarcely above a whisper, "What is that supposed to mean?"

Wilma Blain said mildly, "Why don't we just let the lady tell her tale."

The judge and the DA exchanged a long glance. Then Sears turned back to Kirsten and rolled her finger. Go.

"Erin Brandt was a magnetic, alluring, beguiling diva. More than anything, she wanted a starring role at the Met. She considered it the jewel in her crown. There were obstacles. She thought Kedrick Lloyd, as a Met board member, was in a position to give her what she wanted. She used him."

"The child is Kedrick's?"

"Kedrick thought so. And that was enough for Erin. But still Kedrick could not get Erin a debut at the Met. So to punish Kedrick, she married Dale."

"Why?"

"Dale Steadman is Kedrick's best friend."

Wilma gave a soft unh unh. "That was some woman."

"It gets worse. Kedrick contracted a rare form of cancer known as CML. His only hope lay in a bone marrow transplant from a blood relative. And there was only one."

The DA snapped her fingers. "The attempted kidnap we figured for a burglary."

"This alarmed Erin so much she returned to Wilmington, drugged Dale, set the house on fire, and abducted her own child."

"All this so she could sing?"

"By this time, I think she was after revenge. Kedrick couldn't give her the debut she wanted. So she hit him where she knew he could still be hurt. She demanded money. A lot."

Marcus spoke weakly from the sofa. "The hotels."

Kirsten resisted the urge to turn around. "He was busy selling them by the time we entered the picture. Which means Erin was holding his supposed child up for ransom."

Judge Sears opened the file on her desk, fiddled with her pen a long moment, then turned to the court reporter and said, "You ready?"

"Yes ma'am."

"All right. This court is now in session. I have before me a request from the district court of Manhattan requesting the extradition of Dale Steadman. I am hereby turning this down." Knowing Marcus was beyond reach just then, she glanced from Kirsten to the DA. "Can I leave it to you to pass on the information?"

Wilma smiled. "With greatest pleasure."

"Okay. Next, there is a charge of murder one. I am dismissing this case. All charges against Dale Steadman are hereby dropped."

She closed that file and opened the next. "The case entered against Dale Steadman by Health and Human Services is dismissed. Marcus, if you wish I will consider charges against the young man." When he did not respond, she observed. "He's fallen asleep."

"Let him rest." This from the DA. "He's had a hard day."

"I have a variety of charges filed by Hamper Caisse on behalf of the former ex-wife, Erin Brandt."

"Hamper's dance card is gonna be full for a while yet," Wilma offered.

"Fine. Then I am issuing a blanket dismissal of all charges related to the custody of one Celeste Steadman." She signed a form, then turned to the court reporter and said, "Perhaps you would give us a moment here alone."

When the court reporter had departed, Sears went on, "There is the matter of the child's actual parentage."

Kirsten spoke with utter certainty. "Dale Steadman is that child's only real father."

Wilma met the judge's gaze with an easy shrug. "Works for me."

Judge Sears closed the file. "I have no trouble holding the information we have disclosed here *in camera*." She looked at Kirsten. "Do you know what that means?"

"I have a year of law school."

"Tell me you're going back." This from the DA.

"I'm thinking about it."

"Do more than think." She rose, shook the judge's hand, then turned to help Kirsten lift Marcus to his feet. "When you're done, come find me. We're always on the lookout for somebody good as you."

CHAPTER

6 2

I N ALL HIS TIME AT THE MET, this was Kedrick Lloyd's first visit to the Family Circle.

The stage was five levels below, a greater distance than he would have imagined possible. The Standing Room section at the back of this level was reserved for poverty-stricken fans. These people were so loyal they braved any weather, long lines, endless waits, for the chance to see what otherwise was far beyond their financial reach. Though they shared his passion, Kedrick had never felt any need to meet and greet. They were beneath him. Far more than distance and four thousand higher-priced seats separated them. Until now.

The stage was set for Mozart's *Idomeneo*, a production he had seen perhaps three dozen times. The entire back wall was formed into a pastiche mask of the god Poseidon. The god looked not merely forbidding. He seemed hungry in the manner of one who ate souls yet never grew satiated. His mouth was open and waiting. The dim lighting turned the black eyeholes alive and watchful.

Carefully Kedrick took the dark stairs down to the front railing. His bones were increasingly fragile. Even this descent of nineteen steps was enough to leave him gasping. He used both hands to grip the seatbacks, pausing now and then for air. It would be such a mockery, to come this far and be defeated by a tumble and a broken limb.

He reached the balcony's carpeted front barrier. The brass railing across its top was impossibly cold. He gripped it with both hands and chuckled over the thought that he really should register a complaint.

Order the cleaning staff to warm the rail up for the next one to pass this way.

He paused once he managed to lift himself onto the barrier. More than the exertion was causing his breathing to rasp like wind through dry reeds. For there upon the stage stood an ethereal diva, a lovely woman seemingly trapped in the amber of ageless youth. She wore the full regalia of an opera queen. Her arms were outstretched, her mouth opened wide, her empty eyes focused upon the very last row. But there was no voice to this aria, no lilting power to the silenced voice.

Kedrick released his grip upon the railing and offered the apparition a mock salute. Any place as exalted as the Met really did need its own resident ghost.

He pushed himself to his feet, his hands outstretched like feeble mockery of wings.

He looked down, and decided the orchestra seats were a satisfactory distance away. Now that he was here, he wondered why he had not done this long before. It would have saved everyone so much bother.

He glanced at the stage once more, and stared at the god and his glaring pits for eyes. And the open, hungry mouth.

He then addressed the empty hall for the final time. "Tonight's performance is unavoidably canceled."

CHAPTER

6 3

For once, the weather was with them.

A breeze more in tune with the autumn months ahead blew out of the north, chasing frayed and frothy clouds across a gloriously cool sky. They were back at the border of the private airport, watching the small jet taxi toward them. Kirsten waited a short distance from Marcus' wheelchair as he talked softly with Omar Dell. The court reporter grinned and scribbled busily. A photographer lounged farther back, waiting for the pictures to come. When fatigue began to stain her fiancé's features, she walked over and said, "I'd like a private word with Marcus, please."

Omar signaled to the photographer. "One picture of the two of you together."

The photographer snapped three and would have taken more had Kirsten not declared, "That's enough."

"A word for the record?"

"Marcus has already done that."

The reporter was too full of coming glory to object. "Great to have you two still around and kicking."

Wind and roaring engines from the commercial airport offered them an illusion of privacy. Marcus squinted into the empty sky and asked, "How much longer?"

"They're due any minute now."

The act of reaching for her hand brought the bandages covering his wrists into view. "I never thought I could be so happy being weak."

Kirsten blocked her motions from the others as best she could. She used her free hand to stroke his face, his neck, his shoulders. The proprietary gestures of a woman in love. "Are you okay?"

"Fine." He raised the hand he held and nestled it on his cheek. "Are we okay?"

She leaned closer, kissed him softly. "We're better than that. A lot better."

A shout from the onlookers drew her around. A sleek private jet taxied off the runway and headed straight for where they stood. Kirsten walked over to where Dale stood by the cars. The man's entire being was focused upon the jet. A tremor rocked his frame, revealing the suppressed anxiety of one who had been forced to live on the edge for far too long.

She said to him, "I'd like to ask a favor."

His gaze did not leave the plane. "Name it."

"Ask Goscha to stay here as the child's nanny."

He looked at her then. "Erin's maid?"

"Yes. Have you met her?"

"Once or twice, and not for very long. Erin had her stay and to watch over the house in Düsseldorf. When we went there, Goscha played the ghost."

"She loves your baby, Dale."

"This is the same woman who refused to release my own child to me."

"Same reason, different action. She only knew you in Erin's company. Goscha trusts me to make the right decision for Celeste."

"If I remember correctly, she also butchers the English language."

"I doubt seriously," Kirsten replied, "that Celeste will mind."

The jet's engines whined down, and the side door flipped open. Kirsten said apologetically, "I'm supposed to do this alone."

Dale did not actually push her forward. "Go. Hurry."

She walked toward the gray-cloaked nun who stood blinking in the sudden sunlight. The nun spotted her approach and descended the stairs. "You are Kirsten Stansted?"

"Yes."

"I am Sister Agnes. Please, that is the father?"

"Dale Steadman. Yes."

But the sister made no move toward him. "That horrible man who was with Erin came back and demanded the child. Who was he?"

"Just what you said. A horrible man. He's been arrested."

"Then I acted correctly when I refused to hand Celeste over to him."

"Yes."

"I knew something was very wrong as soon as he appeared. He claimed Erin had sent him. She didn't, did she."

"No."

"The attempted break-in at our convent, it was for the child?"

"Probably."

"Then it is good we hid her. And the news I heard from Goscha is true, Erin is really lost to us?"

"I'm afraid so."

"Goscha was very explicit in her instructions. I was to hand the baby only over to you. The father she did not know. But you she said I could trust. You would know what to do. You would know where the baby would be safest."

Kirsten liked her. So much she was able to confess, "There is a problem."

"Let me guess. Who truly is the child's father." She smiled at Kirsten's surprise. "I knew Erin at her beginnings."

"My fiancé and I don't know how much we should tell the man who believes Celeste is his child. Especially since we don't know anything for certain."

"Your fiancé. How nice. That is the gentleman there with the bandage on his head?"

"His name is Marcus Glenwood."

"And you love him."

"So much."

The gray-clad nun cocked her head to one side. "I detect an unfinished thought. So much it frightens? So much it brings forth truth?"

"Both."

"So there is to be honesty between us. Good. I consider honesty one of my dearest allies." Soft eyes inspected her with the calm of centuries. "Tell your beloved this. All God's own have been adopted to his clan. He will understand this?"

"Better than me."

"If this situation is good enough for God, why not for man as well? You will tell him this also?"

"Yes."

"Then I will share another honesty with you. I was sent to the monastery school when I was nine. Erin was eleven. I became her best friend. Her only friend. I was lonely and she was Erin. Already then she was Erin. You understand?"

"All too well."

"One night we were in the attic smoking forbidden cigarettes. A harmless crime, only the building caught fire and three of the other children burned to death."

"I'm so sorry."

"Thank you. In that moment of initial terror, Erin caught me and made me swear an oath never to divulge the truth. So when I have confessed my sins to the families and my own clan, I have spoken only of my own actions. In seeking to make amends, to bring a rightness to this tragedy, to make up for the lives I caused to be extinguished, I became who I am. For Erin, the response was different. She became *above* all rules."

"She was the star."

"Even then." The nun straightened, seeking to cast aside the weight of many years. "I have remained true to my vow until now, though I am convinced punishment might have saved her. But now she is gone, and my vow is ended. Erin dedicated her life to fulfilling her every ambition."

"That is what killed her," Kirsten said. "It wasn't your fault."

"No?"

"You said it yourself. Erin was Erin."

The nun studied her a long moment, then said, "And I was the one coming to offer you peace."

Before Kirsten could respond, she climbed back inside the plane, then returned carrying a small bundle in crinoline and white. "Go with God, my children."

Kirsten accepted the armload and crossed back across the tarmac. She stopped before the silent, trembling man. And smiled for both of them. "Take your daughter."

ACKNOWLEDGMENTS

North Carolina District Court Judge Alice Stubbs is one of those rare jurists whose name elicits respect even from lawyers who have disagreed with her judgments. It was a regular astonishment just how many people were willing to respect me simply because Judge Stubbs had offered me her help. Initially she granted me a Sunday afternoon to help structure the basic legal arguments of this book. Then, while sitting at the bench and trying cases, she drew me forward both to help with introductions and to explain certain procedures that proved crucial to this story.

As with *The Great Divide*, Kieran Shanahan's assistance proved invaluable. Not only did he aid mightily in structuring the legal portion of the book, but it was while bouncing ideas around in his office that several key points finally solidified into something usable. He has become a true ally in the creative process.

Richard Douglas, Chief Counsel for the Senate Foreign Relations Committee, kindly walked me through the political minefield surrounding the Hague Convention and the crisis affecting so-called "left behind" parents. His concise overview was most instructive.

Helen Oliver is far too nice and sensitive a lady to fit the traditional mold of a divorce and custody attorney. But it is precisely these talents which prove so beneficial to her clients and their young charges. I am honored to have had the chance to see the courtroom world through her eyes.

Bill Young is a full-fledged trial attorney. Which means he lives and breathes the courtroom drama on a daily basis; his office hours are from six in the morning until court opens, then from six in the evening onward. The day he walked me through the courtroom process, he faced eleven different trials—a relatively light load.

A number of people went out of their way to assist in making connections for me. I would especially like to thank Jim Hinkle and Ray Denny for opening a number of doors on my account. One of these vital connections was with Brian McClure, former coach at UNC-W and the first head of their downtown redevelopment program. Brian took most of a day off work to drive me around and discuss the strata of Wilmington society. Thanks also to Gene Miller, another new acquaintance, who started where Brian left off.

Stedman Stevens left Wilmington because he had to—tied to a company who made the incredibly foolish move from the port city to Long Island. It took him nine years to return, and it is doubtful that he will ever depart again, or if his family would ever travel with him. He was a great guide. He and his wife, Lisa, are great pals. Thanks, guys. For everything.

Antoinette Williams and her parents, Eva and Carlyle, were grand representatives of Wilmington. This is one of the treasures of the writing life, being granted entry into worlds where I otherwise would probably have no contact. Thanks also to two further contacts that Antoinette made for me, both of whom have enriched this book: Herbert Harris, journalist and author; and Bertha M. Todd, a woman who truly lives to teach.

I only attempted to create the Reverend Deacon Wilbur because of Reuben Blackwell. He has entered elected politics now, and is forced to measure his minutes out like diamonds. Yet he remained not just available, but eager, even when the time simply was not there. Thank you, Reuben, for everything. And thank you, Neva, for letting him.

Duncan MacMillan is a trial attorney who lives and breathes according to courthouse time. A walk from the courtroom to the front plaza required halting for six different trial-related negotiations. Despite this fact, I outlined what I needed and the man not only gave his time, but walked me across the street and forced himself into the office of a former district judge. Together these two gentlemen tackled one of the book's tough issues and knocked it cold. Masters of the craft, both of them.

André Bishop is Artistic Director of Lincoln Center's Vivian

Beaumont Theater. He kindly walked me through the administrative setup and helped flesh out the character of Kedrick Lloyd. Thanks also to Heinz Neumann, a retired baritone who introduced me to the magic and mystery of Lincoln Center. I am also most appreciative of Harold Grabau's efforts to keep this story and all its details on proper course. My sincere thanks also go to all the staff at London's Royal Opera House, who made time for me the opening week of their summer season.

Jeanne Piland is a diva with the Düsseldorf opera. She has sung all over the world, and embodies the greatness that opera offers. She is also the exact opposite of Erin Brandt in all ways except her remarkable beauty. Through her care and guidance, this character and this story came to life.

Dr. Phillip Unwin has been of enormous assistance with a number of my stories, and it is high time I remember to thank him. He has become my resident guru of ailments, and the medical expert that has helped shape so many crucial scenes. My heartfelt thanks go to him and his lovely wife, Claire.

The number of people at Doubleday to whom I am indebted continues to grow. Special thanks, however, must be given to Jason Kaufman, a truly outstanding editor and very fine gentleman. Thanks also to Michelle Rapkin and Don Pape, who remain trusted advisors and dear friends. My heartfelt appreciation also goes to Eric Major, whose guidance has been essential.

One of the great joys of these books remains the insider's look it has granted me to my father's legal realm. Thanks, Dad, both for all the assistance you gave, for the wisdom you gladly shared, and for forgiving me for choosing a path in life other than law.

As always, my first and my last thanks go to Isabella, my wife and partner and very best friend.

T. Davis Bunn was raised in North Carolina, taught international finance in Switzerland, worked in Africa and the Middle East, and was named managing director of an international business advisory group based in Düsseldorf. He is the author of fifteen bestselling novels, including *Drummer in the Dark* and *The Great Divide*. He lives in Oxford, England, and Melbourne Beach, Florida, with his wife, Isabella.